DOVER MYSTERY CLASSICS

THE MYSTERIOUS MICKEY FINN

Elliot Paul

Dover Publications, Inc.
Mineola, New York

Bibliographical Note

This Dover edition, first published in 1984 and reissued in 2014, is an unbridged republication of the work originally published by Modern Age Books, New York, 1939, under the title *The Mysterious Mickey Finn; or, Murder at the Café du Dome; an International Mystery.*

Library of Congress Cataloging-in-Publication Data

Paul, Elliot, 1891–1958
   The Mysterious Mickey Finn
   Reprint. Originally published: New York : Modern Age Books, 1939.
        p.cm.
     ISBN-13: 978-0-486-24751-9
     ISBN-10: 0-486-24751-1
     I. Title

PS3531.A852M97   1984
813'.52   84-7996

Manufactured in the United States by Courier Corporation
24751103   2015
www.doverpublications.com

CONTENTS

1 *The Rosy-Whiskered Morn in Montparnasse*   9
2 *The End of a Fiscal Year*   13
3 *An Odd Use for Olive Oil*   21
4 *Of Mineral Mesmerism*   29
5 *In Which Twin Cheques Are Signed*   35
6 *The Philanthropist Disappears*   46
7 *The Dragnet is Spread*   54
8 *No Pastures*   68
9 *A Glimpse of a Candle-Light Greco*   74
10 *Murder at the Café du Dôme*   98
11 *The Agent Plénipotentiaire*   103
12 *The Suspects Awake*   109
13 *In Which a Tender Heart is Revealed Beneath a Gruff Exterior*   118
14 *The Sound of a Great Amen*   127
15 *The Seine Yields a Clue*   135
16 *A Shot at Whistler's Aunt*   140
17 *Anchors Aweigh*   146
18 *A Potato-Masher Proves to be a Boomerang*   154
19 *Strange Bedfellows as it Were*   163
20 *Not a Moment too Soon*   170
21 *The Mysterious Mickey Finn*   174
22 *The Lure of a Buddy's Body*   180
23 *Two Hearts That Cease to Beat as One, or to Beat at All for That Matter*   189
24 *Foul Play in an Old Château*   203
25 *A Truck-load of Contact Mines*   213
26 *Of the Odour of Saints and Sinners*   218
27 *The Heart of a Little Child*   223
28 *The Film Saves the Day*   227
29 *Ashes to Ashes, in a Way*   234
30 *The Whole and its Parts*   239
31 *In Which Many Hearts Are Gladdened*   249
32 *The Boyish Silhouette Gives Way to the Curved Outline*   255

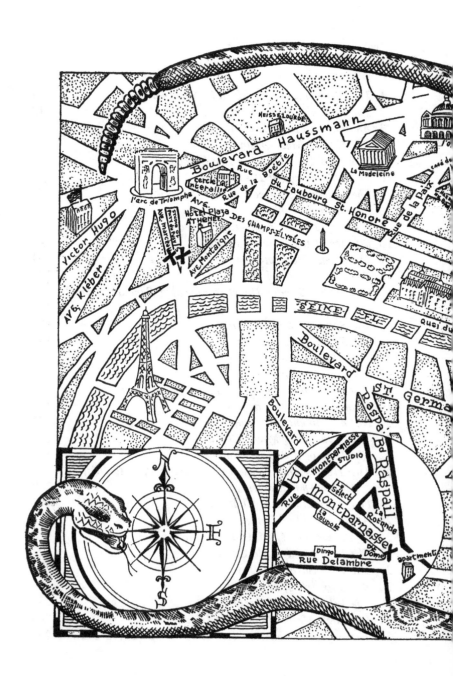

a map of
Paris
for guidance
of the reader

DEAR READER

My purpose in writing this book is to entertain you. I do not think that purpose is served by starting with the murder of a character who must necessarily be a perfect stranger to you. Do not be afraid, as you read the first few pages, that no one is going to die. The casualties are going to be fairly heavy before we get through.

If, however, you do not like this departure from the mould into which such stories unhappily have fallen, I promise you that next time I will introduce a dead body into the preface, before the book is properly started at all.

THE AUTHOR

The characters in this book have had to be toned down somewhat for the family trade, but otherwise are pretty much as they were in the heyday of the American occupation of Montparnasse in the post-war years.

CHAPTER 1

The Rosy-Whiskered Morn in Montparnasse

ELEVEN A.M. is a dull hour on the *terrasse* of the Café du Dôme. The early risers of Montparnasse have already had coffee and rolls, the larger group who are in Paris frankly for loafing and inviting their thirsts, stay in bed until afternoon. The French of the neighbourhood, small shop keepers, butcher boys, dairy girls, bill collectors, and the like, are scurrying to and fro with their minds on their retail business.

On the spring morning in question, Homer Evans, one of the few who were sitting in front of that famous *café*, was there because he had not yet been in bed. He was a tall, broad-shouldered, fair-haired young man who looked sturdy without being athletic, and responsive although indolent. He did not lounge awkwardly over table and chair like a character from Mark Twain, and decidedly he did not sit erect and perform moral gymnastics like an American business man. He looked as if he had lived easily and well, neither rich nor poor, but nobody in Montparnasse knew how he did it, where his funds came from or what his antecedents were. His friends, and he had scores of them, secretly wondered why a man of such brilliance and poise was content to let his talents lie fallow. For while there was considerable doubt as to the artistic merits and abilities of many of the residents of the quarter, Evans could write and paint with the best of them. His output, however, was small. He had written one short monograph entitled 'Democracies, Ancient and Modern' and had painted only one picture, a portrait of his friend and drinking companion, a Norwegian-American artist named Hjalmar Jansen. He had sat for Hjalmar, as he had sat for many other painters, and when the big Norwegian had got through, Evans had borrowed the paints, rags, and brushes and had turned out a work of art that caused other hard-working artists to wince with envy. One of them, plump Rosa Stier, had almost flown into a rage.

'You've no right to do that, damn you, Homer,' she had said. And even Hjalmar Jansen had grunted uncomfortably. 'When I think of the work I put in to train my hand and my eyes, when you consider these poor bastards all over the quarter who'd give their right eye to paint like that ...'

'I swear by all that's holy that I'll never do it again,' Evans said, and he kept his word.

Music, of all the arts, meant the most to Evans, so much that he seldom talked about it. Each year he would spend January and February in Spanish Morocco, usually at Melilla where he knew an Arab *café* in which the musicians played all night long, with their throbbing, insistent rhythm and unending simple melodies. Then he would return to Paris for the best part of the concert season.

He liked particularly to hear finger exercises played, over and over again. He loved to lie in bed and listen to those musical Arabesques repeat themselves and run idly through slight variations. For two years, until the previous December, he had hired a music student to play finger exercises on his grand piano each day between eleven and one, and when the pretty and earnest young girl from Montana had gone back home to teach he had been vaguely uneasy for weeks, although it occurred to him afterwards that he had never known her name.

On the Tuesday morning on which this story opens Evans had not been to bed, not because alcoholic excesses had driven him to carry on beyond the natural ending of a party. He had been showing his publisher and some visiting Americans the night life of the city. They had tasted the right food, and a staggering number of the right kind of drinks, had seen busy people at work in the most commendable of all labours, the continuance of the food supply. Just to remind his guests that beneath the frosting of society are strata with no margins for defending their humanity, he had taken them to the huge square in front of the city hospital, just after two o'clock, at the hour when all the tramps and derelicts are chased out of the squalid bars and from beneath the bridges. Standing in the shelter of the great cathedral, the Americans had watched the furtive army of the disinherited slink across the square on the way to the market where some of them might earn a few *sous* and the others scrape up discarded carrots and cabbage leaves from the slippery sidewalks. It was one of Evans' few acts of self-discipline, mingling now and then with that unholy and wretched crowd, and usually he performed it alone. But his publisher had wanted to see everything, so after a dinner at the Café de Paris, an hour at the Folies Bergère, a drink or two *chez* Weber, and the stimulating popular quarter around the place Clichy, instead of treating his guests to a session of living pictures in the notorious rue Blondel, Homer had confronted them unexpectedly with the lowest of the low, in one of their moments of greatest discomfort. It was his sense of the dramatic, perhaps, and more likely something more. At any rate, it had given his publisher such a shock that, later, he had viewed the miraculous pyramids of carrots and cauliflower, the entire place St Eustache covered with baskets of strawberries, the Bourse flanked with fifty thousand mushrooms, in a daze and had harangued Evans in every market *café* on the subject of his idleness, on the number of books he might have been turning out, on the injustice of burying his thirty talents, in contradiction with Biblical precedent and the practice of right-thinking people everywhere. After the dawn, involving green and gold behind the spires of Notre Dame, after the last bat had zigzagged between the buildings of the rue de la Huchette, Evans had retired to his own quarter, Montparnasse, again to think it over. He had thought it over and once more decided he was on the right track. No books, no paintings, no fame. If he wrote as he could write, no one would publish it, least of all the dapper young president of the Acorn Press, and if the stuff were published, no one would read it. And if someone read it, he would probably not understand it. And if he did by chance understand it, it would make him feel badly.

A negative resolve is not conducive to sleep, so Evans had sat calmly on the *terrasse* of the Select watching the blue deepen behind the Coupole. Then, at the appropriate hour, he had shifted over to the Dôme and had just about decided that after lunch he would take some rest when Hjalmar Jansen appeared.

No doubt 'appeared' is too light a verb to use in connexion

with the hulking Norwegian painter. He lumbered across the street, letting the traffic dodge him as best it could, and before he had approached nearer than fifty yards, Evans could see that his friend had something on his mind.

'What the hell?' Evans asked, startling the Norwegian into recognizing him. 'One would think, by the looks of your face, that the English girl had made you marry her.'

'Worse than that,' said Jansen, making the straw chair creak with his weight as he sat at Evans' table.

'There's nothing worse than that,' Evans said. 'Her feet. . . .'

'This is serious,' Jansen said. 'Hugo Weiss is in town.'

CHAPTER 2

The End of a Fiscal Year

HUGO WEISS was known in every capital of the western world as a multi-millionaire, a philanthropist and a patron of the arts. His home was New York and his refuge, Paris. He financed two symphony orchestras, kept a number of lesser opera companies circulating in America, was the moving director of at least half a dozen important museums. The aura of dollar signs and astronomical figures, of glittering diamond horseshoes, 'la' in altissimo and miles of narrow galleries filled with dim paintings evoked by the mention of Hugo Weiss was so different from that of the Café du Dôme on a spring morning that Homer Evans did not at first receive the import of his friend's remark. It was as if Hjalmar had said, 'They are scrubbing off the dome of St Paul's this morning,' or 'Now is the time for all good men to come to the aid of their party.' Then Homer suddenly remembered that it was because of one thousand dollars advanced by Hugo Weiss that Hjalmar Jansen had been able to stay in Paris and paint during the past year, the fiscal year, from Hjalmar's viewpoint, that was drawing to a dismal close.

'So he's here?' said Evans.

'He got in yesterday,' Jansen said, and sank into a deeper gloom, which was agitated by fitful flashes of awareness that something drastic must be done.

Now Hjalmar Jansen was what might be termed a serious artist. That is to say, when he produced a painting that was distinctly below par he threw it away, sometimes stretcher and all. He had impressed Hugo Weiss at a New York cocktail party, where his hearty voice, rugged physique and capacity for bathtub gin had made him stand out from the city folks present. They had ducked out of the party together and spent the evening at Luchow's where the magic of Weiss's presence had produced real Würzburger.

It would not be fair to say that Hjalmar had done no work since coming to Montparnasse, but his artistic conscience had developed much faster than his skill, so most of the canvases had been chucked out of the window, not a few before the window had been opened. After a failure he would usually get roaring drunk, and get into a fight if he could find a man big enough. Then, if he still felt rebellious, he would hop a Belgian canal barge on which he would ride to the border, through the marvellous canals of northern France, insisting on doing most of the work and on buying all the wine. This would take about two weeks, after which he would settle down to work again. His best painting, a portrait of the proprietor of the Dôme, was hanging inside the *café* and was the proprietor's prize possession. He had accepted it for a bar bill that would, if represented by stacked saucers, reach approximately to the level of the Eiffel Tower. By such expedients, Hjalmar had lived abundantly and made his thousand dollars go far, but it was nearly gone. In fact, there were seven francs fifty of it left, and lunch for himself and the English girl with the tenacious temperament and enormous feet had to come out of that.

The two friends sat silently at the Dôme while Evans reviewed the facts in his mind and Hjalmar Jansen shifted in his seat, twisted his *béret* in his huge hands and tried to decide what to do. By borrowing the portrait hanging in the *café* (and which the proprietor prized almost as much as his licence to do business) Hjalmar would have three paintings to show his benefactor, – three paintings to answer for a year's hard work: the portrait of Chalgrin, otherwise known as M. Dôme, in a severe black frock coat and funereal tie, somewhat after the manner of Fantin-Latour; a nude of the English girl with red hair (and consistent at that) and those expressive British feet in the foreground; and a still life of some old boots that had taken his fancy. Could he explain to Hugo Weiss that he had covered about an acre of canvas, each foot of which had taught him something? What to do? What to do? His wits were not responding that morning, partly on account of his benefactor's unexpected arrival, partly because Maggie Dickinson, the English girl, had been particularly tearful and troublesome at

14

breakfast and had made it clear that she intended, for his own good, to make him settle down.

'Listen, old boy,' Evans said, at last. 'I've been up all night, and involved in a number of things. My publisher has been badgering me, I've beheld starvation in the midst of plenty. I have seen the sun rise behind the spires of Our Lady while the predatory bat was a-wing. It's certain: (1) that Hugo Weiss did not come to Paris expressly to view your masterpieces; (2) that he will still be here to-morrow, since I noticed in this morning's *Herald* that he is to be a guest of honour at the banquet of the *Société des Artistes Français* three evenings hence; (3) that I can give you better counsel after I have had two hours' peaceful sleep. Meet me here at five this evening, when, if the sun holds strong, a long cool drink will be in order.'

'Thanks. Much obliged. I will,' said Jansen, rising quickly and upsetting two chairs in his progress across the *terrasse*. 'So long. Sleep well. At five,' he roared, from the sidewalk, and of the dozen heads behind spread newspapers, only one turned toward the speaker and then back to where Homer Evans was sitting. That one belonged to Ambrose Gring.

No one knew where Ambrose Gring had been born or what sort of passport he carried. He frequented art galleries, the kind that deal in fabulously priced old masters, and seemed to be familiar with the dealers and attendants all up and down the rue la Boétie and in the place Vendôme. He had been at Yale and won a poetry prize, was familiar with Constantinople and spoke Turkish, had followed Kolchak in northern Russia, although no one could imagine him as a fighting man, and had been involved in a notorious affair which ended by having an American widow taken forcibly from his apartment by her male relatives and sequestrated in a private and expensive *Maison de Santé* until she had cooled off sufficiently to give up Ambrose. Gring listened to the voice of Hjalmar because it was his habit to listen to everything. Whatever he saw or heard he made a mental note of, for future reference, and oftener than might be expected, he found odd scraps of information could be made profitable to him, either to ingratiate himself with someone, or to take vengeance for a personal slight, for he was very vain.

15

'This afternoon at five,' Gring repeated to himself, and resolved to be on hand, at a nearby table. He knew that Hjalmar was agitated and that he was perfectly sober, two unusual circumstances which by coinciding made it certain that something important was in the wind. And it was a small wind in Montparnasse that did not blow Ambrose at least a cup of coffee or an introduction to some naïve American girl who was seeing Paris for the first time, and needed guidance.

Homer Evans was aware of Ambrose, sitting two tables in front of him, but that did not spoil the morning for him. He was tolerant of Ambrose Gring as he was tolerant of everyone. In fact he had often admired the eel-like way in which Ambrose got along, without work or visible achievement, without disclosing his past, explaining his present or speculating upon his future. Most pan-handlers worked hard at their trade, so hard in fact that in any other line of work they would have been successful. Not so with Ambrose. The lilies of the field were sweatshop slaves compared with him, and Solomon in all his glory never had a better fitting suit or a niftier tie. It was true that a few years previously some articles bearing Gring's signature had appeared in *Art for Art's Sake*, a commercial review which listed all the important auctions and sales, but no one had seen Gring write them.

As Homer Evans turned to call the waiter, he saw with dismay that Maggie Dickinson, the English girl, looking sterner and more haggard than ever, was heading across the *terrasse*, unmistakably bound for his table.

'I know you don't like to be interrupted, but I must talk to you,' she said, running her skinny fingers through her shock of red hair.

He had risen courteously, and with all his impatience concealed, asked her to sit down.

'You're the only one of Hjalmar's friends who has any sense, or decency,' she burst out, and the ears of Ambrose Gring, two tables in advance, spread themselves a fraction of a millimetre and expressed the utmost satisfaction.

'What's wrong?' Evans asked.

'He's wasting himself, he's throwing himself away.... Oh,

16

don't think I'm jealous. He can run around with other girls if he wants to, but he needs a steadying influence, someone to take care of him, his clothes, his filthy studio, to wake him at the proper hour, to give him breakfast, get his models there on time, take care of his money and see that he eats his regular meals. I don't mind if he drinks. It's natural, perhaps, for him to drink. But he ought to work and he needs a little order.'

'It's hard to say what anyone needs,' said Evans, uneasily.

'He says that he likes plump women, that I'm too skinny, but he says that in the morning. I haven't noticed that he has any aversion to me at night. Of course, he's drunk at night, but he likes me.'

'Of course he likes you,' Evans said.

Her face took on a more desperate expression and for a moment it looked as if she were about to sink to her knees. With clasped hands she said imploringly:

'You talk to him. Tell him to marry me. Nothing else would settle it. He'd feel some stability then, and stop wasting his life. He can paint. You know he can. But he doesn't, and if he does, he throws away the paintings. I'm no judge, but I'm sure the ones he throws away are just as good as the ones he keeps. I can't for the life of me see a bit of difference. . . . You'll talk to him, won't you? Promise.'

Gring's ears moved a full millimetre that time and his face was lighted with his cat-like smile.

'Listen, Maggie,' Evans said kindly. 'I know you're fond of Hjalmar and want to do the best you can for him. But right now I can't think. I've been up all night. . . .'

'I'd like to know why you all sit up all night. It's just the same as the day-time, except for the lamp-light, isn't it?' she said, with pent-up exasperation.

'Suppose you meet me at the Dingo at seven. . . .'

'I'll be there at seven,' she said, and strode away, dabbing at her eyes with a wilted handkerchief.

'Hell. I'm going to bed,' Evans said. 'If only I could be lulled to sleep by Czerny. Good old Czerny and his school of velocity. I'll bet he was steady, all right. No weeping ex-virgins in his life, I'm sure. Or am I? I must look it up. . . .'

And with that he paid the waiter and started for the rue Campagne Première, his mind on fresh cool sheets and dim silences. The day and night preceding had been too eventful for his quiet taste. Everything in moderation, was his motto. He could, on a pinch, stand one event a day, or at best, two. Three were decidedly too many.

His latchkey was in his hand but he did not insert it. Instead he listened. From the piano came to him the familiar five-finger exercises, and for a moment Evans thought his heart was pounding. The western girl, whose soothing music he had missed too severely, had returned. He could see her profile, the proud way she held her head, the graceful slope of her shoulders. She was playing Czerny as she had never played him before, with microscopic exactness and clarity.

The clock struck one, she raised her fingers from the keys and looked at him.

'Good morning,' she said.

'Why, good morning,' he answered. He was so glad to see her that he could say no more.

'You seem surprised,' she said, a little bewildered.

'Quite pleasantly,' he said.

'You didn't get my letter?'

'Your letter?' Obviously he had not received it. With a faint guilty smile he opened the door again, reached out into the corridor and opened his mailbox. In the midst of a two-week accumulation of letters and circulars he found the one postmarked 'Billings, Mont.'

'I might have known you wouldn't read it,' she said, for it was one of Evans' rules of life that mail, unless it is truly important, should be read when the recipient wishes and not when any Tom, Dick, or Harriet sees fit to write.

Homer started to rip open the flap of an envelope from Billings, Montana.

'Don't read it now,' she said, blushing and making a movement to restrain him.

'Why not?'

She hesitated and blushed more deeply. 'You're tired,' she said. 'You haven't been to bed.'

'Is it as harrowing as that ? '

'I didn't mean it to be, but one never knows how a letter will seem. . . .'

Evans had always resented being pampered by women, perhaps because it gave him such unmistakable comfort that he was afraid it might be habit-forming. 'It's true that I'm tired, and I've had a hell of a day. If this keeps up, I'm going to Times Square for a little peace and quiet,' he said.

'I'm sorry,' she said. 'It's of no importance.'

'You know very well that I can't go to sleep until I've read it,' he said.

'Then perhaps I'd better tell you,' she said.

Impatiently he tossed the unopened letter to the tray. 'Be brief,' he said. 'I've appointments at five and seven. . . . Christ almighty. I might as well be Roxy or Charley Schwab.'

'There's not much to tell,' she said.

That brought him to his senses. He stepped forward and placed a hand on each of her shapely shoulders. 'Miss . . . What in hell is your name ? '

'Leonard . . . Miriam Leonard,' she faltered.

'Miss Leonard, I'm not an imbecile, although I've been acting like one. I may be eccentric, wilful, and selfish. I may be an idler, escapist, and expatriate. But I am fairly observant and can associate ideas. You are in trouble. In some way I am to blame, although that phase of the matter eludes me at the moment. . . .'

'I never said you were to blame,' she said. 'I don't know why I came here.'

Evans rubbed his hand across his forehead. 'I've actually got a headache now,' he said. 'Let's have a drink. You'll have to get this off your chest. . . . I suppose you're in love. . . .'

'This has nothing to do with love,' she said firmly.

'Thank God,' he said, and went to the kitchen to mix a couple of drinks. For himself he prepared cognac and siphon, for Miss Leonard a vermouth-cassis, the former to induce sleep, the latter to stir an appetite.

'I'm keeping you out of bed,' she said nervously.

'That's become the regional sport,' he said. 'Now pull yourself together, and don't try to spare me. I know you're not hysterical or coy or deceitful. I owe you a great deal, more than I realized until you went away. . . .'

'I wish I had stayed here,' she said.

'Not possible,' he said. 'Career. Brilliant young pianist. Meets go-getting western man, where men love horses. Vacillates between career and marriage. . . . Wrong either way. . . .'

'That's not the way it was at all.'

'How was it, then?'

'I can't play anything but finger exercises,' she burst out, and bit her lips to hold back tears.

Suddenly Evans saw light, and immediately afterwards felt real dismay. The girl's two hours of Czerny, played too conscientiously, had mechanized her reactions. She might feel all the drama of Bach and the poetry of Chopin when reading a score silently, but once at the piano she would fall into the exact monotonous pattern of the finger exercises.

'I couldn't teach, I couldn't play. I couldn't stay at home and do nothing. What can I do?' she asked.

'Believe me, I'm very sorry,' Evans said. 'I'm sure that something can be done but just at the moment I don't know what it is. Why not let me sleep a few hours, then meet me at the Select at nine o'clock? . . . Perhaps we can work out something then.'

'You're very kind,' she said.

'You've made me feel like a brute,' said Evans, dismally, and started for the bedroom.

CHAPTER 3

An Odd Use for Olive Oil

AT four o'clock Homer Evans awoke, refreshed. He was glad to be in his apartment, which was arranged to his taste; he was thankful that the apartment was in Montparnasse. He remembered coincidently with his waking that he had a few odd bits of advice to formulate for some of his friends but nothing seemed formidable or even annoying. He pulled a cord at his bedside which released a small American flag so that it fluttered just outside one of his bedroom windows. That done, he stretched and flexed his muscles leisurely and stepped into the needle bath.

'A shower bath is an abject copy from nature,' he often said. 'A needle bath, coming at you more or less horizontally, is an improvement by man. Also, it does not half blind you or choke you if you care to sing.'

The American flag was a signal to his barber across the street. Whenever it fluttered from the window, Henri came over with his implements, for Evans disliked shaving himself. It forced a man to make undignified grimaces, he thought. Moreover, it deprived a barber of his means of livelihood.

As he was being shaved, Homer sorted out his various problems. Hjalmar Jansen's predicament was problem 'a' and Evans had no difficulty in finding a solution. The Norwegian needed more paintings. It was almost too easy. First, there was the portrait of Hjalmar by Evans, himself. He would lend it for the occasion. Rosa Stier could be counted on for a half dozen landscapes and still-lifes. Harold Simon must have a dozen finished works on hand. Snorre Sturlusson, the Finn, would kick through with ten or so. Evans knew that Gwendolyn Poularde had fifteen ready for her Chicago show that already had been announced.

But what about the signatures? That stopped Evans but a moment. He recalled having read that Titian's faithful pupils,

21

in order to prevent the master from spoiling his masterpieces by revising them when he was too old, had mixed the colours with olive oil instead of linseed oil, so the repainting could easily be removed.

Olive oil it shall be, then, he said to himself. Let's see. The Coupole has wonderful olive oil, imported especially from Spain. Shaved and dressed, he set out in that direction, in tune with the warm spring air and the impersonal colourful crowd of regulars and tourists that swarmed the sidewalks and chattered gaily, enlivening the avenues for blocks on end.

When he chose a seat on the populous Coupole *terrasse* M. Delbos, the manager, came over to speak to him.

'Good evening, M. Evans,' M. Delbos said.

'How's business?' asked Evans, pleasantly.

'Not bad. We've surpassed the world's record for broken glassware and crockery. Ten thousand francs' worth in a single week, when nine boat trains came in.'

'That's terrible,' Evans said.

'On the contrary, it's good. The weeks when we only have 5,000 francs breakage, the receipts are correspondingly low. Broken glasses mean crowds, hurried waiters. . . . I don't eyen charge the waiters for what they break.'

Homer settled down to a peaceful drink. Problem ' a ' was fairly well in hand, except for the presence in Paris of Maggie, or problem 'b.' He thought hard about that, for Maggie, Hjalmar had said, had been looking forward to the day when the Weiss windfall would be spent and Hjalmar would be obliged to work or starve. . . . The English girl's condition verged on desperation and Evans was ready to believe she would stop at nothing in her efforts to make Jansen a solid citizen and a marrying man. To what extent would it be fair to deceive her? Could he tell her that if she would go back to her respectable parents in Hampshire for a fortnight, he would promise to put the case for matrimony to Hjalmar as forcibly as he could? He would try it, he decided, as a nearby clock struck five.

Also as the clock was striking, Evans noticed that Ambrose Gring was walking along the sidewalk in the direction of the

Café du Dôme and that, upon hearing the sound of the chimes, he quickened his pace.

'Right on time,' said Evans, amused, but his contentment was ruffled nevertheless. Gring was decidedly a nuisance. If he found out what was under way, either he might tell Hugo Weiss slyly, hoping to get a subsidy himself, or he would extract annoying favours from everyone involved in the deception, as a price for his silence. Refreshed as Evans was, however, he soon hit upon a plan to insure them all against Gring's interference. He would use Miriam Leonard to hold Gring's attention while the painters of the neighbourhood were filling Hjalmar's studio with paintings, most of which would surely be no better than those the big Norwegian had lofted out the window. He would tell Gring that Miss Leonard's father had struck oil, thus relieving her from the necessity of remaining in the States to teach piano. He felt sure she would co-operate.

Hjalmar was waiting, fidgeting in his chair and stalling off ordering because lunch had reduced his seven francs fifty to no francs seventy-five, and there was nothing at the Café du Dôme that could be purchased for seventy-five centimes. His mind was on a single track, with a large bumper at the end. When he saw Homer Evans approaching with his pleasant smile, as if care had departed from the world, he growled and tore a handful of straw from the back of the chair in front of him. Ambrose Gring was four tables in advance, the best he could do on the now crowded *terrasse*, but he missed nothing of the gruff Norwegian's perturbation.

Nodding and smiling to his many acquaintances as he strolled up the aisle, Evans paused a moment to speak with Gring, which surprised the latter to the point where he was stuttering like a schoolgirl. When finally Evans arrived at Hjalmar's table he greeted his friend gaily.

'Well, what shall it be?'

Hjalmar shifted his feet uncomfortably.

'Waiter,' Evans said, without further prompting. 'One American whisky. No, make it double. And bring me vermouth-cassis.'

Hjalmar began to growl but Evans interrupted him.

23

'Don't worry about the expense,' Evans said. 'Within the week you'll be rolling in money.'

Gring dropped his copy of the *Boulevardier* and upset his *crème de cacao* in trying to retrieve it. The word money did things to Ambrose Gring. He thought of men and women in terms of dollars and cents. He thought of music, books and pictures in the same way. That's why he liked old masters. A day at an auction at the Hôtel Drouot left him limp with emotion, just the sound of the prices. If he had seen Miriam Leonard in the humble financial state in which he had always imagined her, and Mrs B. Berry McGluck of Grand Rapids, Michigan, sitting side by side, Miss Leonard would have been a blur without form or colour. On the other hand, the McGluck millions from yellow pine machine-made furniture would transform the wrinkled and foolish widow into a dream of fragrance and loveliness.

The slight confusion attending Gring's mishap with his *crème de cacao* reminded Evans that he must retire to a safer spot for his interview with Hjalmar, so after three double whiskies and three vermouth-cassis, imbibed in silence, Evans led the way to a small chauffeurs' *café* in the neighbourhood. There no one understood English and Gring would not dare enter, because of the rough looking taxi-drivers, most of whom were steady family men.

'I've got it,' Evans said, to end his friend's suspense. 'It's all very simple. You need paintings with which to impress Hugo Weiss. Now paintings are the most plentiful objects in this neighbourhood. I don't know how many coals there are in Newcastle, but I could place my bet on the paintings in Montparnasse to outnumber them. And to the casual glance of the ordinary millionaire and director of museums, the paintings look about as nearly alike as the famous coals.'

He paused to borrow a small sheet of paper from the patron of the *bistrot*, who was pleased that two of the likeable residents of the quarter had chosen his modest place.

'Let me see. If you had painted one canvas a week . . . is that a fair speed . . . you'd have fifty on hand. I'll lend you my single effort which you can call a "self-portrait". All paintings are

24

self-portraits, as a matter of fact, even if the artist doesn't know it. I'm putting down Rosa for six. Harold Simon's good for at least a dozen. Moroni Smith will kick in with, let's say ten. Gwendolyn has fifteen all ready for her Chicago exhibition. That leaves six to be accounted for. Whom shall we give the privilege of contributing the six? It isn't everyone who has a chance to get his work looked at by Hugo Weiss. How about Larry Valley?'

'Not that punk,' Hjalmar said. He wasn't yet hopeful but had placed himself without reserve in Evans' hands.

'Flonzaley?'

'He's a cubist. Good stuff, but we'd never get away with it.'

'Well, there's always Pratt.'

'He stipples his colour. We've got to stick to birds like me who smooth it out with a palette knife.'

'The Finn?'

'I knocked out his front teeth in the Viking last week. He's off me, I think.'

'Nonsense. Northerners don't hold grudges. Besides, he chewed a part of your ear.'

'I forgot I had a necktie on,' Hjalmar said. 'You have to be more careful when you wear a necktie.'

'Six from the Finn. By the way, his name is a long one. That will take a lot of olive oil.'

'Olive oil?'

'Sure. To paint out the signature. You'll have to sign your own name fifty times. Are you up to it?'

Hjalmar was all dejection again. 'I knew there'd be a catch to it. These people won't let me paint over their signatures. It would ruin the paintings.'

'You painters are all alike. You don't know the history of your art, or even the chemistry of it, for the most part. If you mix the colours with olive oil instead of linseed, the whole thing can be washed off and it leaves the painting as good or better than ever.'

'Are you sure? I wouldn't want to queer Gwendolyn's show in Chicago.'

'Have no fear. Titian's best pupils used olive oil.'

25

'I'll be damned if we don't try it,' Hjalmar said. His broad face was happy again, his blue eyes were no longer dull but were distinctly mischievous.

'Don't think we're going into this blindly,' Homer said. 'I've thought of all contingencies. . . . I hope. There are a few precautions to be taken. First we've got to get rid of Maggie.'

At that, Hjalmar beamed and brought down his heavy hand on Evans' shoulder. 'By Yesus, you don't say so.'

'I think I can send her away for a fortnight. . . .'

'Longer,' roared Hjalmar. 'Hey, waiter. Leave the bottle of cognac here.'

'You mustn't get too drunk until the operation's over. Then we'll have a party Montparnasse will never forget.'

'A fortnight,' murmured the big Norwegian happily. 'By Yee.' Then he stopped and his face was clouded again. 'But how are you going to send her away ? I've done everything but throw her out the window.'

'Perhaps you're not aware that she wants you to marry her,' Evans said.

'She's nuts to want to marry me. Can't you talk sense to her . . . ? Tell her I'd probably kill her, that I'd be tangled up with every woman for miles around, that she'd starve. . . .'

'I'll have to tell her that she must go away, that you must be missing her while I'm trying to persuade you.'

'She's not such a damned fool as that. She'd know I'd wake up with another tart beside me the morning after she beat it. . . . Sometimes I think the queers have an easier time, so help me Moses, I do.'

'I'll get Maggie out of the way. I'm seeing her at seven o'clock, and I shall tell her she must leave without a word to you, without even seeing you again. Meanwhile, keep this all under your hat. I'll see the painters and collect the paintings. . . . To-night at eleven o'clock we'll fix up the signatures. To-morrow I'll call on Hugo Weiss, tell him what hard work you've been doing and ask him to spare a few minutes to drop around. You must promise "a": not to get drunk. . . .'

'Never mind "b." It will take all my will power to attend to "a", ' the Norwegian said.

As Evans started for the Dingo, the *terrasses* of the New Dôme and the Old Dôme were packed with tourists and habitués. Extra waiters were scurrying along the outskirts, the regular waiters worked incessantly but efficiently in the central areas. At some of the tables there was earnest conversation, at others alcoholic persiflage. The early spring evening was soft and radiant. Evans walked along at his unhurried pace, aware of the reproachful eyes of Ambrose Gring who was wedged in so tightly that he was a moment late in starting for the Dingo. Evans found Maggie sprawled awkwardly over a bar stool, her long shanks exposed, her skinny fingers clutching a ginger beer.

'Maggie,' Evans began, 'I've thought about what you said to me. If I promise to speak to Hjalmar, will you do exactly as I suggest ? '

'I'll do anything. I'll bless you every day for the rest of my life.'

'You won't complain, if things go badly . . . afterwards ? '

'Just to be his wife. That's all I ask.'

'I can't promise anything, but I'll do the best I can. Meanwhile you must go away. . . .'

'I can't. I wouldn't dare.'

'Only for two weeks. If you are right, and he needs you so much, he'll miss you. He'll appreciate all the little things you've been doing for him. I can talk with him more freely if you are not on the scene. You must leave at once. To-night. You have money ? . . .'

'Of course, I have money. But he won't let me spend a cent of it.'

'All right. Take the next train for London. Don't leave a note, don't tell him you're going. When you come back . . .'

'When I come back I'll find another woman, some fat, shameless creature who doesn't care whether he paints or not. . . .'

'That's the only thing I'll promise you definitely. There'll be no other woman on the premises when you return. . . .'

'I'll do it,' Maggie said, desperately. And as Ambrose Gring came through the doorway she repeated, more wildly: 'I'll do it. But I won't stop at murder. . . .'

'Calm yourself,' said Evans, sharply.

'Remember what I say, and I mean it. There's nothing I won't do.' And she rushed distractedly out the doorway.

'Ah, Gring,' said Evans, cordially. 'Have a drink with me. I haven't had a talk with you in ages.'

CHAPTER 4

Of Mineral Mesmerism

'A FRIEND of mine, who admires you very much, was asking for you to-day,' said Evans, in his most charming manner. Ambrose, who, had he been contemporary with Narcissus, would have outstripped the latter so far that the famous piano piece would have been named Ambrose and not Narcissus, turned pale with delight and astonishment.

' Not Hugo Weiss ? ' he gasped.

' Oh, no. I haven't heard from Hugo, although he usually calls whenever he's in town,' Evans said.

' Hugo Weiss calls on you ? ' Ambrose gasped. 'He actually looks you up ? '

'I put him on to a good thing, once, or at least I saved him from wasting a lot of money. It was a matter of a fake El Greco. . . .'

At that Gring almost fainted. 'A fake El Greco,' he repeated, reaching for water. 'You didn't say a fake El Greco ? '

Utterly unable to understand his companion's alarm at the mention of the Cretan-Spanish master, Evans changed the subject at once.

'I wasn't thinking of Hugo Weiss but of Miriam Leonard,' he said quickly. 'You surely remember Miriam, the good-looking young girl from Montana.'

'Miriam Leonard,' Gring repeated, still in a daze.

'Her father has struck oil,' said Evans, and the change in Gring was little short of miraculous. His dark eyes shone, his thin lips parted in a dizzy sort of smile. He clasped his hands in a prayerful way and gasped. 'Struck oil ! Why that means millions. . . . And she spoke of me ? '

'You were the only one she talked about. She gave no other reason for returning to Paris, although perhaps I shouldn't have told you. She's bashful, really timid, you know. Was raised on a ranch. That makes girls shy. An only daughter, too. . . . Well,' he paused to look at the clock, 'I must be going. So long Gring. No doubt I'll see you later. . . .'

Gring was out on his feet, or rather, on his bar stool. He made a feeble attempt to clutch at Evans' departing sleeve, made a hesitant start to follow him when the bar-tender's voice brought him back to earth with an unpleasant thud.

'Twenty-two francs fifty,' the bar-tender said. He knew he could put the amount on Evans' monthly bill but he preferred to get it out of Gring, if he could. The bar-tender at the Dingo didn't have much fun, especially in the springtime, and almost never had a chance to separate Ambrose Gring from any of his francs.

'Oh, dear. Oh, my God,' Ambrose said, and gazed despondently through the empty doorway in the direction of Evans' back. There was nothing to do but to pay. He couldn't afford to offend Evans, or even to lose a jot or tittle of his newly-acquired esteem. . . . Oil. . . . Millions. . . . 'Well, you needn't be so impatient. I'm not going to run away with your old twenty-two francs fifty. So there now,' Gring said, and with that he stamped a well-shod foot, took a leather change purse from the pocket nearest his heart and counted out exactly twenty-two francs fifty. Miriam owed him twenty-two fifty, was the mental note he made as he handed over the coins. Gring never placed coins on a plate or a table. He delivered them personally, with proper regard for their nature and their magic properties. Once the operation of payment was over, he wiped his brow with a mauve silk handkerchief and hurried out into the evening, jostling passers-by as he desperately sought a glimpse of Homer Evans. Every strange girl looked western to him, and he paused, his jaw dropped, his eyes grew bright with anticipation when one by one the regulars of the sidewalk, whom in his perturbation Gring failed to recognize, said: ''ello, chérie' or 'Où allez-vous, cher Monsieur?'

Meanwhile Evans was approaching the Select, where Miriam was waiting demurely at one of the tables in the rear of the terrasse. In order to be sure that she would not be ogled or annoyed by night-faring tourists she was pretending to read a copy of the Saturday Review of Literature. Actually she was thinking: 'He's coming. He's really coming. I'm not sorry I hurried back to Paris. I don't care if they stop making pianos to-morrow. He didn't seem to dislike me. He didn't throw me out.'

'Am I late?' Evans asked.

The clock on the nearby tower began to strike, so an answer was unnecessary.

'I was early,' she said, apologetically.

'I've involved you in a conspiracy,' he said.

How pleased she was that he didn't try to talk about the piano. How marvellously tactful to plunge her at once into another line of thought, she said to herself.

'You are very thoughtful,' she said.

'You won't think so when I tell you about it,' he went on. 'But first, let's order something to eat. I'm starved. I've done more meddling into other people's affairs to-day than in all my life together.'

'In what way can I help you?' she asked.

'I warn you that the assignment is a tough one. You've got to immobilize Ambrose Gring ... you've got to hold him like a bird before a snake. . . .'

Her dismay was eloquent. 'That lizard! What on earth have I to do with Ambrose Gring?'

'I've got to be certain that he doesn't leave his table on the Dôme *terrasse* between the hours of eleven this evening and one to-morrow morning,' Evans said. 'It's a matter of life and death, almost.'

'Would it be asking too much if I begged for an inkling as to why I should immobilize that scissorbill, and if not why, at least how? He never has even so much as glanced at me. I'm not in Bradstreet, worse luck, and although I've paid little attention to your friend Ambrose I'm sure he's fond of money. Of course, I'm stronger than he is, but if I hold him forcibly in place won't he scream? Wouldn't the police interfere, or the waiters? I'd have to give them some explanation.'

'I've attended to all that,' Evans said. 'I've already told Gring that your father just struck oil.'

'Oh,' she gasped. 'You've told him that.'

'I've taken an even greater liberty,' Evans went on. 'I hinted that you had come back to Paris expressly on his account, that you like him, that he ... er ... fascinates you.'

Miriam half rose, then regained a part of her former placidity. 'Mr Evans,' she said, severely, 'if anyone but you had done such a trick, I would crown him with this siphon and leave town.'

'Please let me explain. ...'

'Well. That's a relief. You're going to explain.'

Rapidly and succinctly he told her about Hjalmar Jansen's predicament and the remedy he himself had suggested. Her hearty but not boisterous laugh caused neighbouring drinkers to glance at the handsome couple, all except Harold Stearns, who was taking his drinking with the usual appropriate seriousness and thinking about the Atlantic Ocean because it was between him and prohibition in the United States.

'I'll do the best I can, but how does one strike oil? I've got to have a factual background, or Ambrose will smell a rat.'

'He won't find it strange that you've taken a fancy to him. It will seem to him quite normal. Whenever he gets you on dangerous ground talk about money. You must have seen large sums of it in mints or banks. But above all, don't mention Hugo Weiss and if you see any of the neighbouring painters dashing toward Hjalmar's studio with canvases under their arms rivet Gring's attention.'

'If only it were anyone except Gring,' she sighed. 'However, I'll try.'

They had finished their dinner, there was an hour to spare, so Evans suggested a drive around the lake in the Bois. His favourite taxi driver, Lvov Kvek, former colonel in the recent army of the late Tsar, was not in line so they strolled back and forth along the sidewalk between the Select and the Rotonde, enjoying the contrast between the chorus of American voices on the *terrasse* of the former and the Scandinavian inflexions which poured from the latter. Rug peddlers with fezzes and brightly coloured wares walked to and fro in a half-hearted way, a fire-eater filled his mouth with gasolene, sprayed it out and lighted it, long-haired sketch artists with portfolios braced likely groups of tourists and were enjoying a fairly brisk trade. The foliage oᶠ the trees showed yellow-green around the street lamps. Montparnasse was hitting its evening stride of those unforgetful days gone by when mankind was dancing without thought of the fiddler's recompense.

As Miriam walked beside Evans, he was pleased to note that she could keep in step. He was telling her about Lvov Kvek, about his escape via Constantinople, his days of starvation in Paris because he was proud and spoke no French and his final triumph over economic problems in the Hôtel Voltaire. It seemed that when Lvov was at the lowest ebb of his fortune he had noticed an old engraving on the wall of his narrow hotel room. He had hidden it under his coat, sold it for three hundred francs on the quai (it was worth much more) and then for three francs had bought a modern engraving to replace it. Each week, until he learned enough French to make his living with a taxi, ex-colonel Kvek has asked the manager to give him another room. He was nervous, he said, and couldn't sleep more than a week in any room. The manager was obliging and thus the engravings in room after room were changed without anyone except Lvov being the wiser. It was Evans' custom to use Lvov's taxi whenever he had a long errand and when it drove up he helped Miriam in and exchanged a few pleasant words with the resourceful Russian. From that moment until they returned to Montparnasse Evans said almost no words at all and when, half way around the lake, he noticed he was holding Miriam's hand, he continued to do so, to soften the ordeal with Gring which was to be her lot that evening.

It was not hard for them to locate Ambrose. He was almost in a state of collapse, stumbling from *terrasse* to *terrasse* in search of Evans and the oil princess of Montana. He looked more haggard than the rug peddlers, for, being of a suspicious nature, he had been shaken with the fear that Evans might have thought over the girl's possibilities and that, even as Ambrose hustled from *café* to *café*, Homer might be trying to steal her affections and her millions. His relief, when confronted by Evans and Miriam, can better be imagined than described. He leaned against a plane tree, clutched his coat lapels and an

33

ivory *café crème* hue spread quickly over his rapturous countenance.

'It's you,' said Miriam, and looked straight into his eyes.

'Glub glub,' he answered as he struggled for words and for strength to sustain himself without the aid of the tree. What followed amounted to mesmerism. The girl drew Ambrose toward the *terrasse* of the Dôme and, by much squeezing and willowy hip weaving, got him seated with his back to the sidewalk. Evans, unable to hold back his laughter, had made a hasty retreat.

Meanwhile, across the boulevard Montparnasse trudged a solitary figure, a red-headed English girl with enormous feet and a large suitcase, hoping for a last secret look at Hjalmar Jansen before she started on her lonely pilgrimage. Luckily for the success of plan 'a', she did not see Hjalmar, who was in a secluded corner of the Rotonde with a tall Swedish actress. He had kept his promise anent the grape. He even had kept track of the hour. But Hjalmar had ten minutes to spare and his dynamic nature, further aroused by the prospect of a Maggie-less fifteen days, demanded stimulation of some sort and Jansen was not the man to thwart himself, if he could help it.

CHAPTER 5

In which Twin Cheques Are Signed

THE picture-signing bee went off without a hitch, although Hjalmar had a rather narrow escape from painter's cramp. The next morning, Evans, true to his promise, called on Hugo Weiss at the Plaza Athénée and was surprised to find that Gring had been there before him.

'Come right in, Mr Evans,' boomed the hearty voice of Hugo Weiss. The multi-millionaire was clad in pyjamas and slippers, covered in part by a loose dressing gown of Persian brocade. The remains of a sumptuous German breakfast were spread on a table near the bedside, a stack of unopened mail rested loosely on the floor. There was no valet in the offing, although Weiss's clothes were ranged neatly in the spacious closet. Except for the breakfast dishes and unopened mail, the large, sunny room was in order.

'I was afraid I might be too late,' Evans said. 'All the biographers of American millionaires would have us believe that they are at their desks by eight-thirty, or at least nine o'clock.'

'In the first place, I'm not American; I'm cosmopolitan. Secondly, I'm not a millionaire, but a multi-millionaire. And I never have had a desk. . . . I'm really glad to see you. Where have you been all this time? You saved me, young man, from making a fool of myself . . . from being laughed at by that hypocrite, T. Prosper Stables. . . .'

'It was nothing,' said Evans.

'To me it was important,' the older man said. 'Not financially, of course. I'm more concerned with getting rid of money than with making it. But I'll tell you a secret. I'm vain. I like to think that I'm perspicacious. I don't like to be deceived. . . .'

Evans suddenly felt the warmth of the morning sunshine and mopped his forehead. 'No. Naturally not,' he said, uneasily. At that moment his scheme in Hjalmar's behalf seemed trans-

35

parent and ridiculous. They would be found out, exposed, and Hugo Weiss would be deeply offended. Even worse, he would be hurt. Still, Evans had no choice but to continue.

'I've come to you about a friend of mine, an artist named Hjalmar Jansen,' he began.

'Jansen,' repeated Weiss, trying to place the man. . . . 'Oh, Jansen,' he said. 'The big Norwegian who drinks like a barracuda. Where is he ? What is he doing ? Why didn't he ever come to see me in New York ? '

'You sent him to Paris,' Evans said.

'Oh, yes. Paris, of course. To paint ? Or was he a sculptor ?'

'He paints,' Evans said.

'Tell me all about him,' the philanthropist said. 'Ah, now it comes back to me . . . a garret in Greenwich village . . . Luchow's. That Würzburger. "Take me down, down, down where the Würzburger flows, flows, flows. It will drown, drown, drown all your troubles and cares and woes." Very true, that, Evans, my boy. I had a good evening with the chap, and I'm glad he's getting on. Straightforward sort of man, no nonsense. Didn't try to impress me, didn't pretend a lot of things that weren't so. That's what I like, Evans. An artist with self-respect and sincerity, one who doesn't put on any dog, whose word is his bond. One who's not afraid of work, who goes straight to his goal. . . . That's Jansen, or I sized him up wrong, and I'm seldom mistaken about people,' said Weiss.

'He was hoping you could see his work . . . he owes so much to you. . . .

'Owes me ? Nonsense. Of course I'll see his work. And by the way, do you suppose there's any real beer in this city ? He'd know it, if there is.'

'You're very kind,' said Evans. 'When may we expect you at the studio ? '

'That's the difficulty. People keep me busy, day and night. I'd like to loaf, as you do. I'd enjoy being detached and inconspicuous but in the beginning I didn't play it that way. I thought I wanted power, and all I got was responsibility. . . . Now, the studio. . . . Let's see. To-day I'm all tied up. Some relatives, you know. It'll be refreshing to see that chap Jansen, who wouldn't give a damn what anybody thought. Imagine him dressing up his place for me, the way relatives do.'

Evans was passing a bad few moments. 'Perhaps to-morrow,' he suggested.

'That's it. To-morrow. I'll drop in before I go to that damned banquet of the *Société des Artistes Français*. I hate banquets and speeches, especially in French. What can a man say in French that hasn't been said too many times already? And I don't even know yet what it is they want of me. They're getting good prices for their stuff, that gang. No, Evans. It's the hard-working, obscure young men like Jansen who'll be talked about when we are gone. Mark my words.'

Evans was marking them all too well. He looked forward to the morrow with misgivings. 'About six o'clock?' he asked.

'Make it six-thirty. I hate to keep young people waiting. . . . And, by the way, did you meet that chap who came to see me just before you did? Ambrose Gring, he said his name was, although it doesn't sound likely. What was he up to, do you think? Said he wrote for *Art for Art's Sake* and wanted a story. You know as well as I do that stories in that sheet don't mean a thing. They're thrown in with the ads. He wanted, in particular, to know if I intended to visit any of the private galleries, if I could tell him of any interesting old masters that might be on sale. The whole thing sounds fishy to me. He wanted to pump me for something. What was it? Who is he?'

'His name is Ambrose Gring, all right. . . . At least, that's the only name he's used in Montparnasse. No one has seen his passport. He went to Yale, won a poetry prize, claims he was with Kolchak in Russia. . . .'

'If I'd known that, I'd have thrown him out bodily,' the philanthropist said.

'He did once write for *Art for Art's Sake*, a small job with almost no pay. He seems to know all the dealers. . . .'

'What seemed stranger than anything else, he asked me about oil. Was it a good, safe investment? Were there really millions in it?'

'What did you tell him about oil?' asked Evans, amused.

'I told him that oil belonged to the public, that natural

resources were the property of all and that anyone who took private profit from them was a robber and a scoundrel. That's what I said. And it seemed to disturb him, almost to frighten him. He thought the public was going to seize the oil before the day was over, it seemed to me. Anyway, I had nothing to tell him about my plans. I'm going to keep away from galleries. I'm not going to open any mail. I shall not put in an appearance at any studios except that of your beer-drinking friend.'

'I must leave you,' Evans said. 'I've taken too much of your time.'

'Not at all. Come any day you like. And thanks again for that Greco incident. I should have stubbed my toe, and been the butt of the trade if it hadn't been for you.'

'To-morrow, then, at half-past six,' said Evans, and with growing qualms walked down the long corridor, descended to the lobby and got into Lvov's taxi at the kerb.

Hjalmar Jansen's studio was in the loft of a dingy building in the rue Montparnasse, overlooking the narrow street and the roofs and chimney-pots of the lower buildings across the way. From the rear window might be seen a small gravelled playground which, at hours of recess, swarmed with decorous half-dazed children from the adjacent parochial school. The windows at the back were barred, since the day when Hjalmar had absent-mindedly heaved a painting of a male nude down into the yard just a moment before the children were turned loose by the nuns, three of whom suffered nervous breakdowns. From that time on, no matter how enraged he became because of the inadequacy of his works, Hjalmar was careful to chuck the discarded paintings northward, toward the street. Of course, not a few of these sailed all the way across and rested on the sooty roofs and before coming to rest tore out aerials and clay chimneys. But that was considered by all concerned the lesser of two evils.

The studio was a huge one, having one small corner set off by curtains for sleeping purposes, and a small gas stove and a wooden table in another corner called the kitchen. The plaster walls were bare, marred by stains of rainwater and bearing scars of nails from which canvases had now and then been hung. The works of Jansen, in what might be termed his 'Paris period', were stacked against the radiator, which never got even warm. Hjalmar had northern blood in his veins. The lack of steam heat did not trouble him, but it was a trial to poor Maggie, who, except in the hottest days of summer, had to watch herself to keep her teeth from chattering.

On the evening Weiss had promised to inspect Hjalmar's paintings, which also was the day set for the annual dinner of the *Société des Artistes Français*, Miriam was again assigned to the task of keeping Gring out of the play. When she joined him on the Dôme *terrasse* she found him in a tremulous state.

'Er, oil, my darling. . . . Oil, my dear. Don't you think you should cable your father?' Ambrose began, and the sound of his words confused him. He had intended to lead up to the subject tactfully.

'There's plenty of time for cabling, although I don't know what I shall say to dad,' she said. 'Just think, in Montana it's only about six o'clock in the morning. How I miss the ranch, sometimes. The shorthorns and the buckaroos, the sagebrush and the cactus. What a pity it is that Montparnasse is not in Nevada, just across the state line. One could rope a broncho....'

At this Ambrose shuddered.

'One could rope a broncho,' she continued, steadying her glass so that Ambrose's shuddering would not spill *crème de menthe* on her dress. 'One could ride for hours across the prairie and the hills, and tie up at the Dôme. That would be living.'

'I got a very disturbing tip about oil, straight from one who knows,' Ambrose mumbled.

'Perhaps father should sell the petroleum and invest in olive oil. Shall I cable him to do that?'

In his eagerness, Gring did upset the *crème de menthe*, but Miriam was too quick for him, and got out of harm's way in time.

'Nothing hasty,' he said imploringly. 'Oh, dear. I'm so nervous this afternoon. I feel as if something were going to happen, as if the people we know were looking at me strangely, as if nothing were safe. . . .'

To get him safely away, she suggested a walk in the Luxembourg gardens.

Their departure was the signal for a general exodus in the direction of the rue Montparnasse. At Evans' suggestion, a half-finished canvas was on the easel, wet. Hjalmar had wet it that same afternoon. The paintings to be exhibited were not stacked neatly but were ranged around the huge room with an air of nonchalance and abundance. Only Evans, who was to select them and place them on the easel, knew exactly how they had been arranged. He had placed them, from left to right, in the order of their merit, as best he could decide, so that the year's progress would be evident. His own portrait of Hjalmar, however, he had placed at the end of the stack, not because he thought it was the best. He could not judge it at all. But he hoped, secretly, that before his portrait was reached, Hugo Weiss would have seen enough. Evans didn't know why, but he was reluctant to have Hugo inspect the so-called self-portrait.

Some very decent sherry had been obtained, clean glasses and a couple of trays had been borrowed from the Dôme and Hjalmar had also borrowed a number of kitchen chairs and daubed them a bit with chrome yellow and emerald green for the sake of the *décor*.

Promptly at six-thirty, a taxi stopped at the door.

'Here he comes,' said Gwendolyn Poularde, who was watching from the window.

Hjalmar looked at Evans for reassurance. He would have rushed from the studio and signed on with the first freighter he bumped into, had he not believed it his duty to stand by and take the blame when it should descend on them. The light of early evening seemed to Hjalmar to be brighter and clearer than it had been at noon.

A knock sounded on the door, and he hastened to open it.

'Glad to see you,' said Hugo Weiss, heartily, offering his hand. 'Four brutal flights of stairs, but I got here just the same.'

Evans joined them, having seen that Hjalmar's knees were knocking together.

'How are you, Mr Weiss? I took the liberty of inviting a few friends for the occasion, people who have a tremendous interest in Jansen's work. They've done so much to help him and encourage him, that I thought you wouldn't mind. . . .'

'Of course not. Of course not. Only don't make any ceremony. Trot out the stuff and let me see it. I'm sure, in advance, that it's all right. Seldom make a mistake in sizing up the younger men, if I do make a bloomer now and then on old masters.'

One by one, Gwendolyn, Rosa, Harold Simon, and Sturlusson were presented and Hjalmar, after trying to manage the tray and accidentally lofting three or four glasses of sherry over his left shoulder, asked the Finn if he'd pass around the drinks.

'Unluckily I haven't much time,' Weiss said. 'I've got to attend that infernal banquet. What on earth shall I say ? I don't like respectable painters. They don't even like themselves or each other. Can you imagine four or five of the Salon crowd coming together like this and trying to encourage another artist ? Never. It's here, in the garrets, that honest work is done and honest judgements are made. No pretence. No fake. . . .'

That time even Sturlusson dropped the tray. 'I tink I go,' he said, but thought better of it and sat down moodily in a corner. Evans was trying to decide just where to begin. With a banquet staring him in the face, Hugo Weiss could not be expected to react to still lives of oysters and Gorgonzola, and Homer wanted to delay the portraits on account of his own. Landscapes. That was the note for a sunny evening. He pulled out a very creditable garage by Simon and placed it on the easel. Hugo Weiss looked at it politely, and no one said a word. Evans tried a clump of trees by Gwendolyn.

'Very fresh,' said Hugo Weiss, adjusting his *pince-nez* and trying to be informal. 'For a big hulk of a sailor, who drinks beer like a Viking, that painting seems extraordinarily feminine.'

Evans jerked it away and reached for another garage, this time with some farm buildings to relieve the severity.

'Mmmmm,' grunted the philanthropist. 'Uncompromising reality. You're versatile, my boy. Quite versatile.'

In a panic, Evans made a grab at random and came up with Maggie, against a velvet background, the foreground usurped by her extraordinary feet.

41

'Gott im Himmel,' said Weiss.

From that time on, until the portraits were reached, the show went better. Hugo Weiss, surrounded by sympathetic Bohemians and warmed by the sherry which he pronounced 'excellent' (one grade higher than 'decent') began to joke as best he could and tried to get the others to express their opinions of the paintings as they were shown. Sturlusson had done a few oysters himself, at a time when he was very hungry, and Weiss thought he detected a considerable advance over the oysters done by Rosa.

'What do you think, Mr Sturlusson ? Hasn't our friend made progress ?'

'I think the first are better oysters,' Sturlusson said, and Rosa, not to be outdone, held out for the bivalves of the Finn. That worked out better than when the same pair was asked to decide between a garage done by Gwendolyn and another two-car garage with pump by Harold Simon.

'After all, one don't compare a one-car garage with a two-car garage,' Rosa said. 'The problem is a different one, involving in one case uniqueness of form and in the second case, repetition of form.'

'I must remember that,' said Hugo Weiss, smiling. 'That remark with slight variations would have saved my face any number of times.' He took a small notebook and a neat gold pencil from his pocket, tried the lead, borrowed a real pencil from Gwendolyn and wrote: 'uniqueness, repetition, not to be compared.'

'I may even work it into my speech to-night,' he said, reaching for another sherry. 'You don't mind ?'

'I should feel honoured,' Rosa said, and slapped him on the knee.

By the time they got to the portraits, the atmosphere of the studio had cleared, and also the sharp edge had been lost from the light. Hjalmar was in a sort of trance, incapable of speech or motion, and this made an excellent impression on Weiss, who attributed his embarrassment to natural modesty.

'I'm seldom wrong about people,' the millionaire repeated.

42

The moment came when Evans had to produce the alleged self-portrait and that time Hugo Weiss was what might be called 'electrified'.

'Ah! Amazing,' he said. 'I've never seen a thing like that before.' He got up, walked to the easel, peered at the brush-strokes, turned and scowled at Hjalmar, who ducked as if the millionaire had thrown a belaying pin.

'Young man,' began Hugo, sternly, 'I've known all along you had talent, and industry. I see now you have genius. You must go on, by all means. You must work, work, work, without thought of ordinary cares.' The philanthropist reached impulsively for his chequebook and a fountain pen. 'Let me see. I gave you a thousand dollars. Not enough, my boy. Not enough. This year I'm going to do better. . . .'

Hjalmar, bewildered, made as if to protest.

With a sweep of his hand towards the portrait, Weiss said: 'My reward is there. You've freed yourself from academic shackles, you've got the mud all out of your palette. . . . Gad! And I hadn't noticed the pose, before. How on earth did you do it, my boy? I've seen self-portraits by Rembrandt, Goya, by Cézanne. But in all of them, the eyes were staring straight at you, and followed you wherever you went. A bit disconcerting at times, not the thing for one's home. But you have painted yourself in half profile.'

'Uh, uh. That's torn it,' muttered Rosa, and Evans crushed a sherry glass in his hand, as if it were an eggshell, and a pigeon's egg at that.

'You must have used two mirrors,' Weiss went on.

'Yes. Double mirrors,' mumbled Hjalmar, and they all breathed again.

'By George. I want that portrait,' said Weiss, and grabbed for the cheque book again. He wrote a cheque for the year's sustenance and handed it to Hjalmar, who shamefacedly put it in his pocket without reading it. Then he took his pen in hand and said: 'I'm buying that self-portrait. . . .'

'But, after all . . .' Hjalmar said.

'No, no. Don't try to give it away,' said Weiss, holding up his hand. 'My boy. A painting is either worth a fair amount of money or it's worth nothing at all. I know you'd give me every painting in the room, if I asked for them. . . .'

'Sure,' said Hjalmar, and Gwendolyn half rose to her feet.

'But I want to pay. Why shouldn't I ? And some day, my boy, I want you to do a portrait of me, for my daughter. I've refused to pose for anyone, so far. But if you can do that of yourself I want to know what you'd do with me.' With that he handed Hjalmar a second cheque, shook hands with everyone and started for the door, the portrait, unframed, in his hands. Only Evans had the presence of mind to accompany him. Lvov was in line with his taxi. Evans helped Weiss into the Russian's cab, shook hands, thanked him profusely, and said to Colonel Ķvek:

'The *Cercle Interalliée.*'

The cab started off, turned into the boulevard Raspail. Evans stood watching it, feeling a strange combination of relief and shame. He mounted the stairs again, entered the studio, and approached the group who were slowly recovering.

'Let's see the cheques. I want to see what price you got for that prize portrait,' said Rosa.

Hjalmar handed them over. He still hadn't read the figures, but the awareness that he was all set henceforth and forever was stealing over him, also the fact that Maggie was far away, that Evans had saved him from exile and privation, and that Hugo Weiss was a brick. His musings were interrupted by Rosa's scream. Rosa gasped, flung the cheques towards Evans and rushed to the corner where the Pernod had been set aside.

'My God. He thinks highly of that daub,' Evans said, taken aback.

'Whatever he paid is yours,' Hjalmar said. 'Of course, I know you were fond of that thing, but I'll pose for another. . . .'

'Oh, no,' said Evans. 'Never again. And you know I've all the money I need. The loot is yours.'

'Let me divide it with the gang,' Hjalmar said.

They all protested. They had set out to do an unselfish deed and didn't want it to prove to be a boomerang. They were beginning to enjoy the situation, and to look forward to an epoch-making evening. The cheques were each for twenty-five

44

hundred dollars. Both were made out to Hjalmar and bore the same date.

'Gring's back. We've got to rescue Miriam,' Evans said, 'but first we must decide where she should join us. We're not quite out of danger yet, you know. I've seen Gring snooping around Hugo Weiss's hotel already and if he gets wind of this and tips off Weiss, who dislikes above all things to be deceived, we're sunk."

'I'd better cash those two cheques to-night, in case,' Hjalmar said.

'I think you'd better, too. But where?'

'Chalgrin will take one, Delbos the other. I owe them both enough to make it worth their while,' Hjalmar said.

CHAPTER 6

The Philanthropist Disappears

IT was eight o'clock in the spacious main *salon* of the resplendent *Cercle Interalliée*. Elsewhere, in the same zone with reference to Greenwich, it was eight o'clock, too, but the people did not seem to be so uneasy about it. The odour of expensive food in preparation, in fact in readiness, mingled with the fragrance of tulips, roses, hydrangeas and lilies of the valley. The resultant atmosphere was stirred with talk about art, not for art's sake, but for the sake of the distinguished gathering of men, all clad in the conventional black, with neatly trimmed beards, practically all sporting the *rosette* of the Legion of Honour in their buttonhole. The artists assembled knew that the guest of the evening was to be Hugo Weiss, and they all were sure the dinner would come back to them, like bread cast upon the waters, in the form of donations to funds for the stabilization of art. Only two men, the president and the first vice-president of the *Société*, who by amicable arrangement alternated with the first and second prizes at the annual *Salon*, knew what the multi-millionaire was about to be asked to contribute and for what specific purpose.

The first vice-president, Christophe Paty de Pussy, had formulated the plan. He knew his colleagues had a frightful time investing their money. Established painters were under a perpetual disadvantage in the financial field. If they were careless and lost their earnings the rich bankers would say: ' A man so defective in good sense cannot be a first class painter. After all, we are artists, too. We make patterns with money. The flow of currency must be subtle or bold, as the case may be, just like the flow of line. Monsieur So-and-So, whom I rooked so easily, must be a bad painter.' On the other hand, if an artist-investor showed too much shrewdness, the financiers would shake their heads with apprehension: ' *Maître Un Tel* has his mind on other things than his models. One cannot serve art and Mammon.' In either case, the painter lost out. It had been Monsieur Paty de Pussy's idea that Hugo Weiss and a few other magnates who controlled the world's purse-strings should establish an *Institut Artistique de la Prudence et de la Sécurité* which would handle the funds of Salon exhibitors, guaranteeing a profit of at least ten per cent to members whose paintings were hung 'on the line' and of seven and one-half per cent to those whose works were placed above the line. Post-Impressionists, Cubists, Surrealists and all subversive painters were, of course, to be excluded from the benefits of the proposed *Institut* and *pointillistes* were to be admitted only by a two-thirds vote. The reward to be offered to Hugo Weiss in return for his acceptance of the presidency and his assumption of overhead charges was that the new institute was to be named the *Hugo Schussschicker Weiss Institut Artistique de la Prudence et de la Sécurité.*

'French artists would never accept assistance from an institute with a German name,' said the president, M. Haute Costa de Bellevieu.

'I have never seen them turn down anything that resembled money,' M. Paty de Pussy said.

'It's after eight o'clock and the damned ingrate hasn't showed up yet,' the president said. That was substantially what all the other artists and members of the staff were saying. The committee had been obliged to spread itself. No detail had been overlooked. The menu contained the best that France had to offer, arranged traditionally and to be served with appropriate wines. Members who were likely to doze after eating had been placed at a safe distance from the speaker's place and were to be screened by the roses and hydrangeas, lilies of the valley not having enough height for the purpose. The thing had cost a pretty penny, and some of the younger painters, that is to say, those under sixty-five, were hungry and had begun to fret.

By eight-thirty they were calling Hugo Weiss a pig and before nine o'clock had run through the list of lesser animals. At nine o'clock M. Paty de Pussy asked the *maître d'hôtel* to telephone the Plaza Athénée and inquire if M. Weiss had left.

'M. Weiss left the hotel, alone, at six-fifteen,' the *maître d'hôtel* reported.

47

'Six-fifteen? Ridiculous! The dinner was to begin at eight,' the president said.

'Perhaps he has a mistress,' suggested Paty de Pussy.

'A mistress, at six-fifteen? With wines like Lafitte 1907 and Montrachet '21 in prospect? Barbarous. But one can never tell about these Americans, whatever country they really come from.'

'Find out if he has a mistress,' the president snapped to the *maître d'hôtel*. Within five minutes the *maître d'hôtel* returned.

'Not in Paris,' he said. Both the president and the vice-president grunted in disgust.

'The man's an imbecile,' M. Haute Costa de Bellevieu said.

Paty de Pussy was angry but he also was alarmed. 'Could anything have happened?' he asked.

'Well, speak up! Could anything have happened?' the president snapped at the *maître d'hôtel*. The latter withdrew and in five minutes was back again.

'Something might have happened,' he said. 'A telephone girl at the Plaza Athénée and the Russian doorman both were listen-in on the phone at six, when M. Weiss told one of his cousins that he was going to Montparnasse.'

'Montparnasse?' exclaimed the president. 'Good God! What on earth would he be doing in Montparnasse?'

At that point a reporter from the New York *Herald*, who had been busy in the bar and had not noticed it was nearly ten o'clock, staggered into the main dining room and, negotiating in a creditable manner the slippery floor, approached the president.

'When do we eat?' the reporter asked. 'I'm hungry.'

'When, indeed?' exploded Paty de Pussy. 'When, indeed? Our guest of honour, your countryman, is cavorting in Montparnasse, while the flower of French art cools its heels and a dinner too good for King George is spoiling in the kitchen. It's an insult to France. The fellow should be deported.'

'Can't we start with the dinner anyway?' the reporter asked.

'It would serve him right,' said the president. One-third of the members were already asleep.

'I think, M. le Président, that it might be wise to inform the police,' the *maître d'hôtel* suggested politely.

'Nonsense,' the president said.

'After dinner,' said the reporter. 'This is my first assignment this season with a decent dinner in prospect. Let's put on the nosebag, then I'll go to Montparnasse myself and dig up the man. There are only four places he could be, the Dôme, the Coupole, the Rotonde, or the Select.'

'Or possibly the Falstaff or the Dingo. They have very decent baked beans at the Dingo,' the *maître d'hôtel* said.

'Don't mention baked beans. I'm dying of hunger,' said the reporter. 'Why not compromise? Let's eat and call the police simultaneously. They'll be looking for Weiss and if they find him they'll bring him here.'

Reluctantly the president consented and told the head waiter to wake up the dozing members and to use his own judgement about bringing in those who had clustered around the bar.

'I would not have thought of suggesting the police, had I not remembered that M. Weiss has dined here seven times in the last ten years and that on each occasion he was punctual, scrupulously punctual. In 1919 he was five minutes late, following a conference with the minister of finance, a matter which bore on our national defence....'

Impatiently the president interrupted the *maître d'hôtel's* flow of reason. 'That's it. We'll have to make an announcement.' He rapped sharply for order and said loudly: '*Chers Maîtres!* I regret to announce that our guest of honour, M. Hugo Weiss, has been detained on a matter involving our national defence...'

There was polite applause and without further prompting the members found their places and the waiters distributed the steaming plates of *crême de pommes d'amour Campbell*, a speciality of the chef's when he was put out about something. Meanwhile the *maître d'hôtel* was in conversation with the prefect of police. The prefect was not alarmed. Americans were likely to do anything, he said. However, he agreed to inform the commissariat nearest the Dôme and to start a search for the missing multi-millionaire.

Meanwhile strange things had been happening in Montparnasse. Homer Evans, after watching with mixed feelings Lvov's taxi containing Hugo Weiss disappear into the boulevard Raspail, and having learned that the genial philanthropist had

49

written two cheques for twenty-five hundred dollars to all intents and purposes identical, had telephoned Miriam, knowing that the Dôme's booths were reasonably soundproof and that Gring, however anxious, would not dare to follow her into the booth. Homer had asked her to meet him in fifteen minutes at the Café du Départ in the place St Michel. It had been agreed that Hjalmar was to throw a party and Evans had suggested a rendezvous in the rue de la Huchette, just off the place St Michel, where he knew of a small hotel with an unexploited revolutionary sub-cellar, an arched stone room far below the street level in which no end of carousing could occur without a whisper being heard above stairs. Monsieur Juillard, the proprietor, was an inspired cook, a genial Savoyard, and would enter into the spirit of the occasion, produce a meal that would be historic, trot out the best from his well-stocked wine cellar that in Robespierre's day had been a prison cell. Homer had asked the other participants to scatter and to go to the Hôtel du Caveau separately, without letting the news leak out in the quarter. The hour of assembly, for preliminary drinking, was set for nine o'clock.

Hjalmar, all his good spirits returned and his qualms drowned in excitement, was at the top of his form. Money galore, fame awaiting as the only painter of Hugo Weiss, and Maggie three hundred miles away. He hurried to the Dôme and flashed his cheque on the astonished M. Chalgrin, who, liking Hjalmar sincerely, rejoiced at his good fortune. Of course he would cash the cheque. Who had not heard of Hugo Weiss? He excused himself, after he had looked up the rate of exchange, went to his upstairs apartment and returned with 125,000 francs which Hjalmar stuffed carelessly into various pockets. M. Chalgrin almost went down on his knees.

'I beg of you, I implore you. Let me keep it safe for you,' he said, but Hjalmar, for just one night, wanted to know how it felt to have unlimited funds right in his pocket.

'Don't tell a soul about this,' Hjalmar said, and M. Chalgrin promised, shaking like a leaf. While they were standing there, Chalgrin still shaking and Hjalmar bubbling over with animal spirits, Ambrose Gring came rushing in.

'Where is she ? Where is Miriam ? She's gone !' he shrieked, wringing his hands.

'Have a drink. Who's gone?' asked Hjalmar, knowing Miriam had made a clean getaway and was probably sitting beside Evans in the place St Michel.

In despair, a picture of complete desolation, Gring turned on M. Chalgrin. 'She got away through your side entrance ! She must have ! I was watching the main door every minute.'

'How many thousands go in and out my doors ? Do you expect me to remember ? Sit patiently, and no doubt she'll come back, whoever she is you're looking for.'

Ambrose gasped, pressed his hands to his forehead and dashed across the street toward the Rotonde. Hjalmar swallowed another brace of applejacks, shook M. Chalgrin's hand, and lumbered through the *terrasse*, upsetting two tourists, one table and three beers. One of the tourists, not knowing Hjalmar's *penchant* for fighting and having lost his faculty for estimating the size of objects, rushed after the Norwegian and demanded an apology. The *habitués* of the Dôme held their breaths and those within ten metres scattered to avoid the danger of being hit by flying visitors. But to everyone's surprise and relief, Hjalmar grabbed up the little man, held him in a fervent embrace, and kissed him on both cheeks. Then he hurried on toward the Coupole.

At the Coupole he found M. Delbos, who gladly cashed the other cheque for him and gave Hjalmar 125,000 francs in 5,000 franc bills. No sooner had the bills been stuffed into Hjalmar's already bulging pockets than Gring came dashing in, more frenzied than ever.

'I can't find Evans either ! He's stolen her. I know he's stolen her. . . . You wait. I'll find her, and I'll get even with him. You see if I don't. You're all in league. You're all against me,' Ambrose said.

'Have a Calvados,' Hjalmar said. 'It can't be as bad as all that.' He had a generous expansive nature and when he himself was feeling so good he couldn't bear to have another man sad.

'It can't be Evans who got her,' Hjalmar said, thinking that would comfort Gring. 'Evans is banqueting with Hugo Weiss.

51

I'm sure. No women present. Swanky dinner of some sort. I saw them go away together.'

That seemed to give Ambrose a new lease of energy and, panting with dismay and apprehension, he dashed across the street to the Select.

By nine-fifteen, not one person who had been a party to the deception of Hugo Weiss in Hjalmar's studio that day was to be seen in Montparnasse. They had, without exception, disappeared without trace. The light showed yellow-green around the street lamps and pink reflexions of the quarter's mad glitter could be seen on the clouds above. Through the gay crowd the rug peddlers strolled with their wares, the fire-eater sprayed forth his first geyser of flame. All the seats on the *terrasses* were occupied and extra chairs and tables had been used to extend the area. Taxis arrived and departed. Everyone was carefree and light-hearted except Ambrose Gring, who staggered desperately from *café* to *café*, mumbling and imploring.

At ten o'clock, he could contain himself no longer. He rushed to a telephone, called the *Cercle Interalliée* and begged to be allowed to speak with Evans.

'No M. Evans is here this evening,' the *maître d'hôtel* replied.

'My God! He must be! Then let me speak with Hugo Weiss.'

The *maître d'hôtel* did not lose his head. He merely asked an assistant to call the prefect of police and ask him to trace the mysterious call and listen in, so the rest of the dialogue between the distracted Ambrose and the *maître d'hôtel* was heard by the prefect and a stenographer, while police reserves rushed towards the Dôme to take Gring into custody.

'I demand to speak with M. Weiss. . . . My girl has gone, the people may seize the oil at any moment. I can't find Miriam, I can't find Homer Evans. . . .'

'Would you mind repeating those names?' the *maître d'hôtel* asked, having in mind that the police were on the wire.

'Homer Evans. There's a plot! I don't know what to do. I've looked everywhere. Homer Evans went to your club with Hugo Weiss. I know he did. . . . No, I didn't see him. Hjalmar told me.'

'Damn these foreign names,' said the stenographer.

'H for Henriette, J for Julienne. Yes, that's it. J. Hjalmar Jansen, a painter. He said Homer was with Mr Weiss. That they set out together for the club. . . . Glub. Help. Mamma !'

The conversation terminated in a series of pitiful shrieks as the heavy hands of a quartette of cops tore Ambrose from the phone booth, and rushed him through the crowded *terrasse* and into the wagon.

CHAPTER 7

The Dragnet Is Spread

MIRIAM, with Evans beside her, was sitting on the corner of the
Café du Départ, her back to Notre Dame, with the Conciergerie
on her right and the St Michel fountain on the starboard side.

'We could have done nothing without your help,' Evans said.
Nevertheless he was afraid Gring still might find out what had
happened. 'You're sure he didn't suspect anything?' he asked.

'He wasn't out of my sight,' Miriam said. 'Of course, last
night two men I'd never seen in the quarter sought him out and
spoke with him. I couldn't hear what they were saying, but they
wanted something from Ambrose. Once I thought I heard the
word " Greco " but I might have been mistaken. Come to
think of it, the same pair found him again to-night and they
were disappointed, displeased with what Ambrose had or had
not done, I think.'

'Let's forget Gring. You were magnificent,' he repeated.

'I've never seen such singleness of purpose as poor Ambrose
showed,' she said, this time without a shudder. 'Had he been
attracted to me, in a messy way, the situation would have been
unbearable. But I never have felt so impersonal. It was as if I
were the Goddess of Petroleum in technicolor, thrown upon a
screen amid gushers and bank vaults. Now, if I could keep my
eye on the ball like that I'd make Brailowsky sound like a piano
tuner. And you . . . Why, Homer, with that kind of concentration, you'd be . . . why, you'd be . . .'

'What would I be, if I pulled myself together?'

She gave up. 'I don't like to think of you otherwise than you
are,' she said.

'The great loafer. That's what I want to be. I have written a
book and painted a portrait, only to prove to myself that I don't
have to loaf if I don't want to. But that's what I want to do.
I like it. I hate activity and bustle. I don't want to carry on the
torch of civilization.'

54

'Of course not. You make me feel small,' she said. 'Just a few days ago I thought nothing mattered except thumping away at pianos. Now that doesn't mean anything at all.' And she sighed so happily that Evans had a faint twinge of alarm. He heard a faint roar and saw a couple of frightened bats come larruping out of the rue de la Huchette. 'Hjalmar must be arriving,' he said. 'Let's go to the Caveau.'

It was Hjalmar, all right, and not far behind him was Rosa Stier, who somehow had shaken off the effects of the afternoon's Pernods and was ready to start all over again. The Phoenix had nothing on Rosa, as a come-back specialist, only the fabulous bird rose from ashes and Rosa preferred something infinitely more moist. The Finn, when he appeared a moment later, had with him the Swedish actress and they all grouped themselves around M. Julliard's neat zinc bar, where they were joined by Harold Simon and his favourite model, a black girl from Martinique who was nicknamed 'Cirage'.

'Is this an American holiday?' M. Julliard asked, serving drinks adroitly without seeming to exert himself. There was a night's work ahead of him that might have staggered the kitchen force of the *Cercle Interalliée*, but he liked to work in good company and especially for Evans and Hjalmar, who had used his modest establishment as a refuge many times before. An *habitué* of Montparnasse who goes to a narrow street behind the place St Michel is as safely hidden as if he were in the Marquesan islands.

When Hjalmar and his friends got tired of standing around the bar, they all descended two long flights of dark stone stairs, ducked through low archways and over gravelled corridors until they reached the banquet room, which in its day had been a judgement room used by Robespierre. There they were doubly safe from either discovery or intrusion. Even a man as prominent as Robespierre had been able to carry on there at will, without the people in the streets above, or even the commissaire of police two blocks away, suspecting what was happening in those granite-vaulted chambers. And in the same degree that the placid rows of wine bottles transformed the ancient prison cell next door, the company of revellers, primed with

55

divers stimulants and cheered by their recent success, transformed the grim tribunal into a banquet hall. The first course was not *crème de pommes d'amour en boîte à la Campbell*, as had been served to the frock-coated academicians, but a St Germain to which M. Julliard had brought a true poetic touch as well as the prescribed ingredients. Miriam was conceded by all to be the heroine of the day and was toasted in various languages, including the Scandinavian.

Would it be too cruel to leave that happy company a moment and look upon Ambrose Gring ? Ambrose, his face distorted with fear and his clothes awry, was cowering on the edge of the hard-wood bunk and staring at a blank plaster wall. A rat now and then peered at him suspiciously, then withdrew into its hole. There were, in the vicinity, neither tulips, roses, hydrangeas, nor lilies of the valley.When a draught through the bars of the door stirred the air, Ambrose, fond of money as he was, would have paid ten francs for even one sprig of catnip. He had been heaved rather forcefully into the wagon, in plain sight of all Montparnasse, jolted over cobbles and pavements, placed under a blinding white light, and asked what he knew about Hugo Weiss. He told them all he knew, and did his best at inventing more, but the officers had not thought he had told them enough. Not even half enough. The commissaire had barked and fumed, detectives had roared, threatened, and cajoled in turn. Whatever happens in police stations, hidden from the eyes of the public, happened that evening to Ambrose Gring, and all he could say was that he had interviewed Hugo Weiss at the Plaza Athénée two days previously in the hope of picking up saleable bits of information, and that he had not seen the magnate since. He repeated hundreds of times and under all conditions of light and pressure, that a painter named Hjalmar Jansen, which the prefect's stenographer had written as Iallemaire Gonso, had told him (Ambrose) that Hugo Weiss and a man called Homer Evans (transcribed by the *commissaire* as Jaume Ivan), an alleged North American without visible means of support, had (Hugo and Jaume) entered a cab driven by a dangerous Russian, Lvov Kvek (even the *commissaire* could not make that one more improbable) and disappeared.

56

'You are sure this fellow Iallemaire said " disappeared " ?'
asked the *commissaire*, shaking Ambrose with every word but
especially hard with the words 'Iallemaire' and 'disappeared.'
The *commissaire* had a flair for emphasis and rhythm.

'Not disappeared. He said " drove away ".'

'First you say one thing, then another. Now what exactly did
this . . . this damned painter tell you ?'

'He just said that they got in the cab,' Ambrose said.

'Lock up this imbecile until he can get his story straight,' the
commissaire bellowed, 'and then bring me this unpronounce-
able artist. Also this Jaume Ivan and the Russian Kvek. Also
Iallemaire's *concierge*, if there is such a person and he has a
concierge. If not, we'll consult this Greeng Ambrose again, but
formally.'

'You're not going to let me go ?' Ambrose asked in terror.
'I've done nothing at all. I wanted to find my girl, who's struck
oil.'

'Ah. *Crime passionel*. Her name ?'

'Must I tell you that ?'

'If you like to remain healthy,' the *commissaire* said.

'Her name is Miriam . . . Oil . . . Montana.'

'Ah, Spanish. Take that down. Mademoiselle Montana.
Bring her, and also her *concierge*.'

'Please bring her here. I must find her. You will find her,
won't you ?'

'Patience, *nom de Dieu*. We've got to find half of Montparnasse, and probably not one of them can speak understandable
French.'

'You have no passport. That is enough to hold you thirty
days, after which we can hold you six months or more for
having failed to report that you had no passport. By that time,
if Hugo Weiss is not found, alive or dead, you either will be
guillotined or not, according to the circumstances. Take him
away,' the *commissaire* roared.

'Away' was perhaps too strong a word. They dragged the
half-fainting Ambrose about six yards, opened an iron door
with bars and then shoved. Then, accompanied by two detectives from the prefecture, practically the entire staff of the

Montparnasse commissariat started looking for the missing witnesses, Gonso or Gonsi, Ivan Jaume, L. Kvek, and Mademoiselle Montana. It was not more than an hour before Sergeant Frémont, an officer whose record at the prefecture had rapidly been attracting favourable attention, found a *concierge* who had an artist-tenant whom she described as very big and violent, although *gentil*. The painter, she said, had conducted some sort of reception that afternoon at which a very well-dressed and rich-looking man, unquestionably distinguished, had been a guest. The rich distinguished American had arrived in a taxi, had asked the *concierge* on which floor the painter lived and had mounted the four flights of stairs, only pausing twice for breath and not very long at that.

'He was very spry for a large man,' the *concierge* said.

'And did this distinguished phenomenon reappear?'

'About half-past seven. Maybe a little later,' the *concierge* said. She insisted, however, that her tenant was not called Iallmaire or Gonzo, but was named Johnson, like so many North Americans.

Sergeant Frémont beckoned an officer to accompany him and started up the stairs. He paused for breath only once, not wishing to be outdone by a visiting millionaire. The door of the studio on the fourth floor was ajar and without hesitation Sergeant Frémont walked in, expecting to catch this Gonso or Johnson in some incriminating activity. Instead he saw a huge, empty room, with paintings stacked along the walls, a double cot bed imperfectly screened in one corner, a gas stove in another. An easel stood empty and there was broken glass on the floor, but no bottles or glasses, the same having been removed by the waiter from the Dôme. Quietly and efficiently the sergeant examined the studio and glanced at one of the paintings. It chanced to be Maggie, so he replaced it quickly. The cop stood in the doorway, waiting for instructions. The *concierge*, whose curiosity was too strong to permit her to remain downstairs, appeared.

'Where does this Gonso spend his time? He's not here,' the sergeant said.

'He's never here at this hour. He'll come rolling in about

four in the morning, probably with a new woman since his girl's away,' said the *concierge*.

'Is his girl called Mademoiselle Montana?' the sergeant asked sharply.

'God knows. I never asked her,' said the *concierge*. 'I should have, I know, but the girls come and go so fast I thought she'd be gone before the report could reach the commissariat. This one has stayed longer than the others. Anyway she's certainly not a beauty.'

'When did she go away, and where?'

'She left two days ago, in the evening. Was going to America or England, I think she said. She didn't seem happy, and she assured me she was coming back.'

'I can't produce her to-night, that's certain.' He reached for his note-book and scratched off Mademoiselle Montana. 'And we can't wait until dawn for this blasted painter,' he said. 'Where would we be likely to find him?'

'In one of the big *cafés*. He drinks practically all the time he's not sleeping or painting.'

'Who else was here to-day?'

'Some other painters, one of them a short, stocky woman who looks like a chair, another a French girl who paints trees and garages. I saw some of her paintings when I helped her carry them upstairs.'

'Then the paintings here are not necessarily those of this Gonsohn or Iallemaire?'

'They've all been bringing paintings lately,' the *concierge* said. 'The chair woman brought in some oysters and lobsters that looked good enough to eat, almost. She paints food, for the most part, I think. Each one seems to have his speciality.'

'If the paintings are signed, I can find out all their names,' the sergeant said. 'Bonnet, please stack these canvases according to size and show me the signatures one by one.'

The officer and the *concierge* both got busy, and Frémont began to scowl as it became clear that all of them were signed H. Jansen. The *concierge* looked frightened and guilty.

'*Madame*,' said the sergeant severely. 'Perhaps I should have told you that in this case a kidnapping and very probably murder is involved. Enough of your jokes. You led me to believe, for no reason I can fathom, that these paintings are the work of several odd people, denizens of this quarter whom you know by sight. I find, upon examination, that none of them were painted by this Gonso, and all of them were signed by a party who styles himself H. Jansen.'

'That may be Johnson for all I know. It's hard to spell these outlandish foreign names. And I was speaking the truth when I said that the French girl showed me garages and trees she said were hers, that the chair woman claimed to have painted the sea food and fruit. And I know for a fact that my tenant, who I will never believe is a murderer, painted that undressed girl with the feet, for that is the girl who went to America and I saw her lying right here in her pelt, shivering, when M. Johnson or Jansen was at work,' said the *concierge* with spirit.

'You will have a chance to tell all that to the *commissaire*,' the sergeant said.

'I'll tell it to the President of the Republique, if need be. I'd tell it to a priest on my deathbed, for it's true,' she said.

'I'm inclined to believe you, although it doesn't get me anywhere. You said paintings have been brought in, and that this nudist is Mademoiselle Montana, now in England or the United States. Have paintings been taken out, also?'

'Only one,' the *concierge* said.

'Who took that out, and when?'

'The well-dressed distinguished gentleman took one with him at seven-thirty, a painting of M. Johnson, and it looked just like him, too,' the *concierge* said.

'What devilish luck,' the sergeant said. 'Are any of these other paintings of this Gonstein? No, I thought not. I'll have to take you along to identify him. We'll make the round of the *cafés*.'

'As you like. You won't find anything wrong with him, unless it's a tendency to box when he's drunk, and a certain laxity with women which is pardonable in a man of his age and profession.'

'He'll have to find Hugo Weiss, to say nothing of Kvek, an American dilettante called Ivan and everyone else who attended

60

that party this afternoon. Also to explain about this unimpressive person without papers who says he is Greeng Ambrose. If he's not a gigolo, then I'm not a detective,' said the sergeant. 'There are plenty of gigolos,' the *concierge* said, 'and too many detectives.'

Frémont turned to the cop. 'Pack all this stuff (indicating the paintings) into a car and take it to the *préfecture*. And handle everything with care. For all I know these things may be good, or even valuable. . . . Ah, I have it now,' he said. 'The frock-coated American has been swindled by this mob. He came to buy paintings. They all knew he was coming. No doubt this Gonzo, whose confederate is Mademoiselle Montana, commands a higher price than the French girl or the chair woman or the others. Therefore he signs all the paintings and the American, thinking he has bought a Gonzo, goes away with a painting which might have been painted by practically anyone in Montparnasse. I believe that Mademoiselle Montana, as well as this Ivan and Kvek, scout for customers while Gonzo's associates in the studio turn out canvases by the yard. What you call " quantity production " and " high pressure salesmanship." '

'I think M. Johnson will explain,' the *concierge* said.

'If he knows what's good for him, he will,' said the detective.

They entered the Dôme and found M. Chalgrin standing near the cashier's seat and listening to the clinking of coin. Because of Hjalmar's gathering in the studio, the Dôme had got off to a flying start of broken glass that day and its proprietor had hopes of smashing the world's record for twenty-four hours which was held by the Coupole. The Dôme was an old-established *café*, the Coupole an interloper, according to Chalgrin's idea.

'Why, hello, sergeant,' M. Chalgrin said. 'I haven't seen you since that Rosary game exposure. Congratulations. Now we'll hear no more about the genial Irishman who's on his way to Rome.'

'There are thousands of Irishmen, worse luck,' Frémont said. 'The man I'm looking for now is a party named Gonzo . . .'

'Not Gonzo, Johnson,' the *concierge* said. 'You know. The big painter who boxes when he's drunk. . . .'

'Oh. You mean Jansen, the Norwegian. Why? What's wrong with him?' Suddenly M. Chalgrin gasped, clutched his pocket, leaned against the bar in order to keep his legs from buckling.

'I'm sure he's not a swindler or a murderer,' the *concierge* said.

'I want him, and I want him now. Where is he?' Sergeant Frémont said.

Chalgrin began to splutter, then to wave. The spluttering began to be faintly articulate and the waving slowed down so that Frémont could grab and hold a cheque that had been in Chalgrin's hand. The sergeant glanced at it once, then his usual calm forsook him.

'You cashed this cheque? You gave this Gonzo huge sums of money?'

'And why not? He's been a good client for a long time, he's even painted my picture. . . .'

'Very probably he did not.'

'My dear sir, I was sitting in the room when he did it. I sat there for hours every morning. That cheque is signed by Hugo Weiss. Everybody knows about Hugo Weiss. Why shouldn't I cash it?' M. Chalgrin asked.

'I could give you a dozen reasons, but there's no time now. At what hour did you commit this idiocy?'

'About a quarter to eight.'

Frémont groaned. 'My God. He's had a start of three hours and a half. He may be in Belgium, Luxembourg, on the English channel to join that Mademoiselle Montana. . . . One hundred and twenty-five thousand francs. . . .'

'But the cheque. What's wrong with the cheque?'

'Hugo Weiss has disappeared, evaporated, vanished. No trace of him anywhere.'

'Does that affect the cheque?'

'I'll take the cheque,' the sergeant said. 'Now show me this Gonzo.'

'He's not on the *terrasse*. In fact I haven't set eyes on him since I gave him the money. He started out from here in the direction of the Coupole.'

'Why didn't you say that in the first place? We've wasted

62

valuable time,' the sergeant said, disgustedly, and hustled toward the Coupole with the *concierge* in his wake. There they found M. Delbos standing on the sidewalk, in the shadow of a tree, glancing anxiously toward the Dôme. He had heard the breakage record was in jeopardy and was frankly worried.

'M. Delbos,' the sergeant said, 'is there a painter on your *terrasse*, a kind of Swede named Gonso?'

'Not Gonso, Johnson,' said the *concierge*.

'You don't mean Jansen, Hjalmar Jansen?'

'Perhaps. He also goes by the name of Iallemaire. Lead me to him instantly.'

'What's wrong with M. Jansen?' asked M. Delbos, and instantly all thoughts of the breakage record were swept from his mind. He began to yammer and clutch at his collar.

'Nothing much. Look at this,' the detective said, holding out the Weiss cheque for $2,500.

'Where did you get it? How could I have been so careless?' asked Delbos, reaching quickly for his pocket. To his astonishment and horror, he found his cheque was still there. He hauled it out, started waving it, and the sergeant grabbed his wrists.

'You don't mean to say there are two of them?' He snatched both cheques away and compared them. 'Identical, or a clever forgery,' he said. 'Don't lose a minute. Take me to this Gonzo.'

'He's gone. He went away at a quarter to eight,' Delbos said. 'Sergeant! What shall I do? The cheque I cashed was signed by Hugo Weiss, the multi-millionaire. M. Jansen is an old customer, besides, he owed me quite a bill.'

Sergeant Frémont was visibly annoyed. 'M. Delbos, I think I should tell you that there is kidnapping and probably murder involved in this case. This M. Gonzo is fiendishly clever but he couldn't be in two places at once. Your neighbour at the Dôme, M. Chalgrin, has stated that he cashed a cheque for $2,500 at a quarter to eight and handed the money to this Gonzo, and that they drank six glasses of Calvados together. Now you tell me that Gonzo was *here* at a quarter to eight. A man doesn't swallow six glasses of Calvados in as many seconds.'

'You don't know M. Johnson,' the *concierge* said.

Delbos was too frightened to talk or to think. 'Is the cheque good or not?'

'Our experts will decide whether or not it has been forged, and our legal advisers will look up precedents. I'll have to take the cheque. . . . Bonnet!' he said. 'Go to the Rotonde and the Select and collect all cheques for $2,500 signed by Hugo Weiss.'

The agent saluted and crossed the busy thoroughfare.

'Who are the intimates of this Gonzo? Do you know Mademoiselle Montana, or an American called Ivan, or an alleged taxi-driver named Lvov Kvek?'

'I know Kvek. He's a former colonel in the recent army of the late Tsar, and he drives a Citroën cab. As for Mademoiselle Montana, is she a red-headed girl, rather thin. . . .'

'That's the one. Do you know where she is?'

'She wasn't with Jansen to-night. That's strange. Usually she stays quite close to him, to keep him out of trouble.'

'What kind of company does Gonzo keep?'

'All kinds,' said Delbos. 'But his friend Mr Evans is a fine gentleman.'

'That must be Ivan. Where is he?'

'I haven't seen any of them to-night. That's strange.'

'What's strange? They've made a big clean-up and a clean get-away. You and M. Chalgrin furnished them the money. . . .'

'Don't say that!' said M. Delbos.

'Not only kidnapping and murder, but some new racket connected with the making and marketing of paintings. I found Gonzo's studio filled with canvases he did not paint, each one signed by him. The last seen of Hugo Weiss, the American multi-millionaire, was when he left Gonzo's place in the taxi driven by the confederate, Kvek. Mademoiselle Montana had fled two days previously. Other members of the gang. . . . By the way, was it one of your waiters who served the party in that studio this afternoon?'

'I think the waiter was from the Dôme,' the *concierge* said.

'Why didn't you say so before,' Frémont said, and hurried back toward the Dôme again.

Rug peddlers and sandwich men strolled through the swarms

of merrymakers on the sidewalks, the street lamps showed yellow-green among the trees, and everywhere *agents de police*, singly, in pairs, or in squads, on foot, on bicycles, and in automobiles, were scouring the district for Gonzo, Ivan, Kvek and Mademoiselle Montana. And Ambrose Gring was leaning weakly against the bars, his eyes glued to the doorway, listening for the sound of a familiar voice and murmuring 'Miriam. Petroleum. The people, no, no, no.' Every fifteen or twenty minutes an officer would approach his cell and scowl at him.

'Your cock and bull story has given your confederates a chance to get away. Not one of them is in Montparnasse,' the *commissaire* bellowed.

'You mean she's gone ? The girl has disappeared ?'

'Your precious girl went to America day before yesterday,' the *commissaire* said.

'She couldn't have. It's not true. I talked with her to-night,' Ambrose sobbed. 'It's Evans who's stolen her. It's Evans who's to blame. Can't you do something ? Can't you stop him, before it's too late ? The girl belongs to me.'

'When a multi-millionaire has been kidnapped, or murdered, there's no time to be bothering with one of the trollops of the studios. I tell you, your sweetheart left the country day before yesterday, and not one of the persons you mentioned has been seen or heard from since eight o'clock to-night. It was lucky we landed you, otherwise we'd have nothing to show the American ambassador.'

'I don't want to be shown to an ambassador,' said Gring, his face paler and more haggard than before. 'I want Miriam. ... I want to warn her father. ...'

'What's that ?'

'The people are after the oil. The proletariat. ...' Gring stammered, in a pitiful effort to get his point across.

'My dear sir. We were not born yesterday,' the *commissaire* said. 'If you think that by feigning insanity you can escape the guillotine, let me disillusion you at once. No use babbling about trollops or oil, to say nothing of the proletariat. I can hold you six months more for even mentioning the proletariat. You know that, I suppose.'

Gring, in despair, flung himself on the hard wooden bunk and began to cry.

Frémont, in Montparnasse, was making headway, or at least he thought he was. He spotted the waiter who had carried the bottles, glasses and trays to and from Hjalmar's studio and from him, prompted by M. Chalgrin, got the names of Rosa Stier, Gwendolyn Poularde, and another kind of Swede named Snorre, who had two front teeth missing. On investigation Frémont found that all of Snorre was missing from the quarter, as well as Mme Stier, Mlle Poularde, and an eccentric named Simon, a religious fanatic who spent his time carving out the Gospels on blocks of wood.

The sergeant, leaving a large force on watch for any or all of the missing persons, went back to the commissariat to have another go at Gring, whom he found in a state of collapse.

'Be careful,' the *commissaire* said. 'He's all we have to show the ambassador, or the prefect, either, as a matter of fact. The prefect wouldn't care much but the ambassador will be shocked if our suspect is in bad shape. I should have thought of that in time, before I talked so much about the guillotine. The mention of the guillotine upset the fellow no end.'

'He's not a forceful type,' the sergeant said.

The paintings were stacked in a cell adjacent to Gring's and *Agent* Schlumberger, a whimsical Alsatian who spent his days off painting landscapes and churches, was looking at them, one by one.

'Why, this one's been altered, just recently,' the *agent* said. He turned on the strong white light ordinarily used as an aid to questioning, held up a still life of oysters and lobsters, and said: 'Look here, sergeant. There's another signature underneath H. Jansen. I think we've hit on a smuggling scheme. It's more than possible these are old masters, with scenes and faces painted over them to make them appear of little value. That's been done, you know. A dozen Italian primitives got by the customs in New York last month, because each one had a picture of Garibaldi painted over the original.'

'I'll have every last one of them expertized at the Louvre,' the sergeant said. 'I'm going to get to the bottom of this, if it takes the rest of my life.'

The telephone rang and at the end of the conversation the *commissaire* said: 'The minister of justice is taking a hand. He's having the Seine dragged for the missing taxi.'

'Don't forget to tell him there's a painting of Gonzo in the cab. The grappling hooks might mess it up, and then if it turned out to be something like the Mona Lisa the department would get a black eye. The public is touchy about works of art. The man in the street doesn't care much what happens to people, if they're not related to him or in some way profitable. But let anything happen to a work of art and the whole world is up in arms.'

The phone rang again. 'Every taxi in Paris has been checked, and only one, the Citroën driven by Kvek, is missing,' the *commissaire* said.

'Have all the railroad stations been watched ?'

'Of course, and all the tramways, buses, and airplanes. How a dozen suspicious characters could escape as if there were not a policeman in all Paris is mysterious to me,' the *commissaire* said. 'There'll be an investigation, a shakeup, an international scandal. . . .'

'I thought at first that our list of people came from this Greeng's imagination, but it seems such people exist, or existed up till eight o'clock this evening.'

'I shall hold you responsible for finding them,' the *commissaire* said. 'The prefect will come down on me, and the ministries of justice and foreign affairs will be severe with him. The American ambassador will make it hot for the foreign office. The United States Government will prod the ambassador.'

'I shall find them,' Frémont said, and started for Montparnasse again.

CHAPTER 8

No Pastures

In the sub-cellar of the Hotel du Caveau, rue de la Huchette, roast goose had just been served. The group of artists and friends, little suspecting what was taking place above stairs and in the embassies, city rooms, chancelleries, *préfectures*, commissariats and Montparnasse cafés, had done justice to mixed hors d'œuvres, turbots which were truly noble, and several wines as good as those at the Interalliée. M. Julliard, the proprietor, had called in a fiddler and piper from the dance hall nearby, thereby furnishing not only music but partners for Rosa Stier and Gwendolyn Poularde. The latter had, clutched in her shapely fingers, a volume entitled *Les attributions des huiles diverses*, but the worry about her Chicago show was fading from her mind.

Hjalmar, his pockets stuffed with thousand franc and five thousand franc notes which he mistook now and then for a napkin or handkerchief, sat lustily at the head of the wooden table with Miriam on his right and Cirage on his left.

'Skal,' he shouted from time to time.

In a less boisterous way, Homer Evans was enjoying the party, too. He did not roar and drink from bottles after biting off the neck, or recite Barbara Frietchie in Swedish, jumping up on the revolutionary table when he was Barbara and down again to reply in the person of Stonewall Jackson. Neither did he fill pipes with red wine or carve snatches of the Twenty-Third Psalm on the woodwork of the piano. His was a contemplative nature, and in idle moments he was thinking about Miriam, or problem 'c'. When his eyes began to smart from the smoke, he suggested to her that they get a breath of air. Upstairs, meanwhile, M. Julliard was reading the early morning papers, still wet with ink.

'Any news?' asked Evans as he passed.

'Nothing much,' replied the Savoyard. 'Some American chap got lost.'

'They should stay away from the Alps,' Homer said, from the doorway. The sun was rising in green and gold behind the towers of Notre Dame.

'How lovely ! How unbelievably lovely,' said Miriam. 'Let's go to the end of the street, then walk the entire length of it, facing the cathedral and the sun. It seems to me as if I had never seen suns or cathedrals before.'

Evans started to utter a warning, then checked himself and reached for her hand again. 'Oh, what the hell,' he said to himself. 'Why dampen her pleasure ? After all, I've ruined her career. . . .'

A scream cut short his thoughts. Miriam and he were arm in arm, passing the commissariat where Ambrose Gring's cell faced the door. Thus, the anguished prisoner had caught a glimpse of his oil princess with his dread rival.

'What was that ?' asked Miriam, startled.

'Just a drunk,' Homer said reassuringly. 'The Paris police are gentle and understanding with drunks, but of course a drunk will yell now and then.'

At the barred entrance of Gring's cell a lively scene was taking place. The officer who had been left to guard Ambrose understood no English and Ambrose was in such a frenzy that he forgot to speak French. He was shrieking, squealing, tearing his hair and his clothes, grinding his teeth, and exhibiting other symptoms of emotional instability, and between the grimy fingers of the officer, whose hand was across Gring's mouth, came words which convulsed with laughter Jackson, the *Herald* reporter, and a young Frenchman with an American hat, the two last-named having been just recently snared in the dragnet.

'There he goes ! That's the man you want ! He's stolen Miriam. He's in league with the proletariat. He's going to get the oil . . . the petroleum . . . the wells . . . gushers. . . .'

The *commissaire*, who had been dozing, was awakened by the rumpus and came swearing to confront Ambrose, spurring the officer to such efforts that no sounds at all came forth.

'What has this louse been shouting about ?' the *commissaire* asked Jackson, to whom all the officers had taken a liking be-cause he spoke fairly fluent French.

69

'He thinks someone has stolen his girl, and that the girl and the other man just passed by,' Jackson said. 'Also there is an oil field involved but I haven't made out just how that fits in.'

'Feigning insanity,' the *commissaire* said, and sighed. 'I told him it wouldn't help him, but he continues. He'll wear himself out, then blame us for brutality when the ambassador comes.'

'The ambassador'll identify me and insist that you let me go,' Jackson said.

'How can I let you go ? You're the only one of the lot here who speaks both American and French. Be reasonable. Don't make a complaint and get yourself released just when I need you. You may send out for food or tobacco. I'll have girls, books, or magazines brought in.'

'Well, if you put it that way, I'll have to stick with you, I suppose,' said Jackson. 'As a matter of fact, I'm beginning to like it here.'

'That's very nice,' the *commissaire* said. 'So few people appreciate what we try to do for them.' He turned to the officer who was still holding his hand over Gring's mouth and nose, notwithstanding that the unfortunate Ambrose had passed into a semi-swoon. 'Schlumberger,' he barked. 'I am going to try for a wink of sleep again and I shall expect you to suppress any unnecessary noise until further notice.' And suiting the action to the word the *commissaire* resumed his place behind the counter, rested his face on his palms and his elbows on the desk and in a moment was fast asleep. The following moment Jackson began a series of blood-curdling yells.

'Evans ! Homer ! For God's sake, old man. I'm in quod. I'm in the soup up to my ears. I'm being held for knowing both American and French.'

That was what Jackson thought he was yelling, for he had seen Evans and some starry-eyed young girl, arm in arm, not four feet from the open doorway of the *commissariat*. The only sound that reached the street was 'Ehhhhhh' and all the rest was smothered in *agent* Schlumberger's heavy hand. This time the officer took no chances on having the *commissaire* disturbed. He reached behind him for a billy and with just the amount of force necessary to stun his patient without cracking the skull he brought down his instrument and Jackson went into what seemed to him to be a long tunnel. Upon recovering consciousness, however, he roused the *commissaire* to tell him that Evans, or the American Ivan, the man the whole city was looking for, had passed within a foot of the doorway. Within two minutes the quarter was swarming with police on foot, bicycles, motor-cycles with and without sidecars, horses, automobiles with and without sirens, and even trucks. Had not Evans and Miriam chanced to step into the dim church of St Severin, a block away, to admire the best example of Gothic architecture in Paris, they surely would have been apprehended. As it was, they escaped the notice of the officers who, however, descended into the sub-cellar of the Hôtel du Caveau and found a suspicious gathering of men and women up to their knees in empty bottles and unable to explain in any satisfactory way how they came there, to what country, if any, they owed allegiance, and who were all without papers of any kind. One seemed to be a ringleader. Although very drunk, he tossed around a half-dozen policemen before he noticed they had uniforms on. He had his pockets stuffed with thousand franc notes the officers assumed to be counterfeit. There was some delay while the Hôtel du Caveau was combed from sub-cellar to roof in search of a counterfeiting machine. Then Hjalmar; Rosa and the piper; Harold Simon and Cirage; Snorre Sturlusson and the Swedish actress (who had nothing on but shoes, gloves, and violet knickers); Gwendolyn and an alleged fiddler; and the protesting M. Julliard were stowed into a Black Maria and taken directly to the *préfecture*, where they were joined in short order by Ambrose Gring, limp and burbling, a young Frenchman with an American hat in bad repair, and Jackson who seemed to be enjoying the whole thing immensely. The array of suspects and witnesses had got beyond the capacities of *commissariats* and were being housed in the more commodious *préfecture*.

Eventually, Evans and Miriam strolled back to the rue de la Huchette, entered the Hôtel du Caveau and assumed, because M. Julliard was not behind the neat zinc bar, that he must be downstairs. They made their way down the spiral staircases, through gravelled corridors, under low stone arches, and into the former chamber where Robespierre had made some of his biggest mistakes.

'This is strange,' said Evans. The chamber was empty, except for several hundred bottles, a deflated cornemuse, a shattered fiddle, and a piano on which had been carved 'The Lord is My Shepherd I shwill not schwant pashtures no pastures'.

They mounted again to the street level and helped themselves to a refreshing drink of brandy at the bar, then started to read the morning papers. Miriam scanned a few headlines and a couple of paragraphs, then gave it up and clung to Evans' arm. Evans' head suddenly cleared. Hugo Weiss had disappeared, incredible as it seemed. The papers were unanimous about that, and also they agreed that a Russian taxi-driver, complete with Citroën taxi, had vanished also. Homer's first impulse was to rush back to Montparnasse, warn Hjalmar, go at once to the authorities and explain. Explain what, exactly? That Weiss had been hoodwinked and mulcted, to say nothing of being deceived and victimized; that paintings had been altered, misrepresented and sold for staggering prices under false pretences and with malice aforethought; that a group of well-known painters had lent themselves to fraud, had borne false witness, were in fact, each and severally accessories before and after the fact, and had been present while the fact transpired? It would be not easy to explain why two identical cheques had been written and why two well-known *café* proprietors had been persuaded to cash them almost instantly, but that would be easy in comparison with explaining why all the principals and seconds, except the missing persons, had hid themselves at once in a stone cellar below the level of the Seine. Homer's quick wit grasped the situation with reference to himself and his companion. Montparnasse had been turned upside down to find all the members of the party, the alarm had been given, the dragnet had covered all Paris and the suburbs and at last Hjalmar, Rosa, Gwendolyn, Snorre Sturlusson, and Harold Simon had been found with the guilty money in their possession, in fleshpots that would have done credit to Egypt in her gayest days. Having found no traces of blood in the cellar,

Evans believed that Hjalmar had gone quietly. Doubtless the faithful M. Julliard had gone along to bail them out, or would M. Julliard be suspected, too? Of course. He would be the keeper of the hideout. As he looked closer, Evans noticed even in the bar room evidence that the place had been roughly searched.

'We've got to go where I won't be disturbed until I can think this out,' Evans said. 'I played a scurvy trick on Hugo Weiss, and involved a number of my friends in a swindle. But there's much more than we know about in this disappearance. The least I can do is to devote myself to finding Weiss and Lvov, and if the police take me in I shall be able to do nothing.'

He glanced down the narrow rue de la Huchette and all at once got an inspiration. The Café des Hirondelles was just around the corner, the meeting place of the Arab rug peddlers, where Moroccans and Moors slept in daylight hours, stored their mats and carpets, hung their fezzes, spread their burnooses, and otherwise comported themselves as peddlers off duty.

'Come,' he said simply to Miriam. They walked, arm in arm, to the corner of the rue des Deux Ponts, crossed the street and within less time than it takes to tell it were safely out of sight in a dark doorway which led them to the desk of the Hôtel des Hirondelles. There Evans' knowledge of Morocco and Moroccans served him in excellent stead.

'Salaam aleichem,' he said to the proprietor.

'Aleichem salaam,' Ben Sidi replied. 'What is Mr Evans' pleasure? One of my unworthy rooms?' And he handed out a key politely.

Evans blushed and Miriam giggled.

'I like that man,' she said. 'But we've got work to do.'

'I am honoured by your hospitality,' Evans said to Ben Sidi, 'but my errand here is an important one.'

'I like that,' said Miriam indignantly. 'It may be pressing, but as for importance. . . .'

'Peace, woman,' Evans said, lapsing into the Arab vernacular. And to Ben Sidi he said softly: 'I must see Ben Abou at once. Is he here?'

'I will summon him,' Ben Sidi said, and gravely withdrew.

73

CHAPTER 9

A Glimpse of a Candle-Light Greco

DR HYACINTHE TOUDOUX, the medical examiner, and Sergeant Frémont were having an argument in the *préfecture*, and both had been roundly abused by the prefect.

'If what Julliard, the hideout proprietor, says is true, about the quantity of liquor consumed, the ring-leader Gonzo, alias Johnson or Jansen, cannot be aroused until evening, say between eight and twelve,' the doctor insisted.

'That should give even my homicide squad enough time to find the American Evans or Ivan and his girl,' Frémont said, disgustedly.

The experts of the Louvre had received the forty-nine suspicious paintings which had been numbered, cross-indexed, and should have been sent to the laboratories where after two weeks or so a preliminary report would be made. At the *préfecture* there was a lull, and if there was anything that got on Frémont's nerves, it was the occurrence of lulls in the midst of important cases. This one was broken by the precipitate entrance of the prefect himself, who had in his hand a set of thumbscrews he had borrowed from the Carnavalet museum, the prefectorial gimlet which had been filed for the occasion, and a bucket of ice-water from a nearby saloon.

'The ambassador is on his way,' the prefect snapped. 'I'm going to wake this man at any cost.'

'My opinion is unchanged. Gonzo will not respond,' the doctor said.

The doctor proved to be right. Hjalmar did not as much as wink when the ice-water struck him, nor did he groan when his head was lifted by the ears and let drop on the flagstone floor. Gring, however, in a nearby cell began to yammer and squeal and Ambrose, unshaven, unwashed, and clutching at the bars was not a pretty sight.

'Get him out of here,' the prefect roared. 'How can we show a sight like that to the envoy of a friendly power?'

Gring objected but was thrown out with promptness and dispatch. A moment afterward a genial voice called out at the end of the corridor:

'Does anyone here speak English?'

Jackson and Frémont answered in the affirmative.

'Why, hello, Jackson,' the ambassador said. He was a tall thick-set man with walrus moustaches and he smiled as he ambled toward the cells, silk hat in hand.

Jackson explained briefly what had happened to him. He had started out from the *Cercle Interalliée* with the intention of checking up on Hugo Weiss. Evans, with whom he wished to consult, had not been at home. Neither had he been at the Dôme, where a flock of plain clothes men had jumped on Jackson. The reporter had escaped by throwing several siphons in the air and retreating under cover of the resulting explosions, only to be arrested at the Plaza Athénée. Of all the suspects, Jackson was most lacking in papers. He had no identity card, no police pass, and his American passport, which had been disfigured by accidental immersion in brandy, was in the pocket of a suit of clothes which had been six weeks at the cleaners.

'Want me to get you out, I suppose. Ah, youth,' the ambassador said.

'I'd just as soon stay a while,' the reporter said. 'But you might say a word for that young French chap. He's in because I changed hats with him in the fracas at the Dôme. By the way, the Dôme has established a new record for breakage. Beat the Coupole figure by fourteen kilos of glass and crockery.'

'You don't say?' remarked the ambassador. 'Well, stay here if you like. But at least come out of the cell and interpret for me. I've got to pay my respects to the prefect and find out what they've done about Hugo Weiss. Probably he's out on a bat. I crossed with him once on the old *Dresden* and between us we drank all the beer in first class and tourist and were well started on the third class when the Statue of Liberty hove in sight and I had to pose for some photographers.'

'This door is locked,' Jackson said.

The ambassador turned to the prefect. '*La porte, s'il vous plaît !*' he boomed and the prefect opened the cell door with alacrity.

'I must apologize for the condition of my suspects and witnesses. They ate and drank all night before we caught up with them. . . .'

'Know just how they feel,' said the ambassador.

'He said,' began Jackson carefully, 'that he understands just how they feel.'

The ambassador was by that time strolling up and down in front of the cells. He nodded to M. Julliard, who smiled courteously; laughed heartily when he saw Hjalmar; raised his eyebrows appreciatively at the sight of Rosa Stier and the piper; sighed in front of Gwendolyn and the fiddler; gasped at Simon and Cirage, the former of whom had crawled under the blanket of the latter, exposing a generous portion of the latter in so doing. The Swedish actress evoked an exclamation of true appreciation. It was evident that the statesman in question preferred blondes.

'Got all their names and addresses?' the ambassador inquired.

The prefect all but wrung his hands. 'M. l'Ambassadeur,' he said. 'They were unconscious when we found them, they have remained so ever since. . . .'

'Between eleven and three,' muttered Dr Toudoux.

'Quite all right. Now what about Hugo Weiss? Any trace of him?'

'These are the witnesses and suspects,' the prefect said.

'Nonsense. Hugo's probably on a bat. One time we crossed on the old *Dresden*. . . .'

'He says that M. Weiss is probably blotto. . . .'

'Blotto?'

'Pifflicated. Oorieyed. Mulled. Boiled. Stinko.'

'Then perhaps we'll hear from him between midnight and four o'clock,' said the prefect, catching on.

'I shouldn't worry. Well, I'll toddle along,' the ambassador said. 'By the way, send me those names and addresses as soon as you get them.'

76

'A certified copy,' the prefect said.

'And by the way,' said the ambassador, brushing off the brim of his hat, 'out front I met a chap who seemed to be in trouble. Said he'd asked you to find his girl and a duffer named Ivan, and that you'd made a mistake and thrown him out. Just thought I'd mention it. He's still waiting outside, no doubt.'

'I let him go, but he's to be shadowed every minute of the night and day,' the prefect said. 'He will lead us to his confederates in time.'

'Just thought I'd mention him. Well. Good day and thanks. So long, Jackson. . . .'

'Could you ask the prefect to let me stick around ? He has a way of kicking out his clients. . . .'

'Sure. I understand, my boy. Scoop. Headlines. In at the finish, and all that. Tell him I said you could stay as long as you liked. And ring me up from time to time. If old Hugo's really in trouble we'll have to get action. Better let me know what these people say after they've slept off their jag. That party, Jackson, must have been a whopper. Were you in on it, boy ?'

'No, worse luck. They pinched me at the Plaza Athénée.'

'As good a place as any,' said the ambassador. 'Well. Keep me posted, boy. So long.'

While these events were taking place Homer Evans had by no means been idle. Henri, the barber, had been secretly summoned to the Hôtel des Hirondelles, and he had brought with him false hair, grease paint, and glue as well as his barber's tools. Miriam's hair had been cut in boyish fashion, both she and Evans had darkened their faces, hands, and arms and put on fezzes and burnooses furnished by Ben Sidi and Ben Abou. Also, Ben Sidi had reached into a drawer where he kept an assortment of Arab passports and given Homer one with a saturnine photograph under which was written the name, Ibn Hassan, while for Miriam a youthful one was found. On the ranch as a child she had often wished she were a boy, and here she was, a handsome Arab boy by the side of the man she loved.

It surprised Miriam when Homer led the way, not toward Montparnasse but to the rue de la Boëtie where the art galleries abound. As they strode along he explained what he wished her to do. She was to be an Arab prince anxious to buy expensive paintings. He was her uncle and interpreter. When and if she saw the pair of mysterious men, perhaps dealers, who had visited the Dôme in search of Gring and had seemed disappointed with him, she was to whisper 'Beano'.

In the first gallery they were shown a Bellini painting of a narrow-faced young man with constipation, a Rubens portrait of a flushed-faced ample woman in excellent health, and a Botticelli that was not rugged, but not suffering either. All along the famous street they strode, glancing at Rembrandts, Van Dykes, and on one occasion a rare portrait of Whistler's father. There they nearly had their robes torn off by eager salesmen.

'Amscray, your Highness,' Evans said to Miriam. At last, they traversed the avenue Percier to the boulevard Haussmann and entered still another gallery, one of the dingiest and most expensive of all. And there, when Ibn Hassan made the break about expense not mattering and the usual sound of falling objects preceded the hasty entrance of the partners, the distinguished-looking sheik was pleased to hear 'Beano' in a clear boyish whisper.

'I've just the thing, a few of the best Delacroix,' the taller partner said, and the other rubbed his hands and made little squeals and chuckles of satisfaction.

'To a Mohammedan, the name of the painter you mention has an irritating Christian connotation.'

'He was at his best in desert scenes, Bedouins and all that sort of thing,' the tall partner said.

'Be yourself, Abel,' the short partner interposed. 'The prince doesn't want pictures of the desert. He wants a change. Something green, with cows and vineyards. . . .'

'Vineyards,' snorted Ibn Hassan.

'The Prophet was a teetotaller,' the tall one explained. He seemed to be the forceful member of the pair. He began shuffling through stacks of paintings and discarding them with grunts of dismay. The entire stock of Heiss and Lourde seemed to be blemished either by a too obvious Christian slant, or vines, bottles, glasses, or drinking horns, or at least, Bedouins, houris, oases, camels, or burnooses. Evans was enjoying himself hugely, for the first time since he had become a Mohammedan and a private detective. When Sasha, nicknamed Dodo, the junior and shorter partner, stumbled on a couple of Corots, Evans shook his head.

'There is something over-delicate, a little indecisive, even feminine about this non-believer Corot. I'm sure the prince, who is a manly little chap . . .'

At this the prince was seized with a fit of coughing and drew the burnoose more loosely about certain parts of his person.

'It's the dampness,' murmured Evans. '"*Quelle chose malsaine, la Seine. . . .*" One of your French poets, I believe, admitted that. Are you fond of poetry, M. Lourde?'

'Sure, I like it all right,' Dodo said, good-naturedly. He didn't want to introduce a jarring note.

'We're business men,' said Abel, to add a touch of solidity to the impression the house was giving.

Messrs Heiss and Lourde made a dive at another stack of paintings and Evans moved nearer, so he could get a glimpse of those discarded. He saw Abel give a start of surprise, almost alarm, utter a grunt of disapproval and call the clerk who sat at a desk near the doorway.

'What is that canvas doing here?' he demanded, and Evans' heart gave an extra hard thump at his ribs as he saw the candle-light Greco being whisked away by the frightened clerk, who mounted a stairway to an upper storeroom, mumbling apologies as he mounted. The clerk was followed hastily by Dodo, who skipped excitedly around him like a basketball player about to interfere with a throw. Abel tried to regain his composure, and smiled thinly at Ibn Hassan, who also was trying to be calm.

'Your honour. It's hard to get efficient help these days. The way that fellow handles Old Masters, you'd think they were playing-cards or something. And if we fire him, we have to pay a bonus something fierce and he goes to somebody else with all the trade secrets,' Abel said, nervously.

'In my country he would be left on the desert for the jackals to feed upon,' Evans said. 'But come. The sun is well along on its westward journey. . . . The prince is hungry and athirst. . . .'

Again the prince turned away to cough.

'How about a Goya? I've a choice A-1 Goya,' said Abel, producing what indeed appeared to be a Goya, but Evans shook his head sadly.

'That's a prince, and besides, he's on horseback. His Highness doesn't want paintings of other princes, and he's spent all his life in the saddle. Something remote and soothing. Perhaps that one you just sent upstairs. . . .'

Abel turned a colour that might have been achieved by Tintoretto if he had plenty of ochre and silver white at hand.

'No. That wouldn't do. . . . Er. You'll excuse my bluntness but the painting is only a picture of a coloured boy, and not even daylight, just a candle. . . .'

'The prince is fond of candles and coloured boys,' Evans said.

Miriam looked less gracious and more imperative, and Evans addressed her in Arabic, of which she caught only a few syllables which sounded suspiciously like 'Hold everything'.

'The prince must break bread,' Evans said. 'The prince invariably breaks it about this time of day. We shall return this afternoon, when the sun is at the three-quarter mark and is heading into what you call the home stretch. At that hour, refreshed and ready for choosing, we shall come back to your excellent gallery, and I hope you will do us the honour to let us see that coloured boy and candle. I was sent to you by a mutual friend and acquaintance, one Ambrose Ben Gring. . . .'

'Is he an Arab? I've always wondered just where he came from,' Abel said.

'Who came from?' asked Dodo, who had joined them from the loft.

'Gring,' Abel said, and it was apparent that both of them were deeply disturbed.

Evans and Miriam salaamed and after promising again to return, the one in flowery speech and the other with a gracious gesture, they left the agitated partners and the gallery, now in comparative disorder. Both Abel and Dodo followed them to the sidewalk.

80

'Perhaps His Highness would prefer that we brought the paintings to his hotel,' Abel suggested. 'Just tell us where you are stopping. . . .'

Evans shook his head. 'His Highness would not put you to that unnecessary trouble. We shall return, never fear. The word of a Believer is as good as his bond, and the words of two Believers are twice as reliable.' He pointed to the sun, which was blazing from its appropriate angle. 'When the sun is there' (he shifted his pointing finger to the three-quarter mark) 'you shall see us again. The blessings of Allah will be with us in the interim,' he said.

'I hope,' added Miriam as soon as they were out of earshot.

'The best asset of a good detective is luck,' Evans said. 'Remember what Lefty Gomez said before the World's Series. *Mieux la chance que l'adresse !*'

'Let's have a long drink, and then tell me what this is all about,' Miriam said.

'My dear young woman,' Evans said. 'When you are in a burnoose, you must do as Mohammedans do. If one of those thousand of cops who are hunting us from pillar to post, and especially in *cafés* and bars, should see two Bedouins drinking brandy and soda, even the dullest of them would smell a rat.'

'God ! Let's change to White Russians,' she said.

Quickly they took a taxi to Montparnasse, having gained confidence in their disguises, and there they had the added good fortune to bump squarely into Tom Jackson who had secured his pass to go in and out of the *préfecture* and was seeking Homer in the hope of getting a little light on the situation. They had not been in the quarter two minutes before Abel Heiss and Dodo Lourde came dashing on to the *terrasse* of the Dôme, demanding the whereabouts of Ambrose Gring. M. Chalgrin informed them, erroneously, that Ambrose was still in the jug.

Quickly Evans hailed another taxi and gave the address of a small saloon in the avenue Percier, near the galleries of Heiss and Lourde. Jackson told his story on the way.

'The longer I live, the more admiration I have for Lefty Gomez. *Mieux la chance que l'adresse.* It's better to have luck than skill,' Evans said.

'Lefty Grove is better, but that's neither here nor there,' Jackson said.

'What shall it be ? Brandy and soda ?' the waiter asked.

'For us, Vichy,' Evans said. 'When one is disguised as an Arab, one must feel like an Arab, too.'

'They must feel rotten,' said Jackson. 'Well, now you talk.' Evans suddenly abandoned his air of jocularity. Unmistakably he was in earnest, which startled Jackson and surprised Miriam even more.

'I wish I had minded my own business in the first place,' he said. 'This affair, in spite of its comical aspects, is serious. In fact, it is desperate. That's not too strong a word. You see, ordinarily when crime is committed, it is done by one criminal alone, whose style and psychology may be studied. Or it may be the work of a gang, with a dominating leader but, generally speaking, of similar temperaments and habits. This maze of iniquity in which we all have been innocently involved, is not so simple as that. No, indeed. Not nearly as clear and straightforward.'

'I'm still in the fog,' Jackson said.

'As you know,' Evans said, 'I'm not a man of action. I deplore action. All my life I have avoided unnecessary exertion and fuss. I do not work because I have money, not unlimited wealth but enough. Quite enough. My duty is to spend it, to keep it in circulation.'

'Of course, no one blames you,' Jackson said.

Evans continued even more earnestly. 'Having more time for contemplation than most of my friends, and an idle man cannot have other idle men for friends, I am able to view their problems calmly and objectively and in a few instances have given them sound advice. I deplore advice, too, mind you, but I also dislike to see my friends worry, especially if a solution of their difficulties is clear to me.'

'In short, what is called a heart of gold,' Jackson said.

'You get the drift,' said Evans. 'Now the other day, it already seems ages ago, Hjalmar Jansen came to me in a lamentable condition. . . .'

'It must have been in the evening,' Jackson said.

82

'That would not have startled me,' Evans said. 'But he came in the morning, when I was sitting peacefully on the *terrasse* of the Dôme. Hugo Weiss had just come to town unexpectedly ...'

'Why would that upset a big Norwegian roughneck like Jansen?' asked Jackson.

'Between you and me,' Evans continued, ' Hugo had financed Hjalmar in Paris for a year, the year was nearly up and Hjalmar wanted another cheque from Hugo.'

'You don't mean he bumped him off just for that ...' the reporter said, shocked and indignant.

'Jackson,' Evans said, 'if you're going to interrupt and jump at conclusions ...'

'I'm all wet. I'm all wet,' Jackson said. 'I won't do it again. But remember. The sun is approaching the old home stretch ... '

'I know,' said Evans. 'Let me proceed. Hjalmar was shy about bracing Hugo because he had only three paintings to show. He had painted many more, but, being a conscientious artist, had thrown them away.'

'That's fine. I hate paintings. They give me the creeps. Either they look like something else, and keep reminding you of it, or they don't look like anything else and keep you wondering who's nuts, you or the guy who painted them.'

'Then why did you cover the banquet of the *Société des Artistes Français?*'

' My God,' said Jackson. 'Am I already a suspect? I was sent there because I knew less about art than anyone in the office. That's the policy of the *Herald*. Then if there's a kick about the story, the management can say: " It was the reporter's fault. He didn't know his job. We'll fire him."'

'Ingenious, but hardly square,' Evans said. 'Ah, well. In all countries and in every field of activity, ethics are being swept away. The law of the jungle.... But I must get back to my story. Hjalmar had only three paintings. He should have had forty at least. It occurred to me that there were plenty of paintings in Montparnasse, and a number of good scouts among the artists who would be glad to help a friend in need. In short, I was ass enough to propose a hoax to Hjalmar, personally to solicit paintings from our mutual friends....'

'But the signatures. . . .'

'That was where my erudition got me into further trouble. Nothing like erudition for getting one into hot water, my boy. I had read somewhere that olive oil, if mixed with paint, rendered it capable of being scrubbed off without injury to the painting underneath.'

Jackson smiled. 'I see it now,' he said. 'By God, that's a good one. That's why they have sent all those paintings to the Louvre to be expertized.'

Evans shuddered. 'You haven't heard the worst. I called on Hugo Weiss, and partly because of a favour I'd done him years ago, he agreed to visit Hjalmar's studio. Meantime we got the show ready. Fifty paintings by Stier, Sturlusson, Simon, Poularde, and one modest offering of my own, my only painting, in fact. Weiss showed up punctually, acted like the prince of good fellows, drank a half bottle of sherry, looked over the paintings one by one and finally not only reached for his cheque book to give Hjalmar another year's study but bought the painting which had been done by me. He wrote two cheques, one for the daily bread, the other as payment for the painting. With the painting under his arm he said good-bye and good luck, then descended the stairs. I descended with him and hailed a taxi, a taxi driven by a Russian soldier and gentleman I have trusted and respected for years. They drove away.

'On returning upstairs I found that the cheques were for $2,500 apiece and again was foolhardy. I advised Hjalmar to cash them at once, that evening, so he took one to the Dôme, the other to the Coupole. Then we all lit out for the Hôtel du Caveau; that's off the beaten track, you know, and we didn't want to be disturbed. We had a little party. . . .'

Jackson could not refrain from breaking in again. 'A little party ! Is that what you call it ?'

'Well,' Evans said, 'I didn't stay until the end. Neither did Miriam.'

'The end hasn't happened yet,' Jackson said.

'Unfortunately not,' continued Evans. 'Some time after dawn, I suggested to Miss Leonard that we get a breath of air.'

'The only sissy,' Jackson muttered.

'He is not a sissy,' Miriam said indignantly. 'The smoke was getting in his eyes.'

'Ah. Smoking was permitted, then,' Jackson said.

'We took a little walk in the neighbourhood, then stopped in at St Séverin . . . marvellous Gothic, St Séverin.'

'Probably it looked better than usual,' said the reporter.

'When we got back to the hotel, our friends and M. Julliard, the proprietor, were gone.'

'But not forgotten,' added Jackson. 'They were as far gone as any crowd I've seen since the garage massacre in Chicago, only your friends are more unlucky. They've got to wake up and face the world again.'

'I've got to get them out, but that's a mere detail,' Evans said.

'They'd be delighted to hear you say so, if any of them can hear yet,' said the reporter.

'First, we've got to find Hugo Weiss. He's in real danger,' said Evans.

'You think he's dead ?'

'I think he was kidnapped, and I've an inkling of what's behind it,' Evans said. 'And it's no small potatoes involving a few fake signatures and $5,000 worth of perfectly good cheques. That's why I want your help. . . .'

'It's yours,' said Jackson. 'I don't understand the disappearance as well as I did when you started talking, but count me in for whatever I can do. I interviewed Weiss when he got off the boat train and he was very decent about it. The man was tired, didn't want it advertised that he was in the city, and still he remembered his manners. The big shots are likely to be like that. Any guy who's always having rows with the press is sure to turn out to be a palooka.'

Miriam, thrilled but happy, was taking an independent shot at the sun, in an amateur way. 'I may be wrong,' she said softly, 'but isn't that damned chariot of Apollo on one wheel at the corner ?'

'You have spoken well, O woman,' said Evans. 'And you, too, O reporter,' lapsing into the Bedouin mannerism again. 'The next step, Jackson, depends on you. I want you to go into

85

the gallery of Heiss and Lourde, just around the corner. You will find a pale inefficient-looking clerk who's none too bright, and two partners, one tall, the other short, respectively called Abel and Dodo. They will appear to be crazy, but actually they are only anxious.'

'With your gift for understatement in mind, I know about what to expect. . . . A little party. . . . Great snakes ! A little party. . . . Well, what do I do ? Slug the tall anxious partner and sideswipe the other ?'

'Please,' Evans said. 'If I had wanted strong arm work I could have sent Miriam, or Mademoiselle Montana. This requires finesse. . . .'

'I like that,' Miriam said.

'There's work for everyone,' Evans assured her. 'You, Jackson, are to enter this gallery, say you are an American. . . .'

'I've never yet been taken for a Chink.'

'. . . . an American whose father has struck oil.'

'Mr Evans has an oil fixation,' Miriam said. 'You'll get used to that.'

'I'm all attention,' Jackson said. 'I'm a mug from Oklahoma. They'll be booking me as Mr Oklahoma within the hour, probably. . . .'

'Say you came to Paris to get culture and by God, you mean to have it. Thump on the desk when you say by God, and scare the clerk. We want him to be nervous.'

'I'll be nervous enough for both of us,' Jackson said.

Evans went on smoothly. 'Look through what they show you, and ask if they haven't something with prairies and great open spaces. . . . I know for a fact that there's not a Remington in the place. Then mention casually that you were sent there by a couple of Arabs and let it drop that you just saw the same Arabs sitting on a *terrasse* in the place St Augustin. . . . Then, a moment later, when you're alone with the clerk. . . .'

'But the partners ?'

'They'll be running to the place St Augustin. Allowing four minutes for the run, ten minutes at least for the search, and six minutes for the trek back home . . . they'll be out of breath and tuckered . . . you ought to have twenty minutes with the clerk. At the end of fifteen minutes we'll come in, Miriam and I, and I'll take over, but you'd better stick around. . . .'

'Wild camels couldn't drive me away,' Jackson said. 'Well. I'm off, Caligari. . . .'

'Not so fast. You haven't had your most important instruction. As soon as Abel and Dodo are safely away, go to the clerk in a brusque free and easy way and say, loudly, like an Oklahoma rancher, " Have you got any of these here Grecos ? If so, son, trot 'em out and be quick about it." Then you must take notice of the clerk's reactions, remember every word he says.'

'But when he gives me one of them Grecos, whatever a Greco might be. . . .'

'Stall, and hold it firmly in your hands. Don't let it get away until I come in. . . . Of course, be careful not to tear it or punch holes through the canvas with your finger. Even a moderately-sized Greco is worth anywhere from $300,000 to half a million dollars. . . .'

'Holy cats ! I'll be shivering all over. I'll make an aspen look like a billiard cue.'

'Brace up, and get started. The longer you wait, the more anxious the partners will be.'

As soon as the reporter had gone, Evans turned to Miriam with a look on his face she had never seen before. 'We have fifteen minutes, and I've got to think. Don't speak, turn off your sex appeal, try to be non-existent. Exactly a quarter of an hour from now, rouse me. If I can count on that I can really concentrate, without thought of the time.'

Obediently she moved away from him, so her robes were no longer touching his, and riveted her eyes on the *bistrot* clock while Evans went into a sort of trance. There were no outward signs, such as pallor, closed eyelids or twitching of muscles. He sat immobile and Miriam could feel the force of his intelligence like a strong electric current in the room, gaining in voltage relentlessly until it seemed that she could bear it no longer. In tension such as she never before had experienced she sat so stiffly that her muscles ached, eyes glued on the clock which never had moved so slowly. She was sure that hours were passing, but the hands indicated only seven minutes when a voice at her side said, 'Relax, my dear, I'm sorry to put you through this, but it had to be done. Fortunately it didn't take long, and now I see better what's before us.' He glanced through the window, up and down the street. No detectives, plain-clothes men or other Arabs were in sight, so he said pleasantly to the waiter, who had been made drowsy by Evans' feat of concentration without knowing the cause, 'Slip us two brandies, straight, and be quick.'

As she raised the liquor to her lips, her hand trembled so that she almost spilled a few drops, but the sight of Evans, raising his glass with the calmness and precision she had learned to expect from him, soothed her and she was able to swallow without choking although the brandy was rather bad.

'It was almost too simple,' Evans said.

'Your gift for understatement . . .' she murmured.

'I was obliged to find out how Hugo Weiss was spirited out of Paris,' Evans said, apologetically. 'Really, it should have come to me before.'

'Can you tell me ?'

'Just you. No one else, not even Jackson, who will be of great assistance. It said in the paper that all railroad stations, bus lines, tramways, and air lines had been watched, that pedestrians and automobilists, even farmers and drivers of horse-drawn vehicles had been stopped and questioned. What other means is there for leaving Paris ?'

'You're sure they left ?'

'Positive. With two such resourceful men as Hugo Weiss and Lvov Kvek on their hands, to say nothing of a Citroën taxi, our precious band could not hope to stay in Paris and remain hidden. It just could not be done, and such experienced thugs as the ones in question would know better than to try it,' Evans said. 'With all ordinary means of transportation and exit closed to them, what remained ?'

'The river,' Miriam said. Evans at first was crestfallen, then looked at her admiringly.

'That's what I concluded,' he said.

'I'm sorry I guessed,' she said. 'You see, there's a river on my father's ranch and whenever a steer was missing, we looked for his body downstream.'

In the ordinarily hushed premises of Heiss and Lourde a strange scene was unrolling, as the French say, while Old Masters stared disapprovingly from the walls. A man, obviously from North America, wearing a black French hat and carrying an army raincoat over his arm in a way that might have concealed any number of weapons, had entered, tossed his raincoat into a Louis XIV chair, planted the palms of his hands on the desk, eyed the clerk with determination and shouted:

'Ah'm Tom Jackson, pardner. What's your moniker, if that's a fittin' question in this man's country?'

The clerk had begun to burble, and in the back room where they were lurking and peering nervously through the peepholes expecting an influx of Arabs, Abel Heiss and Dodo Lourde began to wince, then to fidget and to bumble.

'Well, let it pass. Let it pass. It don't matter what a man was back East, it's what he is to-day, hombre. Ah say it's what he is to-day,' and with that Jackson gave the desk a trial thump, to test its resonance.

The clerk was still speechless.

'Ah want a few yards of this here art, something pretty that a man can look at when he's in from the range, a good bunch of cattle and an alkali stream, or maybe buffaloes and a couple of Indians. Say, buddy, did you ever see Custer's Last Stand? If you'd seen that, you'd know what Ah want, and when Ah wants a thing, stranger, Ah wants it pretty bad. By the way, you speak English, don't you?'

At this the clerk shook his head to indicate a negative reply and ducked, expecting that the shooting would surely commence. Jackson, however, refrained from violence and repeated the essential part of his request in French, making a hash of the word 'shorthorns', but otherwise intelligible.

'Perhaps this isn't the place,' he said. 'A couple of Arabs sent me in, said you had art to burn.'

The mention of Arabs brought Abel and Dodo into sight with such dispatch that Jackson was the one who ducked that time.

'Hold everything, strangers,' he said. 'Ah come on a peaceable errand. Mah friend the sheik, he says, Tom, when you get a hankering for old paintings, just you mosey over to see Heiss and Lourde. There you can't go wrong. . . .'

'Exactly, exactly, the sheik . . .' blurted Abel, while Dodo wrung his hands, which had had several thorough wringings that day and were due for a couple more.

'Just a little something with shorthorns . . .'

'The Fragonard portrait of the old Comte de Sartrouville. The count was a famous cuckold,' Abel said.

'You speak English, pardner, but you don't get mah drift. What Ah mean is cattle, steers . . .'

'You mean livestock,' Dodo said, glad of a chance to be helpful. 'We've got some Corot sheep that would send you running to a restaurant, mister.'

'Never mind the mister, call me Tom,' said Jackson, and then belatedly wondered if he should be using his right name. 'Mah friend the sheik, now he's democratic. Ah saw him sitting right there in one of the open air saloons, big as life, and his boy friend with him . . . Ah says to him . . .'

Abel had begun a sort of rigadoon or St Vitus dance and Dodo was hopping from side to side. The former was the first to be able to speak. 'The sheik. Where is he? Where was it you saw him?'

'Why, do you all know the sheik? He was a-sittin' right there in one of them *cafés*, down here in the place St Augustin, not ten minutes ago. He says to me . . .'

Whatever it was that the Arab had said to Jackson was lots to the ears of Abel and Dodo who had crashed through the doorway side by side and were well around the corner.

'It must make a man nervous, having so much art around the place,' Jackson said. Then he approached the terrified clerk, whose teeth were chattering, banged on the desk so heartily that a Second Empire inkwell jumped half a foot, fixed his antagonist with a glittering eye and said :

'Pal, Ah'll tell you what Ah'll do. Ah'll compromise. If you ain't got no prairies or animals, Ah'll buy one or two of them Gonzos . . . .'

90

Jackson was as well-meaning a chap as the next reporter, but he hadn't been to bed for some time, had received his instructions hastily, and all during a troubled night had been hearing about Gonzo. So he confused Gonzo with Greco without realizing his mistake. The effect on the clerk was catastrophic.

'Gonzos?' he gasped.

'Gonzos. You got me that time, buddy. And when Ah gets a hankering for Gonzos, Ah don't mean maybe. It ain't a question of what they cost. . . .'

'But we haven't any Gonzos. . . . I never heard of him,' said the clerk, already terrified. Jackson's manner changed.

'Now look a-here, pal. Ah got it straight from mah friend the sheik that there's Gonzos in this here joint. . . .'

'I assure you, Monsieur, that I have never seen a Gonzo.'

'Ah didn't come in here aimin' to make no trouble, pardner, but Tom Jackson's not the man to be trifled with. You can ask anybody in Oklahoma and they'll say the same thing. Now Ah'll give you five minutes to trot out one of them Gonzos, and the best in the house is none too good for me.' Jackson took out his watch. 'An', pardner. Don't try no false moves, either.'

'I'd be glad . . .' the clerk began, and probably would have fainted had not the door opened and Miriam, followed by Ibn Hassan, entered. Evans, or Ibn, or Ivan saw at once, to his surprise, that Jackson had not got his hands on the Greco. The clerk, prayerfully thankful for the entrance of the Arabs, appealed to Evans at once.

'Your honour. Have you heard of a painter named Gonzo?'

'Who has not?' Evans answered haughtily.

'This little runt here, for one,' said Jackson. 'Ah came in here, not aimin' to make no trouble, and Ah says to him: "Trot out a Gonzo. . . ."'

'Perhaps you meant a Greco,' suggested Evans, suavely.

The clerk began jumping up and down with relief.

'All right, friend, make it a Greco, only make it snappy, pardner. The service in this place ain't what we're used to in Oklahoma.'

This time the clerk was actually in tears. 'But, monsieur, the Grecos . . . I've strict instructions . . .'

91

'You've never had instructions as strict as what you're gettin' right this minute,' Jackson said, slipping his hand around to his hip pocket and clutching a briar pipe as if it were a shooting iron. 'If you-all don't have every Greco in this joint out here on the table before I count ten, then there's a-goin' to be some preachin' that you won't hear.'

The clerk had just so much stamina and no more. It had been exhausted. There was none left whatsoever. Yammering and shivering he ducked into the back room, ran up the stairs and came down again with a canvas about the size of the Mona Lisa, only tipped the other way. On it was painted the picture of a coloured boy leaning on a table by candlelight. It was a matter of a split second before Jackson had a firm grip on the frame.

'Now that's something like,' he said.

'Is that all you have?' asked Evans, kindly, but fixing the clerk with a glance that brooked no refusal.

The clerk rushed up the stairway again and was about to bring down another Greco when the outside door of the store burst open and not without a brisk struggle two Arabs, one tall and the other short, were propelled into the gallery by Abel and Dodo. The dealers' astonishment at seeing Evans and Miriam was almost equalled by Evans' dismay at seeing the real Ibn Hassan, whose passport (having been stolen) was reposing in the folds of Evans' burnoose. There was a decided resemblance.

The tableau was as follows: Abel and Dodo, having loosened their clutches on the new Arab's robes, were staring first at Miriam and Evans, then at Jackson who still had the candlelight Greco in a grip of steel. Upstairs the clerk was cowering, expecting to be shot, then fired. The real Ibn Hassan was the first to regain a measure of composure. Gravely he salaamed toward Evans, then toward Miriam.

'These Christian dogs have something on their minds which is hidden from these old eyes,' Ibn Hassan said. 'Their ways are not our ways, and are indeed mysterious.'

'True,' murmured Evans, in Arabic.

'What a break. He really knows the lingo,' said Tom Jackson to himself.

The real Ibn Hassan stepped nearer to Evans and continued:
'We were walking peaceably, my nephew and I, and thinking of the Koran when these fellows set upon us and begged that we accompany them, insisted, in fact . . .'

'I noticed,' said Evans. 'Their manner of insisting, O countryman, is known in their parlance as " the bum's rush ", and is only applied to gentlemen in extreme cases. Their need must, indeed, be urgent.'

Instead of being reassured, the real Ibn Hassan's distinguished countenance grew black and he turned to Abel and Dodo. With a scornful finger pointed toward Evans, the tall Arab said:

'That man is an impostor. He has been drinking what no Son of Allah permits to pass his lips, and a very bad quality to boot.'

'You must have sneaked one, then got too close,' Jackson murmured. The clerk upstairs began screaming 'Police', in which he was joined by Abel and Dodo.

'Impostors. Police. *Au secours.*'

Evans saw that the jig was up. 'Follow me ', he said, taking hold of Miriam's hand and rushing for the rear exit as fast as his burnoose would permit. Jackson was almost abreast of him with the candlelight Greco flapping like a sail in his hand.

'What am I to do with this, chief ?' he grunted.

'Drop it and scram. I know these little alleys,' Evans said, turning just in time to catch the oncoming Dodo neatly on the jaw, in such manner and at such an angle that Dodo's falling body tripped the real Ibn Hassan and brought forth a stream of Arab curses that Evans, had he had time, would have been glad to note down. As soon as Jackson and Miriam were safely outside, Evans jerked the key from the lock, followed them out, banged the door behind him and locked it from the outside, tucking the key into his burnoose as he ran.

By a circuitous route, the fleeing trio, led by Evans, found refuge in the Cernuschi Museum where the single attendant was sleeping at his desk. There Homer persuaded Jackson to find Sergeant Frémont, and try to convince him to give up the idea of arresting Evans, who had been of service to him in a famous suicide case not long before, and to meet Homer at nine o'clock at the Café de la Paix.

The late afternoon crowd was milling to and fro on the sidewalks of Montparnasse, so far away. Residents mingled with tourists (when it couldn't be avoided), merrymakers rubbed shoulders with philosophers and poets. The sandwich man and the chap passing out handbills were doing the usual, waiters scurried or ambled, according to their respective temperaments, drinks flowed, coursed, gurgled, dripped, and dribbled. But one element was lacking from the customary scene. There were no rug peddlers in sight The dragnet had been spread once more and all Arabs, Bedouins, Riffs, Turks, Armenians, Syrians, Moroccans, Algerians, and the like, had been caught in its relentless mesh and were severally and surlily assembled in a hall at the *préfecture*, not knowing why or what to expect. Among them was the real Ibn Hassan and his boy friend, and the former was the least philosophical of any of the sons of Allah. He had denounced an impostor and as a reward the ungrateful dogs of infidels had chucked him in the can. The bum's rush and the clink on one and the same day, to say nothing of a lost or stolen passport, was too much for Ibn Hassan's peace of mind.

Of course, because of burnooses, fezzes, and complexions, sons of Allah are jam for dragnetters. There is nothing easier to spot and dragnet than a man with flowing robes. Not less than two hundred were dragnetted in the first half hour, including a batch of disciples of Raymond Duncan and two Maharajahs, one with Maharanee. Frémont was slowly going mad. Not enough had it been for a world-famous millionaire to disappear and half Montparnasse devote itself to suspicious actions. The art world was in eruption everywhere, and a new volcano had started spewing trouble all over the boulevard Haussmann and the rue de la Boëtie.

It would be unnecessarily brutal to relate what the minister of justice had said to the prefect, on the subject of the release of Ambrose Gring, because the mysterious Ambrose, whether sane or insane, was the crux of the Heiss and Lourde affair. Gring had plotted something, a huge robbery, no doubt, and had sent his accomplices, a roughspoken American gunman known as Oklahoma Tom, and a pair of crooks disguised as Arabs and had nearly got away with one of the most valuable paintings then in Paris. There had been some discrepancy in the testimony of the partners, Abel Heiss and Dodo Lourde, also the clerk, M. Dinde, who was on the verge of a nervous breakdown, but nevertheless insisted in his delirium that the canvas chosen by the picture bandits, or Gring mob, had been a priceless Gonzo. The curator of the Louvre denied the existence of an Old Master named Gonzo. Heiss and Lourde were being held under guard in their place of business while Montparnasse was not only being combed, but practically being filtered for the missing Gring and the picture bandit trio disguised as Arabs and Americans.

But although the word Gonzo meant nothing to the experts of the Louvre, it meant a good deal to the sergeant, the prefect, the minister of justice, and others who were waiting for Hjalmar Jansen to wake up. Dr Hyacinthe Toudoux hovered near Hjalmar with his watch in his hand, now and then stooping with a stethoscope, feeling the pulse, testing the breath with a lighted match and becoming more officious each moment. The prefect had seen at once that the two sensational cases of the day were linked, and therefore had passed the entire buck to Sergeant Frémont, who had been relieved of his duty in Montparnasse exclusively and had been given a roving commission wherever art was erupting or even rumbling. And no one, not even Tom Jackson, disliked art as thoroughly as did Sergeant Frémont. It was in this mood that the reporter found him, and instead of bringing out what they had in common, a healthy detestation of painting, and especially oil painting, Jackson blurted out his plea for Evans and held his breath while the sergeant had one of the closest bouts with apoplexy the reporter had ever witnessed.

'The Café de la Paix, indeed,' he shrieked, when once he got his breath.

'That's what he said. I'm only trying to help you, sergeant.'

'And Evans thinks the case is not yet of adequate dimensions, that we've been trifling. That the ambassador, premier, presidents of at least two republics, and the prefect don't mean what they say when they tell me that either I must produce Hugo Weiss or my resignation. I have heard that you Americans have considerable nerve, *culot*, we call it. I have underestimated your capacities,' the sergeant said.

'You're going around circles,' Jackson said. 'Why not let Evans straighten you out? You have pinched Gring because he telephoned Weiss, which ought to have proved that he knew nothing of the disappearance; you let Gring go because the prefect doesn't like his face. You are holding Abel Heiss and Dodo Lourde virtual prisoners in their gallery because they have been mixed up with Gring, whom you want and do not want alternately. Our friend Evans is a big-hearted man. He goes about doing good deeds almost constantly.'

'Tell him if he's not here, with his papers, in half an hour, I'll spread the dragnet,' Sergeant Frémont said.

'You've had the dragnet spread already nearly twenty-four hours and Evans slips in and out of it when he pleases. Do you think he'll show up at the Café de la Paix unless I give him the "all clear" signal? You need help badly, sergeant. You're not doing well with this case, so far, and I'm not the only one to notice it. Even the people in the streets are beginning to think you were merely lucky in solving the Rosary game. . . .'

Jackson paused. He was not a total washout as a psychologist, and the expression he saw on Frémont's face warned him that he had better try another tack.

'Ah, there's my raincoat,' Jackson said, seeing the garment in question on the sergeant's desk. 'I must have left it here.'

What Jackson did not see was that the coat had been tagged carefully as 'Raincoat. Exhibit A. Found, with no identifying marks and pockets empty on premises of Heiss et Lourde. According to testimony of Witness Dinde, coat was left behind by member of picture bandit gang.' In his haste, and his indecision as to what to do with the candlelight Greco, Jackson had, indeed, left the raincoat slung across the Louis XIV chair. In fact, the raincoat, if a couple of hundred Arabs and the like may be disregarded, was all the sergeant had to show for his raiding and dragnetting in the vicinity of the boulevard Haussmann.

96

The sergeant did not lose his head. 'Oh, so it's yours? You must have forgotten it somewhere? You know, Jackson, these army raincoats are very much alike. Are you positive it's yours? Could you, for instance, testify in court. . . . ?'

'Of course,' Jackson said, relieved that he had sidetracked the sergeant's anger so successfully. 'There's a hole in the left pocket, a hole that one franc will slip through but which is just too small for two francs.'

The sergeant was listening but also pressing buttons. Buzzers were ringing in the guard room, gongs were sounding in the corridors. Before the sergeant had time to speak again, a dozen of the toughest officers in Paris had crowded silently into the room.

'Monsieur Jackson,' Sergeant Frémont said, 'you admit the ownership of the raincoat, but you are wrong about where you left it. You left it in the gallery of Heiss et Lourde, where you were occupied with holding up the clerk, M. Dinde, at the point of a gun, and later, when Messrs Heiss and Lourde returned, you fled through the back door with your accomplices and a priceless Gonzo.'

'Not a Gonzo, a Greco,' Jackson said. 'And I didn't take it.'

The sergeant turned to the officers. 'Put this gentleman into the cell known as the Goldfish Bowl, after taking his papers, his money, his necktie, belt, and shoelaces. Watch every move he makes, take note of every word and if he appears to be thinking try to make some intelligent guess as to what he is thinking about. We are on the right track at last. The Café de la Paix, indeed.'

A tall Arab, who had recovered a bit of his desert philosophy and was watching through a door ajar said to a Duncan disciple he took for a Moroccan: 'That method of persuasion, you see, O companion in misfortune, is called by the infidels " the bum's rush ".'

CHAPTER 10

Murder at the Café du Dôme

THE *commissaire* of the Montparnasse district was unlike the prefect in many respects. He liked lulls. There was nothing, in his way of thinking, as restful as a good lull in the midst of an exacting case. Consequently, when after having been informed of Gring's release he had curled up in an easy chair for a quiet nap, he was annoyed at being awakened merely to be informed that his superiors had decided they must have Gring back again. The *commissaire* roused himself, called his men together, and before embarking them on the man hunt felt called upon to give them detailed instructions. Now the problem was simple in itself. The prefect wanted Gring, but merely to say to such a fine body of men as the officers of that precinct: 'Go get Gring' seemed inadequate.

'There's no use looking for Greeng Ambrose on the *terrasses* of *cafés*, especially the Dôme where he sits for hours. I have noticed a tendency among you, while dragnetting is in progress, to sit at *café* tables and drink wines and liqueurs which later appear on your expense accounts. This must stop. We are in a period of national economy, the franc is losing value, the budget is so unbalanced that several clerks were injured yesterday in attempting to carry it from the House to the Senate. Therefore, if any man in my unit is found sitting at *café* tables in the course of this man hunt, such officer will be fined one week's pay. I have never been unreasonable with my officers, nor denied the importance of thirst. Any officer who wants to snatch a quick one at some little bar, and does so without wasting the republic's time, will not be fined unless he does it too often. That's all, men.'

The officers went their ways but in the search for Greeng Ambrose, they avoided like the plague the Café du Dôme, the Coupole, and even the Select and the Rotonde. And, as fate would have it, Ambrose, exhausted and discouraged, had found himself unable to stagger back and forth a moment longer in his search for Miriam, and had slumped into his favourite chair of the Dôme's *terrasse*. Little did he suspect, as he asked for a *crème de cacao*, that he was being sought again by all the minions of the law. His capacity for thought had narrowed down considerably, because of worry and fatigue, and what little was left he tried to apply to Miriam and Evans, so that longing and fierce hatred passed alternately over his unshaven face. For a while the alternation of those expressions and the consequent distortion of a countenance that at best was not attractive, kept timid customers from taking the only empty chair on the *terrasse*, the chair beside Ambrose at his small table. Finally, however, the chair was occupied. Moments, then a couple of hours passed and meanwhile the man who occupied the chair had left the *café*, as had many of the customers who were planning an early dinner. The rush hour of the apéritif had passed, the crowd was somewhat thin, waiters, sandwich men, tourists, etc., carried on rather indolently, and officers, singly and in pairs, in plain clothes and uniforms, on foot, mounted, or motorized, were trying to comb the quarter without rendering themselves open to suspicion of having violated the *commissaire's* strict orders. For most of the officers, the problem was simple. For *agents* Moue and Serré, however, the situation grew complicated, and *Agent* Moue, from the sidewalk in front of the Dôme *terrasse*, gave a quick involuntary glance at the merrymakers and said:

'M. Serré, that fat-head in the centre, alone at the little table, looks like Gring, Ambrose.'

'It may be a trap. After all, a week's pay . . .' Serré said. He was the soul of caution.

'Hey, Gring. Come here,' shouted Moue, hoping to entice their prey out of his sanctuary.

Ambrose Gring did not move an eyelash.

Both officers shouted, then bawled, and two waiters, after finding out what they wanted, approached Gring's table to inform him he was about to be taken into custody. Would he kindly step off the *terrasse* to the sidewalk? Gring did not appear to hear them. His eyes were half open, his face and hands were pale.

'Bring him over here, in the name of God,' shouted *Agent* Moue. 'The man must be deaf, dumb, and blind.'

M. Chalgrin, aware that something unusual was taking place, came anxiously out from behind the bar. 'What's all this ? What's all this ?' he demanded. One of the waiters told him that the officer wanted to speak with Ambrose and had been forbidden the *terrasse*.

'Indeed, I shall complain to the prefect. Am I to be deprived of the patronage of detectives and *agents* ? Are they to be sent to other *cafés* ? Is there, perchance, a rakeoff ? Graft ? I shall, as a taxpayer and a business man, insist on a shakeup of the entire department.'

Just then a woman screamed. 'He's dead !'

'Impossible,' said M. Chalgrin. 'I've had trouble enough.'

Other clients had taken up the cry, however. Some were crowding around Gring's table and others, anxious not to have their merry-making spoiled by a corpse or corpses, tried to go away. Both were rebuked by M. Chalgrin, the former for disturbing the area to be known as 'X ', the latter because each one of them had become suspect and suspects, M. Chalgrin knew, should be detained.

'Do you want him brought to the sidewalk, dead or alive ?' asked Chalgrin.

'Touch nothing,' said the cautious cop. 'I shall telephone the *commissaire* for instructions.'

Serré made a dash for a neighbouring *bistrot* where there was a phone. The *commissaire* was at his desk impatiently waiting for news.

'*Agent* Serré,' Serré said.

'Well, what of it ? Have you got him ?'

'I know where he is, but I wanted to ask . . .'

The *commissaire* exploded. 'In God's name, if you know where he is, why don't you bring him in ? He'll go away.'

'I think it's unlikely, sir,' said *Agent* Serré. 'In fact, the man is dead.'

'Dead ? Impossible,' shouted the *commissaire*.

'Several alcoholic foreigners and M. Chalgrin of the Café du Dôme have pronounced him dead,' the officer said.

The *commissaire* waited to hear no more. With surprising agility for a man of his age and habits he started running toward the Café du Dôme and was on the scene almost before *Agent* Serré had returned to his post on the sidewalk.

'Come here, you dunderheads,' the *commissaire* shouted. 'Because I warn you about drinking, you let a murder take place right under your noses.'

'Who said it was murder?' demanded Chalgrin. Some of the tourists and merrymakers screamed.

'Has anything been touched, the table, the glass and its contents?' Cautiously the *commissaire* sniffed. 'Smells like cocoa to me. There might be at least have been a bitter almond odour. Here, you two blockheads, take a sniff, each one of you.'

Even the cagey Serré admitted that the liquid smelled like cocoa.

'It's *crême de cacao*. He always drank that, God knows why,' the proprietor said. 'Well. Can't you take him away from here? My night's business will be ruined. No one wants to sit on a *terrasse* with a corpse.'

'You might screen off the area,' suggested the *commissaire*.

'Screen off, hell. Some drunk would push the screen down, then there'd be a panic, and if any of my clients got hurt in the crush I'd be responsible.'

The *commissaire* was not the brightest officer in the world but he was not the dumbest, either. He decided to pass the buck.

'Inform the prefect,' he roared, and to the crowd, which had gathered from all corners of the quarter and was blocking the traffic on both boulevards and all the side streets, he said, in a more moderate tone: 'Keep back, but no one is to leave the vicinity'. Since few of them had had any intention of leaving the vicinity before dawn, there was no murmur of protest. The word that Ambrose Gring, formerly a quarterite and, according to the latest papers, one of the picture bandits, had died and that murder was suspected had permeated every nook of Montparnasse. The proprietors of the Coupole, the Select, and the

101

Rotonde were tearing their hair. It was true, they knew, that while Gring's corpse was actually on the Dôme *terrasse*, the Dôme's business would suffer, but for days afterward curiosity-seekers would want to view the spot marked X and, if possible, to sit in the chair about to be labelled G, and the more daring of them would insist on sipping a *crème de cacao*, an expensive drink. To their credit must be said that none of the afore-mentioned proprietors thought about murdering anyone in order to furnish a counter attraction, but their thoughts and comments on the deceased were less sympathetic or charitable than otherwise they might have been had he died in a tramcar to the Jardin du Luxembourg, for instance.

Sirens announced the arrival of the prefect and Sergeant Fremont, whose loud words, nevertheless, were overheard by some of the loiterers along the sidewalk.

'It was your idea, not mine, letting that lizard roam at large again,' the sergeant said. 'Now he's got himself killed, and at the least convenient time.'

'I told you to have him followed and watched,' said the prefect. 'The responsibility is yours.'

'Then later you told me to put every man I had at work collecting Arabs,' said the sergeant.

'You couldn't even collect the right Arabs. Of all the Arabs in existence, I only gave a damn about two, and those were the two you failed to collect,' the prefect said.

'Well, here we are,' said the sergeant, as the official car ploughed its way through the crowd and brought up at the corner of the boulevard Montparnasse.

CHAPTER 11

The Agent Plénipotentiaire

JAMES JOYCE was making the sixth revision of page two thousand and forty of his *magnum opus* called 'Work in Progress'; Harold Stearns was sitting at the Select bar, murmuring that murders were unusual, therefore banal, consequently uninteresting; Gertrude Stein and Alice Toklas were drinking brandy and soda, Gertrude the brandy and Alice the soda; Ernest Hemingway was in the Bois thinking what he would do if the Bois was Wyoming, the swans were wild ducks, and he had a gun.

Homer Evans and Miriam Leonard, however, were sitting on a Han stone slab, 202 B.C. – 220 A.D. in the Cernuschi Museum where the single attendant still slept at his desk.

'Are you going to be reticent and mysterious, or shall your helpers be enlightened from time to time?' Miriam asked. 'You said you got exactly what you wanted in the gallery,' she continued. 'If that is true, your wants verge on the eccentric. I got one of the principal frights of my life. My old dad may not have stuck oil, but he'll cut off my allowance and beat hell out of me if I figure in the police news.'

'We shall spare your parent any undue alarm,' Evans said. 'Perhaps this all will be clearer if I tell you that the candlelight Greco I saw this morning, contrary to the intentions of Heiss and Lourde, was not the same painting as the candlelight Greco produced by poor clerk Dinde, after some prompting by reporter Jackson. And both paintings were painted on very old canvases.'

'One would not expect to find Old Masters on a new canvas, would one?' asked Miriam.

'All too often, that is precisely what one finds,' Evans said, 'and then one knows one has been stuck. I must go back some years and tell you first of my little favour to Hugo Weiss, which involved, strangely enough, still another candlelight Greco on very old canvas, too. The copy, for a copy it was, had been done with great skill, so skilfully that it passed for an original with a number of experts. I, however, had just been perusing an odd volume on chemistry and knew that a certain crimson Greco used later had not been found at the time the master did the candlelight series. And there was a touch of that same crimson in the candle flame of the painting for w'ich Hugo Weiss was to have paid a huge sum. That would not have hurt him. He was also to have been exposed by a rival of his, another millionaire-philanthropist who hated Hugo and would go to any length to get the best of him. I saved not only Hugo's purse but his face. He has been kind enough to remember that and it may have been a factor in inducing him to be so well disposed towards our friend, Hjalmar. I can't help feeling a certain responsibility. Hugo must be found, but just now I'm consumed with impatience for the taxi driver to return with our clothes. I must confess that I feel a deep anxiety for the safety of Ambrose Gring.'

'He can't be that important,' Miriam said.

'Ambrose himself is certainly unimportant, but he either has, or is suspected of having, information which is dangerous in the extreme. If it is worth the while of interested parties to risk kidnapping such a prominent man as Hugo Weiss, would men in such straits hesitate a moment in doing violence to Gring ?'

'Why don't you have him arrested again? A word to Sergeant Frémont. . . .'

'Precisely what I intend to do, but delay is fatal. . . Ah, here comes our indispensable taxi. How fortunate the attendant sleeps so soundly.'

The taxi driver tiptoed in with two bundles of clothes in his arms, grinned appreciatively at the sleeping guardian of the Oriental treasures, and indicated by grimaces and gestures that he had something important to convey. It was a matter of moments before Miriam and Evans had descended to the facsimile of the tomb of Liang Hse, B.C. 224, and emerged in their everyday clothes. The fezzes and burnooses Evans had tucked into a mortuary vase, the date of which was still in dispute. Miriam, of course, still had her boyish haircut but her hat—

Schiaparelli 1870 – 19. . – concealed the fact that her ringlets were missing.

> 'She had a quick and roving eye,
> And her hair hung down in ringlets.
> A nice girl, a decent girl,
> But one of the roguish kind.'

They all tiptoed past the attendant, who, had he waked and saw they were dressed differently, would have made them pay again. They entered the taxi and drove to the corner of the Avenue Velasquez, where the driver halted and turned towards Evans.

'Your friend, the barber, was in that Arab joint, much excited. Said he had found the man who was causing you trouble, wanted to speak with you right away,' the driver said.

'Henri? What could he have wanted?' Evans asked, in surprise.

'He was not only excited but unreasonable. He had an idea that Ben Sidi and Ben Abou could tell him where to find you. They're a smooth pair, those Arabs.'

'Well,' Evans said, 'I can see Henri some other time. Henri can wait. We have graver matters to attend to now.'

'I hope he'll take good care of my ringlets,' Miriam said.

'Now,' said Evans, with more animation than he had shown since his exposure by Ibn Hassan, 'we must have a chat with the ambassador.'

The ambassador was enjoying what he called an old-fashioned cocktail, although it had no fruit in it and very little sugar or water. He received Evans without formality, since he had known Homer's father as a boy, and in fact, had been confirmed by him.

'Well, Homer. What's up? Decided to let me find a job for you at last? Ought to do something, young man. Don't know why exactly. Never thought it out to the end. But that's what a lot of chaps seem to think. Man ought to work,' the ambassador said. Then he noticed Miriam. 'Gad, my boy. Didn't notice the girl. Maybe you're going to marry and settle down. Lots of chaps think a man ought to marry. Close thing to decide.'

Miriam was pleased, but equal to the situation. 'I wouldn't think of disturbing Mr Evans' remarkable peace of mind and his effortless way of living,' she said.

'Close thing,' said the ambassador. 'Lots to be said on one side or the other. That's the worst of most questions. Two sides and all that. Nothing ever gets done. Well. Nice to see a good American face. Miss 'em here, you know, in the off season. Then too many at once. Give and take. Ah, well.' He sighed and reached for his whisky.

'I'm sorry to disturb you,' Evans began. . . .

'Nonsense. Glad to see you, my boy. But don't make work for me. Had to spend half the day on that Hugo Weiss affair – cables, phone calls, young chaps in the office all upset. Even had to drop in on the prefect, just to make a show. He promised me a list of addresses. . . . You know, Evans, I think Hugo's on a bat. We'll have to hush it up. Do the same for us, I'm sure.'

'I'm afraid it's more serious than that,' Evans said.

'You don't say,' the ambassador sighed. 'Well, if it's serious, something must be done. But what, my boy?'

'I want your permission to examine his correspondence,' Evans said.

'Why, sure, my boy. Why not? If the police haven't rummaged around and lost it already. Energetic chaps, the police. Have to be, no doubt, but I often think they'd get farther if they took their time.'

'As I understand it, you yourself asked the prefect not to open Hugo's mail.'

'So I did. So I did. Privacy and all that, Evans. Had to say something to those chaps, you know. But you and Hugo are friends. I'm sure he wouldn't mind if you took a peek . . . But what makes you think the case is serious? Only gone one day. That's not so bad. If the police had been sicked on me every time I took a little vacation. . . .'

'I have reason to believe he's been kidnapped,' Evans said.

At this the ambassador was all attention. 'Kidnapped,' he said. 'Can't be kidnapped. No ransom note. Always is a ransom note when a chap is kidnapped.'

'This case is unusual,' Evans said. 'Some powerful interests want Hugo out of the way for a day or two.'

'Well. What's the harm of that, if they let him go again? He'll get back at 'em. Smart chap, Weiss. Played poker with him on the old *Dresden*. Nobody's fool.'

'There is much in what you say,' Evans continued. 'Had Hugo's philanthropic and business rivals taken charge of him themselves we wouldn't have to worry. But it is more than possible that the spade work, as it were, was turned over to some parties who are not quite as scrupulous where human life is concerned. There's been such a row about the case, the disappearance. . . .'

'I know.'

'The point is this. If the thugs who did the actual kidnapping get frightened, the natural thing for them to do would be to get rid of Hugo, and that means also getting rid of my friend Colonel Kvek and a Citroën taxi. Here's the difficulty. The evening Weiss disappeared, I and my friends, whom you saw at the *préfecture*, played a little joke on Hugo. Harmless little prank, I assure you, but the police misunderstood, arrested all of the crowd except Miss Leonard and me. And because I'm missing that fathead of a prefect is sure I did away with Weiss. All the police in France are on my trail, and as a matter of fact, I'm the only one who can help them find Weiss. If I show up at the *préfecture* they'll throw me into jail and hold me incomunicado, and Weiss may lose his life. . . .'

'Gad, boy, don't say that. What is it you want? I'll do anything you think best.'

'Could you have me appointed special agent of the U.S. government to co-operate with French authorities in the finding of Weiss and the exposure of an important smuggling ring?'

'Nothing easier! Miss Archibald!' he roared.

A trim young woman dressed rather severely appeared as if by magic, notebook in hand. 'Mary,' the ambassador said, 'ask this gentleman what he wants done and then do it. If it's necessary to phone the Secretary of State, I'll talk with him myself. But find out just what I ought to say. No beating around the bush.'

107

'Surely, Mr Ambassador,' said Mary. Evans followed her into the alcove and explained what was needed. Within half an hour he had a special diplomatic passport, an appointment to the secret service, and a special commission on parchment, with no less than fifteen ribbons and seals, authorizing him to act in behalf of the United States in the matter of Hugo Weiss' disappearance and whatsoever matters not herein 'set forth which, in his judgement, would further the interests of all concerned, and promote Franco-American co-operation and amity. There was a clause authorizing Homer to open American mail to or from any and all persons, firms, societies, associations, etc. A certified translation, subscribed and witnessed by a notary from the Ministry of Foreign Affairs and the American ambassador in person accompanied the commission, for the benefit of all and sundry who could not read English.

'Keep me posted, boy. . . . And let me know if I can be of service. Good-bye, Miss Leonard. Good American face. Figure, too, for that matter. Sporting of you not to want to ball a man all up and marry him. Come in again, any time,' the ambassador said, as they left.

'He's an old darling,' said Miriam. Evans had not neglected to secure for her a suitable commission to act at any and all times as his secretary, clerk, assistant, or amanuensis, and this she clutched with youthful pleasure, never having had anything like it before. 'Oh, here it is in French, too,' she said, scanning the parchment happily. 'How thoughtful you are.'

CHAPTER 12

The Suspects Awake

It was just before eight o'clock when the body of Ambrose Gring was removed to a waiting ambulance and taken to the mortuary where it was placed on a slab. Dr Toudoux was to perform an autopsy at the earliest possible moment but the most pressing duty he had was to preside over the awakening, of the suspects and witnesses from the Hôtel du Caveau. During his long and gruesome experience, the doctor had never heard of a death from *crème de cacao*, but he had found no bullet holes, no wounds from sharp or blunt instruments, no symptoms of organic disorder, and, most annoying of all, no bitter almond odours.

Rigor mortis had not set in, if anyone gave a damn about that. It was evident that Gring had had so little *rigor vitae* that it was doubtful if he could produce a satisfactory *rigor mortis* which would be useful in determining the hour of death. M. Chalgrin insisted that the murder took place between two o'clock and seven o'clock, but he had made himself so unpleasant about the delay in removing the body that no one in authority was disposed to accept his statements sympathetically.

The routine work had been accomplished without mishap. The glass and its contents, wrapped in a silk handkerchief, had been carefully transported to the laboratory, first to be examined for fingerprints and later to be tested for poisons. Everyone available had been questioned, but no one except one waiter had noticed that a man had sat for a while at the table now labelled G, and that waiter, having served several hundred clients that day, could not be sure whether the man in question was white or coloured, what language he spoke, or whether he had been in conversation with the deceased. At each step of the investigation, the prefect grew more sarcastic with Sergeant Frémont and the latter more disgusted with the world, his profession, his superiors, inferiors, and equals, and especially with

Montparnasse. Photographs had been taken of the spot X, the table and chair, the glass and bottle, and several tourists had been trampled in the rush to get into the pictures.

'I shall expect prompt results,' the prefect said. 'We are not living in anarchy. If men can disappear from your district, can die without resort to guns, knives, clubs, garrottes, darts, serpents, or bitter almonds, there is need for a shake-up in the department.'

Sergeant Frémont had to come across, or lose his prestige completely. 'I have already obtained results but you have been too busy to hear about them,' he snapped. 'I have the American Oklahoma Tom, the picture bandit trigger man, in the Goldfish Bowl. Furthermore, if you care to accompany me at nine o'clock to the Café de la Paix I will produce for you the American Ivan, who may be in Arab costume.'

'I shall hold you to that,' the prefect said. 'Come. We've little time. First we must wake up that collection of roisterers and give Gonzo his preliminary grilling.'

Amid the whining and howling of sirens, the official cars departed, leaving Montparnasse, except for the dearth of Arabs, much as it always had been.

The *préfecture* had been the scene of ominous preparations. *Agent* Schlumberger, who had been left in charge of the Caveau suspects, had been in touch with a cousin who led the trumpeters of the *Garde Républicaine*, and also, through an interpreter, had led the Arabs to believe that their prompt release depended upon how lustily they gave the old Arab battle cry when martial music sounded. When the prefect and Sergeant Frémont entered the corridor, eight squads of trumpeters in blue coats, with red trousers, gold epaulettes, and helmets decorated with long white feathers, were lined up in front of the cells. Dr Hyacinthe Toudoux pulled out his watch.

'Not a note before eight o'clock,' he said.

The real Ibn Hassan was peering through the doorway of the assembly hall, ready to give the signal for the Arab yell, and Jackson, looking foolish without necktie, belt, or shoelaces, watched the proceeding from the brightly lighted Goldfish Bowl.

110

'I insist on speaking to the ambassador,' he said.

'This is no time for joking,' Officer Schlumberger said.

Precisely at eight o'clock the signal was given and the trumpeters let loose with all their wind. The din was stupendous, and when augmented by the frantic war cries of two hundred mad Mohammedans, became hideous.

The first response was from the Swedish actress, who, thrusting aside her blanket, stood erect in her plum-coloured knickers and declaimed, defiantly:

'Shoot if you must this old grey head.'

Her cell-mate, Snorre Sturlusson, began to sing Finlandia. The black girl, Cirage, threw herself, Pocahontas-fashion, across Simon's head, to protect him from what she supposed was to be massacre. Gwendolyn Poularde, with true French sense of proportion, said: 'Well, well'.

About eight measures of the call to arms had been played before Hjalmar stirred. He rubbed his eyes, raised himself to a sitting posture without opening them, finally got to his feet and stretched.

'Holy mackerel,' he said. 'I've got drunk and joined the army.' Then, seeing M. Julliard standing nearby, he asked: 'How much of a stretch are we in for?'

'This is not the army. We are under arrest,' M. Julliard said.

Hjalmar, paying little attention, felt in his pockets, which were empty, and many things came back to him. He leaped toward the bars, shaking them like harpstrings. 'Hey, you,' he roared at the prefect, 'I've been robbed. Someone's taken my money. I had lots of it when I came in here. Don't think you're going to get away with anything.'

While Hjalmar's remarks were being translated to the prefect, the other members of the party set forth complaints and demands of their own; for information, drink, food, liberty, whatever came first to their minds. The *Garde Républicaine* trumpeters were winded, but the Arabs, hearing Hjalmar's roars and understanding, from their tone, that they were in defiance of the prefect and all infidel authority, howled with glee and approval. Jackson, in the Goldfish Bowl, was yelling at the top of his voice and gesticulating violently. And since his grandfather, Habakkuk Jackson, had been master of a famous clipper and had taught him to make himself heard against the wind in a storm, Jackson was able at last to attract Hjalmar's attention. The latter was mildly surprised at being addressed as Gonzo, but the whole situation was bizarre enough to allow for such minor discrepancies.

'None of you can speak French. Don't any of you speak a word of French,' Jackson shouted.

'Who says so ?' Hjalmar replied.

'Homer Evans. He said not to speak a word of French. They're going to grill you in a minute.

'The hell they are. I want my money. I lost a lot of dough.'

'I think they've got it at the desk,' Jackson said.

At this, Hjalmar brightened and began rattling the bars again, until the plaster loosened and fell to the floor in chunks. M. Julliard touched him gently on the elbow. 'They thought your money was counterfeit,' he said.

'Counterfeit ! That's a good one. Right out of the cash drawer of the Dôme and the Coupole.'

'They've nabbed all the paintings from your studio. Sent 'em to the Louvre to be expertized,' Jackson yelled.

'The Louvre ! Ho, ho. That's rich !' Hjalmar was beginning to get into the spirit of the thing. He had slept off the liquor and was ready for more, only he wanted to clear up the point about his money. He wanted to be sure it was safe at the desk.

The prefect, who previously had been unable to distinguish a word because of the din, caught on to the fact that the prisoners were exchanging information. Sergeant Frémont had known it, and had tried to listen in, without success. In the *préfecture*, the prefect was running the show, and after the way Frémont had been treated that day, the sergeant was not anxious to help his superior. In fact, the more of a hash of the investigation the prefect made, the better the sergeant was pleased.

'Take this man to my office for questioning, and forbid these other prisoners to speak to one another,' the prefect said. 'I'll talk with them one at a time.'

112

Six *agents de police* with drawn revolvers approached Hjalmar's cell and one of them gingerly unlocked the door. The big Norwegian looked at the half dozen smaller men, grinned good-naturedly, and after shaking hands with M. Julliard, allowed them to lead him down the corridor. In the office, the prefect confronted him angrily, while Sergeant Frémont stood by.

'Where's my money?' Hjalmar began.

'Young man, I will do the questioning...' the prefect said.

'Question all you like, but first tell me where my money is. My friend of the press....'

'Enough. Your friend of the press, as you call him, is Oklahoma Tom, trigger man for the picture bandit mob. You are Gonzo. Don't deny it. Your accomplice who escaped to America or England is the red-headed Mademoiselle Montana.'

'Listen, chief, I need some coffee and I want my dough, that's all,' Hjalmar said.

'How much money did you have?'

'About 250,000 francs.'

'Do you habitually carry that much money on your person? Is your art as profitable as that?'

'I don't mind telling you that I never had that much before. I'd had a great stroke of luck. Good fortune.'

'Tell me about this great good fortune.'

'Well, you see. It was like this. More than a year ago, in New York, I met a rich man named Hugo Weiss.'

The prefect turned to the stenographer. 'Are you getting every word?' The stenographer nodded.

'You met Hugo Weiss? I suppose he befriended you,' the prefect said.

'I'll say he did. He gave me a thousand bucks, so I could study in Paris a year, then we went to Luchow's and drank a lot of beer. Würzburger, it was. Fine beer, Würzburger.'

'A disgusting drink,' said the prefect. 'When one thinks of the wine....'

'Wine's all right, too,' agreed Hjalmar. 'But that night we had beer.'

'And then?'

'Then I came over here.'

113

'That interests me very much. I have had examined minutely the records of all passenger steamship lines and the name Gonzo does not appear on any of them for the past ten years.'

'My name is Jansen, not Gonzo.'

'There are no Jansens listed at the time you mention.'

'I didn't come on a passenger liner. I'm a sailor. I worked my way across,' Hjalmar said.

'And then jumped ship?'

'Well,' Hjalmar said, 'nearly everyone jumps ship. Otherwise the ship would take you right back where you came from.'

'A good beginning for your course of European study. Illegal entry into France,' the prefect said.

'Oh, come. I had a passport once.'

'No papers. Nothing in order.'

'I found a studio. . . .'

'In the rue Montparnasse. We have ransacked it thoroughly. . . .'

'Not much to ransack. . . . Although, I say. I hope you were careful of the paintings. . . . Some of them . . . er. . . .'

'You will please tell your story chronologically. Whatever we have taken, in the interest of justice, is safe in our hands.'

'I painted a year, my money was almost gone when Mr Weiss appeared in Paris. A mutual friend, Mr Homer Evans. . . .'

'The American Ivan,' the prefect said, aside to the stenographer.

'Mr Evans called on Mr Weiss, invited him to visit my studio, and Mr Weiss did so. . . . Last night or night before last. . . . By the way, is it Thursday or Friday? And how about some coffee?'

The prefect hesitated and stammered. 'Go on about Weiss,' the prefect snapped. 'The law is not interested in your appetites or your inability to follow the days of the week.'

Hjalmar stifled a brief impulse to sock the prefect on the jaw, then he thought of his two hundred and fifty thousand francs. He wanted them back in his pockets. He could remember the comforting feeling of them, stuffed every which way, crackling when he moved.

'Weiss came to the studio.'

114

'Alone'?'

'Sure.'

'What time ?'

'Half-past six.'

'What did he do there ?'

'Looked at the pictures. Evans showed them, one by one, about fifty. . . .'

'Forty-nine,' the prefect corrected.

'Then Weiss wrote me a cheque for the coming year's expenses and bought a portrait, giving me another cheque for that. I cashed 'em. . . .'

'Before Weiss left the room ?'

'No, after he'd gone. . . . He beat it about half-past seven. Said he had to meet a lot of stuffed shirts at the *Cercle Interalliée.*'

'Did this American Croesus refer to the flower of French art as a bunch of stuffed shirts ?'

'Flower of French hell. Say, *M. le Préfet.* You may be a good prefect, although I haven't seen any signs of it yet, but you're all wet about art. Let's stay off the subject, if you don't mind. No use quarrelling.'

'Why did you cash the cheques instantly, and both of them ?'

'Wanted to feel the dough in my pockets.'

'You were cautioned by M. Chalgrin. . . .'

'He's naturally cautious. . . . I'm the other way. I'd never had a lot of money and I wanted to enjoy it, not to let somebody else keep it for me. . . . Say, if you think this talk is all phoney, give Weiss a ring. Call him up. Ask him all about it. He's at the Plaza Athénée.'

The prefect rose menacingly and came very close to Hjalmar.

'Oh, he's at the Athénée ? What makes you think he's there ?'

'That's where he is stopping,' Hjalmar said.

At that point the prefect could suppress his rage no longer. His face assumed an expression that veered between explosion and frustration. 'Take this man away, quick, before I kill him,' the prefect shouted.

Hjalmar, ruffled by the man's tone, got set. 'I want my money, and I want it now,' he said, pounding on the desk.

115

Now Hjalmar did not pound with the restraint that previously had been shown by Jackson in the gallery of Heiss and Lourde. The prefect's inkwell, which outweighed that of the witness Dinde by a pound, not only jumped but erupted like a geyser, covering the prefect with a particularly vile solution of official violet ink. This was followed by such a wallop in the jaw as had never been stopped by the prefectorial mandible. 'Now, do you hear, you fathead. I want the money now. Two hundred and fifty thousand . . .'

At that moment the number of police and attendants who jumped on Hjalmar did not reach two hundred and fifty thousand but it was well up in the three figure column. Those nearest he tossed into the air, swatting them with his fists, side-swiping others with his elbows, disabling still others with his knees and feet. Fortunately he had no necktie on, but unfortunately he had no belt, either, and his trousers started slipping down around his knees, adding to an already staggering handicap. Rabelais has truly said that a man without breeches is in no condition to right wrongs. The Arabs, scenting battle, roared and yelled approvingly, knowing that if Hjalmar was even in moderate form a number of unbelievers would get plenty of what all good Mohammedans prayed constantly that Christians should receive. Rosa Stier, hearing the racket, started protesting in her rich baritone. Cirage squealed. Olga shouted: 'Who touches a hair of that grey head dies like a dog. March on, you blighters.' Jackson added to the din by singing happily: 'Bury me not on the lone prairie.' At last the combined police force got Hjalmar into a cell and locked the door, then busied themselves with their injured companions. Dr Hyacinthe Toudoux was wiping violet ink from the prefect's eyes.

'I warned you against awakening the man too soon,' the doctor said.

'Never mind that. Shall I be blind? I can't see,' the prefect roared.

'I have never had experience with such vile ink before,' said the doctor. 'Time marches on, and will tell.'

The groans of the wounded and the sharp odour of drugs and medicaments added to the disarray of the formerly orderly *préfecture* as Sergeant Frémont set out for the Café de la Paix.

He did not see, as he left, a distraught, lanky red-headed girl on her way across the square in front of Notre Dame, nor hear her murmuring, with a broad Hampshire twang: 'Hjalmar's in trouble ! He needs me ! The police are foreigners and fools, but they'll have *me* to deal with. I'm a British subject, thank God, and I'll stand none of their nonsense.'

CHAPTER 13

In Which a Tender Heart is Revealed Beneath a Gruff Exterior

'I'M getting increasingly anxious about Gring,' Evans was saying to Miriam.

'That's the only anxiety I cannot share with you,' she said. 'My documents, sealed and attested, say that I'm your stenographer, secretary, amanuensis, and slave, but there's nothing in them about worrying over Ambrose Gring.'

'Don't joke about it. I've a terrible presentiment,' said Evans.

She accepted his mood. 'Well, whatever happens, you'll be in the best tradition. A private detective who stoppeth one of three murders is doing as well as can be expected.'

'Since I was forced into this distasteful business I'd hoped to better the record,' he said.

'Always the perfectionist,' she murmured.

'Another factor also is troubling me. . . .'

'Is it Henri, the barber, by any chance?'

'Look here, young woman,' Evans said, severely, although he was secretly pleased. 'If you're going to anticipate all of my conclusions. . . .'

'I'm sorry that I spelled that word . . .' she quoted.

'Why should Henri be seeking me so feverishly in the Hôtel des Hirondelles? He's never bothered about me before, unless I flagged him. We've a good half-hour before I'm supposed to give myself up at the Café de la Paix. Let's toddle along to the rue Campagne Première, if you don't mind.'

'But the police?'

' They'll never think of looking for me there.'

'I hope you're right,' she said.

Their next taxi was driven by an American ex-service man, coloured. It brought them to the little shop where Henri the barber worked and lived, but there was no sign of Henri. Instead Henri's wife grasped Evans by the arm and began to cry. Where had he been? Why was her husband acting so strangely? Henri had come home, said he must find Evans, then later he had returned, pale and frightened, mumbled that he must get away, that somebody was after him.

'My dear woman,' Evans said. 'You must calm yourself. Your husband is safe, I'm sure. I called him this morning for a rather difficult and unusual tonsorial job, which he performed with credit. If later he wanted to see me, no doubt he has picked up some information which may be useful. Dry your eyes and go to bed. When Henri comes, he'll wake you.'

'Small chance. Ah, men,' she said, but in a less hysterical manner. It was clear that she was trusting Evans, and the knowledge of that fact added to Evans' dismay.

'We might try the Dingo,' Evans said. 'It's possible the bartender may have seen Henri.'

At the Dingo there was a small crowd, all intent on alcohol and each other, and none of them knew that on the *terrasse* of the Dôme not a hundred yards away a grisly drama was being enacted, and badly enacted at that. Joe, the bartender, greeted Evans uneasily and motioned for him to follow to the kitchen.

'Have you seen Henri?' Evans asked.

'Now how did you know I was going to ask about Henri?' the bartender said, almost indignantly.

'I'm nothing but a repository for inconsequential personal information,' Evans said. 'That's what I've become.'

'The cops are on your trail. I suppose you know that,' Joe said.

'Well-meaning fellows,' said Evans. 'Nearly always mistaken, but really not vicious, you know.'

'Well, you know your own business,' Joe said. 'But they haven't found Weiss yet and they claim you're mixed up in the kidnapping, or whatever it was.'

'Absurd,' said Evans.

'That's what I told 'em,' said Joe, 'but those saps never pay any attention to what I say.'

'Now what about Henri?' Evans asked.

Joe's honest face clouded. 'He's been coming in here now and then. Likes beans.'

'I know.'

'He reads a lot, too. French translations of the old Nick Carters.'

'Harmless and entertaining,' Evans said.

'Yeah. Within limits. But he got hepped on Mickey Finns.'

'Mickey Finns ?'

'You know. Knock-out drops. Read about 'em and wanted to try one. Well, one thing led to another, and you know how I am. I can't refuse a guy nothing. So one day this Henri he wanted to sneak out on his wife, had met a tart in here and wanted to know about Americans, probably. You know how it is. Well, he got the idea that if he slipped his wife a Mickey, she wouldn't wake up when he beat it and would sleep until after he came in. I fell for the plan, gave him a Mickey, and he said it worked. In fact, I've done it more than once.'

'Still harmless and entertaining,' Evans said.

'Yeah. But to-day didn't look so good. Henri wasn't himself. He wasn't just out for a little cheating. He was worried about something. Said he had to find you. And he got another Mickey, a little stronger than usual. That was about five o'clock this afternoon.'

'Tell me about a Mickey Finn,' Evans said. 'Does it fail to work if the patient is worried or agitated ?'

'Not so's you'd notice it,' Joe said. 'I never use 'em myself, except when I have to – if someone starts getting nasty, or spilling something he'd be sorry for if it got out. I have to look after the interests of my customers. . . . They trust me, you know.'

'Well, I've got to amble,' Evans said. 'Thanks, and don't worry about Henri. His wife's still conscious, unless he's been there in the last five minutes.'

'I think Henri's a very considerate man,' Miriam said. 'Imagine taking all that trouble to spare his wife pain. Some men would flaunt their conquests.'

'I'm glad you appreciate the value of discretion,' Evans said.

'Oh, I do. I do,' she said. 'Don't worry about that.'

'I've got enough to worry about. Damn Henri. I wish I could be in several places at once. I want to have a talk with Abel

120

and Dodo. I want to reassure myself about Gring and get him to a place of safety. I must find Hugo and Kvek, get our friends out of jail, retrieve the paintings from the Louvre. . . . And I can do nothing more until our precious police officials agree not to run me in whenever I show my face. That's the first step. Convincing Frémont. It's going to be rough going. Come on.'

'Where to, boss ?' asked the American Negro at the wheel.

'The Café de la Paix, and not too fast. I've got to think as we joggle along.'

'I won't disarrange your innermost ratiocinations,' the driver said and slipped smoothly into gear.

Evans was silent as the taxi moved steadily out of Montparnasse. 'The pieces simply won't fit together,' he said. 'Ah, well. If the answers were too apparent, I suppose even Frémont would solve the problem. He's the only one on the force with any flair. The prefect's a politician, and a traitorous one at that. The *commissaires* are given their jobs on account of long service and few arrests; that's the standard of promotion. The cop who makes the least trouble wins a sergeantcy, and so on.'

'There seem to be hundreds of cops around here,' Miriam said, glancing apprehensively from the window. They were gliding along the avenue de l'Opéra in the neighbourhood of the Café de la Paix.

Evans rapped on the window. 'Hold everything, chauffeur,' he said, and the cab pulled up at the kerb without a jolt. To Miriam, Evans said: 'That unspeakable fathead of a prefect must have ordered my arrest. The dragnet's out again.' He did not pause long in indecision, however. Pointing to a small bar in the rue Daunou he said to the driver: 'You know Sergeant Frémont ?'

'Of Rosary Game fame ? Certainly, boss.'

'Ever seen him ?' The Negro grinned.

'In first class embarrassing circumstances, sah,' he said.

'How come ?'

The face of the Negro grew serious. 'A chauffeur's like a priest, you know. Can't spill nothing.'

Evans pulled a thousand franc note from his pocket and dangled it gently. 'This is a cause of life and death, of guilt and innocence. You wouldn't want a whole jailful of good Americans framed. . . .'

'If you put it on a patriotic basis, I place country above professional ethics,' the Negro said, reaching for the note.

'Good man,' Evans said, and to Miriam: 'What should we do without Lefty Gomez?'

The Negro smiled bashfully in Miriam's direction. 'Should I tell you this in confidence, boss?'

'I know all about life, theoretically,' Miriam said. 'Also, I'm Mr Evans' official assistant and amanuensis.' She flashed her imposing documents and the Negro turned pale.

'I hope I'm not getting into anything judiciary,' he said. 'I didn't really desert the army, boss. You wouldn't haul me in?'

'Not if you come clean about the sergeant,' said Evans, showing his papers with the ribbons and seals. 'I'm a special agent of the United States government, but of the civil branch. Military peccadilloes are of no interest to me, except as means to an end.'

'I'll come across. It's my bounden duty,' the Negro said. 'You see, the sergeant, when he was on that Duke Ormington case, got acquainted with the cast of the " Blackbirds " that came here from Harlem with a show. There was one girl, especially, who took his eye. She liked him, too. You know how Frenchmen are with coloured women. Polite. Admiring. Seem to get all young again.'

'Naturally,' Evans said.

'They call it changing your luck, out west,' Miriam said.

'There was one drawback,' the driver said. 'If Hydrangea had been yellow, or even light brown, the sergeant could have passed her off as a Spaniard and no talk would have been caused. As it was, Hydrangea was the blackest of the troupe. The sergeant was afraid his wife would get wind of the affair, and he was more afraid of the prefect, who hated women of all sorts. So they had to be discreet and Hydrangea vouched for me as discretion personificated. I took them everywhere, and when things got hot, pretended to be Hydrangea's escort. Boss, them was days. I got enough swell clothes to last me till almost now.'

122

'You've been of great service to your country this day, and I shall see you're properly rewarded,' Evans said. 'Now I want you to drive alone to the Café de la Paix, find Frémont, who'll be pacing anxiously in front of the *terrasse*, and simply tell him that Hydrangea's come back and is waiting for him in the little *café* I've indicated.'

The Negro started trembling with fright. ''Fore God, boss, I don't dare do that. He'll lock me up forever. He'll beat me till he uses me up. Hydrangea's a sore point with him, boss. He never got over it when she went back to Harlem.'

'I'll square it with him,' Evans said, and Miriam grunted.

Reluctantly, the chauffeur started away. Miriam took a seat and ordered a whisky. 'Can't we get a sandwich before we're thrown into the *conciergerie* ? I haven't eaten so irregularly since the 1922 roundup when some rustlers stole the grub and ran a bunch of shorthorns off the range.'

'Just a few minutes with Frémont, then I'll order you the best meal in France,' Evans said. As he was speaking, Sergeant Frémont broke in, but it was not the lethargic Sergeant Frémont who had haunted the corridors of the *préfecture* that day. It was a man filled with eagerness and hope, to say nothing of vitality and joy. When he caught sight of Evans his expression changed with such ferocity that the Negro abandoned his taxi and started running down the street.

'Patience,' Evans said. 'I happened to-day to learn of the whereabouts of Miss Hydrangea Palmerstone Waite. . . .'

The sergeant lost his ferocity and became wistful again.

'Where is she ? Let me see her.'

'Not so fast,' Evans said. 'I have been led to believe that you had the ridiculous idea of arresting me.'

'That can wait. Everything can wait except Hydrangea. Monsieur Evans, you wouldn't believe what a woman she is. Why, I have neglected case after case of the gravest import just to see her dance, to watch the supple motion of her limbs and try to realize that when the show was over she would be mine, hidden from all other eyes.'

'I'm afraid the chauffeur got my message wrong,' Evans said. 'Miss Hydrangea's not here in Paris at the moment, but I know

123

where she is and can persuade her to come. . . . On one condition.'

Sergeant Frémont sank pitifully into a chair. 'She's not here ? Not in Paris ?' he murmured.

'Another whisky,' Miriam said to the waiter.

'On one condition,' Evans said, producing his impressive set of papers. 'You will see that my government has given me charge of the Weiss case, as special plenipotentiary agent. That will excuse you, if the prefect finds out. I'll have the ambassador settle with the prefect in the morning. Meanwhile, to-night I must be free, and I promise you results.'

The sergeant was slowly coming out of his fog of disappointment, so Evans talked fast. 'Sergeant,' he said. 'This case involves millions of dollars, and an internationally important kidnapping. Fortunately there's no murder in it yet.'

'Who said there was no murder ?' demanded the sergeant, still fumbling the papers with indecision. 'That mackerel Greeng Ambrose . . .'

Miriam screamed. 'He's not dead ?'

'God. How unutterably thoughtless I've been,' said Evans.

'Greeng was poisoned on the *terrasse* of the Dôme between two and seven o'clock,' the sergeant said. Then he added: 'I can't think. I don't know what to do. Hydrangea.'

'Sergeant,' Evans said kindly, 'I know all about your tragedy. Hydrangea was fond of you. . . . She wanted to stay here with you. . . .'

'Yes.'

'But on account of the language, she got homesick, began to waste away. She herself hardly understood what was happening. Surrounded by strange tongues, she thought everyone was talking about you and about her. She was afraid she'd bring you disgrace. Several of the girls had had frightful experiences of the sort at home, you know. Involved with white men. Ruined them, the men, of course. We've got the most barbarous notions about race in our country. Scarcely credible, you know. Wives can practically name their own figure of alimony if they can drag a husband into court with a coloured girl. . . .'

'But won't it be the same ? Won't she waste away again ?'

124

'Ah, I've thought that all out,' Evans said. Miriam tried to stuff her handkerchief into her mouth but the former wasn't big enough. A sound escaped that was about halfway between the tinkle of a breaking liqueur glass at the Coupole and the gurgling of the waters of Beef Creek just at fly time. Evans glanced at her reproachfully. 'I've thought it all out,' he said. 'I've made the acquaintance of a coloured model, a black girl called Cirage. Most extraordinary woman. Intelligent. Warm-hearted. She'll take an apartment with Hydrangea, teach her French, explain all the foreign ways, act as a companion during the long hours you are tracking down the denizens of the underworld. ...'

Frémont clasped Evans' hand with fervour. 'Monsieur Evans, I'm in your hands. My life. My job. My future. ...'

'Problem " e",' Evans muttered. 'Will this series never end?'

Suddenly Frémont rose like a jack-in-the-box, tearing his hair. 'What did you say was the name of the future companion of my beloved?'

'In the quarter she is affectionately known as Cirage,' Evans said. 'Her real name is Marie-Thérèse Eugénie Berthe Mortelle.'

'But I've spoiled everything. I've arrested this Mademoiselle Cirage. She's in jail this very instant,' the sergeant said.

'She won't hold it against you if you let her go right away. Release Madame Stier, by the way, also the Swedish actress, Olga, and those reputable painters MM. Simon and Sturlusson. Yes. I forgot Mlle Poularde. By all means release her, and we must get those paintings you sent to the Louvre. I'll explain everything later. But pacify the prefect to-night. ...'

'If you could see what your friend Gonzo has done to the prefect, you would understand that pacifying my superior to-night is not a job to be undertaken lightly,' Sergeant Frémont said.

'I'll send a cable to Hydrangea,' said Evans.

'If I let these people go I'll have to have them shadowed,' said the sergeant. 'I can say it's necessary in order to find their confederates.'

'Good man,' Evans said. 'I won't be unreasonable. I know

125

that Gonzo and Oklahoma Tom seem to have incriminated themselves. They're innocent as lambs. . . .'

'Lambs ! If your pal Gonzo is an American lamb. . . .'

'Gonzo's a trifle impulsive, when he's crossed,' Evans said. 'He was crossed by the entire staff of the *préfecture*, and twenty-two of them will be eligible for hospitalization and convalescent pay. And this in time of national economy,' Frémont said.

'Nevertheless, I'll need him to-night. Without Gonzo we can't hope to solve this case. He's the only one who can lead us to Hugo Weiss,' said Evans.

'Then we're lost. Merely on the assault and battery charges he's piled up since we got him in jail, the prefect would hold him fifteen years. You didn't see the prefect, all covered with violet ink.'

'You stir in me the only desire I ever have felt to see your prefect,' Evans said. 'By all means, in violet ink. It takes an artist to put on just the right touch, old man. You'll begin to see their merits before this case is over. But come on. We've got to get going.'

CHAPTER 14

The Sound of a Great Amen

THE next step was to go to the cable office in the boulevard des Capucines where Evans dispatched the following:

MRS CORALYE MCLANE
1923 SEVENTH AVE.
NEW YORK CITY

SHIP IMMEDIATELY PARIS FORMER BLACKBIRD HY-DRANGEA PALMERSTONE WAITE stop FUNDS AFRICAN NATIONAL BANK   HOMER EVANS

'That will fetch her,' Evans said. Miriam looked at him in awe, swallowed hard once or twice, then shrugged her shoulders.

'Did them a little favour in Harlem years ago,' Homer said.

Then they went to Maxim's for a snack, ending up with brandy Carlos III.

'In honour of Lefty Gomez,' Evans said to Frémont.

'Gomez? A Spanish philosopher? A *gourmet*?'

'A philosopher, indeed,'.Homer said. 'Now for business. We've got to talk with that brace of lilies known as Heiss and Lourde. But first perhaps I should explain to the sergeant how I happened to cause a slight disturbance in the gallery this afternoon....'

'You don't mean that you're at the head of those picture bandits?' Frémont asked, rising indignantly to his feet.

'That's an over-simplification,' said Evans. At that point a messenger burst in and the sergeant, fumbling with a telegram, began to splutter.

'They've got Miss Montana, and she's gone nuts,' he said.

'Maggie. Great God, I'd forgotten her,' exclaimed Evans. 'And don't tell me that a barber has disappeared from the rue Campagne Première.'

The sergeant's face clouded. 'If our great governments are to work together, there must be mutual frankness,' he said.

Rapidly Homer told him about Henri, and when he mentioned the Mickey Finn and its properties the sergeant looked as if he had heard the sound of a great amen.

'Michael Finn,' he repeated. 'Harmless soporific. Puts wife to sleep.' The sergeant began to trip and to caper. 'The man's a genius,' he continued. 'What, exactly, is this Fine Michel or Michael or Mickey Finn? Can it be bought in pharmacies?'

'The moment my friends are released from your antiquated jail I'll tell you where to obtain Mickey Finns,' Homer said. Fervently the sergeant grasped Homer's hand.

'I shall never forget your kindness,' he said.

Without further ado the trio set out for the boulevard Haussmann where they entered the gallery of Heiss and Lourde. Abel was sitting at the desk with his head buried in his arms and was groaning. Dodo, who as a groaner had slightly the better of the senior partner, was pacing back and forth in front of Bellinis, Delacroix desert scènes, Rembrandts, and a little known portrait of Whistler's Aunt Harriet in which the family resemblance was strong. One burly cop, five feet four, was leaning against the door, dozing, and another brace in uniform guarded the stairway leading to the upper storeroom where the plain clothes men were playing what they called in their innocence contract bridge. Everyone except Abel jumped to attention when the sergeant entered.

'As you were,' the sergeant said. 'Then clear out of here, all of you. I have with me the special agent plenipotentiary of the government of the United States. . . .'

At the word 'government' Dodo made a dive at the door which, had it not been the best plate glass, would have given way. Abel, aroused from his lethargy, was not far behind him. Sergeant Frémont grabbed their respective coat-tails and hauled them back.

'Not you. We have something to say to you, and we are confident,' his tone grew ominous, 'that you both will have a lot to say to us. The officers can go. We shall not need them further, unless, of course, Messrs Heiss and Lourde do not talk fast enough. In that case the officers will be called back, with necessary implements.'

128

The police and plain clothes men filed out, glad to be relieved of their dull vigil among the masterpieces of the ages. The last one had not rounded the corner before Abel let out a shriek. His eyes protruded, his Adam's apple worked up and down like the piston of a pump. With a lean finger he pointed straight at Evans: 'That's the sheik,' he screamed.

'And that's the prince,' joined in Dodo, pointing at Miriam. 'We've been framed. We've been spied upon. Government agents. . . . How do you get that way? We haven't done a thing. Not a sale in a fortnight.'

'Peace, partners,' said Evans. 'Just sit quietly, you, Abel, at the desk. There's an automatic in the middle drawer, within easy reach of your hand. . . .'

'Merciful God,' said the sergeant, leaping on Abel's scrawny neck. . . .

'Spare yourself, sergeant,' Evans said calmly. 'I removed the slugs this afternoon. Besides, Abel has never fired a gun in his life. He hates violence. Abhors rough work of any kind. We're dealing with the smoother type of ruffian. . . .'

'You can't pin a thing on us,' Abel said. 'I don't know what your game is, but it won't work with me.'

'And you, Dodo,' Evans continued, ignoring Abel completely. 'Ensconce yourself in that chair you pretend is Louis XIV, when the upholsterer who stuffed it was only ten years old on the day of the king's funeral.' He turned to Frémont, whose eyes were bulging. 'It isn't that a Louis XV chair is less valuable than a Louis XIV. Dealers simply are nervous about telling the truth. They shun the truth by instinct, knowing that it frequently leads to trouble. True stories about art objects may be checked. Minor discrepancies naturally occur. Clients become distrustful. But when a tale is made up of whole cloth, no one ever finds a flaw. Still, I have a hankering for truth, myself. I want for the first time to introduce its healing ray into the musty corners of this establishment. I should like, if you don't mind, to have you distract these gentlemen with a few tales of necessary police brutality while I have a look upstairs. But first, could you call one of your faithful minions back? I want him to do an errand.'

The sergeant shouted 'Bonnet' from the door and the officer who first had accompanied him to Hjalmar's studio and who was present at the discovery of the mysterious cheques, stepped up promptly and saluted.

'Monsieur Bonnet,' Evans began . . .

'Monsieur Evans is special *agent plénipotentiaire* of the United States government. Take orders from him as if they came from me,' the sergeant explained.

Evans bowed his thanks. 'Monsieur Bonnet,' he said. 'Would you mind toddling over to the Plaza Athénée, mounting to room 465 and gathering up all letters, telegrams, or other communications which may have accumulated there ?'

'But that's the Weiss room. The ambassador's forbidden . . .' interrupted Frémont.

'The ambassador has given me *carte blanche*,' Evans said.

Bonnet bowed in turn, and retired. Evans motioned Miriam to follow him to the upper room. Swiftly he glanced at one canvas after another, taking them one at a time from a stack against the wall. 'Ah,' he said, when he tackled the second stack. 'I thought so.' He drew forth a painting and when he laid it face up on the table, Miriam gasped.

'The candlelight Greco,' she murmured.

'Not *the* candlelight Greco, *a* candlelight Greco, and one, I fear, that the worthy master never had the pleasure of seeing. Before I review the history of the candlelight series, real and bogus, I think our friend the sergeant should be summoned. He hates paintings, but likes anecdotes. And since the sergeant should be with us, why not invite Heiss and Lourde ? They might learn something about their stock and their trade, and just possibly they might let fall a few pearls of information. Just possibly, you know.'

'I'll herd them all up here,' Miriam said, and started resolutely down the stairs. At the landing she called to the sergeant: 'Bring those rustlers topside. The *agent plénipotentiaire* wants to talk with 'em.'

'You heard what the lady said,' the sergeant snapped, and shaking with foreboding, Heiss and Lourde rose furtively and preceded the sergeant up the stairs.

130

'Ah, gentlemen,' Evans said, quietly. 'Just in time for the little talk on Greco. Not Gonzo, sergeant, do not confuse the Cretan master with our friend who uses violet ink to such splendid effect. Greco, whose real name was Domenico Theotocopoulos, was born about 1547, suffered under Titian while learning *sub rosa* from Tintoretto, embarked for Spain in 1576, painted as long as he could stand it for that prize bigot and purveyor of atrocious taste, Philip II, then set up a studio in Toledo, where, among other things, he tangled with the Inquisition in the matter of the length of angels' wings.'

'Monsieur Evans, I detest art, and know less than nothing about it,' the sergeant interrupted.

'You are kindred, then, with Heiss and Lourde. Both of them were put into the art business by relatives who couldn't trust them in banks. . . .'

Abel began making choking noises. 'No use to protest,' Evans said. 'I couldn't be trusted in a bank, either. When I see huge packets of big bills. . . .'

Dodo groaned with such feeling that Evans desisted. He turned to the sergeant and said, seriously, 'Sorry to bore you with a bit of history, but it's vital to the case. What I'm getting at is that Greco . . . we'll eschew his real name as being too difficult . . . dashed off a series of candlelight paintings, mostly for his own amusement. Got fed up with angels and saints and politicians. Wanted to experiment in rendering the effects of artificial light. The results were marvellous, like everything the Master tackled. Now it was generally conceded among experts and historians of art that Greco painted five candlelight pictures, all with the same Negro boy as model, the same table, table cover, wall, etc. They were not copies, merely slightly different paintings. You follow me ?'

'I don't see what this has to do with Hugo Weiss,' the sergeant said, disconsolately.

'Sure. You hit it there, sergeant,' Dodo said. 'This plenipotentiary guy's full of apcray.'

The sergeant silenced Dodo by stamping on his foot, a trick he had learned from the Fakir Yenolob in the Carats case.

'I'll get right down to business,' Evans said. 'Ah, here's

131

M. Bonnet with an armful of mail. Place it right here on the table, please. And perhaps you'd better remain. You like art, M. Bonnet?'

'I had always wanted to paint,' Bonnet said, 'but my father insisted that I join the police force. He was a painter, but not a very good one.'

'Exactly,' Evans said. 'Now, to resume about the candle-light Grecos. There were five in existence, up to 1923. One was the property of T. Prosper Stables, a wealthy American financier and, incidently, a bitter rival of our missing friend, Hugo Weiss. Stables is a surly fellow, liver practically gone. Hates Weiss but Weiss is only sorry for him. Has more money than Weiss and makes a great show of philanthropy. The Stables candlelight Greco was adjudged by several experts to be the best of the series. Another is in the British Museum, the third in the Hermitage collection in Leningrad, a fourth in Vienna, and the fifth is being held for speculation by the American Can Corporation.'

'Then this must be a fake,' the sergeant said, making a grab at Abel's collar.

'Not so fast,' Evans said. 'In 1923 a sixth candlelight Greco was, according to the story put out by a firm of British dealers, found in an attic in London. Some British soldier, ransacking in Spain, had taken the canvas home and his grandchildren had found it in the attic, along with some letters, yellowed with age, which proved beyond a doubt that the painting had come from Spain. The 1923, or sixth candlelight Greco, was touted as being better than Stables No. 1, so naturally Hugo Weiss put in a bid for it. Just before that I had seen the painting myself, and for a while, was fooled. The canvas was actually old. It had been woven in the early sixteenth century by the same weavers who had done the cloth on which the Conde de Orgaz was painted. No mistake about that. Had it not been for the candle flame, the 1923 Greco would have got by me, but I had just been brushing up a bit on chemistry and history of art and I knew that the crimson in the candle flame. . . .' He paused to point to the flame on the picture before him. . . . 'That crimson,' he continued, 'was not known until the last years of Greco's life, a long time after he had finished his candlelight experiments. I did not give the show away, not liking to meddle....'

Dodo groaned louder than ever, and dodged the sergeant's heel.

'I did, however,' Evans continued. 'slip a word to Hugo Weiss. I disliked Stables, for personal and family reasons, and didn't want him to gloat over Hugo when the hoax was discovered.'

'Where did you get this forgery?' the sergeant roared at Abel.

'Patience, sergeant. I'll answer that in time. First I must tell you how Mr Stables learned that art is simply wonderful for dodging income tax and concealing assets.'

'My head is aching,' Frémont said.

'So's mine,' said Dodo.

'Perhaps M. Bonnet wouldn't mind bringing in some aspirin. About sixty grains, officer, please. I've more to unfold, I assure you, gentlemen. I've merely sketched in the background.' With that he reached down to the nearby stack of canvases and pulled out one which he held toward the light.

'*Nom de Dieu*,' Frémont said, indignantly. 'Another of those pesky Negro boys and candles. Let me take these crooks to the *préfecture*. Why wait?'

'My dear friend. I have told you repeatedly that this case is not a simple one, not merely petty swindling. Our first object is finding Hugo Weiss. Then we can proceed at leisure with these smaller fry.'

Abel and Dodo winced, and were about to speak resentfully when the sergeant did the double heel trick, a variation of his own on the Hindoo original.

'Ouch! Have a heart,' the dealers whined.

Evans faced them scornfully. 'Ah, no. These are not the master minds. Theirs not the brains to conceive this great network of falsification and chicanery. Theirs not the wealth to be hoarded and withheld from the public need. Theirs not the hands so skilful that they can simulate the brushwork of that divine and original master whose real work . . .' he tossed the second candlelight painting contemptuously to the floor, 'is worth more to the square inch than the hearts of such cats'-paws as these.'

133

'I simply adore him when he talks like that,' Miriam said to the sergeant. Since the romance of Hydrangea and Frémont had been brought to light, Miriam had felt drawn to the gruff officer who was capable, in spite of the sordid nature of his occupation, of soaring to emotional heights and inter-racial ecstasies.

'I'm sorry we can't give this pair life terms,' said the sergeant. 'But who are the big shots?' he added nervously.

'All in due time,' said Evans soothingly. 'What we must guard against first is that Hugo Weiss's brief candle is not snuffed before it's time. I've already made a boner in the case of Gring. Someone blundered there, and gravely.' He looked hard at Heiss and Lourde, and his voice grew harsh, so suddenly that Miriam trembled and the sergeant made a grab for his gun. Pointing a scornful finger almost in their faces, Evans rooted them with terror to their seats.

'On the evening of May 24th,' he said, 'you sought out Ambrose Gring. What for?'

There was no sound but the quick intake of terrified breaths.

Abel was the first who dared speak. He cowered and said: 'We want a lawyer. We're not saying a word.'

'We didn't bump off that guy, and we can prove it,' Dodo said. 'Jeese, we were sitting right here and the place was lousy with bulls.'

'I didn't ask you who killed Ambrose Gring. I'm sure you don't know, if that's any comfort to you.'

'Hell,' the sergeant said. 'They'd have made such a fitting pair of culprits. Are you sure they didn't kill him? Could they not have administered a slow poison? That's it. Slow poison. I'm going to put the cuffs on 'em, and send for Doc Toudoux's report.'

'They will talk more freely without handcuffs,' Evans said. 'Again I ask you,' he said to Abel, 'what you wanted with Ambrose Gring.'

'He'd worked for us before,' Abel said.

'What kind of work?'

'Collecting information.'

'You're a sucker to spill a thing,' Dodo said, and dodged the sergeant's ready heel.

134

CHAPTER 15

The Seine Yields a Clue

AMONG the many men and women involved in the Weiss case, none took it harder than Officer Schlumberger, known as 'the Sunday painter'. Being an Alsatian, he took practically everything hard. He suffered in his civic pride, as a member of the police force, because men of prominence could disappear without trace. He was sure his *commissaire*, and particularly the prefect, were making fools of themselves, that of all the witnesses and suspects held, none was guilty of the kidnapping. But most of all, Schlumberger was worried about the forty-nine paintings which had been sent to the Louvre. Were they, in fact, old masters in disguise? Was France being drained of precious art treasures through the machinations of clever Americans?

The good patrolman had had fairly rough sledding since the Weiss case had broken. His *commissaire* had insulted him publicly, he had come in for all sorts of extra duty. Against his better judgement the forty-nine mysterious canvases had been turned over to the experts of the national museum, who Schlumberger thought were boobs. Had they not spent huge sums for fake Watteaus? Had they not covered the walls of the Louvre with bogus Rembrandts? Schlumberger did not lose his head. Unlike his superiors, he did not go off his rocker at the least provocation. He was the phlegmatic type, so he left the musty *préfecture* on the pretext that he must get something to eat and as the hour of midnight was striking, and, unknown to Schlumberger, the dealers called Heiss and Lourde were sweating under Evans' merciless questioning, the officer leaned his elbows on the parapet of the bridge by Notre Dame and tried to ease his thoughts by watching the endless flow of the Seine. How miraculous, a river! the good officer thought. He gazed at its brown rippling surface, inhaled its dampness and the odour of the ancient stone walls. On and on. To-morrow and to-morrow and to-morrow. Water from the fragrant slopes of northern France, trickling, accumulating, finding its grooves and channels; bearing commerce and pleasure craft, the delight of gay children, a last refuge for the despairing. What secrets could not the Seine divulge? What horrors had it cloaked in its time?

Officer Schlumberger's hair began to rise and a prickly sensation crept upward from the base of his skull. The brown placid surface of the Seine was stirred by a floating object. The officer did not hesitate. He tore loose the huge stuffed life preserver from its case on the parapet, grasped the strong new rope firmly and hove. Only one detail, in his haste, he overlooked. He forgot to let go of the rope. Therefore, the weight of the life preserver jerked him clear over the low stone wall, and after a sickening descent he felt the cold smack of that same brown surface of the river he had admired but a moment since.

'Glowb ... uggle ... Glowb' were the sounds that bubbled up as he sank. It was hard swimming in full uniform, weighted down with club, automatic, badge, handcuffs, etc., but Schlumberger was not the man to drown without struggle. And neither did he forget in his plight the floating object that had lured him to his ducking. It was not a body, not even a bundle of clothes. His heart leaped when he saw that it was a canvas, without frame, an oil painting.

His yells attracted the attention of the river patrol, and within twenty-five minutes, during which he clung to the rough stones of the quay and cursed the service, two patrolmen launched an emergency boat and were trying to row it toward him, with indifferent success.

'Pull yourselves along by the wall if you can't row, you saps,' Schlumberger shouted.

'You ought to be thankful we don't let you drown,' a patrolman said.

A brisk dialogue continued until finally Schlumberger was able to crawl over the bow, without upsetting the craft. He glanced at the wet painting and let out an exultant yell: 'Gonzo! By Jove. It's the missing self-portrait. I'll be promoted. I'll be rewarded by the rich American.'

'This guy is whacky,' No. 1 boatman said.

'Let's get him out of here in time,' No. 2 said, bumping the quay awkwardly with the stern.

Once his feet were on dry land, Schlumberger wasted no time. He lit out for a telephone booth to learn the whereabouts of Sergeant Frémont. Schlumberger had no confidence in the prefect, and was sure that if such important evidence came to his attention first he would hash it up somehow. The officer was determined to place the precious Gonzo in the hands of the sergeant. A bored voice at the *préfecture* gave him the address of Heiss and Lourde and it was the work of a moment to hail a taxi. It was the work of several moments, however, to find a driver who would take him in, wet and dripping as he was, and muttering ejaculations of joy over a water-soaked picture.

In the upper room at Heiss and Lourde's, Evans had reached the point in his questioning at which he demanded to know why Abel and Dodo had wanted to confer with Gring on the night of May 24th. It was at that point that a lull occurred in the examination. For Heiss and Lourde refused point-blank to talk. Both Abel and Dodo closed up, not like clams which may easily be pried open, but more like the vaults of one of the banks in which they could not be trusted by their relatives. Miriam was urging both Evans and the sergeant not to be gentle on her account. If they wanted to give the pair a thorough going over, with or without the implements from the Carnavalet, it was jake with her, as she expressed it. She went so far as to offer to help, by holding instruments in readiness and passing them when needed. But Evans had scruples about torture, not because it was cruel but because it was crude.

'Look here, you pair of weasels,' he said. 'You are, as I have told the sergeant, men of small capacity. You are merely the tools of brainier thieves. But you have in your diminutive reptilian minds a few kernels of information which are necessary to me. I'm going to extract them, never fear. I'm going to leave you wrung out like dishrags. If you see fit to delay, so much the worse for both of you.'

Just then, however, they all were electrified by the sound of a taxi with defective brakes and Officer Schlumberger, soaked to the skin and muddy, dived through the doorway and up the stairs, flapping the portrait and shouting: 'The Gonzo. I've got the missing Gonzo.'

Evans, although possessed of unusual composure and poise, was not above astonishment. He frankly gasped and practically gurgled as he seized his own masterpiece and held it to the light. Then dismay and pain crossed his countenance.

'There's a hole in the forehead,' he said.

Miriam, all gentleness, was at his side. 'Oh,' she said. 'I'm so sorry.'

Sergeant Frémont was glaring at Schlumberger. 'What do you mean, breaking in here like this, and bringing another painting? As if we didn't have enough paintings. Forty-nine in the Louvre, all tagged and labelled; about a thousand in this dump, and half of 'em fakes. . . .'

'Say sixty per cent,' Evans said, trying to cover his disappointment. Then he clutched the painting closer, stared at it and 'By Jove', escaped his lips. 'Sergeant, don't rag our friend, the officer. He's brought us exactly what we need, a message.'

'Message? You've lost your mind,' the sergeant said. 'There's nothing written on that thing except H. Jansen, and we've got his signature fifty times on paintings and twice on cheques. In what way does one more scrawl, " H. Jansen ", advance our interests?'

'The hole in the forehead. Does that tell you nothing?' Evans asked. 'And we may be sure, now, that the kidnappers went upstream.'

The sergeant grabbed the painting and after a moment grunted. 'The hole was punched carefully. It wasn't accidental,' he said, already ashamed of his obtuseness.

'Ah,' said Evans. 'Nothing could be surer. The hole was punched with care. Therefore we may assume that it was placed with equal care. In the centre of the forehead. Does that mean anything, Sergeant?' Without waiting for an answer he turned to Bonnet. 'Please bring me at once a large map of France. Don't lose a minute.'

It was surprising to Miriam to note the change that had come over Evans. Gone was all his indolence. He radiated energy and decisiveness.

'Sergeant,' Evans said. 'Have this pair of buzzards thrown into the dirtiest cell you have. Collect all the candlelight Grecos in the establishment. You'll find six, if I'm not mistaken. Lock these doors and have the premises guarded so that not even a cockroach (*Stylopyga orientalis*) could squirm in or out. . . .'

'They are not cockroaches. They're water bugs (*Phyllodromia germanica*),' said Dodo, defiantly. And he stuck out his tongue just in time to bite it when the sergeant stamped on his instep with his heavy heel.

'And now,' Evans said, 'there's not a moment to lose. Sergeant, I must insist on the release of Hjalmar Jansen. We've got a night's work to do, and Hjalmar must help us.'

'But the prefect. He'll never stand for it.'

'Damn the prefect. Get him for me on the phone.'

At this prospect of passing the buck, the sergeant fairly beamed. 'Schlumberger, get the prefect on the phone,' he said, and the Alsatian made haste to do so. 'Here he is,' he said, a few seconds later, and added, under his breath, 'the louse'.

'*M. le Préfet*,' said Evans in his incisive perfect French. 'I am Homer Evans. . . . Stop roaring and listen. I am also the duly appointed *agent plénipotentiaire* and representative of the American secret service detailed on the Weiss case. . . . Yes. You'll see the papers in due time, and you'll get a call from the minister of foreign affairs, and if you're obstructive and stubborn you'll get a sealed letter from the president of the republic. . . . Yes. You are serving a republic, you know. . . . You should understand the word.'

Frémont was simmering with happiness. He had been bawled out publicly and privately so many times by the prefect that to hear the latter addressed as Evans was addressing him added months and perhaps years to the sergeant's life. The prefect was a royalist, among other things, and hated the sound of the word republic.

At the phone, Evans' tone changed. 'Ah, that's more reasonable,' he said. 'I won't quibble. You may place the man you insist on calling Gonzo in custody of Sergeant Frémont who will be responsible for him. You can tell the press that the prisoner is to be taken to the scene of the crime. Anything you like. Now I shall expect Jansen here within ten minutes. Good night.'

CHAPTER 16

A Shot at Whistler's Aunt

GASTON HONORÉ CRAYON DE CRAYON, prefect of the Seine, sat nervously at his desk in his now empty office of the now nearly empty *préfecture*. There was still a trace of violet ink in his eyebrows and more than a trace of rancour toward Gonzo, alias Jansen. The prefect had disliked all the suspects and witnesses at sight, with the possible exception of Oklahoma Tom, but his rarest spleen was reserved for the big Norwegian who had smeared him with his own writing fluid, tossed several squads of his choicest officers around the room, and who was the rightful legal possessor of 250,000 francs, then in the prefect's vault. The prefect did not have exactly the same feeling about money as had the late Ambrose Gring, but believed that any large sums of it lying around properly belonged to the pretender to the throne of France and in any case should not be left in the hands of Americans.

In the laboratory of the famous Dr Hyacinthe Toudoux the body of Greeng, Ambrose, was stretched upon a slab, with certain important parts missing which were then being tested for arsenic, strychnine, henbane, hemlock, in fact all the well-known and little known poisons. Nothing was going well with the medical examiner. Litmus papers which should have turned pink when dipped in the fatal *crème de cacao*, came out green, and in extreme cases a bright heliotrope. Liquids which should have been clear foamed and fizzed and vice versa. Now and then the prefect opened the door, gazed at the grisly proceedings sarcastically, snorted and left the room, only to drop in at the salle Ste Anne for a quick look at Maggie, who persisted in denying that she was Miss Montana and shook her thin talons at Monsieur Crayon de Crayon, promising him that if and when the British found out what was happening to her he would be drummed and flogged through the fleet.

The female guards, on the occasion of each brush between

Maggie and the prefect, roared with laughter and dealt one another playful slaps on the rump and shoulders that would have floored an ordinary patient and disabled for life one who chanced to be frail. Maggie was saying to the prefect precisely what the lady bassos and baritones would like to have said, and for that they began to accord her the kindest of treatment, sharing with her huge chunks of Lyon sausage containing enough garlic to nullify all the tests known to Hyacinthe Toudoux and washing it down with red ink that would have taken the gilt off the celebrated and ancient public clock across the street on the Palais de Justice. Maggie, always quick to respond to kindness, thawed in turn and entertained the lusty companions with 'The Bastard King of England', a ballad which reads, in part:

'His only nether garment was a leather undershirt,
With which he tried to hide the hide
But couldn't hide the dirt.'

'Let it pass,' said Evans, cryptically. 'Let it pass. We've a night's work to do, if ever Monsieur Crayon de Crayon will hang up that phone.'

Simultaneously, in the establishment of Heiss and Lourde, Heiss was handcuffed to Lourde, they both were handcuffed to Bonnet, six candlelight Grecos were tossed into the waiting wagon and a moment after the wagon had been cranked, primed, and pushed down an incline to get the motor started, in came Hjalmar Jansen, dragging a contingent of police like a comet's tail behind him. Less boisterously he was followed by Jackson, still wearing the French boy's hat.

'Holy mackinaw! I need a drink,' said Jansen, shaking Evans by the hand.

Schlumberger, who was dry by that time, offered to go out for a bottle of quetsch.

'Make it half a dozen,' Jansen said. 'They've still got my dough in the *préfecture* but Julliard says it's O.K., so my credit ought to be good.'

'I should like the honour of buying liquor for the author of that excellent self-portrait, M. Gonzo,' Schlumberger said.

141

'Oh, that,' said Hjalmar, bashfully, then he started in surprise. 'Cripes,' he ejaculated. 'How did you get your painting back? Evans?... Hell. There's a hole punched through it. What a shame.'

'That hole,' said Evans, 'is precisely what will solve this case. That innocent little aperture will lead us to Hugo Weiss.'

'Is it true, all this talk about his being kidnapped?' Hjalmar said.

At this Sergeant Frémont exploded. 'Monsieur Gonzo,' he said, 'did you think the police department was moving heaven and earth simply to offer a demonstration?'

'No offence, sergeant,' Gonzo said. 'After all, the joke's partly on me. I've been thrown in the can, my money, necktie, shoelaces, belt, etc., have been taken away. I've been goaded to violence, threatened....'

The sergeant smiled. 'Violet ink,' he murmured. 'Let me pay for half the quetsch.'

Evans, meanwhile, had busied himself with the map of France. 'Ah,' he said at last, with his finger on a spot some distance north of Paris. 'Hole in forehead. That's the work of that excellent officer and gentleman, Colonel Lvov Kvek. Let's see. Forehead. *Front*. *Front* is French for forehead.' Homer glanced at the map again. 'It happens,' he went on, exultantly, 'that about two hundred and twenty kilometres, by water, north of the Pont Notre Dame lies a small village on the banks of the upper Seine called Frontville. Does that stir any comforting thoughts, sergeant?'

The sergeant did not try to hide his admiration. 'You mean the missing men are at Frontville?'

'They were at Frontville yesterday,' Evans said. 'It's my guess that they are there right now, unless the kidnappers have got the wind up.... It was a mistake, making all this row in the press about Heiss and Lourde. That may frighten the gang ...and that would be dangerous for Weiss and Kvek....'

Evans held up his hand for attention, and everyone in the room listened breathlessly to what he said:

'Friends,' he said, 'it's true that there is every reason for haste, for immediate action. But all of you have a part to play.

142

I cannot say which one will have to take a sudden initiative. You must understand in a general way what this is all about. And to make it clear, I must go back a few years. You are aware, no doubt, that in 1913 the Congress of the United States passed an income tax law that proved to be very embarrassing for the higher brackets. At once, rich men set about devising ways of concealing assets and dodging taxes. Money in large sums is hard to hide, but one clever chap in the employ of a dyspeptic multi-millionaire named T. Prosper Stables thought of a brilliant scheme. In short, the plan was this. An agent in Europe would buy a painting, either an old master which could be snapped up cheaply, say at $30,000, or a fake which could pass the experts of various public museums, with or without the aid of palm grease. This painting, representing a $30,000 outlay, would be resold to a firm which was, under cover of course, another agent of Mr Stables, and the price which Stables would pay to himself would be about $150,000. This process is repeated until the multi-millionaire comes out in the open and buys, from Heiss and Lourde (a Stables concern, but off the records) a Greco for $500,000. This Greco enters America tax free and is given to the Skowhegan Museum. It cost $30,000. Stables, by legal hocus-pocus, retains actual control of it. He saves an income tax of $250,000, enjoys the use of nearly half a million dollars which has passed out of existence as far as the government is concerned, is touted as a great philanthropist and a judge of high art.

'You have seen enough already, sergeant, to realize that there was about to be a wholesale unloading of fake candlelight Grecos when we came on the scene. Sales had been arranged, six different museums had accepted the so-called gifts, Stables stood to gain about $3,000,000, all told. Cats'-paws like our friends Abel and Dodo were about to rake in a small commission which to them seems large. Have I made myself clear?'

'How does Hugo Weiss come in?' asked the sergeant, impressed but more baffled than before.

'Has it not occurred to you yet that, since Hugo Weiss was warned years ago about the fake candlelight paintings of Greco,

143

his presence in Paris at the moment of the great unloading was dangerous to the Stables plan ?'

'My head aches,' the sergeant wailed, reaching for the aspirin which Miriam held in readiness.

'Heiss and Lourde feared that Hugo would upset the apple-cart if he moseyed around the galleries,' Evans continued. 'That involved the unfortunate Ambrose Gring. Gring had done odd errands of snooping for the Stables interests before, and it is my belief that Abel and Dodo sought him at the Dôme, asked him to call on Hugo, which he did, as the reporter for *Art for Art's Sake*, to find out, if possible, whether Hugo intended visiting galleries. Gring failed, I also believe, because Miriam noticed the next time Heiss and Lourde showed up for an interview with Gring that they were dissatisfied and disappointed.'

'So they bumped Gring off,' the sergeant said. 'I could see they were guilty in the first place, but you confused me with all your talk. Let's phone the prefect. . . .'

'Not so fast,' Evans said. 'Gring is dead, worse luck. We'll find his murderers in time. Just now we must concentrate on Hugo Weiss, who is in Frontville, not far from Châtillon-sur-Seine. Stables and his tax-dodging crowd have not resorted to strong-arm work before and are very likely to have selected to spirit away Hugo a band of ruffians whose instincts would prompt them, in case of alarm, to kill their victims, bury the bodies and scatter to their various lairs.'

'Can't we get going?' Hjalmar asked. 'But say, Evans. What about Gwendolyn's show ? We can't spoil that for her. . . .She's in a state about it and they won't give her any satisfaction at the Louvre.'

'It's only fair to look after Gwendolyn,' Evans said. Then he beckoned to Agent Schlumberger. 'Schlumberger,' he continued, 'go across to the *bistrot*, like a good fellow, and get a carafe of olive oil. You will find in that corner several modern paintings for which Heiss and Lourde have paid the painters very shabbily, considering the value of the work. Paint out the signatures and sign them all " Poularde ", being careful to mix the paint with olive oil. . . .'

144

Sergeant Frémont began to splutter.

'Select fifteen, if possible, with garages, trees, and farm buildings, and have them shipped by air to the Arson Galleries, Chicago, at the state's expense.'

Frémont had left off spluttering, and had begun to emit assorted noises. Evans turned to him and good-naturedly clasped his shoulder. 'That explains the mysterious fifty Jansens,' he said. 'Hjalmar didn't have enough paintings to show Hugo Weiss, so we had to garner a few. Harmless little prank. . . .'

'Harmless, if one forgets the extracting under false pretences of 250,000 francs, enough to keep five French families alive to the end of their days.'

'All families, French or otherwise, live to the end of their days,' Evans said. 'Our problem now is to postpone the end of Weiss's days, and those of my friend Kvek.'

'Well, let's go,' said Hjalmar, and Jackson grunted approval. 'How do we get to Frontville? And shall we shoot or bring in those gangsters alive?'

Evans turned to the waiting officers and borrowed five automatics and ammunition belts. 'Can you shoot?' he asked Miriam, handing her a gun, experimentally.

For answer she took the automatic, smiling, and instantly every occupant of the room leaped into the air. The automatic spoke once, then Miriam crossed the room and brought back with her the portrait of Whistler's aunt. In the forehead, at the spot corresponding exactly to the round hole in the Gonzo self-portrait, was a neat bullet hole.

'Will I do as a member of this scouting party?' she asked, smiling modestly but eagerly.

Sergeant Frémont reached again for the aspirin, this time swallowing all that remained. Miriam turned to him gently. 'Buck up, sergeant. Remember. At the end of the rainbow is Hydrangea. . . .'

'And don't forget the Fine Michel, or Mickey Finns,' the sergeant said, taking heart.

CHAPTER 17

Anchors 'Aweigh

H AD the French poet, already quoted by Homer Evans, lamped the Seine in the hour preceding the dawn, she would not have written those peevish words, '*Quelle chose malsaine, la Seine*'. She would have fallen under the spell of the river's quiet dignity and perpetuity, to say nothing of its enigmatic promise, its intangible threat, its surface like idle fingers on dark ivory, the venerable trees (*Platanus orientalis, Salix fluviatilis*, and the like), the walls that had echoed secret sorrows, the bridges that had been crossed, the signal lights of blue-green and scarlet reflected in streamers. In short, the poet would have forgotten the mists, vapours and dampnesses, the odours, chills and yearly floods in cellars and would have started off something like this:

> '*La Seine, quand même et après tout,*
> *Est forte jolie de la source jusqu'au bout.*'*

The rescue party, armed and ready, led by Evans on behalf of the United States, Sergeant Frémont for the third French Republic (1871–19–), also included Miriam, Hjalmar Jansen, and Tom Jackson, ex-reporter for the New York *Herald*, who hoped, if he turned in a good story, to get his job back again. According to Evans' swift instructions, relayed by the somewhat sceptical sergeant, the prefectorial launch had been tied up at the Pont d'Alma, at the feet of the famous Zouave who serves as a gauge in high water season and a rather questionable decoration at other times of year. As has been mentioned, it was just before daylight, the hour when it is supposed to be darkest but actually is not. The starlight was thinning, the bridge lamps were looking slightly apologetic. Night-faring scavengers were pawing over ash barrels and garbage cans, the central markets were bustling. Montparnasse was rising

---

* Anyway and after all the River Seine
Is lovely from beginning to its end.

to the peak of its nocturnal gaiety, assisted by Rosa Stier, Harold Simon, the doughty Finn and the intrepid Olga, the sprightly Cirage, and the *concierge* of Hjalmar's residence in the rue Montparnasse who had heard of the return of some of the ex-prisoners and had eased herself around to get the lowdown on Hjalmar's 250,000 francs, 645 of which held more than an academic interest for the good woman.

The American Negro, whose name was A. Melchisedek Knockwoode, had stopped running because of understandable exhaustion and was walking rapidly north, just passing Enghien. He knew, or thought he knew, what police sergeants were likely to do to the bearers of false tidings, especially when the tidings raised such a furore of hope as those he had borne Sergeant Frémont. As far as A. Melchisedek Knockwoode was concerned, Hydrangea Palmerstone Waite was just another coloured girl of the shade known as soot and who, unwittingly, had got him, Melchisedek, into one of the tightest holes he had been in since Montfaucon in the Argonne. He was going to think the thing out to the end, but not before he had reached what he believed would be a place of safety.

The remains of Ambrose Gring were still in the laboratory of Dr Hyacinthe Toudoux, and periodically were viewed by the prefect who liked the looks of them no better than when they had been alive and assembled. The medical examiner was in a state bordering on the jitters and had been obliged to repeat 'Every day in every way' and a round half dozen Hail Marys in order to restrain himself from throwing a beaker of *crème de cacao* and muriatic acid at the head of his chief the last time he had popped in and said, 'Well. The man's dead, all right. What else have you found out?'

The candid answer could only be 'Nothing, sir', but doctors can seldom afford to give candid answers.

'There is a trace of something or other besides *crème de cacao* in the contents of the stomach,' Dr Toudoux began. 'It does not respond in the orthodox way to any known tests and is so mild that earthworms have no difficulty in swimming in it.' He held up another beaker containing fishing worms who seemed to be resigned, if not content.

147

'What do the governments of several countries care about earthworms ?' the prefect demanded. 'In God's name, get down to cases. How and why did this wart on the body politic come by his death ? He wasn't stabbed, choked, drowned, or thrown from a high window. Neither was he shot, gassed, hanged, or guillotined. You can find no poison. Why not say he died a natural death and let it go at that ?'

'I feel sure his death was anything but natural,' said the doctor. 'In fact, I shall refuse to sign any certificate to that effect.'

The prefect dashed from the room, smashing a row of test-tubes as he dashed. He did not know that one of his lady bassos, thinking it might annoy him, was phoning the British Embassy anonymously to let it be known that a red-headed girl claiming to be a British subject was being held incomunicado in a tepid bath and was calling loudly for her government to help her.

Heiss and Lourde were playing pinochle in the prefect's office and complaining that the cards had been marked with violet ink. They had spilled nothing because no one had asked them any questions. The candlelight Grecos had already passed most of the experts in France so they did not anticipate any trouble from the Louvre, and they were in blissful ignorance of what had happened to Whistler's aunt and the fifteen modern canvases that were now signed 'Poularde' and were on their way to the Arson Galleries, Chicago.

'Dismiss the boatmen,' Evans said to Sergeant Frémont as they boarded the *Deuxième Pays de Tout le Monde* which was the name of the prefectorial launch. 'Jansen knows the river, every inch. He's got a master's licence.'

'But what if the engine stops running ?' the sergeant asked. Like so many romantics, mechanics was Greek to him.

'Even Miriam could take it apart with her eyes shut,' Evans said.

'Ah, you Americans,' sighed the sergeant. 'My Hydrangea, though, is the clinging feminine type. I'm sure she would scream at the sight of a gun or an engine. She'll be seasick, I'm afraid, poor girl. What is the earliest date she might arrive ?'

148

'She's on her way,' Evans said. 'To-night we've other work to do.'

Hjalmar was at the wheel and already had started the engine. The sergeant and Jackson took places amidships. Miriam sat with Evans in the bow, her hand resting lightly on the smooth automatic. Evans smiled. He was trying to keep his mind on the object of their journey but he could not stifle a feeling of pride because of the way Miriam was behaving. It stirred a latent love for his own far country and the institutions which made such resolute women possible. Desirable? Feminine? Yes....

'Damn Walt Whitman,' he said, aloud.

'I know. A woman waits,' she murmured, her eyes sparkling.

'Let's hurry up and finish this case.'

Skilfully, almost exultantly, Hjalmar had swung the launch into mid-channel and was heading rapidly upstream. From the river, and especially in a low-lying craft like the *Deuxième Pays*, old Paris has an unexpected allure. Walls and towers take on new proportions, perspectives are shortened, altitudes lengthened. They passed the Grand Palais and in no time they were streaming past the Louvre where they believed the forty-nine paintings were reposing. As a matter of fact, they had been mixed up with a batch of 19th-century works destined for provincial museums and had been scattered from Dijon to Arles in small consignments incorrectly labelled. On the left, the Samaritaine was receding in all its superb ugliness which verged on the poetic.

'Which way?' asked Hjalmar as they were about to breast the tip of the Ile de la Cité.

'Port,' Evans said.

Ah, centuries of yore! Ah, history! The *conciergerie* at the crack of dawn. Notre Dame backed with cirrus clouds like rose-tinted angels. The spire of the Sainte Chapelle. The ominous Tour St Jacques. Gaining speed and momentum they slid between the old city and the Ile St Louis, the fragrant Halle aux Vins behind which they heard the roar of lions, tigers, jackals and hyenas in the Jardin des Plantes. That brought the cautious members of the party to an awareness of the dangers before them. The cautious members, of course, were Frémont and

149

Tom Jackson. The latter, like many good men, was a wow on land but on the water, even a narrow river like the Seine, he began to think at once of the beauty of Panurge's immortal thought: 'Happy is he who plants potatoes, for he has both feet firmly on the ground.' The combination of the motion of the launch and the jungle cries of wild beasts was a bit too much for Oklahoma Tom.

'I think I'll go downstairs and lie down,' he said.

'Where do you think you are?' railed Hjalmar, good-naturedly. 'Don't say " downstairs". Say "below". And take a good swig of *Quetsch*. . . .'

'Kwaup, gug, gug,' said Jackson and dived down the short companionway.

The others, nothing loth, passed a bottle around, and when it reached Hjalmar he finished it and tossed it over the side.

'Should have left a note for my friend the prefect in the bottle, I suppose,' Hjalmar said. 'Cripes. It's good to get out in the air.'

'You're in my custody, remember,' the sergeant said. 'If any of you get lost, I'll lose my job.'

'Don't worry. I've got 250,000 francs I'm going to get or else take 'em out of the prefect's hide,' Hjalmar said.

At that prospect the sergeant smiled and chuckled again. He didn't know much about Gonzo as a painter, but as an inker of prefects and a helmsman he was tops. The big Norwegian found the channel effortlessly, roared greetings to friends on passing tugs and barges and to the *café* keepers along the shore. The river folk had long since taken the big roaring artist to their hearts and even Evans was reassured by his friend's handling of a boat and his standing with the bargemen and long-shoremen.

'We'll be safe as far as Chatillon,' Evans said, consulting the map again. 'There we'll disembark and do some reconnoitering. What's Frontville like, Hjalmar?'

'It's just a clump of houses across from a wooded island.'

'An island, you say?'

'It's about a hundred metres long. A few shacks the barge-men sleep in sometimes, also four or five big dugouts.'

'Dugouts ? What for ?'

'It was an ammunition dump during the war. The army kept high explosives there, where the airmen wouldn't look for them. Plenty of shelter. Tall trees. And if the stuff blew up, almost nobody near enough to get hurt. Not dumb, the Frogs. . . .'

The sergeant drew himself up stiffly. 'Your tribute to my countrymen is overwhelming,' he said.

'What the hell ? I like your country well enough to live here,' Hjalmar said. 'I've just got myself in jail trying to stay here, haven't I ?'

Jackson came up from the cabin, looking pea green.

'Don't quarrel when a pal is dying,' he said.

They were passing through a rolling countryside, with red-roofed villages and distant hills, white roads cut straight across the flats and twisting around the hills and through the gullies. Fertile rural France, the envy of less-favoured lands, the mother of peaceful sturdy folk to whom life itself is an end. The Frogs, indeed, were not dumb along the Seine that morning. They were ploughing rich dark earth, or moving at a rate consistent with human comfort along chalk-white roads lined with double files of poplars (*populus nigra italica*). Their horses were glossy and strong, their cattle knee-deep in lush grasses.

'I shall die if this gets more beautiful,' Miriam said. Her fingers were not toying with her automatic then, but were raised to the level of her white young throat.

'Can you swim ?' Evans asked.

For answer she rose and only his quick grasping of her slender hips prevented her from executing a perfect backward dive into the rippling current.

'I'll take your word for it,' Evans said. 'And please don't show off any more in front of the sergeant. He can stand just so much excitement and no more. By the way, that was a real Whistler you punctured this morning. Don't shoot anything else, not even paintings, without my O.K.'

'I'll be good,' she said. 'Let's have another drink.'

'You'll all be zigzag before we get to Bar-sur-Seine,' the sergeant said woefully.

'Hell. You never have seen us drunk aboard ship,' Hjalmar

151

said. 'It isn't like *café* drinking, where a man has to be a little careful.'

'I'm responsible for you, drunk or sober,' the sergeant groaned, and his hollow voice was echoed by that of Jackson. 'I may as well take a drink,' he said. 'I couldn't feel worse.' Miriam was singing like a thrush: 'I shall have an old age full of rum and riot.' She paused to turn to Evans again. 'You will find the man who killed poor Ambrose?' she said. 'I feel somehow responsible.'

'His last thoughts were of you,' Evans said. 'Of you and oil, no doubt.' Then he added, seriously: 'I'll revenge the poor chap, never fear. But I'm puzzled about that feature of this tangled affair. Now if Heiss and Lourde had been extinguished. ... God! What a fool I've been! Sergeant! Hjalmar! Run her nose to the next telephone booth. I've got to get in touch with headquarters at once.'

'And pray, what for?' asked the sergeant.

'To stave off a couple more murders. ... No, make it three, I forgot the poor clerk, M. Dinde.'

There was a gentle impact as the nose of the *Deuxième Pays* touched the bank in front of the *Rendez-vous des Imprévoyants* just west of Bar-sur-Seine. There the river was broader and still, tall grass fringed the sloughs, treetops touched over narrow creeks and tributaries and the song of the merle (*merula merula*) mingled with the delighted 'Bonjour' the proprietor was extending to Hjalmar. While Evans was phoning, the rest of the party gathered at the bar and this time even Sergeant Frémont broke down and swallowed a small brandy. The prospect of three more murders in his absence had done things to Frémont. He knew that, somehow, he would be blamed.

Evans did not call the prefect. He wanted action and no argument. It was a matter of no more than thirty minutes to get through to the minister of justice.

'I'm Homer Evans,' he began.

'Perhaps you want the ministry of war,' the minister of justice suggested. He was no mean passer of the buck, himself.

'The special envoy of the American *sûrete generale*,' Evans continued.

152

'Ah, yes. Of course. That disappearing millionaire. . . . M. . . . M. . . .'

'Weiss.'

'Yes. By all means. Weiss. Have you found him? Your ambassador, droll fellow, assured me the man was probably out drinking. Is he, in fact, on a bender. . . . ?'

'I'll have news of him before the day is over,' Evans said. 'Just now I've another matter of frightful importance. Will you please phone the prefect and have two suspects, Abel Heiss. . . . No. Not Weiss. Weiss's name is Hugo. " H " for Henriette. No. Not Henriette. Abel Heiss. H-E-I-S-S. And his partner Sascha Lourde. Now you've got it. Heiss and Lourde. And a clerk named Dinde. Heiss, Lourde and Dinde. Have them sent to your office at once, under guard, and keep them there. Don't let anyone go near them.'

'Suspects are customarily held at the *préfecture*,' the minister said.

'If these men lose their lives, the press will know I warned you,' said Evans, severely. 'Now. Will you act, or must I call my ambassador?'

'I'll do what you ask,' the minister said. 'You Americans have no regard for precedent, but I like your ambassador. Makes no trouble at all. Always gay and carefree.'

'This evening you shall have Hugo Weiss,' Evans promised. 'If you carry out my suggestions, I'll bring him to your office first, for press photographs.'

'No stone shall be left unturned. Heiss, Lourde, and Dinde. Good day.'

The phone clicked and Evans joined his companions at the bar. Jackson was almost himself again. Not quite, but he was definitely on the mend.

'Lie down, little dogies,' he was singing, while Miriam was explaining that dogies in American, did not mean *chiens* or dogs but the brothers, sadly altered, of *vaches* or cows.

'There's no logic in your language. I suppose logic would be out of place in so vast a country,' Sergeant Frémont said.

CHAPTER 18

A Potato-Masher Proves to be a Boomerang

THE proprietor's wife, on the approach of Hjalmar, had locked her daughter, Gaby, in an upper room, and was guarding her grimly.

'My own mother was a hard woman,' Madame Sosthène said to the pouting girl. 'My own mother was hard, but not quite hard enough. You shall profit by her errors.'

Had Homer Evans not been so intent on his telephone call, had his sympathy not been so boundless and so catholic that it could be aroused in the interest of the safety of even such un-promising specimens as Heiss and Lourde, he undoubtedly would have noticed in the back room a slim but wiry man who, although he wore riverman's clothes, did not wear them well. The stranger seemed to be enormously affected by what he heard the rescue party saying. Outstripping the merles (*merula merula*) and also the swift *Carduelis elegans*, or goldfinch, that unsavoury character set out through the woods at a frantic clip and finally spied a motor cycle, the owner of which, having stopped for a *tête-à-tête* with his girl, was, in Rabelais' words, already found useful in this story, not in a position to right wrongs or retrieve receding Harley-Davidsons. The speed with which the stranger left those parts may be partially explained by his name. It was Barnabé Vieuxchamp, and his late grand-father, after having sired the father of Barnabé, had fled to America where he had raised another family under his Ameri-can name, Barney Oldfield.

Meanwhile Evans put in a call for Dr Hyacinthe Toudoux. That good doctor was having such troubles with the remains of Ambrose Gring that he was exclaiming, when the phone rang:

'Damn this ex-gigolo. If he were still alive I would do away with him myself.'

This is what the doctor heard:

154

'I'm Homer Evans, the *agent plénipotentiaire* of the United States in the case of Hugo Weiss. Your reputation, Dr Toudoux, has spread far beyond the borders of France, and even of Europe. Not only your monograph *Resuscitations effectives des ivrognes, avec notations pratiques sur le delirium tremens*, but your larger work on the use of hot apple sauce and aromatic spirits of ammonia are well known to my countrymen.'

'I think I was cheated, then, by my American publisher,' Dr Toudoux said, indignantly. 'The returns were far from satisfactory.'

'Too profound for the lay minds, or even for most professionals,' said Evans comfortingly.

For the first time since the Weiss case had begun, Dr Toudoux thawed a bit.

'You are kind to say so. Are you a doctor of medicine, Monsieur Evans, may I ask?'

'Only an amateur chemist, a *dilettante*,' he said.

'You're not a *dilettante*,' cried Miriam, indignantly. 'You mustn't say such things about yourself.'

'You are engaged in the autopsy of one Ambrose Gring, are you not?' Evans asked the doctor.

'I insist that the death was not a natural one,' the doctor said.

'I'm sure you are right, and the prefect is wrong. Natural death, indeed! Of course you have covered the routine; strychnine, arsenic, Prussic acid, cyanide, and the like.'

'Child's play,' said Dr Toudoux. 'And with maddening results.'

'Organs O.K.?'

'Unusually sound for a man who took no exercise except, possibly, amatory exercise, and with such types even that is likely to be languorous,' the doctor said.

'May I make a suggestion? I want you, Doctor, to have full credit in this case. For obvious reasons I must stay in the background . . .' Homer said.

'I shall be delighted,' Toudoux said, graciously. 'If you should help me make a greater ass of the prefect than he already is I would be your friend for life.'

'In America,' Evans began ... 'There's no danger of your being overheard?'

'Not the slightest. Proceed. In America...' the doctor said.

'In America there is a specific not known to doctors generally, called Mickey Finn. It consists of a few drops of liquid which, when poured into any ordinary drink, will induce unconsciousness for several hours, beginning within ten minutes after taking. The effects, on rugged types, are not serious. Slight headache, excessive thirst, remorse, imperfect memory of events just preceding... That sort of thing, you know.'

'I follow you,' said Dr. Toudoux. 'I have read of these Michael Finns and have made several attempts to learn more, but none of the American physicians or chemists has included them in his list of published studies and findings.'

'Ah, that's the rub. The making of a perfect Mickey Finn is an old professional secret, probably originating with the Incas, and the precious formula belongs not to the doctors or medicine men but to the cupbearers or bartenders. It has been passed on from father to son, and guarded safely from outsiders. It has been used to quiet obstreperous clients in tippling houses, to protect reputable drinkers from talking too much, to secure crews for seafaring vessels. Now when I was at the University I had to select a subject for a thesis and I chose " The Mickey Finn." Unfortunately for my scholastic record, however, after I had put in two years of work unearthing the secret of making Mickey Finns and the history of their development through the ages, I decided it would be unsporting to publish my results. Bartenders are among our most useful citizens. They have always been the friend of mankind. Let them keep the secret they had cherished, I decided, and had to spend another two years on a thesis about red flannel underwear.'

'Are you going to do me the honour of imparting the secret to me?'

'First I must have your promise never to divulge the formula or to let it be known that you know it,' Evans said.

'Monsieur Evans,' the doctor said, fervently, 'I am a war veteran, a knight of the Legion of Honour, an official of the French Academy of Science and, in 1910, led the French

156

fencing team to defeat in Rome. And that defeat, monsieur, occurred because I insisted on conceding a doubtful touch which my best adversary, with tears in his eyes, asserted he had not accomplished. The word of a Toudoux. . . .'

'Enough, doctor. . . . We understand one another .. Now please memorize this, don't write it down. Examine the contents of my late acquaintance's digestive organs for *Oleum crotali confluenti*, that is the oil of the prairie rattlesnake. This oil, you will find, if you find it, is slightly more soluble than that of the diamond rattlesnake, the timber rattlesnake or the smaller variety found in the High Sierras. Then search carefully for traces of *Tinc. Argalli spicati Texarkanae*. This is by no means the common *marijuana* from which reefers are made but is a variety of locoweed found only in Texas and Arkansas. Test also the *crème de cacao* that was left in Gring's glass. I'll phone you again as soon as I can.'

'I shall never forget your courtesy,' said Dr Toudoux. 'There is much international misunderstanding, even among nations such as ours which are allied. That is not the fault of the men of our profession, the searchers after truth. *Oleum crotali confluenti.* Is there not amity and poetry in the flow of those words ? And *tinctura argalli spicati arcanae.* The identical metre used by the lyrical Englishman, Keats, in propounding his famous riddle: Oh, what is so rare as a day in June.'

'Exactly,' said Evans. Then he called the minister of justice again to check up on Heiss, Lourde, and Dinde. To his dismay he learned that Abel and Dodo had been released and that their bodies had not been found.

'And the clerk, Dinde ? Where is he ?'

An earsplitting shriek from the proprietor's wife cut off further remarks. What happened in the next few seconds, Evans himself could not be sure about until sometime afterward. He saw an object hurtling through the air, aimed straight for the open door, a wicked compact grenade with long wooden handle of the type known as 'potato masher' in the world war. It was coming on, end over end. It couldn't miss the group. With one arm he flung Miriam clean over the bar, knocking over the patron who fell also to the floor. The split second

157

during which his life should have passed before his eyes was occupied by a wistful glimpse of his former self, in pre-detective days, sitting quietly in his seat at the Dôme thinking easy thoughts and sipping. . . . There was a flash, not as Evans expected of high explosive and jagged fragments of iron tearing into flesh. The flash was a grey one and consisted of Hjalmar Jansen's powerful right arm. That was all that Evans saw, but just afterward he saw the ungainly missile hurtling in the opposite direction, away from his friends and toward the *Deuxième Pays*, whose engine was barking furiously.

Midway between the bar and the shore, and not ten feet in the air, the grenade exploded. There was a sudden awful flowering of white and silver flame, collective impacts like hail among the leaves. Four bottles broke and their contents trickled down on Miriam who had not recovered sufficiently from her toss to stand up again. But Evans' attention was all on Tom Jackson who had put his hand to his forehead, looked foolish, then dead white and was sinking slowly to his knees, and collapsing forward.

'They're stealing the boat,' roared Jansen, and started hell bent for the landing. Three men were in the *Deuxième Pays*, one at the wheel, another at the engine, the third lying flat on his belly in the stern.

'Look out. He's got a machine gun,' Sergeant Frémont said. He was too prudent to follow the foolhardy Norwegian, too brave and conscious that he represented his country among strangers to throw himself on the ground. Whether Hjalmar heard the warning or not, was impossible to say. He kept going, the *Deuxième Pays* made headway from the shore.

'Oh, you superb idiot! You bloody splendid fool,' said Evans, moved beyond his usual phlegmatic acceptance of things. For Hjalmar without a pause at the landing had dived three metres out into the Seine and was making after the launch with his powerful Australian crawl. The sergeant wept, Evans shut his eyes, Tom Jackson fainted. Miriam, who had raised her head above the bar, was the only one to act. Her automatic spoke for a second time, then she bit her lips and looked at Evans in dismay.

158

'I'm so sorry,' she said. 'You told me not to shoot without instructions.'

The import of her apology did not dawn on Evans until later, for he was watching the stranger in the stern who seemed to have lost interest in the proceedings. His hand lay idly on the Sho-Sho gun, his eyes stared vacantly into space. Jansen whipped up his pace, his huge arms flying like flails while his churning feet kicked up so much stir in the water that *Goujons* (*Gobis gobis*) and *lottes* (*Boarces viviparus*) fled in terror downstream.

'He's holding his own. Ah, God. These incredible Americans,' Sergeant Frémont said, and shamefacedly put away his gun which he had drawn unconsciously when he had heard Miriam's shot.

'I'm so sorry ...' Miriam repeated, looking at Evans imploringly.

'You have saved Hjalmar's life,' he said, simply, but his eyes said much more, so much, in fact, that Miriam blushed and had to clutch the bar to keep her knees steady.

No matter how stout the heart or strong the sinews, man cannot pit his strength and speed against a well adjusted gasolene engine with a desperate driver. Jansen was dropping back, and had to give up the chase.

'Why for Chri' sakes, didn't you shoot ?' demanded the bandit at the wheel, spinning furiously to avoid a snag.

'Can't you see the bugger's dead ? Somebody shot him,' said his confederate at the engine.

Now the man at the wheel, while willing to shoot, was not at all willing to be on the receiving end. The sudden awareness that beside him was a corpse, who not thirty minutes before had been his pal, upset the helmsman to such an extent that he sideswiped the snag instead of clearing it, there was a coughing protest from the engine and the clogged propeller promptly came to rest. The *Deuxième Pays* was not more than a thousand yards from where it had started, and was feeling the gentle nudge of a sandbar on her bottom. It was a close thing whether the two remaining thugs hit the water first, or whether Evans, on the steps of the *café*, first yelled:

'Come on. The engine's stopped.'

'I'm responsible to the prefect for that boat,' said Sergeant Frémont, and the thought spurred him to some rather decent sprinting. Evans was in the lead, Hjalmar, dripping wet as he was, a close second. Miriam, who had outrun many an enraged steer to a corral fence, was keeping in the money. Tom Jackson, who had quickly recovered consciousness and had been reassured that the wound was only a flesh wound and had missed his brain by a safe three millimetres, was too weak to run but he cheered. Sosthène, the proprietor, was ruefully checking up on the broken bottles. His wife was spluttering: 'I told you there'd be trouble when those bandits came up the river.'

'What bandits?' asked Jackson, his reporter's instincts quickly asserting themselves.

'The ones who had the snub-nosed tugboat and the big grey barge. I said to Sosthène that I didn't like the look of that barge the minute I set my eyes on it,' the proprietress said.

'Were the men who stole the boat the same bandits?' asked Sosthène.

'To hear you talk you'd think we had an unlimited supply. Of course. Those crooks from Paris. Could hardly steer. Who else would be passing here at four o'clock in the morning?'

'Is that an unusual time for a barge to pass?' Jackson asked.

'When it's heading upstream,' the proprietress said. 'They stopped for a drink and some food. Ate as if they were starving. That's strange, too. There are plenty of restaurants along the river banks.'

'What day did they pass, and what did they do with the barge?' asked Jackson.

'They passed on Friday morning, just four o'clock it was. What they did with the barge I can't say. As far as I'm concerned, I hope it sinks with all on board.'

'Did they carry any cargo?' asked Tom, fidgeting with his bandage which consisted of a clean bar towel.

'Hay,' she said disgustedly. 'And they'd busted open some of the bales. That looked funny, too. I didn't see any animals aboard.'

160

While Jackson was exercising his idle curiosity, Evans, Hjalmar, Miriam, and Sergeant Fremont, in the order named, were streaking through the woods, scattering leaves, twigs, bark, and brush as they streaked, slapped by branches, bruised by stumps and torn with briers. Miriam, it must be said, was less rumpled and untidied than the others, she having had years of experience at cross-country running on a fairly tough range while the others were more accustomed to slippery decks, cindered tracks or resounding pavements. Frémont, in fact, had never been in the country before, except in the month of August, and on those occasions he had fished and not sprinted.

At last, Evans caught sight of the stranded *Deuxième Pays*. The two thugs had disappeared into the thicker forest on the opposite bank. In less time than it takes to tell it, the four able-bodied members of the Weiss expedition had waded and splashed their way to the sandbar, boarded the craft and were making a quick survey of the situation.

Hjalmar had gone at once to the stern where lay the body of the hapless trigger man. Since it had slipped into a somewhat undignified position, Hjalmar grasped it by the coat collar and lifted it to the stern seat.

'One to one, by God,' he said, referring to the score. 'They got Gring, we got this chap. Not much choice.'

Miriam was keeping carefully towards the bow of the *Deuxième Pays*. It was one thing to shoot a target, or a wounded steer, or even a portrait of Whistler's aunt. To have picked off a fellow creature, no matter how vicious, was new to her. She kept telling herself that doubtless she would get used to it, but definitely she had not as yet done so. She looked rather pitifully at Evans who immediately understood.

'Throw a tarp over the stiff,' he said to Hjalmar, who was prodding the body thoughtfully and trying to remember about *rigor mortis*.

'I'll chuck him down into the cabin,' said Hjalmar. 'If there's a leak, by God, we'll stuff him into it.'

'*Nom de Dieu*,' Sergeant Frémont said. 'You all forget I have a job and a family to support. I've got to list his papers.'

'If you find a paper on that mug, I'll buy you a new uniform.

161

You'll need it, after that run through the briers,' Hjalmar said.

A quick search proved that Hjalmar's surmise was true. The deceased triggerman had no more papers than a jack rabbit might have carried. 'How about thumbprints?' Hjalmar grunted, good-naturedly. 'It's better to go back with them than nothing at all.'

'We shall take back the entire body, if we get back ourselves,' the sergeant said. 'I was reluctant at first, Mr Evans, to believe this case contained the dangers you hinted at. What has happened just now has caused me to change my mind.'

'Just a mere hand grenade and Sho-Sho gun, and a trio of mobsters?' asked Evans, mockingly. 'Before we get through, I'm afraid we'll run greater risks than those. I'm decidedly displeased with the situation. Our kidnappers have been warned and have taken the offensive. I had hoped to surprise them.'

'If they knock off old Hugo, I'll tear out their livers and eat 'em steaming,' Hjalmar said, and the look on his face seemed to indicate that he would be as good as his word.

'I come not to bury Hugo but to save him,' Evans said. 'We must beat those chaps to Frontville, or our philanthropic friend is doomed. But how shall we get there? By what means of locomotion, or propulsion? We have no Harley Davidson, our motor boat is aground.'

'Look,' Miriam said. 'There's a bunch of horses. Why not rope 'em and cut right across the country?'

The answer was four splashes, as Evans, Hjalmar, Frémont, and Miriam herself, in the order named, hit the Seine again and made for the adjoining meadow.

CHAPTER 19

Strange Bedfellows as it Were

HEISS and Lourde were enjoying their new-found freedom with certain reservations. They had passed through many trying experiences, such a rapid succession of them as had not ruffled the shady course of their business career since they had passed off a false Giotto mural in the pre-war days, only to discover that they had received in exchange an even more phoney Cimabue. To boot, the enormous frame of the Cimabue was not gilded according to specifications but covered with radiator paint.

The recent advent of Hugo Weiss, on the eve of what was to be a clearance sale of candlelight Grecos, had been the precursor of more disturbing events than Giotto and Cimabue had ever dreamed of. First, Gring's mission had failed and he had been murdered. Then after having their hopes raised by Arabs who simply ached to be fleeced, the Bedouins turned out to be U.S. Government agents. Then the police had swarmed all over the place. From the frightful grilling by Evans they had been miraculously saved by a summons from the prefect. They were at large at last but could it be a trap, they wondered. Abel took the affirmative, Dodo, with less conviction, the negative. There was no decision. For want of better occupation they strolled back to their place of what loosely, perhaps, could be termed business. It was empty, save for the water bugs and old masters.

'I have a terrible feeling that I have forgotten something,' Dodo said, rubbing his arches which still throbbed from the sergeant's heels.

His timid remark brought Abel to his feet. 'The cops have got the Grecos. They should be shipped to-morrow at the latest,' Abel said.

'Maybe the prefect'll give 'em back. He wasn't as tough as I thought he'd be,' said Dodo.

'You sap. That's part of the third degree. First one slaps us around, then another pulls a Florence Nightingale. They nab us, then turn us loose. They're playing with us like a cat with a mouse. . . .'

'Worse,' Dodo said. 'But what are we going to do ? We can't lose the sales, our only big clean-up. You know it looked too good from the start. Six Grecos at a wallop. Now I ask you, what can any guy do with six Grecos all the same size. . . .'

'Shut up. I got to think,' Abel said. It was evident that his thoughts, such as they were, did not incline toward the bright or cheery side. However, he said at last: 'We got to get a set of new ones. That's what we got to do.'

'All this grilling's scrambled your brains,' Dodo said. 'Who can turn out six Grecos overnight ?'

'You know who,' Abel said.

'He's never done more than three Old Masters a week,' Dodo said. 'I'm not talking about guys like Millet with two peasants digging clams and just a couple of trees or steeples, brown like gravy. This man Greco's stuff is all complicated and cock-eyed. You can't *ad lib.* when you copy a guy like that.'

'The new process. What about that ?'

'Do you think it would work ? Can our man snapshot candlelight ?'

'He's got to,' Abel said. 'I'll put the screws on that guy. He's been getting away with a lot of guff, his social standing, all that hooey. The higher his social standing is, the more harm I could do him if I opened my trap.'

'He's got a great eye for copying,' Dodo said. 'You got to hand him that. Give him a painting and he'll turn out another just like two peas in a pod. Naturally, such a talented guy is temperamental.'

'Now that we've got his name I'm going to take him down a peg,' Abel said. 'I've been kicked around enough.'

They jammed hats on their heads, Abel choosing a flat broad-brimmed derby and Dodo a rakish felt of what is known to the trade as 'assignation green '. A good three minutes before the special agents of the minister of justice swooped down the boulevard Haussmann hoping to take them into custody again, the enterprising pair were walking rapidly in the direction of the avenue Pierre Premier de Serbie, a quarter where no dragnet

164

had netted much of anything since the days of Millerand. In front of a large ornate apartment building characteristic of the 1890s, they paused, straightened their coat lapels, glanced uneasily up and down the silent street, and pushed the button which opened the front door. The *concierge*, taking a cursory look at them, snapped: 'Service entrance'. Abel, however, had his dander up.

'Service entrance be damned. We're not selling anything. We come to make a professional call,' he said.

'What floor ?'

'The top.'

'No one home,' the *concierge* sniffed.

'Then we'll wait on the landing,' Abel said and shoved Dodo into an elevator built for two. The elevator clanked and thumped its way almost to the top floor, so near that Dodo was able to pry open the outside door and be boosted to the floor level, after which he braced himself against the framework and pulled Abel up after him. In response to their tug at the bell cord a man servant opened the door.

'The master cannot be disturbed,' the servant said.

'He's got to be disturbed,' Abel said. 'We've got to see him right away.'

'Out of the question. The master's orders are that while he is painting he cannot be interrupted,' the servant insisted. It was clear that he did not like the looks of Abel and Dodo. In the first place they were too young to be calling on the master. Furthermore they were not wearing ribbons of the Legion of Honour and they bore hats in their hands the like of which the servant had not seen since the day he had been obliged to fetch his master home from an exhibition of Toulouse-Lautrecs.

'Good day,' the servant said, coldly, and started to close the door. It was Dodo who acted, in that instance. The heel trick of the Fakir Yenolob had been tried on Dodo so often that he had picked it up, so he brought down his heel smartly on the arch of the servant's foot and before the latter could regain his poise both Abel and Dodo had slipped past his guard and were in the hallway. The ensuing scuffle brought the master, palette and brushes in hand, to the doorway and he was none

165

other than Paty de Pussy, vice-president of the *Société des Artistes Français* and the author of the plan for the proposed *Hugo Schussschicker Weiss Institut Artistique de la Prudence et de la Sécurité.*

'What does this mean?' he demanded.

'Stow it, *maître*. Climb down,' Abel said. 'Tell this trained seal of yours to go hide himself. We got to talk to you.'

'Adolphe, put them out at once,' Paty de Pussy said to the servant, who was nursing his foot.

'He can't put us out,' Abel said. 'Why not call the police? Dodo and I have just been released from the *préfecture*. Some of your swell friends would be surprised, if it got out that we were in your studio.'

'This is an outrage,' Paty de Pussy said, but less aggressively. 'It was distinctly understood that all transactions were to take place through an intermediary. . . .'

'You don't read the papers,' Abel said disgustedly. 'The intermediary's dead. He was murdered at the Café du Dôme.'

At that Paty de Pussy dropped his mask of hauteur and showed himself capable of some very quick embarrassment and anxiety. 'Go, Adolphe,' he said, 'go soak your foot in mustard water until I call for you.'

He beckoned Abel and Dodo into the spacious studio, closing nervously all the doors and even the skylight. His hands were trembling, his manner betrayed the deepest agitation. It was not the death of Ambrose Gring that had upset him so, but the fact that Gring had been overdue in the Avenue Pierre Premier de Serbie with the payment for six candlelight Grecos not only forged with extreme skill but having been painted on the old fifteenth-century canvas that had baffled the experts of several countries.

'Gentlemen,' Paty de Pussy implored. 'Set my mind at rest, if you can. When M. Gring was found dead, did he have on him any considerable sum of money?'

Abel caught on at once and spat disgustedly on the Aubusson carpet. He could put up with avarice in the lower classes but when a man who had never known want showed such a passion for money Abel had no sympathy for him.

'You mean your pay ?'

'My . . . er . . . emolument,' Paty de Pussy said.

'Nothing doing. That batch of Grecos haven't been paid for, and they won't be paid for, either. . . .'

Paty de Pussy rose and started waving his arms. 'Not paid for. You mean . . . not paid for. This is a swindle. I've fallen into the hands of bandits and assassins. *Canaille*.'

'The cops have confiscated all of them,' Abel said.

Paty de Pussy wilted into a Louis XIV chair. 'I'm disgraced. I'm a ruined man.'

'Take it easy,' Dodo said. 'We haven't squealed on you. What do you think we are ?'

The master was too frightened to be reassured : 'You've come to blackmail me,' he said.

'Not at all. If you'd let us talk, we'd tell you why we came.'

'Do so. I beg of you, do so,' the master said.

'Nobody's wise to them Grecos except a mug named Evans, a stranger to all of us. He's out of town to-day and I've got it on good authority that he won't come back. Not to-day or any other day. See ?' Abel said.

'I refuse to have anything to do with murder, unless it is political murder and therefore justifiable,' Paty de Pussy said, drawing himself up to his full height.

'Calm yourself,' said Abel. 'I ain't asking you to do no rough stuff. What we want is another batch of Grecos, six of 'em. And we want 'em the first thing to-morrow morning. *If* we get 'em, you won't be exposed. We won't even tell the cops we know you. You won't be charged with grand larceny and conspiracy. Your name won't be mixed up in no murder case. You'll be sitting pretty. See ? But, on the other hand, if you should act upstage, or stall or anything, well, I wouldn't be able to promise you the guillotine, maybe, but whatever France has short of that, you'd get. And what headlines. Scion of French aristocracy ringleads mob. Salon prize winner baffles art world with forgeries. Juicy ? Eh ?'

'Eiffelturish,' murmured Dodo, rubbing his hands. 'Listen, Abel. Wouldn't it almost be worth it to expose him ? Think of the show there'd be. In court, in the Santé. Society broads fainting in the crush at the courtroom. Just think of what M. Pussy's mug would look like, in two column cut, with inserts of real and fake Grecos on each side.'

Paty de Pussy had reached the end of his resistance. Perspiration had wilted his collar and was trickling down his back and the calves of his legs. His hands were trembling so badly that Abel had to call a halt.

'Lay off, Dodo,' he said. 'If he gets the shakes he won't be able to do anything but Pissarros or Van Goghs. We got to have Grecos, and no mistake.'

'You know how them Greeks are,' Dodo said. 'So crooked they can't paint a guy with a straight face. All right. No more mental cruelty, if you say so. But let's get down to business.'

'Yes. To business,' Abel said. Then he added kindly to Paty de Pussy: 'You see? We're tender-hearted. We don't want you to lose your fees, neither for the half-dozen you've already turned in nor the six you're going to do to-day. What the hell. It won't hurt you to work all night for once. Got a blue light?'

The vice-president of the *Artistes Français* nodded and tried to compose himself. Abel, too, tried to introduce an element of calm into the proceedings.

'I know,' he began suavely, 'that it seems unreasonable to you, asking for six Old Masters in eighteen hours, but we must ship them early to-morrow morning. Otherwise all of us will lose out. The six the cops have will be sent to the Louvre. That don't mean a thing. This guy Evans who knows so much that isn't good for him will find himself behind the eightball. Now we're going to let you in a secret, something big. One of our associates has just developed a method of sensitizing canvas so it will take a photographic print. Do you get me?' Abel smiled delightedly. Paty de Pussy was still in the fog but his hand was no longer shaking, merely shimmering a bit. Abel continued:

'Don't you catch on? We sensitize a canvas, a piece off that roll you got in Toledo. We make a photograph of a Greco, enlarge it to natural size, print it on the canvas and then you get busy with the colours. You know as well as I do that most of the time copying Old Masters is wasted in the draughtsmanship,

168

in getting the exact lines and proportions. Am I right or wrong ?'

Paty de Pussy nodded. The winter of his discontent was letting up a little. It was true that with an accurate drawing, photographically shaded, on the canvas, he could do a rapid job of colouring. 'I'll do the best I can,' he said. 'But for rush work like that I ought to get a higher fee.'

'Time and a half for night work,' Dodo said, magnanimously. 'Let's go. Fix up an El Greco palette, and for the love of God, watch that crimson in the candle flame. Greco didn't use cochineal till he was almost as old as you are. I got that straight.'

'Indeed. I'm glad to know that,' Paty de Pussy said. 'I must use a crimson lake, or alizarin, and ten to one it'll crack within sixty or seventy years.'

Dodo beamed. '*Maître*,' he said, 'if it lasts even forty years, I'll kiss you on both cheeks in Heaven.'

'I trust you'll take no such liberties,' Paty de Pussy said, coldly. 'The fact that we enter into a commercial agreement does not imply social equality.'

'Have it your own way, only get started mixing colours. My partner'n I will do the photography, and we're goin' to do it right here. Have Adolphe fix up plenty of salami and eggs and get in a few cold bottles of beer,' Dodo said.

CHAPTER 20

Not a Moment Too Soon

THE wild race to Frontville was proceeding at an ever-increasing pace as the horses and their riders warmed to their respective tasks. Evans, in the lead, galloped recklessly through the woods, dodging trees, his mount leaping fallen timber and stumps. The map he held in his hand, fluttering like a banner, and from time to time he glanced at it and changed his direction slightly.

'There's the island,' he cried at last. And as the two gangsters from the *Deuxième Pays* broke cover at the same instant, he added: 'Rope them, Miriam. Quick.'

With practised hand, Miriam let fly with the long halter rope she had already knotted and coiled. The noose slipped over the shoulders of the panting gangsters and it was the work of a moment to dismount and tie them up. Imagine the surprise of the rescuers when, engaged in that pursuit, they saw Tom Jackson trot into the area, his head still wrapped in a bar towel. He had acted on the tip from Mme Sosthène, had found the huge grey barge, and on it, hidden deep in the hay, the taxi of Lvov Kvek.

Swiftly Evans gave his instructions. They mounted, Jackson taking Miriam's horse and the girl vaulting lightly up in front of Homer. There was a splash as the hooves hit the water, a moment of floundering in the channel, then the tip of the island was gained. As he rode, Evans made a quick survey of the situation. Then a bullet whipped the air just over their heads and Evans saw a man running from a clearing in the centre to the northern extremity. Another fugitive, taking an easier route, dived in straight opposite Frontville, where at the landing a brick-red snub-nosed tug was waiting.

There was not an instant of indecision in Evans' mind. Why, if the gang was to make its getaway on the tug, should one of them head for the opposite end of the island? And where did all the old-fashioned ammunition and firearms come from ? The dugouts, of course. The dugouts contained explosives. Impossible to say how much T.N.T. It was to Miriam he turned without hesitation. 'Ride the man down,' he said hoarsely, slipping from the horse and pointing to the north. 'If he stoops or kneels, shoot him instantly.'

With that Homer started running toward the clearing where the dugouts were, with Hjalmar and Frémont close behind him. There were three entrances, all looking very much alike. Selecting the middle one, he motioned his companions to enter the others, one left, one right. There was an ominous silence everywhere, broken only by the heavy breathing of the trio. Jackson, without instructions, had started towards the tug boat, met a rain of machine-gun bullets and dropped into a wallow for safety.

The dugout Evans had chosen had steep ladders of decaying boards and there was an odour of stale cigarette smoke. He ripped off a blanket from a chamber entrance well below the surface of the ground and saw the body of Hugo Weiss, the head wrapped in a cement sack, hands and ankles bound with wire. With frenzied effort Evans slung the multi-millionaire over his shoulder and mounted the ladders again, his heart straining, his breath rasping his throat and lungs. Rungs broke, he slipped, his burden shifted, but foot by foot he worked his way upward and after what seemed hours to him reached the surface. There he did what for anyone else would have appeared to be an insane act. Still holding the unconscious Hugo on his shoulder he made straight for the river, and as the earth seemed to rise with a dull roar dived deep into the current and clung to the bottom with all his remaining strength. Around him flying rocks, stumps and clods of earth slapped the surface and odd-shaped masses sank down to the river bed beside him. When he could hold his breath not a second longer he rose to the surface, breathed deeply, then dived again for Hugo.

Miriam, scratched and almost naked, was senseless on the ground, her horse lying almost on top of her. She had started after the running fugitive, as Evans had directed, but just as the man was stooping her horse's foot had caught in a rabbit hole, the animal had fallen headlong, stunning Miriam and breaking its own neck. That it had fallen almost across her body had saved her from the flying debris.

As he tore the gag from Hugo Weiss's mouth and listened for the beating of his heart, Evans was sick with foreboding. Weiss was alive, badly smothered and half drowned, nevertheless he could be revived, Evans thought. It was of his companions and the stout-hearted Kvek that Homer was thinking. Was it possible that they had not been blown or crushed to atoms ? And Miriam ? What could have happened to her that had given the fleeing gangster time to throw the switch ? Homer did not dare let up on the artificial respiration he was giving Hugo Weiss until the millionaire's lungs were free of water. He could only pump away miserably, trying not to accelerate the rhythm. Miriam ! How lovely she had been ! How miserly he had been with his praise or appreciation ! Hjalmar ! Never perhaps to roar or paint again ! Frémont's career ! A brutal end to the Colonel's brave struggle to re-establish himself in a strange and hostile world. Tom Jackson!

Had Evans known what had transpired since last he had called the roll, he would have worked on Hugo with more gusto. The builders of the dugouts, those Frogs whom Hjalmar had conceded were not too dumb, had pointed them carefully away from the town of Frontville. If the enemy spied them out and blew them up, filled with high explosives, the Frogs had figured that the force of the explosion would be spent in the other direction, towards the empty wood. How right they were had been demonstrated by the afternoon's proceedings. Hjalmar, at the bottom of the left hand dugout, had found Kvek, also bound and gagged, had lugged him out in a jiffy, and had started toward Frontville, thinking that if there were no vodka there, at least there would be brandy. And for reviving a weary Russian nothing weaker than brandy will do. The explosion, when it came, knocked him flat on his face but all flying objects were propelled in the other direction.

Frémont, having found his dugout empty, had noticed, as did Jackson, that the tug was getting under way and had been taking pot shots at the helmsman when the great roar behind him made him shoot so high in the air that he winged a chicken hawk (*Buteo borealis*) who was circling over a Frontville hen-coop.

Each member of the party, except Miriam, was mourning the others when all at once they started to circulate. Frémont found Jackson, Hjalmar, and Kvek, who needed nothing but untying and a drink. Then they stumbled on Miriam and lifted her off the horse as if it had been a muskrat. Respectfully they felt for broken bones, found none, wrapped the girl in Lvov's coat and started around the shore. Within two minutes they saw Evans and the limp Weiss, and got there just as Weiss was beginning to blink his eyes and mutter questions which slowly took form and made sense. He wanted first to know where he was, which was reasonable. Then he recognized Evans and Hjalmar and came as near to beaming as a man can who has chewed a cement sack for thirty minutes and then been held under water until he was half drowned.

'You bring me luck, my boy,' he said to Hjalmar, as soon as he was partially himself again. 'What an adventure!'

'You had a close call,' Evans said, 'and the adventure's not over yet. I imagine,' he continued, smiling, 'that the rest of it will prove most gratifying to you. Indeed, most gratifying.'

Then he noticed that Colonel Kvek was bearing the unconscious girl in his arms, and his agitation, had Miriam been able to witness it, would have caused her to swoon again.

CHAPTER 21

The Mysterious Mickey Finn

A SCENE of a different character was taking place in the *préfecture*, specifically in the ward Ste Anne. A tall, hollow-cheeked man, Lord Stewe, was holding a tall silk hat in his hand. He was flanked by a squad of under-secretaries, all with grey-striped trousers, frock coats, and tall hats as well. They all were being held off by a squad of lady bassos and baritones while the prefect, M. Crayon de Crayon, was being sought. One of the bassos, in fact, was humming a topical ditty which began:

> '*Hail jolly ambassador Stewe*
> *There's nothing the bugger won't do.*'

The message sent by the frantic Maggie had reached the British Embassy, and when calls for help by British subjects reach the right party, tall hats begin to move.

'I beg your pardon, ambassador,' the prefect began.

'First, monsieur, I should like to talk with Miss Dickinson,' the British ambassador said.

'We have no Miss Dickinson, only a demented girl named Mademoiselle Montana, member of the picture bandit gang,' the prefect said.

'For the sake of form, I should like to see what you have,' the ambassador said suavely.

'Certainly, if you wish,' the prefect said.

Now Maggie was a stalwart girl, but several hours in a tepid bath, with only garlic sausage and wine for nourishment, will do much to cool the ardour of a lovesick maiden. Maggie had been thinking, not of Hjalmar and the chilly studio in the rue Montparnasse, but of England, her respectable parents, her quiet, comfortable home, and of a village lad who, during her brief stay there, had begged her to give up carousing in modern Babylon and let him take care of her in a steady way. At the time, she had not even thought of the lad seriously. She had burned for Hjalmar, for self-sacrifice and abuse. The immersion therapy in the salle Ste Anne had accomplished the transformation. When the ambassador showed up, he clinched the matter.

'You're evidently British,' he said, sternly, while she tried to cover herself with the bath curtains. 'What, may I ask, are you doing here?'

'I came looking for a man,' she stammered, awed by the formal clothes and official manner. 'My bloke had got himself pinched. No tellin' what for.'

'Why was this girl detained?' the ambassador demanded of the prefect.

'She admitted consorting with a desperate criminal, Gonzo, who has beaten up two dozen of my policemen and showered me with violet ink, to say nothing of swindling an American out of 250,000 francs....'

'Americans ask for swindling,' the ambassador said. 'You may do what you like with Americans, or Gonzos, but I must insist that you clothe this young woman and release her immediately.'

'She came here of her own accord. She'll only come right back,' the prefect said.

'I'll see that she doesn't come back. She will leave for England at once, and will not return. I will take it upon myself to guarantee that she receives no further visas.' Then he turned to Maggie. 'Young woman,' he said, 'it does not befit respectable Englishwomen to run after desperados, and foreign desperados at that. You should return to your native village, your worthy parents ... er, you have worthy parents, have you not?'

Maggie, almost hypnotized, nodded.

'I thought so,' the ambassador continued. 'Fly to them and ask their forgiveness. Say I recommended that they forgive you without any nonsense. And isn't there a swain ...? There ought to be a swain.'

'There is. He's a good, honest lad, and steady, too,' Maggie sobbed.

'Tell him I recommend that he forgive and forget. That's it. Forgive and forget. Only, Miss Dickinson, don't give him too

175

much to forget. Take it a bit easy with the confessions, my girl. A steady young swain shouldn't be overburdened with pages from his lassie's past. Might use them as an excuse to drink too much and brood.'

'If you'll only let me out of here, I'll do as you direct, sir,' Maggie said, shivering, and the interview was closed.

In the laboratory of Dr Hyacinthe Toudoux, all was formaldehyde and roses. The good doctor was holding triumphantly in his hand a beaker. He dipped in a bit of blue litmus paper and it turned just the right shade of pink. A drop of a certain acid produced bubbling and effervescence, a spoonful of another clouded the contents, five minutes over a Bunsen burner cleared them again.

'*Crotali confluenti,*' the doctor murmured. 'How different, indeed, from the timber snake or the huge rattler of the Everglades. What oil ! I can never thank M. Evans enough. And the *Argalli spicati Texarkanae.* There's a weed to do one's heart good. The only thing that puzzles me is that a stiff dose of this Mickey or Michael Finn, so-called, will not kill a lady-bug (*Megilla maculata*), a white-footed mouse (*Peromyseus leucopus*), and least of all a guinea-pig. How could this unspeakable mackerel (he indicated Ambrose's scattered remains) have managed to die ? The anaesthetic and soporific properties of this ancient Inca secret, the Mickey or Michael Finn, are excellent on all insects and animals. Likewise its hypnotic and anti-aphrodisiac qualities. Ladybugs pass out for six hours, white-footed mice, two hours and fifteen minutes, and guinea-pigs sleep soundly for at least forty-five minutes. I must consult with M. Evans again before I sign the certificate. Ah ! Natural death, indeed ! Prefect, bah ! Perhaps this will teach him not to interfere in scientific matters that are beyond him. I shall not let him forget Greeng Ambrose. I shall put Greeng back together tenderly.' And with that Dr Toudoux began humming a song:

> '*Hélas, pauvre Yorick,*
> *Je vous ai connu bien dans le temps.*'*

* Alas, poor Yorick, I knew you well.

Back in Frontville, the rescuers and the rescued were having a chat in the neighbourhood saloon. Evans first congratulated Colonel Kvek on his presence of mind in sending the message, and assured Weiss that the Gonzo self-portrait could easily be repaired. Two powerful speed cars were obtained from the Chatillon garage and the party was divided as follows: Kvek and Hugo Weiss, with Sergeant Frémont, set out for Paris. It was agreed that Weiss was to remain in hiding, at the residence of one of his cousins, until Homer gave the word. To Hjalmar and Jackson, Evans assigned the task of rounding up the horses and riding hard to the Café des Imprévoyants to head off the bandits on the snub-nosed tug. In the other speed car, Evans himself and Miriam burned up the miles to the boulevard Haussmann.

On the subject of concealing the millionaire and of gunning for the higher-ups, Sergeant Frémont was more than doubtful. Stalking master minds simply was not done in the Third French Republic. Before the separation of the party, Weiss and Kvek had related briefly the kidnapping episode. Their taxi had been intercepted near the Pont Royal, both had been jabbed with hypodermics and they had regained consciousness aboard the large grey barge named the *Presque Sans Souci*.

'We'll hear the details later,' Evans said, and in clouds of yellow dust the speed cars roared away.

'Do you think those men will ever come back to see us again ?' asked the daughter of the tavern-keeper.

'You should have been here when the Americans came through in 1918,' he said.

The girl smiled. 'I missed that by less than a year, Pa,' she said.

The tavern-keeper grew suddenly thoughtful. 'So you did,' he said, irritably. 'So you did.'

The premises of Heiss and Lourde had the shutters drawn, but after some banging Homer and Miriam aroused the guards and were admitted. Instantly Evans telephoned the *préfecture* and asked to have Dinde sent to him, together with all the confiscated candlelight Grecos.

The pitiful clerk's teeth were chattering, his muscles were twitching. Homer at once reassured him.

'Monsieur Dinde,' he began, 'no harm will come to you. I've sent for you to do you a favour. Your employers, from time to time, have expressed dissatisfaction because of your lack of initiative, is that not true ?'

'Every day. I try . . .'

'Precisely,' Evans said. 'Now I'm giving you a chance to make good. Messrs Heiss and Lourde are detained elsewhere. Their business is at a standstill. I want you to wrap up those paintings, send them where they are supposed to go, and then, when your employers return they will be overjoyed not to have lost the sales.'

'How can I ever repay you ?' Dinde said, tears of gratitude in his eyes. The clerk reached behind a false Tintoretto depicting Christ throwing the money changers out of the temple, and opened the door of a hidden vault in which three sets of books were kept, one for the French government, one for publicity purposes, and one for the partners themselves. It was from the third set that Dinde hastily copied out six names and addresses, all small museums in the United States. Within half an hour, the paintings were packed separately, and addressed.

'I'll attend to the customs certificates,' Evans said. 'Now, M. Dinde, go home and get a good night's sleep. The authorities will trouble you no further, neither will my friend Oklahoma Tom. He's just a diamond in the rough, you know. Means no harm.'

The customs office was only a few blocks away. A brief word from the minister of justice put the inspector in an accommodating frame of mind and soon each package was properly stamped and certified. The contents were antique and duty free, the certificates stated. When the inspector looked closely at the addresses he stopped and scratched his head.

'Say, what is this ?' he asked. 'I shipped another batch exactly like this, not twenty minutes ago. Same museums, same addresses. Grecos, too.'

'Indeed,' asked Evans, fingering a thousand-franc note, 'may I ask who brought them ?'

'An express man brought them, a guy named Jean Bart. He has a little business of his own, just a couple of trucks, in the

178

boulevard Sebastopol,' the inspector said. 'But, say, shall I forward this duplicate shipment just the same?'

'By all means,' Evans said. 'Let nothing deter you.' And he handed over the thousand francs.

'They'll be on the way in less than a minute,' the inspector said.

Homer was already on the way to the boulevard Sebastopol, and thinking hard.

'More fragments that won't fit,' he murmured.

CHAPTER 22

The Lure of a Buddy's Body

THE proprietor of the Rendez-vous des Imprévoyants, having been fatigued and almost thrown off his feed by events of the morning, had given up wondering who, if anyone, was to pay for the bottles broken by the fragments of the hand grenade, and had shuffled upstairs for a well-earned nap. Likewise his wife, having released her vigilance over her daughter when Hjalmar had got safely away, had rolled in on the other side of the broad family bed and was dreaming of the days in which she had outwitted her own mother. Gabrielle, or Gaby, was sitting on the small *terrasse* and wishing she were a motor boat so that big strong men would fight over her.

The *Deuxième Pays* was still resting on the sand bar just around the big bend and in it, where Hjalmar had hurriedly tossed them, were the remains of the late trigger man known as Eloi le Mec.

Before setting out from the island, Hjalmar and Jackson had bound more thoroughly the mobsters Miriam had lassoed and turned them over to the two Chatillon officers to guard.

'We can make it to the Rendez-vous a good half hour ahead of the tug, and I wouldn't be surprised if the men aboard the tug stopped off there for a bite to eat, maybe to make a getaway. It's the most likely point along the river, plenty of woods, un-frequented roads. Not bad as a hideout,' Hjalmar said.

'Won't they stop at the barge and try to escape in the taxi?' Jackson suggested.

'It would take 'em too long to lift it out of the hold. Besides, the whole country's on the lookout for that taxi,' said Hjalmar.

They set out at a brisk trot and soon were galloping. A short time afterwards, when Gaby heard hoofbeats she made haste to close the front door of the *café*, in the hope that her mother would not be aroused by the sound. Sure enough, when

180

Hjalmar and Tom vaulted from their horses' backs Gaby was alone to receive them.

'Hello,' she said, edging up to Hjalmar and smiling coyly.

'Where have you been hiding?' he asked, always cheered by a pretty face and a receptive attitude.

'Ma made me go upstairs when you were here this morning,' she said. 'Ma's a hard woman, Ma is.'

'Where is she now?' asked Hjalmar. Then he remembered the pressing business at hand. 'Listen, kid,' he said, 'I'll tend to you later. Just now I've to talk to your pa.'

'Darn it all. I never get a break,' Gaby said, but Hjalmar chucked her under the chin and reiterated his promise to devote himself to her interests at the first possible moment.

'Cross your heart,' she said.

Hjalmar grinned and crossed his heart and the girl crept reluctantly upstairs to wake her father. Sleepily Sosthène descended, pulling up his trousers as he came.

'Four bottles,' he said. 'Who's going to pay for them?'

Hjalmar slapped him on the shoulder so heartily that he lost hold of his trousers and had to start all over again with them.

'You'll be paid double, and more if you give me a hand,' Hjalmar said.

'I must insist that you incite no more bombardments,' Sosthène said. That more trouble was coming he had already surmised.

'We've got to take 'em by surprise,' the Norwegian said. 'The kidnapping gang are on their way here, in the snub-nosed tug. I've doped it out that they'll heave-to near the stranded *Deuxième Pays* to get the body of their buddy, so the cops won't be able to produce it as evidence. You see, once the cops know their buddy is Eloi the Mec, and can prove it, the rest of the mob can be traced.'

'Me, I'm a peaceful man . . .' Sosthène began.

The sound of voices had awakened Mme Sosthène, who stuck a tousled head from the upper window. 'Them four bottles. Who's going to pay for 'em?' she said, then she spied Gaby, who was trying to hide behind one of the horses. 'Gaby, you come up here this instant.'

'Aw, Ma,' Gaby said.

'Do what your ma says,' Sosthène said, half-heartedly ...
adding for Hjalmar's benefit: 'I'm not aimin' to be mixed up
in more shootin' scrapes. I'm going to close the shutters and
let that snub-nosed tug go by, buddies' bodies or no buddies'
bodies.'

'Sounds like something in a bathtub,' Tom Jackson said.

There was no time to be lost. Hjalmar had to think quickly.

'All right,' he said, so Mme Sosthène could hear. 'If you let
'em get by the *Deuxième Pays*, they'll stop here and loot your
bloody shop. That's what they will do.'

'Sosthène, you do what the gentleman says. Do just as he
says, and I'll hide the stock in the bushes,' Mme Sosthène said,
pulling up her stockings as she hurried downstairs. On the way
down, she passed Gaby going up and took a healthy maternal
swing at the girl.

'Aw, Ma, I ain't done nothin' yet,' Gaby wailed. 'But I'm
a-goin' to,' she added under her breath, looking back at Hjalmar.

Hjalmar was giving Sosthène hasty instructions. He was to
row Hjalmar and Jackson to the sand bar where the *Deuxième
Pays* was stranded. Jackson, being nearer the size of the late
Eloi le Mec, was to change clothes with the corpse and huddle
in the cabin as corpselike as possible, while Hjalmar, automatic
in each hand, was to hide beneath some nearby gunnysacks.
Then Sosthène was to return with the corpse to the *bistrot* and
await the all clear signal, three shots in rapid succession. That
would mean that the kidnappers had been captured and tied
up, in which case Sosthène would row back to take them all
ashore.

Swiftly Hjalmar elaborated his plan to Tom, as soon as they
were alone. The danger lay in that swivel machine gun in the
stern of the tug. As far as Hjalmar knew, there were three of
the mobsters left. Two would board the *Deuxième Pays* to lug
the corpse, the third would remain at the machine gun. Hjalmar
told Tom to play dead until he was aboard the tug, during
which time Hjalmar would lie low, also, but with all the thugs
covered from beneath the shelter of the gunnysacks. The

182

moment Tom hit the deck, Hjalmar was to fire a shot in the air. The three thugs would turn their heads involuntarily toward the *Deuxième Pays*, at which moment Tom was to knock the machine gunner cold with the butt of his automatic while Hjalmar arose, gun in each hand, and told the others to stick up their hands. Tom would then frisk the pair still on their feet, Hjalmar would board the tug also and the manoeuvre would be rounded out by tying up the victims.

The only catch was the possibility that the thugs might see at once that Jackson was an American.

'How about *rigor mortis* ?' Jackson asked. 'Has it had time to set in, or not ?'

'Take a chance on it. Be stiff and unwieldy,' Hjalmar said, then added quickly: 'Here they come.'

The snub-nosed tug, indeed, was rounding the bend and Hjalmar's practised ear told him at once that his surmise had been a sound one. The tug was slowing down, and after what seemed an interminable time, the slap of a hawser hit the deck of the *Deuxième Pays*. The noose had slipped neatly over the steering wheel. There was a thud of feet, gruff voices, and Hjalmar saw two pair of heavy boots, followed by corduroy trousers legs, on the short ladder into the cabin.

'Here's the stiff,' said one of the thugs, and Tom Jackson felt himself picked up roughly and lugged across the cabin and up the stairs. That was the moment he had dreaded, the first exposure to the daylight, with the eyes of the two kidnappers focused on him. Sure enough, he felt a tightening of the muscles in the arms which were holding him.

'This ain't the Mec,' roared the thug.

'Duck,' yelled the partner, for Hjalmar, seeing a hitch had developed in his plan, had sprung to his feet, automatics in hand.

'Hands up,' Hjalmar yelled. The pair aboard the *Deuxième Pays* stuck up their hands with such alacrity that Jackson, whose head as he was dropped struck squarely on a binnacle, felt everything swim darkly around him and, considering the circumstances, was quite as well satisfied.

The machine gunner aboard the tug could not shoot without

riddling his pals, and to riddle one's pal is against the un-written law of the Paris underworld unless the pal is buzzing one's moll. Since there was no moll known to the substitute triggerman within one hundred kilometres, he leaped to the engine room and pulled the lever to the point marked 'Full Steam Ahead'. Unfortunately for him, he forgot that the tug was tied firmly to the *Deuxième Pays*. There was a hideous jerk, which nearly caused Hjalmar to lose his balance and did result in toppling headlong the two gangsters he was covering. They had the presence of mind, however, to keep their hands up as best they could and Hjalmar, never unnecessarily severe, took the will for the deed and spared their lives.

Sosthène, at the *bistrot*, intead of hearing three shots in rapid succession, saw the snub-nosed tug go steaming past with the *Deuxième Pays* in tow. He waited for nothing further, but started full speed into the woods. Decidedly he didn't like the look of things. Mme Sosthène, less easily daunted, dragged the corpse to the doorway, yelling and shaking her fist.

'You can't leave this in my saloon,' she shouted.

'Sorry,' yelled Hjalmar, without turning his head. He was thinking hard again, which he had had to do too often that afternoon. He was getting fed up with cerebration under strain, still he had to carry on. Before the next bend was reached he had evolved a tentative plan.

'Say, you mugs,' he said to the prostrate pair, 'are you sick of living?'

Sulkily they refused to answer. He prodded them with a hobnailed boot. 'Speak up,' he said, ' or I'll drill you full of holes.'

'Our lives are as dear to us as the next man's,' said the elder.

'Maybe you'd like to prolong them a bit,' Hjalmar suggested.

'If we can do it with honour,' the spokesman replied.

Hjalmar began to roar. 'With honour. That's a good one. Honour ! Jesus Christ ! That's rich.' His rumbling laughter was the first sound to reach Tom Jackson's ears.

'What's the joke?' asked Tom, sitting up and rubbing his eyes.

'With honour,' chuckled Hjalmar.

184

'Have you gone nuts ?' Jackson asked. 'And where are we ? Holy mackerel, we're afloat.'

'They spotted you as an American,' Hjalmar said.

'I might have known,' Jackson said. 'It always happens, no matter what I wear or say. Well, what next ?'

'Frisk these bozos,' Hjalmar said, 'only keep them between you and the tug. Otherwise, Robinson Crusoe there might take it into his head to pop you off.'

The frisking netted four potato mashers, two revolvers, some brass knuckles, a rusty pair of high forceps and a crumpled roll of flypaper. Jackson, smeared with blood and in the corpse's clothes, was as near to not looking American as he could ever hope to be.

'I was telling these gents, when you woke up, that if they wanted to live a while, they'd better order their pal on the tug to run her nose into the bank and then hold up his mitts,' Hjalmar said. 'If he's any kind of a buddy, he'd do that to save his buddies' lives.'

'More likely he'd cut the hawser and make his getaway solo,' the elder thug said, sadly, in an undertone.

'In that case I'd have to use you as a screen and shoot him in his tracks,' Hjalmar said.

'Better make that clear to him first,' advised the younger mobster.

'Thanks. You do the talking,' Hjalmar said.

The request and alternatives were shouted in argot to the helmsman *pro tem.* 'How do you stop the damn thing ?' he yelled.

'Turn the lever to the place at the bottom of the dial where it says " zero",' the elder explained. 'Then turn the wheel counterclockwise. That'll do the trick. And make it snappy. This gorilla who's got us covered hasn't got much patience. He's not a flatfoot, either. He ain't made it clear yet just where he stands.'

'I'm a friend of the guy you kidnapped and tried to blow into smithereens,' Hjalmar said, his face darkening.

The older thug became plaintive. 'What could we do ? We had to scram. We couldn't leave a lot of incriminating evidence, now could we ? By the way, were the old guy and that Russian caught in the explosion ? I got a bet here with Barnabé.'

'We saved 'em,' Hjalmar said.

The elder sighed with relief. 'To tell you the truth, I'm glad to hear it. I always liked those guys. Most parties you kidnap are snooty as hell, or else they are weepers. It was good to meet a couple of victims who can take it.'

The helmsman was still weighing the possibilities of surrender or attempted flight. To help him decide, Hjalmar took a quick shot at his hat, which went into the air like a clay pigeon. Before it hit the water, the man was in the engine room fumbling for the lever. But there his courage failed. He didn't dare show himself at the wheel. Hjalmar, aiming with more care, shot one of the spokes and sent the wheel spinning counter-clockwise.

'That does it,' he said, and held himself in readiness for the shock when the tug would hit the bank and the *Deuxième Pays* the tug.

'Tell me what's wanted,' Tom Jackson said. 'I don't know much about navigating but I know what I like.'

'First hop aboard the tug and drive this bunch of flypaper into the muzzle of that machine gun,' Hjalmar said. 'When we all get aboard, tie up this brace of outlaws while I go below for the third. Then jump ashore and catch the line I'll heave to you. Make it fast around a stump.'

Everything went smoothly at the landing. The timid gangster gave himself up peaceably, and all three were bound hand and foot, dumped into the cabin of the *Deuxième Pays* and chained to the ladder. Tom was posted at the head of the stairway to watch them and to shoot them playfully in the legs if they made a false move. Hjalmar was busily at work, roaring his favourite ballad: 'Never show your bloke to a lady friend'. He had backed the tug away from the bank, set the lever at half-speed, and was heading the craft skilfully into the current, on the way back to the Rendez-vous des Imprévoyants, where there were liquid refreshments, a corpse, and a telephone. Also food, which neither Jackson nor Hjalmar had tasted since morning.

Mme Sosthène was still standing at the *bistrot* door regarding the corpse with hostility and shaking her fist downstream. When she saw the snub-nosed tug returning she bristled with indignation.

'Gaby, to the attic,' she said firmly.

'Aw, Ma. Let me stay down this one time. You'll need some help at the bar now Pa's away,' she said.

'Then you stay right out in the open where I can see you,' the woman said.

'Oh, goody, goody,' said Gaby, and her mother, hard as she was, was forced to suppress a smile. She was thinking of herself and the A.E.F. The sound of Hjalmar's singing brought her sharply to the present again.

'You'd better come back. Four bottles owed, and this slob's remains to be took away.'

'We want eggs and French fried potatoes, stacks of 'em,' Hjalmar shouted happily. 'Get busy in the kitchen.'

The captive thugs stirred uneasily and Jackson fingered the trigger of his automatic. 'Don't worry. We won't starve you,' Jackson said. 'You've got to be fed up well to stand the grilling.'

'Rough stuff isn't legal,' the elder gangster said. 'The law of July 16, 1839 . . .'

'If you talk fast enough the law'll protect you,' Hjalmar said. Then to Jackson: 'Shall we turn 'em over to the bulls at Châtillon or shall we take 'em to Paris in this old wagon? She doesn't steer badly, blast me if she does.'

'How about our barge?' demanded one of the gangsters. 'Can't you take that along, toc? If our lawyer's the man he always was, we won't be idle long.'

'Kvek'll want his taxi,' Jackson said.

'I suppose we might as well take the whole works along,' Hjalmar said.

While Mme Sosthène busied herself at the stove, Hjalmar struggled with the telephone. He got the number Hugo Weiss had given him and soon was talking with the sergeant.

'I've got 'em all, and the launch, the tug, the barge and the taxi. We'll get into Paris between eight o'clock and nine tomorrow evening. Let Evans know,' Jansen said.

The sergeant did his best to be gracious in thanking Hjalmar and congratulating him on his excellent work, but in the back of Frémont's mind was the approaching quest of the higher-ups and he could not think of that without increasing uneasiness. It was well enough for the obliging foreigners, who did not understand the customs of the country, but he was a policeman and knew no other way of making his living. Once he got the reputation of being presumptuous with higher-ups, his career, in spite of the clean-up of the Rosary Game and the finding of Hugo Weiss, would come to an inglorious end. The reflexion that Hydrangea was being borne nearer and nearer, as fast as the *Ile de France* could travel, caused a flutter of his heart that obliterated all else for a moment. Still, Hydrangea was not a girl who knew the value of a dollar, much less that of a franc. Without employment, he might lose her again.

'My friend,' shouted Colonel Kvek, clutching the sergeant and spilling vodka down his neck, 'how can you look so sorrowful? Think of me, an outcast, an exilé, a To-the-Société-Citroën-for-one-taxi-debtor. And I laugh . . . Ho ho ho ho ho. I drink. Glug glug glug glug. I sing! hear me. *Poi, lestotszhka poi.* I sing. I schwallow.'

'All right. Another small brandy,' said the sergeant, trying to resign himself. 'Just the same. To be out of a job.'

'I rejoice in being out of a job. Ah, Weiss. That's something you never can feel, the exuberance, the ecstasy of being unemployed. We must drink again, and smash our glasses,' Kvek bellowed.

'You should have crossed that time on the old *Dresden* . . . .' Weiss hiccoughed happily, tossing down his vodka and laughing as his glass resounded against a seven-branched candelabrum on the window sill.

CHAPTER 23

Two Hearts That Cease to Beat as One, or to Beat at All for That Matter

I N the boulevard Sebastopol Evans had no difficulty in finding the freelance expressman. 'He was something like a priest,' the latter said, but fifty francs fixed that up and Homer was astonished to learn that the No. 1 copyist was none other than Paty de Pussy, and furthermore that in de Pussy's studio Heiss and Lourde were hiding.

'I thought Gring was the go-between,' Evans said to Miriam. 'I certainly didn't visualize direct dealings between Paty de Pussy and such lowly types as Abel and Dodo.'

'But Gring is dead ... so they say. Wouldn't that explain, perhaps?' Miriam said, hesitantly.

'You have reached the nub of the situation. Of course, Abel and Dodo, by bullying Ambrose or having him followed, found thè address they were seeking. Nevertheless, six Grecos cannot be painted in a single night. Not by anyone living or dead.'

'Shall we go to see Paty de Pussy?' the girl asked.

'First I must catch up a few loose ends,' replied Evans.

They found a public telephone near the place du Chatelet and learned from Weiss that Hjalmar had collared the entire kidnapping gang and would proceed down river at daylight with the tug, the barge, the prefectorial launch, Tom Jackson, the arms, knives and blunt instruments, explosives and ammunition, the corpse of Eloi le Mec, the motorcycle stolen by Barnabé Vieuxchamp, and the proprietor and his wife and daughter from the Rendez-vous des Imprévoyants. Sosthène, who had come in from the woods after Hjalmar had fired three shots in rapid succession at intervals of five minutes over a period of two hours, was in a state of nerves. Jansen had pacified him by offering him the food and drink concession on the voyage down river. An impromptu bar and grill had been

189

set up on the huge grey barge, the *Presque Sans Souci*. The big Norwegian had had the binding ropes adjusted so the captive kidnappers could drink and pay Sosthène from a pile of their money that had been collected at their feet.

'It's a shame to miss such a trip,' Weiss said, after giving Evans all the details that had been reported to him. 'Still, we're having a lively party here. Wish you could drop around.'

'Would you mind if I sent you our good friend, the ambassador?' Evans asked. 'I think he's entitled to the honour of turning you in, when the moment comes.'

'By all means. Certainly. A topping idea,' Hugo said, and the tinkle heard over the wire bespoke the destruction of another glass.

The ambassador was nothing loth. He was delighted that Hugo was safe, although he persisted in believing that the philanthropist had been on a bat and had cooked up the kidnapping story because of the unlucky flood of publicity.

'I'll toddle right over,' the ambassador said. 'Gad. This reminds me of the old *Dresden*. We'd cleaned up the liquor in the first and second class ... Boy, if it hadn't been for the Statue of Liberty ... Well. Got to toddle. Like old times, by Jove.'

Evans and Miriam crossed the bridge thoughtfully, side by side. Dusk was settling over the Seine and obscuring the familiar towers. Birds were asleep in the trees along the quai, bookstalls were closed and padlocked, the quai aux Fleurs was deserted.

'I'm sorry,' Evans began. 'My next errand is one I shall have to do alone.'

Miriam was hurt but tried not to show it. 'That's not fair,' she said. 'You shall not take the risks. . . .'

'Oh, risks,' he said, relieved. 'This isn't a risk. It's likely to be messy, that's all. I've got to pay my respects to Dr Hyacinthe Toudoux and ... er ... his laboratory, you know. All sorts of odds and ends lying around. Bad smells.'

'I understand. Poor Ambrose,' she said. 'Well. It takes a lot to tear me from your side but in this case I won't object. That is, unless I have to go too far away.'

190

'Wait on one of the benches in front of the *préfecture*,' he said. 'I'll have an officer keep his eye on you, if you like.'

'I can take care of myself,' she said. 'Only don't be too long. I'm hungry.'

'Of course. What a brute I am. We haven't eaten since yesterday, or was it the day before ? I won't be a minute,' said Evans and hurried into the *préfecture*. He saw the prefect's door ajar but did not want to speak with him or to make any report until all the fragments were in place and the *Presque Sans Souci* had arrived. As he passed, however, he had the feeling that the prefect had seen him and also, for some reason, wished to postpone the interview. That set him thinking as he hastened down the corridor and knocked on the doctor's door.

'Come in,' said Dr Toudoux. Then, seeing who it was, he came forward and embraced Evans heartily. 'Ah, what *Oleum crotali confluenti* ! Such divine snake oil as I have never seen before ! How did you hit on it, my boy ? And the *Argalli spicati Texarkanae*. A touch of genius, Monsieur Evans. Only one point still baffles me. How did the beggar die ? I've tried the stuff on ladybugs, white-footed mice, guinea-pigs and even, in the interest of science, fed a fairly stiff dose to the prefect's pugdog, Frou Frou, who messes up the corridors in a most disgusting way.'

The remains of Gring, respectably assembled, were covered with a sheet. Evans tapped them thoughtfully before he spoke. 'That's why I came here, doctor. To clear up that angle of the case. I wouldn't presume, of course, in view of your experience and reputation . . .'

'That's all right, my boy. Scientists can work together. It's when that miserable prefect sticks his nose in that I boil.'

'I understand,' Evans said. 'It chances that I had the doubtful pleasure of Gring's acquaintance and happened to know of his activities just before he died. Now ordinarily a Mickey Finn is harmless. As you have so aptly proved, it wouldn't kill a ladybug, much less a pugdog or white-footed mouse. However, take into consideration the fact that Gring, at the time he drank the

191

fatal *crème de cacao*, was in a state of physical and moral collapse. His *élan vital*, never much to brag of, was at its lowest ebb. You see, he had just lost, or thought he had lost, a fabulous fortune in oil. Petroleum.'

'Ah, gushers spouting and streaming into the air, black oil inundating the prairies. He had lost some of those, you say? Poor chap. Perhaps I've spoken of him harshly. I didn't think he was a man of affairs. I took him, frankly, for a pimp. The loss of oil, indeed, would explain his death from such an innocuous cause. I shall put that in the certificate. Extreme fatigue and financial ruin contributing factors. Ah! Science after all is the safest mistress to woo. No moth can corrupt, nor thieves break through and steal. Think of it. Losing gushers. I've only seen them in the movies, of course, but they must be dashed hard things to lose. But pardon me. I'm being selfish. I'm so elated at having solved, with your indispensable aid, the toughest problem that ever was stretched on this well-worn slab that I forgot your search for the multi-millionaire. Have you, too, been successful?'

'Between you and me, and the *corpus delicti*, I have found Hugo Weiss, the Russian colonel, the taxi, and all the kidnappers, only one of them dead.'

'Less work for me, thank God,' said Dr Toudoux.

'Not a word of this, not even to the prefect. . . .'

'Least of all to *that* heel. I was tempted to try a bit of the *crotali confluenti* on him and hope for the worst.'

'Good evening, then. I'll see you again to-morrow evening. Until that time, good-bye. Remember. Not a word.'

'I led my team to defeat in Rome . . .' Dr Toudoux began, but Evans was already on his way down the corridor. He was thinking hard again. When he had decided to pass up the prefect he had not suspected that the prefect was not anxious to meet him. What could that mean? Homer hesitated only a moment, then rapped sharply on the prefect's door. There was no response. Evans rapped again, more sharply. Almost hysterically, in fact. He was suddenly obsessed with a feeling that something had gone wrong, most frightfully wrong. Trying the door, he found it was locked. He put his shoulder to it, shoved, and the lock gave way so easily that Evans found himself lying across the prefectorial desk, surrounded by splinters and violet ink. The room, aside from that, was empty.

An urgent premonition drew him to the window. From there he could see clearly the bench on which Miriam had been sitting. The bench was empty, too. With an oath Evans tore the window open and vaulted through, running madly to the side-walk. There were only a few pedestrians walking idly, not an untoward sight or sound. But Miriam was nowhere to be found. Homer tried to calm himself. She might have gone inside a moment. . . . Girls do, even the handsomest of them, he reflected. With his heart beating furiously, he steeled himself to wait. He took out his watch and clenched it in his fist as the second hand crawled around. One minute. Two. Three. He could bear it no longer. He rushed back into the *préfecture,* almost upsetting Agent Schlumberger.

'Where is that boss of yours ? I must see him this instant,' Evans demanded. The prefect was nowhere to be found.

All the nonchalance had gone from Homer's manner. His face was white and set, his fingers clenched. No longer was he engaged in an impersonal problem which he could view in cold blood. Gone also was his former slight uneasiness about involving the sergeant in a clash with the higher-ups. As he rushed down the avenue de la Justice, the most casual passer-by could see that he would stop at nothing.

Not two minutes later, the dim doorway of the Hôtel des Hirondelles swallowed him up. Ben Sidi greeted him with his customary politeness.

'The peace of Allah descend on you and your . . but pardon me. I see you're in a hurry,' the tactful Arab began.

Desperate as he was, Homer Evans could not forget his manners.

'I thank you for your solicitude, O honourable Ben Sidi Abdel Mamout,' he said, salaaming. 'Our common foe, the police, have not laid hands on me as yet.'

'In my country they would be left on the desert for the jackals to feed upon,' said Ben Sidi with feeling. 'Twice this week they have raided my peaceful establishment.'

'Exactly,' Evans said. 'But have you seen my barber, the one who helped me look like a Believer?'

Soundlessly Ben Sidi beckoned to a bell hop, uttered a soft question in Arabic, and nodded:

'Knowing that Monsieur Henri, the barber, was in your confidence, O friend, I have kept him hidden.' And with that he led the way to a small secret chamber where, in fact, Abdel Krim and Vincent Ben Shee'an had been entertained when visiting Paris in the course of the Riff wars.

Henri was on the verge of collapse, and when he saw Homer, threw himself at his feet, in a manner of speaking, instead of jumping out of the window, as he had started to do when his door was suddenly opened.

'This Unbeliever is not at peace with the world,' Ben Sidi said, and Evans tried to calm the barber.

'Henri,' he said, 'if you wish to save yourself, tell me everything. I know that you were accustomed, from time to time when philandering, to give your wife some sleeping medicine...'

At that Henri made a dive for the open window and was restrained by Ben Sidi's ready hand.

'I think that was decent of Henri,' the Arab remarked, gravely. 'A little thought for others, an example of tenderness, is never amiss.'

Henri, by that time, had got hold of himself a little.

'I didn't mean any harm,' he said. 'I went to the Dingo to get one of those American Mickey Finns....'

Ben Sidi salaamed.

'I'd been thinking of you, Mr Evans,' Henri continued. 'I knew you were in trouble and that Gring was mixed up in it somehow. Never trust a man who shaves himself, Mr Evans.'

Homer promised, and the barber continued: 'I saw Gring on the Dôme *terrasse* and it came over me right away that you might like to see him, and that the boss here (pointing to Ben Sidi) might know where you were. On the way, a plain-clothes man who had seen me buy the Mickey took me to the station. There the prefect frisked me, asked me questions about the Mickey and I was so scared I told him all about it. He took it away....'

194

'That's all I need to know,' Evans said, and started abruptly to leave the hotel. However, it occurred to him that if the gangsters in question would strike at Miriam, how much more likely it would be that his own life would be blotted out before his mission was finished. The Arab scribe, Ben Abou, was adept at Infidel shorthand, and to him Homer dictated rapidly what he knew of the picture ring, enough to ruin everyone concerned. Four copies were to be made and delivered: one for the American ambassador, one for Hugo Weiss, one for the minister of justice, and the fourth for Evans himself.

That accomplished, Homer reached for the unlisted phone. Long ago it had become clear to him that the desperados he had pitted himself against would by no means let a barge load of incriminating evidence float down the river unchallenged.

Within ten minutes, he was in communication with Hjalmar at the Rendez-vous des Imprévoyants. Rapidly Homer outlined the situation, then asked Jansen at what point he thought the attack would be made.

'At Charenton,' Hjalmar said promptly.

'Exactly what I thought,' Evans said. 'The river is very tricky just above the town and there is frequent blasting in the nearby quarries. Also there are numerous roads leading in and out, like spokes of a wheel. There are crowded factory areas, and woods with solitary houses. Guard the boats every minute of the night, don't take any chances with the prisoners, and, above all, stay sober, you and Jackson. If you are attacked, I'll be on hand, but out of sight at first. So long.'

Notwithstanding Homer's fearful anxiety, he had to keep a firm grip on himself and think about the fragments. Thus it was that, instead of proceeding at once to Paty de Pussy's studio, he sought out Dr Hyacinthe Toudoux.

'Dr Toudoux,' he said, 'you have on record and on file all confiscated drugs, liquids, powders, or pills found on suspects, have you not?'

'But certainly, Mr Evans,' he said.

'Two days ago a man named Henri Duplessis was arrested in a raid of the Hotel des Hirondelles,' Evans began.

'Just a minute. Duplessis. I'll look under " D ".' He

rummaged in the files, first calmly then with growing impatience, until he was stripping out folders like a bear tearing bark from a tree. 'That's strange,' he said. 'No record.'

'I thought so,' Evans said, grimly. 'There was taken from that man a small phial containing a Mickey Finn.'

'Ah, a clue. The fatal Mickey Finn.'

'That phial should have been turned over to you. It was not. I want you to come with me,' Evans said, and led the way to the prefect's office. It was closed and locked again, but the door had not been repaired. Once more Evans put his shoulder to it and shoved, and again the door gave way. Without consulting further his astonished companion, Homer started pulling out the drawers of the prefect's desk.

'As I expected,' he said, when the bottom drawer was opened. In it was a small phial.

'But it's full,' the doctor said. 'That can't be the one.'

'One moment, doctor. Let's go back to the laboratory,' said Evans. In the laboratory he took off his coat, rolled up his sleeves, and borrowed a white apron. With unerring precision he reached for test tubes and beakers and lighted the Bunsen burner. He poured a few drops of the phial's contents into an empty test tube, added an acid, and nothing happened. Dr Toudoux watched him, fascinated. The blue litmus paper did not turn pink in the mysterious liquid, neither did the same chemicals that caused the *Oleum crotali confluenti* to cloud, bubble and clear again produce orthodox results. Evans sniffed, then grunted and smiled.

'I should have thought of that,' he said. 'It's just plain *Oleum machinae scribendi*, or typewriter oil.'

'*Merde alors,*' snorted Hyacinthe Toudoux. But Evans was pulling off his apron with an air of satisfaction.

'You don't mind if I keep the phial and its contents. I'll return it for the files after it has served its purpose,' Evans said.

'Whatever you wish. This case becomes more baffling every hour,' the doctor said. Evans did not hear. He was already streaking through empty offices, in the hope of reaching the side entrance without being observed and trailed.

'*Enfin,* my friends Abel and Dodo ! We are about to have

196

our long-deferred interview. I promised, once, to wring you dry of information like a lemon cast from the squeezer. I shall try to do better than that. And as for that hypocrite, Paty de Pussy. . . . Here. Taxi,' he said, and gave the address in the avenue Pierre Premier de Serbie. Feverishly he pressed the button and the grilled door swung open.

'Excuse me, sir. But whom did you wish to see?' asked the *concierge* with deep respect.

'M. Paty de Pussy,' Evans replied.

'I regret that M. Paty de Pussy is not at home. I saw him leave between four and six o'clock and he has not yet returned,' the *concierge* said.

'Between four and six,' Evans repeated, with evident disappointment. 'You couldn't fix the hour of departure a little more definitely, madame?' he asked, fingering suggestively a fifty-franc note.

'I should say about five-fifteen,' said the *concierge*, accepting the gratuity with a smile.

'I'll go up anyway and wait. He should be back soon, I think,' Evans said.

'As you wish,' the *concierge* said.

Evans entered the elevator, which protested his weight with a series of squeaks and groans. Having had long experience with French elevators, he did not push the button for the top floor but for the floor just below. The elevator got away to a rumbling start, and clanked like the clapper of a broken bell. At each floor it slowed down, hesitated, clicked, then gathered its strength to continue. Evans glanced at his watch impatiently. 'Five-fifteen,' he murmured. 'He's been gone a good four hours.'

A moderate pull at the bell cord evoked no response from Paty de Pussy's apartment, neither did a peremptory jerk. The same lack of success followed a light tap on the panel and a series of staccato knocks. 'The servant not at home. That's strange,' Evans said, and started searching the stair carpet for hairpins. Finding one just above the fifth floor he returned and picked the lock with ease. Very cautiously he turned the knob, pushed open the door a fraction of an inch at a time, and entered without turning on a light. He located the switch, however, in case of future need, and also observed that the chandelier was in the centre of the ceiling of the spacious salon. As his eyes grew accustomed to the semi-darkness he gave a gasp and rushed back to the light switch, drawing his automatic. The room was not exactly flooded with light when he turned the switch. Paty de Pussy was too economical for that. But of the forty-odd bulbs in the antique chandelier, approximately eight of them flickered into dim red lines of wire which shed enough illumination to disclose the bodies of two men, one short and one tall, hanging limply, their heads awry, from the chandeliers. Below them, on the polished hard-wood floor were two hats, one flat-crowned derby and a felt of assignation green. There was also a pool of amber liquid two millimetres in depth and between two and three square feet in area.

From where he stood at the light switch, Evans could see that the men were dead, and that they were, respectively, Abel Heiss and Dodo Lourde. He bit his lips with mortification. 'I've blundered again,' he said. 'I should have come here first. If this keeps up, there'll not be a shred of evidence left, no witnesses, nothing.'

He did not approach the bodies, for a strong premonition made him feel that he was not alone in the apartment. Switching off the lights again, he proceeded along the wall, past the miniature fireplace, a bust of Louis XV by Houdon, and an empty easel.

'Ugh!' An involuntary exclamation of horror escaped him. His hand had touched something soft and wet. Risking discovery, he switched on the lights again to find that his hand was covered with alizarin crimson and *terre verte*. He seized the palette he had stumbled on and began murmuring.

'By God, it's the Greco palette,' he said to himself. 'Not a false colour, not a single tone off-key.' He laid the palette aside carefully, hoping he had not obliterated the fingerprints of Paty de Pussy.

Leaving the salon, Evans turned the knob of a small room in which he found the curtains reinforced with dark blotting paper to shut out all the light. A red lamp was glowing from the ceiling, however.

198

Strange,' Evans grunted. 'A developing room.' His attention was diverted by a roll of canvas in the corner. Instantly, his heart in his mouth, he turned the main light switch and picked up the canvas reverently. 'You mysterious wonderful fabric,' he gasped. 'To think that Greco's hands have lifted you, that his eyes, which saw as none others, have rested upon you. At least, if all my friends and witnesses die because of my laxity, I shall rescue what remains of you from further ignoble usage.'

'Blub,' said a figure Evans in his excitement had not observed. It was that of a man in his shirt-sleeves, leaning over a shallow soapstone tub, his feet scarcely touching the floor, his face within an inch of the amber surface of some liquid corresponding to that on the floor beneath the bodies of Abel and Dodo. Tearing himself away from the precious Greco canvas, Evans loosened the bonds from the man's hands which had been tied behind him, lifted him from the edge of the tub and jerked the gag from his mouth.

'Thank you kindly, sir,' said the butler. 'I heard your ring but, as you can see. . . .'

'Of course. Quite understandable. You are . . .'

'Adolphe.'

'And your master?'

'He was called away urgently, sir. Won't you step into the salon?' Adolphe led the way, but his air of aplomb deserted him as he saw the ghastly tableau that awaited him. He would have rushed to the centre of the room to sop up the amber liquid had not Evans restrained him.

'Perhaps you can explain?' Evans asked, severely.

'Before God, sir, I know nothing about it. These men practically forced an entrance here. They have, or had, some hold on my master. Not only did they order him to paint, but they took possession of his developing room and kept me running back and forth with salami and beer. Salami, sir. I give you my word. Can you imagine, in a country where *charcuterie* has been raised to the level of the fine arts . . . guzzling greasy salami and thin bottled beer . . . ?'

'I understand your feelings, but go on,' Evans said.

'The master's getting on in years. He shouldn't be driven so.

199

After hours of work, I was given six paintings to dry with the artificial dryer. . . .'

'Ah, an artificial dryer,' Evans said.

'Then I packed them carefully, addressed them to some museums in North America. Just after the expressman had left with them, there was a call for M. Paty de Pussy. . . . I'm not sure but I think it was from M. Haute Costa de Bellevieu. Anyway, it was urgent and my master left, without his muffler and umbrella. That was between half-past four and half-past five. I saw him to the door and watched him descend the stairs. The elevator does not go down with passengers. No sooner had he disappeared than I was seized by some masked men, three of them at least, gagged, bound and thrown into a laundry basket.'

'A la Falstaff,' Evans said.

'Falstaff got in voluntarily. There's a difference, sir.'

'I stand corrected,' said Evans. 'Where, in the meantime, were Messrs Heiss and Lourde ?'

'In the developing room, sir. I couldn't hear what happened, but half an hour later one of the masked men opened the lid of the laundry basket, carried me to the developing room, which was then empty, and tried to shove my face into the developer. Another man said : " Come on. He's only the butler. He didn't see nothing." " Better leave no loose ends," said the man who had me, and he shoved my head down again. Another man who seemed to be the leader said : " Come on. We got work to do ", and I was left as you found me. Another inch and I would have drowned.'

'Adolphe,' Evans said, 'I'm going to trust you. I believe every word you have said. I want you to take a taxi at once to this address.' He scribbled an address on some drawing paper. 'Take this to Sergeant Frémont, whom you'll find there, and bring him back here with all possible speed. Tell him, though, by no means to notify headquarters until he talks with me. Is that clear ?'

'God, sir ! You don't know what it means to be sent on an errand that doesn't involve salami. I shall carry out your orders faithfully. But, sir. Do have a thought for my master. He owes me a lot of money, of which there's no record. I shouldn't want anything to happen to him,' Adolphe said.

'My good man,' said Evans, 'if anything happens to your master, I shall be in a worse fix than you are. Now be on your way.'

'Very good, sir,' said Adolphe, and reached for his hat.

Evans opened his cigarette case and took out a cigarette. He had no matches. There were none in the studio, since the Paty de Pussys suffered with asthma and had not smoked for three generations. In the kitchen he found a few sulphur matches and coughed while waiting for the acrid fumes to pass. 'Now for a look round,' he said. 'I want to be posted when the sergeant comes in.'

He approached the hanging bodies of the picture dealers with smouldering regret. 'How ironic,' he muttered. 'This precious pair have never been wanted for any honest purpose before, and here they are, as dead as El Greco or François Ier, or Abraham, Isaac, and Jacob, for that matter. Death, the great commoner. The disher-out of equal shares. They are dead, all right, but what a clumsy job. First, the masked men try to drown them in developer, find it too slow, then lug them into the salon and hang them with picture wire. No fingerprints on picture wire. Well. They died between five and six, no doubt about that. And they were murdered by unknown persons wearing masks. Let's see what the developing room has to disclose.'

In his first cursory examination of the developing room Evans had not noticed the huge frame which had been used for making prints. It was brand new and, moreover, corresponded in size to the candlelight Grecos. A bottle marked 'Sensitizer 489' was half empty. In a flash, the method of turning out Grecos while you wait became clear to Evans. The canvas was sensitized, the natural-size photograph printed on it, leaving only the colouring for the artist to perform by hand. Homer was sniffing the sensitizer and looking forward to an interesting day in the laboratory, once Miriam had been rescued and the chief assassin brought to justice, when the door burst open and Sergeant Frémont entered.

'Heiss and Lourde,' exclaimed the sergeant, aghast, his gaze riveted on the two lifeless bodies, which had been set lightly a-swing by the draught from the open door. Evans steadied them carefully, a handkerchief wrapped around his hand.

Miss Leonard has been kidnapped, whisked away from a bench in front of the *préfecture* while I was spending a moment with Dr Toudoux. We've got to find her, and find her quickly. ... These unfortunate cats'-paws may as well stay where they are. Adolphe will guard them. Come on,' Evans said, catching the astonished sergeant by the sleeve.

CHAPTER 24

Foul Play in an Old Château

'HE didn't say, " Don't take a drink ". He said, " Stay sober ".
That's different,' Hjalmar said.

'O.K. Two more brandies,' yelled Jackson.

'Can't I serve 'em just this once, Ma ?' begged Gaby, who
stood beside her perspiring parent behind the bar aboard the
Presque Sans Souci. At Hjalmar's request, the contents of the
bar and restaurant had been transferred aboard the grey barge;
the prisoners, evidence, artillery, ammunition, and the extra
police guards from Chatillon had been brought on board also.
Quarters had been allotted to everyone, the evidence had been
locked in a large locker which was within reach of Hjalmar's
arm. The prisoners and the corpse were forward, seated on the
bare deck from which the hay had been swept so the quick could
smoke without setting fire to the ship. The tug was moored to
the bow, the launch to the stern. All were in midstream.

'If anybody thinks he can get aboard us now, he's crazy,'
Hjalmar said. He was convinced that the danger point was near
Charenton.

Sosthène and his wife were happy, because of the money that
was pouring in. They had made in the first two hours aboard the
Presque Sans Souci more money than in the previous six
months on shore. Prosperity did a lot toward thawing Mme
Sosthène, so she said to her daughter:

'Well. Drat you. I suppose you'll outwit me sooner or later.'

'Goody,' said Gaby, happily, and started aft with the tray.

Forward the gangsters were bellowing and singing sentimen-
tal songs so loudly that the birds in the surrounding woods
trembled fearfully in their nests among the branches of the trees.

'As long as we keep going I don't see how anyone can board
us. We've got guns. We have all the advantage. If anyone
shows up and says he's a customs officer we'll scuttle his damn
dory. This is official business. We've got prisoners, evidence, and

203

a stiff. I'm skipper and by God what I say goes. Not one man living comes aboard this ship, unless he is Homer Evans or Sergeant Frémont. And let me tell you, Tom, if any harm comes to that western kid, I'll kill every thug we've got for a starter. I'll strangle 'em with my hands and then start looking for the others.'

'I'm with you. But she's smart. I think she'll take care of herself.'

'Homer's worried,' said Hjalmar. 'We can't let old Homer down.'

'By no means,' Jackson said.

'Come around when you're in Paris.' Hjalmar was saying to Gaby. 'I'll paint your picture, before and after. . . .'

'If I can get away from Ma. She's hard, but she's softening up a little,' said Gaby, and tripped back to the bar. Catching sight of her, the prisoners roared and howled bawdily, to which Gaby replied with a contemptuous little gesture she had gleaned from an old copy of *La Vie Parisienne* she had found beneath her father's pillow. In short, aboard the *Presque Sans Souci* there was more lusty cheer than might have been expected from a company of men, some of whom were in chains and awaiting the dungeon, others who were being stalked and hunted by the most relentless criminals outside prison bars. Tom Jackson, sipping his cognac, must have had some such thought, for he exclaimed:

'I often wonder what the vintners buy
One-half so precious as the stuff they sell.'

'Moderation's the word,' Hjalmar answered. 'If I seem to be getting drunk, don't hesitate to tell me. We've got to get back Miriam and those 250,000 francs.'

'I'll swatch you like rat before scat-hole,' Jackson said, and wiped the pungent steam from his glasses, the better to perform the vigil.

Below them and around them flowed the black waters of the Seine, and overhead were the silently shifting constellations, Orion; the bear; the dippers, large and small; and winking

204

benevolently, as if it had the *Presque Sans Souci* under its special protection, shone that guide to mariners and travellers, that distant and cold star with its five encircling suns—Polaris. Polaris, star of the north, faithful beacon, giver of direction. In the dewy woods the birds and small animals had grown accustomed to the sound of roistering and were getting in some of their soundest sleep before dawn.

Homer Evans, with Sergeant Frémont, in the office of the minister of justice, could not see the foregoing scene in detail, but his imagination, as usual, did not play him false. For one fleeting second he wondered if Hjalmar was staying sober. Then he dismissed the doubt as unworthy of his husky Norwegian friend. Hjalmar would be fit for duty, Evans was sure of that. At the time that was about the only thing Homer could be sure of.

'Sergeant,' he said, 'we must use our brains. For what they are worth we must exploit them. Our friend you have aptly re-christened Gonzo, together with Jackson, or Oklahoma Tom, are in midstream aboard the barge awaiting the dawn. If Gonzo is able to pilot the tug, the launch and the *Presque Sans Souci* with their tell-tale cargoes to the berth along the Seine near the Pont Royal, all the plotting and murdering our enemy has done will go for naught. In the boulevard Arago, a head will fall. That's the way our journalists put it.'

'The guillotine. Upon my word, I'll get up early that morning and watch the performance ... unless, of course, Hydrangea dissuades me. Her heart beats ever for the doomed, the disinherited, the unfortunate. ... Anyway, the *Presque Sans Souci* must get through safely. It's a good idea, transporting the prisoners and evidence by water. I'd hate to chance it by land,' the sergeant said.

'How is it possible to attack an armed barge? What methods would occur to our foe? What means would he have for carrying them out? He can't make a show of force openly. There'd be a riot call. Hjalmar will stop at no one's command except yours or mine. Twenty, even forty men couldn't board her, with him at the head of the ladder, and sheltered from gun fire. Men in boats alongside might toss in incendiary grenades, but

205

before they got half near enough, Gonzo's machine gun would riddle their dories. No. That won't do. . . . They haven't time, I think, to sink a hidden obstruction in the channel. They can't stand off a few miles and use artillery. Charenton is a crowded industrial suburb. A trial shot, to find the range, would cause havoc on either shore. What remains ?' Evans asked.

'My head aches,' said the sergeant miserably. 'Ought we not to bargain, if our enemies are as powerful as you suggest ? Why not drop the case, in return for Mlle Montana ?'

'Another aspirin, sergeant. It'll buck you up no end.'

For a while Evans gazed at the maps he had had sent over from the ministry of war. Suddenly he slapped the desk and half rose, so abruptly that Frémont swallowed ten grains of aspirin without water or wine to wash them down.

'I have it. Look at this. Contact mines. They manufacture contact mines in that little factory. Naturally it's in a somewhat secluded spot. The mines are transported to the sea by means of the river. The sight of a few of them, being loaded, unloaded, or transported would cause no alarm.'

'I can't believe,' said the sergeant, 'that they would dare blow up a barge in the Seine.'

'They could make it appear like an accident. You know. Have a commission appointed, an investigation by some minister who wants a few favours done. Time passes. Public interest dies out. Nothing happens.'

'Too often that's what takes place,' the sergeant said.

Evans grabbed the sergeant's hat and placed it on the latter's head, then reached for his own. 'On our way. . . .' He hesitated. 'But wait. One more glimpse of the maps. Is there, for instance, a country estate near the factory, some wooded acres walled in and guarded and owned by a prominent Royalist ? . . . Ah ! Here ! By God ! Of course !'

He pointed. The sergeant groaned.

'Impossible,' the sergeant said, when he read the name of the proprietor.

'Nothing surer,' said Evans curtly.

The sergeant threw away the rest of the aspirin. 'Farewell, career ! Farewell, monthly pay cheque ! Adieu, my ebony goddess, Hydrangea ! You were loved and lost by a little man who dared aim too high, who imagined, in his folly. . . .'

'Remember what I promised you. Promotion,' Evans said. 'You seem to forget that we, too, can play politics, that we can pull wires with the best of them.'

The woe on the sergeant's face was so eloquent Evans could not laugh at his friend. 'Farewell, farewell ! The moth of petty-officialdom is winging toward the flame of high politics ! Not an ash will remain. Just a wisp of smoke. Ah, Hydrangea ! You who are gazing this moment at the sea, counting the waves as they recede from between us. Will you be charitable, or merely sore ? Should I console myself with the old phrase of those about to die : "I could not love you, dear, so much, loved I not honour more". Ah, honour ! Honour cloaked in disgrace and dismissal. Honour without the monthly pay ! Gone are the dreams of bliss, of fragrant moments insured by the Fine Michael or Mickey Finn. I pit my automatic against a factory full of high explosives. I follow a friend, a dreamer who has no job to lose and whose monthly money comes from God knows where. Come, friend ! Let us haste to our destruction. I'll remonstrate no more.'

'Promotion with glory,' Evans repeated, and led the way.

Before taking the driver's seat in Frémont's official car, Homer turned off the siren. There were, he knew, odds and ends still dangling. There was the Chatillon racer, parked illegally in front of Heiss and Lourde's; the car from the *préfecture* standing near the Hôtel des Hirondelles; the multi-millionaire, the Russian colonel and the ambassador in their cups and even buckets, the pitiful Dinde who was as good as dead, Evans thought. And, of course, the corpses of Abel and Dodo suspended by picture wire from Paty de Pussy's chandelier. Furthermore, there was Paty de Pussy and his host, Haute Costa de Bellevieu. The missing prefect could not be ignored, or the phial of *Oleum machinae scribendi*. Lastly, and of more importance than all the rest, there was Miriam, who had followed him so faithfully and more than once had saved him from disaster.

'I'm glad you're going to drive,' the sergeant said. 'That raises the chances of an accident.'

'We must stop for a sandwich, some coffee, and must obtain two pairs of heavy driving gloves,' Evans said.

'Don't mention food to me,' the sergeant said. 'I have eaten chicken and noodle soup, stuffed fish, roast goose with parsnips, potato cakes, boiled beef with horseradish, *blini, apfel strudel,* frosted cake. . . . I can't go on. In all my career I have never seen such appetites as those of Hugo Weiss and Lvov Kvek. The vodka, brandy, wine. . . .'

'All right. You get the gloves while I eat,' said Evans, pulling up at the Chicago Inn. Swiftly he ate a club sandwich, some coffee and apple pie and had an armful of provisions wrapped up to take with him in the car. Frémont reappeared with the heavy gloves, still muttering and shaking his head. They streaked along the boulevards, through the suburbs and entered Charenton by a side road. In a dark lane, they ran the car off the road and hid in in a clump of trees. Evans drew on the gloves and motioned to the sergeant to do likewise. Rapidly they set out on foot until they were within a hundred yards of a high stone wall, covered with ivy and topped with jagged glass set in concrete.

'Stop,' whispered Evans. 'We must see how well the place is guarded.'

The step of a sentry, in the shadow of the wall, warned them that it was guarded well. Sentries were all around, posted not more than fifty metres apart. Evans asked the sergeant to remain motionless where he was. He himself crawled forward inch by inch, pausing only once to place a smooth stone the size of his fist inside a leather driving glove. The sentry, unsuspecting, was whistling '*Oh, les fraises et les framboises,*' but at the exact second the impromptu weapon descended and the sentry ceased to whistle, Homer took up the tune in exactly the key.

Sergeant Frémont sighed admiringly. 'Is it possible that the young man can save me after all ? That was quick sure thinking. He is not a windbag by any means. Ah, Hydrangea ! Dark as this night. . . .'

Meanwhile Evans had blended his own silhouette with that of the unconscious sentry, and by moving the fellow a yard or

208

two was able to hang him by the coat collar to the overhanging branch of the tree.

'Won't you ever let up on that tune about the strawberries?' called the next sentry to the northward, impatiently.

'As you wish,' Evans said, in a husky voice.

'We'll all catch cold,' said the conscious sentry. 'These woods are bristling with draughts and dampness.'

Evans had dropped to the ground and was crawling in the other sentry's direction. Within five minutes, the latter too was unconscious and was suspended from a limb, not in such a way as to suffocate him but merely to make it appear from a short distance that he was erect and on the job.

'All clear,' whispered Evans to Frémont. 'Now for the wall, and be quick. No telling how much time we have.'

With his foot on the sturdy sergeant's shoulder, Evans was able to reach the top of the wall. The heavy gloves protected his hands from the jagged points of glass. On the top he crouched and pulled the sergeant up after him. Together they dropped to the ground, inside.

A low growl sounded and in an instant a pair of huge dogs were upon them, but Evans had a way with dogs. No sooner did they feel the touch of his hand than their tails began to wag. He fed them a club sandwich which they ate with evident relish and came back for more. It is an erroneous belief of the French aristocracy and others that watch-dogs should be half starved.

The house, or château, a massive structure, looked like a huge Swiss cuckoo clock in the darkness. One window was alight in the rear. On approaching nearer, however, Evans saw that the front and side windows were curtained heavily. After a rapid survey of the premises, and having learned that there were four sentries, two at the main gate, and two along the driveway, Evans made for a small shack which must have been intended for gardener's tools. While the dogs watched with friendly curiosity, Evans picked the lock, opened the door noiselessly and pointed.

The sergeant's hair bristled and his eyes almost popped from their sockets. Side by side, half obscured by gunnysacks, were

209

four contact mines. Evans was on his knees, studying the mechanism. He found a screwdriver, loosened a number of screws, drew off an ugly-looking screw cap and peered inside. There was the deadly trinitrotoluol, enough to destroy the entire estate. The sergeant gasped when Evans reached in and drew out the frightful load, wrapping it in a gunnysack.

'Bring me dirt or sand,' he whispered.

In an empty sack the sergeant packed some sand from a nearby sandpile and Evans placed a quantity of it in the shell of the mine. Within ten minutes, all four mines had been rendered harmless and the explosives had been buried in the sandpile for future reference.

'Now for Miriam,' Evans said softly. 'She must be in that house.'

'Breaking and entering,' wailed the sergeant. 'No warrant. No authority. Ah, Americans.' Nevertheless he followed with alacrity.

'These people never open a window,' Evans said. 'We'll have to break a pane of glass. Too bad we've none of that flypaper.' The words had not left his lips before there was a hideous hue and cry. The outside sentries had discovered their unconscious companions, the dogs started barking and running toward the gate, the front door of the house flew open and three masked men, one tall and much older than the others, hurried out to find out what was wrong. All were armed with automatics.

'Search the grounds! Turn on the searchlights,' ordered the leader curtly. 'And bring in those sentries. They must have seen and heard something.'

Instantly Evans made his decision. The house was unguarded for the moment, the focus of attention was outside. He shoved against a side windowpane, in the shadow of a vine, and was lucky once more. The fragments fell on a thick Aubusson carpet and made little noise, not enough to attract attention. Inside the house, he made at once for the stairway and ran upstairs, one flight, two flights, softly carpeted. Frémont was behind him, aghast but willing to carry on. Footsteps in the corridor told Evans that the upper rooms, in the attic, were guarded. As I thought, he said to himself. That's where Miriam is held prisoner. There was only one thing to be done. Fitting his silencer carefully to the muzzle of his automatic he crept up to the head of the stairway. The sentry's back was turned. Homer aimed carefully, meticulously, in fact, and fired. Rushing forward on tiptoes he caught the man's body before he fell. As he had planned, Evans had grazed the sentry's scalp, enough to stun him but not deep enough to cause his death. After all, he thought, I may as well save work for Dr Hyacinthe Toudoux. The centre room that had been so carefully guarded was locked and bolted, and no keys were in the guard's pockets. The silencer still on his gun, Homer shot away both hinges and flung himself inside. To his surprise and horror he found, not Miriam, but Paty de Pussy, handcuffed to a heavy oak chair.

'Where is Miss Leonard?' Evans demanded. 'I know exactly what part you played in this miserable affair. I have the canvas, the palette, the sensitizer 489, the bodies of Heiss and Lourde....'

'The bodies?' repeated the old man, feebly. 'The bodies.' His limbs began to tremble and shake.

'You didn't kill them. I know that, too,' Evans said. 'I want just one thing from you, the whereabouts of Miss Leonard, and if that information is not forthcoming before I count ten I will drop you out of that window head downward.'

Paty de Pussy drew himself up as nearly erect as he could and looked Evans squarely in the eye.

'I do not know Miss Leonard, or where she is,' he said.

'How long have you been here?'

'About six hours, I suppose.'

'You were called on the phone by Haute Costa de Bellevieu?'

'The moment I get free, I shall send my seconds to him with a challenge...'

'At daylight, in the Bois, I suppose,' said Evans.

'The Paty de Pussys have never submitted to such indignities,' the old man said.

Outside the house, all was confusion. A search was in progress and had netted the searchers no results. Through a slit in the draperies, Sergeant Frémont was watching the tool house and was rewarded by seeing the tall masked leader go there quickly, unobserved by the others, take a rapid look inside, and hurry away. Then the sergeant thought he heard a noise in the room next to the one in which Evans was talking with Paty de Pussy. The door was also locked, but Frémont was able to break it down with his shoulder. Evans was at his side as the panels crashed.

'Miriam,' he cried, involuntarily, and instead of seeing Miriam he found himself looking down at the prefect of police, bound hand and foot, gagged and chained to the window casing.

Homer tore the gag from the prefect's mouth and held the cool muzzle of his automatic against the prone official's forehead.

'Just one bit of information. Where is Miriam Leonard? I'll say " Liberté, Égalité, Fraternité", while you're deciding, then pull the trigger. "Liberté, Éga – " '

'Don't shoot. I'll tell you all I can,' the prefect said. Sergeant Frémont was shaking in a manner that put even Paty de Pussy to shame. Good-bye to glory, to groceries and dry goods forever, he was thinking, while Evans prodded his chief with the automatic.

'It wasn't my fault . . .'

'I know all about that. Where is she?'

'The car that brought me here has gone back to fetch her,' the prefect said.

'She'll be here any minute, then?'

'Within half an hour, say between half and three quarters, if there are no flat tyres,' said the prefect.

'Come on,' Evans cried, leaving the old painter and the prefect as they were, and the guard unconscious on the floor.

CHAPTER 25

A Truck-load of Contact Mines

WHEN Aurora, Goddess of the Morning, got around to touching with her rosy fingers the roof of the Rendez-vous des Imprévoyants, the surrounding woods, the topmost spars of the *Presque Sans Souci* and the distant bends of the Seine she turned in a very creditable performance. As a dawn, *per se*, the one that greeted Hjalmar's watchful eyes had nothing to be ashamed of in comparison with the famous dawns of history. The colours were at first restrained, then a bit blatant, and in time had the good taste to moderate themselves so as not to distract the sober citizens who had work to do. The sound effects were noteworthy, for the birds, having been put on their mettle by the volume and cacophony of the prisoners' chorus the night before, outdid themselves.

'Pipe down, you feathered buggers,' roared Hjalmar before he tried to awaken all hands. 'I can't tell whether you're for us or against us.'

Forward, the corpse and the prisoners were motionless, the former propped against a crate of canned peaches, the latter snoring and cursing in their heavy drunken slumber.

The *Presque Sans Souci* had an engine of its own, a rusty one and not too powerful, but good enough for cruising downstream. With the disabled tug and the launch in tow, the huge ungainly barge reached that stage described too cautiously by the New England poet:

> 'She *seems* to feel
> A thrill of life along her keel.'

By noon, Mme Sosthène had so much money in pitchers and buckets behind the bar that her easy-going husband was for retiring from business and buying some little farm that struck their fancy along the way. Madame, however, was all for sticking it out to the end of the voyage, in order that Gaby might have a magnificent *dot*.

213

In distant Charenton, Homer Evans and Sergeant Frémont were streaking it down the stairs of the ominous house in the forest, across an Aubusson carpet, and out through a broken window pane. Risking discovery by the masked men and the guards who were assembled at the main gate for detailed instructions, they raced to the rear wall, and because of their heavy gloves, were able to vault it uninjured.

'We must intercept the car at a safe distance from here,' Evans said. Swiftly he formulated a plan. In coming to the estate, they had followed a long deserted lane before turning into the private roadway. Homer remembered a sharp 'S' curve, where the trees were thick on each side. They ieaped into the car they had hidden, and had just got back on the road when the sound of another motor was heard faintly and was evidently approaching the private drive. Had Evans' practised ear not detected at once that the vehicle was a heavy truck, he might have jumped at a false conclusion. Of course, it was possible, he thought, that the conspirators might have transported Miriam in a truck, after having nailed her into a packing case. More likely, it seemed, the truck was intended for the transportation of the now innocuous contact mines. He communicated this quickly to Sergeant Frémont.

'The annoying feature is, that the truck blocks our way,' Frémont said. 'It wouldn't do to meet it. We'll have to back off the roadway again.'

This they did and were well concealed when a large truck, looking larger in the thin light of dawn, rolled past. The moment it had entered the service gate, Evans and the sergeant were off again. They reached the 'S' curve, concealed the roadster, and clutching their automatics, sat down on the running board to wait. Instead of hearing the purr of a motor, as they had hoped, they were startled by the sound of footsteps. Automatics in hand, they lay prone on the damp ground, fingers grimly on the triggers. Evans was the first to speak. With difficulty he restrained himself from laughing aloud, for plodding wearily along the road, ragged and forlorn, was Melchisedek Knockwoode. His energy was almost spent. His face was the picture of woe.

214

Knowing that the terrified chauffeur would bolt at the slightest sound, Evans let him pass, then slipped up behind him, and got hold of his belt.

'Melchisedek,' he said.

Melchisedek turned the colour of half-cooked liver, his eyes rolled, he frothed at the mouth, his limbs began to jerk and tremble. When he saw the sergeant standing nearby, he collapsed and had to be revived with brandy and the remaining sandwiches. Slowly he grasped that he was among friends, that his sins had been forgiven; in fact, that he was about to be rewarded. Frémont, whose thoughts of Hydrangea had been stirred anew, was offering to make him his official chauffeur. Evans promised him a complete British officer's outfit, with medals, decorations and swagger stick, to use along the boulevards on his days off. Melchisedek was not a physical coward. Indeed he had proved that beyond the least doubt in the Argonne and the lowest dives around Memphis and Brest. It was an atavistic dread of irate authority, a truly Biblical awe of the law and tablets, that had driven him from Paris and his taxi. He bucked up, also, when told that Hydrangea was on her way to Paris, for he longed for news from Harlem and the sight of a good American coloured face and figure.

As soon as Melchisedek was calm, Evans told him briefly that Miss Leonard had been kidnapped and was being taken to a lonely château in a car that would pass any minute. It was agreed that Melchisedek should take the sergeant's roadster to the concealed portion of the 'S' curve, and meet the oncoming car in an awkward place. Frémont and Evans would appear suddenly, one from each side of the lane, get the drop on the kidnappers, and take over, if possible, without gunfire.

'Here they come,' Homer said, as the sound of an engine reached their ears. Silently, each man took his station. The kidnapper's car was a limousine, and not of a recent model. 'God,' Evans said to himself, 'it weighs four tons. If . . .'

The bulky limousine, moving at a reckless rate, had too much momentum for its squealing brakes and crashed into the front of the roadster. Melchisedek slid from the seat to the floor in a shower of broken glass, saved from going through the wind-

215

shield only by his instinctive grip on the steering wheel. The road was blocked, however, and in an instant Frémont was on one running board and had covered the driver while Evans boarded the other side and threw open the door.

Two men were sitting with Miriam between them.

'Hands up, and be quick,' Evans ordered. Then as they obeyed, he said gruffly to Miriam: 'You gave me the fright of my life.'

Her limbs were stiff, from sitting in a cramped position so long, but she was unhurt and stepped from the limousine to the ground.

'I knew you'd find me,' she said. 'Only . . . I hope it hasn't prevented you from doing what you wanted to.'

'Go to the sergeant's wrecked car, see if the coloured man at the wheel is badly hurt, and get yourself an automatic. There's one under the driver's cushion and it's loaded. Then come back here. We must take no chances,' Evans said. 'And don't worry about the case in general. I'm glad you'll be in at the finish, and it's coming soon.'

Frémont was still covering the chauffeur, but he was worried about the truck. It would be quickly loaded and would return. He had seen Evans remove the explosives, and still he was decidedly nervous about the prospect of a collision on the sharp 'S' curve. Also, he was anxious about Melchisedek, for even if the latter had survived the first smash-up, he might succumb if the light roadster were telescoped from behind by a truckload of contact mines.

In a moment, Miriam had lifted the unconscious Negro from the floor of the roadster, had staunched a flow of blood from a cut on his cheek and stretched him out in a shady spot near the roadway. She found the automatic and, with it in her hand, returned to Evans' side.

'It's good to have your help again. I've been lost without you,' he said, ashamed of his first abrupt greeting.

'To hear you say that, I'd be kidnapped twice a day,' she murmured, and the kidnappers, true Frenchmen, smiled wistfully, their hands still in the air.

'The truck, *nom de Dieu*. The truck,' Sergeant Frémont said,

216

from his perch on the opposite running board. 'I think I can hear it now.'

'Quick,' Evans said. 'Make the chauffeur get out and precede you to that grove. Miriam, go with them and tie him up.' To the pair in the rear seat he said, 'Get out on this side, one after the other, and walk straight toward that clump of birches. One false move, and I'll shoot.'

Everyone obeyed, and none too soon. There was the chugging of the heavy truck, a shriek of brake bands, loud curses, and the truck piled up on the two empty cars, driving what was left of the roadster half-way through the limousine. Miriam, once again, was equal to the occasion. Appearing casually on the road where the disgruntled truck driver was pacing up and down, she said:

'Good morning. Don't feel badly, monsieur. My car was busted, anyhow.'

'I told the damn fools at the château that they should send a car ahead of me,' he said. 'You'd think I was carrying gumdrops the way those guys act.'

'What are you carrying?' Evans asked, stepping from the thicket, and showing the driver his credentials.

'I knew there was something fishy about this job,' the driver said. 'One of the guys from the château asked me if I'd do a job of hauling, said the count was an expert on high explosives. Something about the bloody national defence. There's usually something fishy when guys get to talking about that.'

Evans introduced Sergeant Frémont, who had tied up the chauffeur, under Miriam's direction, in what is known as the Deadwood style. Jacques Goujon, the driver, blinked at the sight of so much authority.

'How would you like to see men like the count take charge of this country?' Evans asked.

'I'd just as soon give it to the lousy Portuguese,' Jacques said, and grinned.

Succinctly Evans told him that the government would pay him double time for his truck and its load, until the case was finished.

'Can I collect from those other mugs, too?' he asked.

'If you can,' Evans said, and smiled.

CHAPTER 26

Of the Odour of Saints and Sinners

THE sun, great giver of light and heat, had scarcely taken in the first trick, when Jacques Goujon, now special deputy of the Paris Police, spread gunnysacks on the tailboard of his truck for Evans and the sergeant, and made room on the driver's seat for Miriam, who was heavily armed. Melchisedek had been left to guard the prisoners, still tied together in the Deadwood style, not without, however, having first exacted a promise from Evans that he would be relieved before the hour when stags (*Cervus elaphus*) are wont to drink their fill. It was not stags that made Melchisedek nervous but hoot owls (*Strigidae scops*). He had heard, according to his own statement, enough hoot owls the night before to last him his natural span.

The contact mines, which had been covered with hay and a tarpaulin, were to be delivered at a little used shed by the river's brink, two miles or so upstream from Charenton. During the last several wars, this shed had been utilized as an emergency loading station when particularly dangerous explosives had to be handled.

'I suppose you have observed nothing about the hay on which we are sitting,' Evans said, as they jolted along.

The sergeant could answer truthfully in the negative. The jolting itself had been enough for him to think about. True, he had seen Evans remove a certain amount of T.N.T. from the evil-looking objects now behind them but the sergeant had not peeped in to make sure that Evans had not overlooked a kilo or two of the stuff.

'I'm not a rustic, I'm a city man,' the sergeant said. 'Still, Hydrangea has spoken of the hay fields, or cotton, was it? You have so many crops in North America.'

'This is not alfalfa (*Medicago sativa*), and fortunately, too, for alfalfa is common in this country. What I hold in my hand

218

here is timothy (*Phleum pratense*) and very good timothy at that,' said Evans.

'It's one and the same to me,' the sergeant said. His mind was veering from T.N.T. to his prefect whom he had left trussed up like a rabbit on a strange Aubusson rug.

'It won't be one and the same when you take it to court,' Evans said.

'If I take hay to court, it'll be my luck that the judge has hay fever and will think I did it on purpose.'

'Seriously,' Evans said. 'This is very important. It chances, my friend, that the timothy now in my hands corresponds exactly with a few wisps I observed in the trousers cuff of Tom Jackson. He had just visited the *Presque Sans Souci.*'

The sergeant caught on so quickly he nearly fell off the tail-board. 'Ah, *ça!* We've only to find the hayfield.'

'We skirted it this morning, just before I immobilized the first sentry,' Evans said.

'We left my prefect immobilized, too. Don't let that slip your mind,' said Sergeant Frémont. 'It will be hard for me to explain.'

'The fragments are fitting together, and high time,' Evans said. 'The prefect will find his proper niche.'

'The least I'll find is Devil's Island,' murmured Frémont. 'Ah, Hydrangea. Would you follow me to Guinea, among the serpents, Corsicans and butterflies?'

'At this moment,' said Evans, glancing at the sun, 'Miss Waite is only sixteen hundred and four-tenths miles away.'

'What a curse is distance!' Frémont sighed.

The truck had turned into a deeply-rutted and deserted road two hundred yards from the Seine. The terrain was sparsely wooded and had been somewhat littered by cows and other domestic animals.

'Be careful,' Miriam said, as they all descended but Goujon. Jacques kept his seat.

'What next?' he asked, laconically. 'Some guys were supposed to meet me in the shed and unload these firecrackers. I'll be damned if I try to lift 'em alone.'

'Continue to the shed, but slowly. Complain afterwards about

219

the ruts, and the danger of exploding the T.N.T. Or maybe those men don't know about the T.N.T. ?'

'They're from the château,' Jacques said. 'They know, all right.'

'And now,' said Evans, as soon as Jacques had started away. 'A little jaunt to the Grapes Movietone. They have a studio nearby and I'm eager to see my old friend the director.'

'God,' groaned the sergeant. 'In the midst of a case, we must take time off for a picture show.'

'Not so fast. We must have evidence. Justice in France, successor to Greece and Rome, is not the high-handed procedure of our western frontier.'

'Shall I ever make myself clear ?' said the sergeant in despair. 'Evidence, not only in France, but in Rome, Greece, Tyre, Sidon and also China, no doubt, is not to be used against higher-ups but the small fry you speak of with such disdain. The miraculous draught of fishes were not marlin or sailfish. Each one was small, and in itself, insignificant.

'I'm not going to regale you with a film, but only to borrow a camera, and the director's roadster,' Evans said.

This done, they hurried back to a knoll which afforded a view of the shed and the river. There Evans set up the camera, concealed it with leaved branches, and waved to Goujon who was waiting for them on the other side of the stream. Hastily they joined him and went with him to his boarding house for a sumptuous country meal. There were cold pickled mushrooms, fresh young onions, beans, carrots and parsnips, a *lotte* fresh from the river and a chicken which had been well treated before and after its death.

'Is it true that in America certain detectives who ought to know better drench their stomachs with bottled beer ?' the sergeant asked.

'It takes all kinds to protect the public,' Homer answered.

Miriam was not fidgety, exactly, but she wondered about the case from time to time. Evans noticed her uneasiness and smiled.

'The *Presque Sans Souci*, with Captain Gonzo at the helm,

220

will not reach the danger point in the river bed until between four and six,' he began.

'Can't you fix the time a little closer?' asked the sergeant, from force of habit.

'All right. Say between five and five-fifteen. Meanwhile the mines will be laid.'

'But, God, man. There are other barges on the river besides the *Presque Sans Souci.* Do you mean . . . ?' the sergeant gasped.

'Not a hair of a bargeman's head, nor a barnacle from a skiff's leaky bottom shall come to grief,' Evans said. 'That is, if we are careful. These mines will not be strewn about as if the Seine were enemy waters. Another method must be found to insure that the barge in question, and no other, will be contacted by the deadly firing pins. Now how is that to be done? I propose not only to find out for myself, but to take certified and witnessed pictures of the event. I take it you all will want to accompany me?'

Before they set out, however, Evans called the landlady's son to his side. He had a way with children, and instead of calling the boy 'Bobo' or 'Little Cabbage,' he addressed him by his name, Jean-Baptiste. To the truck driver's surprise the boy responded, and in a few minutes returned panting with a copy of the local paper, the Charenton *En-tout-cas.* Scanning the pages, Evans gasped and said to the sergeant:

'We must not under-estimate the master mind. He's diabolically clever. Brilliant but anti-social. You see. He's invited the entire membership of the *Société des Artistes Français* for a house party at the château beginning this evening. What an alibi.'

'Corsicans. Tarantulas,' groaned the sergeant. 'I am to go into court with a wisp of exotic hay and a few eccentric foreigners, to be confronted with four score of the most decorated and distinguished men and savants in France.'

'Cheer up,' said Evans. 'We will furnish you with evidence, all right. This afternoon we shall photograph the mine laying operations, this evening we will watch the château. The *Presque Sans Souci* will reach the danger zone about five to-morrow

221

morning. Then we'll ride into Paris and I'll elucidate as we go. . . .'

'Thank God for that,' Frémont said. 'But how are you going to get a word to Gonzo ? Tell me that !'

'With pleasure, if the subject is not too delicate,' Evans said. 'Gonzo, or Jansen, is a resourceful man. He has aboard a valuable corpse called Eloi le Mec, who died some time ago. Now in the case of certain saintly men, it is said that after death, decay and the accompanying phenomena do not occur. Eloi le Mec was not of that illustrious number. He was low. If there is anything in the theory, and it works both ways, we would be able to smell him in Charenton right now. What will Gonzo do, to avoid arousing suspicion, and also for the comfort of his crew and prisoners ?'

'Go on. I'm waiting !' the sergeant said.

'There is an ice plant on the shore at the point he will pass about noon. . . .'

'Gonzo will heave-to a moment, get a large supply of ice, and store Eloi in the hold, well wrapped in ice and hay,' said Evans. 'I sent him a telegram at the ice plant from the Grapes Movietone studio. We'll stop a moment there a little later for his reply.'

CHAPTER 27

The Heart of a Little Child

MIRIAM entered, refreshed by a dip in the pool and the piquant conversation of the landlady. Seeing the sergeant so downcast she went to his side and lightly touched his forehead.

'Courage, sergeant,' she said. 'To-morrow we'll all be back in Paris.'

Frémont winced. 'It would be far better for me to start right now for Estonia. There's no extradition from there,' he said, rising reluctantly to his feet. Goujon stretched and turned to the Madame.

'We'll need another feed between seven and seven-ten,' he said. 'Get busy.'

Obediently she left the room, although advised by her bright little son to tell that big palooka to go to hell. A lively scene ensued because the little chap insisted on going along with Evans. He had sensed that something exciting was afoot. Goujon was for chucking little 'Bobo' into an abandoned well that was handy in the garden. Frémont had the Continental idea that children should not go about without female relatives or nurses until they are safely through college. But Miriam had taken a fancy to the sprightly little fellow, so Evans finally gave way and said:

'What's the harm?'

They set out, Miriam and Jean-Baptiste in the roadster and Goujon and Sergeant Frémont following in the truck. Up river, as Evans had said, they found a ferry, with a precarious raft. Nevertheless, it got them all across, and the ferryman promised, for a generous consideration, to keep an eye on the vehicles until such time as the passengers should return. As they walked through the woods, Evans explained to the boy how necessary it was, if he was to be a good detective, to be quiet and to attract no attention.

'How old will I be before I can take a poke at that big mug who eats us out of house and home?' the child asked.

'Between eighteen and twenty-four, I should say,' was Evans' answer.

'Aw, gee! Can't you fix it closer than that?' the boy asked.

They were near the knoll that afforded the view. A view that is 'afforded' is much softer in character than one that is 'commanded'. The view in question was much as it had been when they had left it, allowing for a shifting of the angles and length of the shadows and the redistribution of domestic animals in the pastures. Evans, however, tested the camera, checked the focus, then sat down behind a clump of bushes.

'Can a guy smoke here?' asked Jacques.

'Quiet, all of you,' Evans whispered. His sharp eyes had detected a movement among the branches on the far side of the river, just opposite the shed. Three men in new overalls were struggling with a reel of what appeared to be three-quarter-inch twisted cable, with eight strands of two hundred wires each around a core of copper. A launch zoomed around the bend and as the cable was loaded aboard a raft, towed it to the shed where, out of sight of the camera, the mines were threaded on the cable, reloaded on the raft and, well-weighted, were placed in the channel under cover of the tarpaulin. Homer, intent on the camera, and trusting to its telescopic lens, was more concerned with the technique of the photography than with watching the proceedings with his naked eye.

'New overalls,' he said. 'Trust these aristocrats to inject a false note whenever actual work is concerned. New overalls, stiff and clean at three in the afternoon.'

When the mining operations were over and the pseudo-workmen had left the scene, Evans sent the sergeant and Jacques Goujon back to the truck while he and Miriam, together with the thrilled young Bobo, started for the movie lot on foot. Homer held the camera and the precious contents under his arm while the boy took pleasure in lugging the tripod.

'Won't you let mademoiselle shoot just once? I never seen a gun go off, except in pictures,' the child begged. Smiling, Evans reached for his silencer and slipped it over Miriam's automatic.

'What shall I hit for you?' Miriam asked, touched by the boy's eagerness.

'That guy who's been watching us through the bushes near the old red cow,' said Bobo, and suddenly the ping of a bullet cut the air, then another. Between pings, however, Miriam glanced at Evans who had thrown her, the boy and the camera into a slight depression in the damp pasture.

'Shoot,' Homer said. Miriam shot.

'Oh, gee! Oh, gee, mademoiselle,' panted Bobo breathlessly. 'You got him! Gee! You got him. How old will I be...'

'Wait here,' Evans said, as he sprinted towards the bush near the old red cow, who had continued chewing her cud philosophically throughout the whole dramatic scene. The body of a slender young man, a brace of converted duelling pistols dangling from his lifeless hands, was prone on the ground, and from a surprisingly small neat round hole in his forehead a drop of blood was oozing.

'Identical with the shot at Whistler's aunt,' Homer murmured. 'She can't help showing off, but then, dear girl, she's young. But who is this young chap who has come to such an early end, and who took such liberties with my coat?' for he had noticed that the second shot had passed through his tropical worsted sleeve and pongee shirt as neatly as if the converted pistols had been buttonhole scissors. Kneeling, he rummaged in the pockets of the youth, but found no papers. This was disconcerting in the extreme. Evidently the corpse was of a good family, and if the news of the shooting got bruited about before five-fifteen in the morning, Evans' well-laid plans might well be thwarted. Hastily he covered the body with branches he stripped from the alders and young evergreens, rejoined Miriam and the boy, and said they must be on their way.

'Can't I take just one peek at the corpse? Mademoiselle, here, says she shot him right in the middle of the forehead, and we got a bet up that she didn't,' Jean-Baptiste said. 'Gee! This is the best time I ever had. If it only had been that truck driver ... but, Gee, I can't have everything.'

'Take a quick look, and be sure to cover him up again. His

225

head's nearest the back end of the cow. Don't scratch around there too long. You might attract attention,' Evans said.

Happily the boy set out on the run, and after a few moments caught up with Miriam and Evans as they were strolling up the deeply-rutted roadway.

'You win, darn it all,' he said, and handed her without flinching a grimy twenty-five centimes piece.

'Take it,' Evans whispered. 'He'll feel hurt if you don't.'

'How well you know the hearts of little children,' she said, and sighed.

CHAPTER 28

The Film Saves the Day

THE nearest stag, as the crow flies, to the château outside Charenton was on the outskirts of Rambouillet, approximately sixty kilometres distant. He was turning his proud antlers to get a good look at the western sky, in order that he might be prompt at the pool when the stags' drinking hour sounded. The dearth of stags drinking their fill around the secluded château was more than compensated by the abundance of *Artistes Français* who were motivated by the same general idea. The fill of a septuagenarian painter varies widely, from approximately a thimblefull of diluted red wine to a respectable number of litres of assorted wines and liqueurs. There was, at the impromptu rustic bar, for each according to his capacity. Before passing on to the scene of merrymaking in the host's ancestral park and wooded acres, it should be noted that Homer Evans had by no means neglected to fulfil his promise to Melchisedek.

A good half hour before even the most impatient chronicler could call it 'eve', the roadster and truck, in the order named, drove up near the grove of birches where the three kidnappers, bound in Deadwood style, were disregarding the Biblical injunction not to kick against the pricks.

The two arrogant young men from the rear seat were still demanding to be taken to a telephone where the matter could be fixed up. Instead, Evans had them loaded on the truck, covered with branches and leaves, and transported to the Madame's boarding house where Goujon, unobserved, let them down gently into the abandoned well where they had ample room to stand but from which they could not possibly escape unaided. To stifle any sounds they might feel the urge to utter, Goujon had been instructed to cover the well with a scrap of elephant iron left behind by the A.E.F. in 1917.

Hjalmar's message had been received at the Grapes Movietone office and was characteristically brief:

ARRIVING FIVE FIFTEEN SOBER

227

The film of the mine-laying operations was being developed by a trusty developer who was under some obligation to Evans and consequently eager to do his best. He was to make two copies, one to be sent at once to the minister of justice, another for the ambassador, the original for Evans himself.

'Tell me,' piped up Jean-Baptiste, who could not be persuaded to leave Evans' side: 'Has rigor mortis set in yet on that guy we plugged this afternoon?'

The sergeant, alarmed, grabbed Bobo by the ear.

'What guy? I haven't been told about any man being plugged,' he said.

'Sorry. Slipped my mind,' said Evans, and tersely recounted the pasture incident.

'Hardly worth mentioning, I suppose,' the sergeant said sarcastically. 'I've so much to explain already. Probably the target so casually perforated by Mademoiselle Montana is only a first secretary or at most, a cabinet minister's son. But no matter. No matter. No report to local police, no medical examiner, no depositions or affidavits. Ah, well. Easy come, easy go.'

On the grounds of the château festivities were in progress. Distinguished-looking groups played croquet or sat in nooks on stone benches on which the arms of the Bourbons had been carved. There were two schools among the *Artistes Français*, one which feared the dampness of the evening and wore mufflers, the other which held that country air was beneficial at any time of day. There were paintings in the château and statues scattered through the grounds, but no one paid the least attention to them.

'I'm beginning to be worried about the prefect and Paty de Pussy,' Evans said. 'Neither of them are in evidence.'

He and the sergeant were concealed in a shapely stack of timothy hay. Miriam had been urged by Evans to get some rest and was sleeping in another haystack nearby. Melchisedek and Goujon were waiting near the 'S' curve.

At ten o'clock most of the artists went home in practically the same condition Bobo had been sent home, fast asleep. But, as Homer had expected, a number of them were assigned bedrooms in the spacious house. No sentries had been on guard

228

while the artists were outdoors, but when the last of them had tottered up the central stairway, Evans saw the host make a quick inspection of the premises. As he passed within a yard or two of the haystack, Evans got a full glimpse of his face and thought he saw on the usually haughty countenance a self-satisfied smile.

Long after the arch-conspirator had returned to the house, Evans thought about that smile. Just what did it mean ? The man knew that someone had eluded his guards the night before, had smashed a window, entered the château, shot and stunned the sentry in the attic and had seen in the upper rooms, bound and held as prisoners, the prefect of police and the vice-president of the artists' organization. Why so content ? The look on his face had been sadistic, but it held a sort of refinement of sadism, a highly developed appreciation of all shades of violence and suffering. Was it the prospect of the explosion, the effects of which were incalculable ? Four contact mines of the type in question might well wreck the town of Charenton, or even cause the ammunition factories to blow up.

'I have it,' Homer said at last and slapped the groaning sergeant on the shoulder.

'You have what ?' the sergeant asked. 'Or perhaps you'd better not tell me. I'm practically a dead man now but I want to keep my sanity.'

'I've figured out what the master mind intends to do with his first vice-president and the prefect,' Evans said. 'He will have them gagged or, perhaps, anaesthetized, and placed in the shed by the river side. The explosion, of course, if it occurred, wouldn't leave a trace of them. . . . We'll keep watch here. No need of trying to enter. By Jove, I believe the man thinks he's scared me off, that the sight of such prominent citizens trussed up in his attic was a lesson to me. What arrogance ! What insufferable smugness ! I shall take great pleasure in pulling him off that high horse of his.'

'For me, huge snakes and scorpions. Black fever. Knouts and chains,' murmured Frémont, turning over in the hay and burying his face in his hands.

The stars were shifting their positions like jewelled dancers

229

of a stately minuet, and up river in the balmy night, Hjalmar
Jansen was roaring a chanty as he spun the wheel:

> 'She was only a poet's daughter,
> But she never was averse.'

Tom Jackson was leaning over the bar, talking with Mme
Sosthène. Sosthène was serving the last of the prisoners who
was able to sit up and swallow. The *Presque Sans Souci* was
proceeding at eight miles an hour, for the channel in those
stretches was easily navigable at night. The reporter strolled
over to the helm.

'Are we on time?' he asked.

Hjalmar glanced at the chronometer. 'Ahead by half an
hour,' he said.

'Gad! I shall paint, after this, as I have never painted before,' Hjalmar said. 'That is, if someone doesn't spill the beans
to Weiss. In that case, I'll go to sea.' And his rollicking voice
rolled out again and was echoed in the woods on either side:

> 'La peinture à l'huile,
> C'est bien difficile,
> Mais c'est beaucoup plus beau
> Que la peinture à l'eau.'*

At midnight, Evans crawled softly to the other haystack to
waken Miriam.

'How beautifully she sleeps, our plucky little American girl,'
he murmured to himself. 'Not many women have the art of re-
taining their looks in slumber. Ah, well. No use crossing
bridges, and all that. Shake a leg, Pride of the Range! Signs of
life, O Flower of Open-Space Womanhood! The cock hath
crown. I have a feeling that something will soon take place.'

Her eyes opened, reflecting the starlight, and she smiled. Before they had time to crawl to haystack 'a', a horse and wagon
appeared on the lane, moving in a ghostly fashion without the
slightest sound. Two men sat side by side on the wooden seat.

'Can you beat that? Padded hooves,' Evans said. 'They've

---

* Painting in oil
  Is lots of toil,
  But it's much better
  Than painting in water.

come to get de Pussy and the prefect. As soon as they enter the gate, we must make a dash for the roadster and get to the shed ahead of them.'

When a faint streak in the east betokened the approach of the punctual Aurora, Evans, waiting on the knoll, was rewarded by the sight of the wagon. The horse had gone lame and was limping along with the utmost difficulty. While two coffin-like boxes were being lifted from the wagon Evans waited, then made a sprint for the shed, followed by the bewildered sergeant and the others. Before the two men could drop their load, Homer was upon them. One he caught right on the button with a left hook, the other he tripped and left to Frémont. Miriam arrived in time to tie up the pair and leave them, roped to the boxes, in the shed. Their pleadings and piteous cries rent the dawn, or at least put some wrinkles in it.

'Where to?' asked Miriam. Her sleep had refreshed her, and she was set for more action.

'The studio. We've just time for a preview of the shots we took this afternoon. It would be safer to look them over, while there's still time,' said Homer.

In five minutes they were seated cosily in the preview room of Grapes, Inc. When the first few feet of film unreeled, Evans grunted with satisfaction.

'Clear as day. That was a wonderful camera,' he said.

'You ought to stay in this business,' the operator said.

Silently the scene of the afternoon's mine-laying spread itself before them. At Homer's suggestion, the operator had slowed down the action so every last detail could be observed. The effect on the sergeant was most gratifying. He roused himself from the slough of despond and again was buoyed up by faith that Evans would pull him through, somehow. Miriam was all attention, Jacques and Melchisedek stunned with admiration. Their surprise, when their leader leaped from his seat with an agonized cry and started hurdling seats and racing for the door, was so intense that for a moment they lacked the presence of mind to follow, and when they reached the open air the faint sound of the whistle of the *Presque Sans Souci* was borne to their ears on the morning breeze.

231

'Ahead of time,' gasped Miriam, her heart in her mouth as she ran. Had she known what was in Homer's mind as he paused in his mad race to wave them all back, she would have been more agitated than she was. For Evans had seen on the screen that the truck load of mines Jacques had left in the shed contained six and not four of the deadly instruments of death and destruction.

Hjalmar, aboard the barge, was singing lustily and all hands were in the bow to have a look at Charenton. He had been lucky all night in his navigation, had had tailwinds all the way and was proud of the time he had made. When Evans was a hundred yards from the shed, the *Presque Sans Souci* was not much farther. Ten seconds passed, a shot was heard, then another. Homer was firing as he ran, and thinking even faster. In front of the shed, a masked man was tugging at the cable. The problem was not the man on the near bank but the other one, across the stream. There was no time to swim. If the barge got between, Homer would have no way of fending off the horrible consequences. Every one of his companions would die, be literally blown to atoms.

A man emerged from the woods on the opposite bank and kneeled. Miriam, by that time near enough to grasp something of the situation, shot him dead. Evans, to her surprise, started running downstream as if in headlong flight. Her jaw dropped and her fingers trembled so that she missed the second masked man who dashed from the bushes to relieve the first. Homer Evans running from danger ? Tears blurred her eyes as she took a futile shot at the cable-cutter, and the huge grey barge slid into the field of vision, shielding the man completely. Then she began to weep with joy, and clasp her hands. For by straining every nerve and muscle, Evans had gained the proper angle and his automatic barked. Miriam, watching him, knew from his almost prayerful attitude of relief that the bullet had gone home across the broad bows of the *Presque Sans Souci*.

Evans, still panting from his fright and exertions, came to her side.

'Shame to kill those fellows. Doomed to death, they thought. Suppose they drew lots. What is it about perverse causes that spurs our brethren to such extravagant courage? For any worthy cause, scarcely anyone will raise a hand, let alone being blown to bits. Well. Let's have a word with Jansen. Then for the final round up.'

Almost gracefully, the large grey *Presque Sans Souci* was sliding up to the Charenton docks, her crew in high spirits, her weird cargo intact.

'I could have told you there were six of them things, but nobody asked me,' Jacques said gruffly, when Evans explained briefly how near to extinction they all had been. 'I got four from one shed and two from the cellar.'

'By no means brilliant on my part,' said Evans ruefully. 'Eh, sergeant?'

'I didn't count them either,' Frémont said.

CHAPTER 29

Ashes to Ashes, in a Way

MIRIAM, Frémont, and Evans went directly to the dock to welcome Hjalmar and his passengers. Jacques and Melchisedek were given brief instructions. After loading the boxes containing the prefect and Paty de Pussy, the two wailing expressmen, the three dead cable cutters, the three kidnappers from the abandoned well, and the lame horse aboard the barge, they got in the truck and drove across the pasture to fetch the corpse with the converted duelling pistols. Homer, after hearty greetings and a brief tour of inspection, was organizing his posse for a quick raid of the château. Hjalmar and Jackson gleefully agreed to accompany the punitive expedition into the surrounding woods. Meanwhile, Evans had snatched a moment to telephone Hugo Weiss, the ambassador and the minister of justice, urging them to charter a taxi and hasten to Charenton without delay.

'Sergeant,' Homer said, noting Frémont's dejected air, 'since you are reluctant to rile the big shots, perhaps you'd just as soon stay on the barge while we stalk the master mind ?'

The sergeant drew himself up to his full five feet five. 'Monsieur Evans,' he said gravely, 'there is a gulf of miscomprehension between us Latins and you who have Anglo-Saxon blood. When we are troubled, we frankly say so. When we mourn, we do not hide. If you have mistaken the expression of my forebodings for faint-heartedness, I can only say that I have given you credit for more acumen than you have.'

'Forgive me,' Evans said, extending his hand.

The truck was free by that time, and the clock said five to five. They rumbled along the road, enjoying silently their reunited companionship and that rare exhilaration an escape from horrible death affords.

In the grove of birches near the 'S' curve, they left the truck and started for the timothy field outside the wall but which

234

commanded a view of the rear of the château and a part of the grounds. Evans, Hjalmar and Miriam led the way, Sergeant Frémont and Jackson were close behind them, Jacques and Melchisedek brought up the rear. The latter was fingering his rabbit's foot assiduously.

'The rest of you hide in the haystacks and wait for my signal,' Homer said. 'The sergeant and I will try to smoke out our quarry. Above all, don't shoot any *Artistes Français*. There are at least fifteen of them on the premises, all innocent of any wrong doing.'

'They're lousy painters,' grunted Hjalmar.

'Unhappily, in our present state of civilization, that's not a punishable crime,' Evans said.

No sentries were in sight. They had the fields and the woods all to themselves. Evans looked at his watch. 'It's after five-fifteen,' he said. Still there were no signs of life in the grim château. At five-thirty Homer said he'd wait fifteen minutes more, and at a quarter to six he was about to arise when he saw a tall man, wearing wine-coloured pyjamas and slippers embroidered with the arms of the Bourbons, walk rapidly across the yard.

'There he is,' Evans whispered, and his hand went instinctively to his holster.

'I'll be damned. It's Haute Costa de Bellevieu,' Jackson muttered. 'What a story. The old reprobate. The hound.'

'He's got some papers in his hand, and he's distraught, all right,' the sergeant said.

'Damaging proofs,' Evans said. 'He's frightened. Thinks his subordinates bungled. We must see what he does with the papers.'

Then even Evans' saturnine countenance blanched with fear and horror. 'Quick. Deep into the hay,' he cried, for Haute Coste de Bellevieu had paused at the sandpile, had taken up an iron shovel and just as the last of Evans' party disappeared as far into the depths of the haystacks as possible, the enraged aristocrat plunted the shovel viciously into the sandpile.

What followed beggars description and even contemplation. The château and the grounds seemed to rise into the air and dissolve, great trees were flattened, clouds of smoke and dust obscured the woods. The ground heaved and tipped like an ice-floe and the rain of falling objects was like a sudden cloudburst. Fragments of wood and ironwork, small pieces of human bodies; limp birds struck dead in flight, copies of *L'Action Française* and *L'Art pour l'Art*, monogrammed chamber pots, torn paintings, *faiences*, and stone benches thudded all around the dumbfounded members of the posse from under whom the haystacks had been blown *in toto*. Luckily none of the party was hurt, although all were bruised and battered.

'What happened? Did you blow him up on purpose?' Hjalmar said. 'You might have let us in on it.'

'Perhaps it's just as well,' said Evans philosophically. 'After all, the victims among the artists had passed the Biblical age. And now, our friend the sergeant won't have to buck their influence in court. ... Well, we may as well go back to the barge.'

Sergeant Frémont was kicking his heels and murmuring, 'Hydrangea. Promotion. Spectre of Devil's Island, farewell.'

'No use waiting around here,' Evans said. 'Everybody's dead and unrecognizable where the château used to be. It had slipped my mind, until I saw the beggar with a shovel, that I had hidden the T.N.T. in that sandpile. Suppose he never knew what struck him. Lucky the concussion didn't set off a powder factory in Charenton. Come on! We've got a brisk walk ahead of us, then breakfast.'

'What's the matter with the truck?' asked Jacques. 'I ain't walked that far in years.'

'The truck will be demolished,' Evans said. 'It wasn't lucky enough to be wrapped in a haymow, as we were. Nothing but hay or sawdust would have saved us. I thought, truly, we were gone that time.'

'What about my truck? Do I collect, or not?' asked Jacques.

'Full value, and a bonus,' Evans said.

'Don't give him a nickel,' said little Bobo who had come up and had overheard the conversation. 'The big heel'll only get fried.'

The party had scarcely boarded the *Presque Sans Souci* when

236

the ambassadorial limousine drove up and out stepped Hugo Weiss, the ambassador and Colonel Lvov Kvek. All wore tall hats, frock coats, grey striped trousers and patent leather shoes, all carried gold-headed canes. Anyone would be hard put to decide which of them looked more distinguished, and which of them carried his load of liquor with more aplomb. Very likely it was the colonel who was enjoying himself the most, on account of his long years of privation and struggle. He was slightly regretful, however, that all the windows in town had been broken, for he doted on the sound of tinkling glass.

In the galley of the barge, Mme Sosthène was turning out mountains of eggs and French fried potatoes. The prisoners, up forward, were agog with curiosity. In the hold was a large fresh supply of ice and stretched upon it were the corpses, then numbering five.

'Been up to some kind of hell, my boy?' asked the ambassador, shaking hands with Hjalmar, then with Evans.

'The master mind got away,' Jansen said, with an expressive gesture toward the sky.

'Ah, well. Another time. Never know when to stop, these criminal Johnnies,' the ambassador said.

Another smart limousine drove up and the minister of justice stepped out, followed by Dr Hyacinthe Toudoux.

'Where's the prefect?' he demanded.

Evans pointed to the prefect's box, which was amidships, near the bar. 'That box to the left. Maybe we'd better let him out.'

'This is an outrage,' shouted Paty de Pussy from the box on the right.

'Uncrate them and give them some breakfast, but keep them tied up for a while,' Evans said.

'Well, Evans, my boy. Tell us all about it,' said the ambassador, accepting a glass of applejack from Sosthène and allowing Gaby to take his hat and stick.

'First let's have breakfast, then start down river. I'll explain on the way. It will help pass the time,' said Homer.

Sergeant Frémont blinked. 'I think there's no doubt of that,' he said, glancing nervously at the minister of justice, and more nervously at the prefect, who was being lifted from the box and placed in a nearby chair. The prefect, however, did not berate the sergeant or anyone else. He was in the throes of black despair.

'That noise. The explosion. What was it?' he asked.

'Your colleague ... er ... got away, as Mr Jansen puts it. He was blown into smithereens.'

'I should have met him on the field of honour,' said Paty de Pussy, stretching his sword arm and rubbing it tenderly, for it was badly cramped.

'Snug little barge you have here. Where'd you get it?' asked the ambassador, as Mme Sosthène served him a large helping of eggs and potatoes. The smell of coffee cheered even the manacled prisoners. For some time all else was forgotten while the company fell to.

CHAPTER 30

The Whole and its Parts

'MAKE yourselves comfortable,' Evans said, as he passed around cigars. The company had been assembled in a large circle on deck, even the prisoners and five labelled corpses for which Homer had need in his elucidation. Jackson had a wad of copy paper on his knee to note down dates, names and addresses.

'Before I begin,' Evans said, 'I must urge you all to ask no questions until I have finished. Then, if everything is not clear, I shall be glad to answer if I can. This affair, which began officially with the disappearance of Mr Weiss (the latter bowed genially and smiled) has much deeper roots.'

Sergeant Frémont groaned.

'First of all, let me say what you all know quite well. There is a more or less clandestine organization in France, the members of which want or pretend to want the restoration of the monarchy. With some of them, it is a matter of birth, habit, rather sloppy thinking. With' others of the more unstable type it is an obsession verging on insanity. Let us leave them for a moment, after having remarked that the cause they represent is always badly in need of money.

'The coffers of Europe have been fairly well drained by partisans of dethroned royal houses. America is the only hunting ground where solicitors for kings or almost anything else have some prospect of success.

'In America, in 1913, an income tax law was passed and the rich have been devising tax dodging rackets ever since. There is a multi-millionaire in Delaware named T. Prosper Stables, who controls large industries, scores of banks, and who fancies himself as a patron of the arts.'

At this, Hugo Weiss began to mutter, then desisted.

'One of Stables' employees thought out a prize scheme by means of which wealthy men could evade the heaviest part of

239

their taxes and conceal their assets effectively. I will outline it as briefly as I can. A painting is bought in Europe for, say, five thousand dollars. The buyer "A" sells it to "B" for fifty thousand. "B" sells it to "C" for two hundred thousand, and so on until the price has been whooped up to half a million.'

At this one of the minor gangsters became so excited that he slipped off the egg crate on which he had been sitting. 'Jeese. We're only pikers,' he said.

Homer smiled good-naturedly at the interruption. 'Of course, Messrs A, B, C, D, and all the others are one and the same man, Mr T. Prosper Stables acting through his badly-paid agents and employees.'

Weiss began to beam and slap his knee.

'What is the connexion between U.S. tax dodging and the royalist movement in France, you may well ask?' continued Evans. 'That link occurred by hazard. The gentleman who was blown to bits this morning was a leader of the royalists, a clever schemer and an influential man. He had at his command a horde of fanatical followers who had pledged themselves to obey orders without question. M. Haute Costa de Bellevieu was in America in search of cash for his movement at the time Stables needed to build up a European ring to handle Old Masters. They got together, M. Haute Costa de Bellevieu agreed to organize and operate a series of agencies and agents, none known to more than one of the others. Stables, in turn, agreed to turn over part of the profits of his philanthropy to the royalist cause.

'You have met, or seen, in the course of this investigation, several members of the ring. At first glance, the late Ambrose Gring would seem a strange choice, but I discovered what is not generally known about Ambrose, namely that he is the son of a member of the royal house of Portugal, out of a famous Can-Can dancer I need not name.'

'The bastard,' murmured Miriam.

'That dash of royalty,' continued Evans, 'entitled Ambrose to be taken care of, somehow, so Haute Costa de Bellevieu entrusted him with a simple job. You see, once he got started in the affair, de Bellevieu could not see the reason for buying

240

authentic paintings, with all the attendant difficulties, when fakes could be cooked up in short order. Gring put him in touch with M. Paty de Pussy . . .'

'You shall receive a call from my seconds,' the old painter spluttered.

Evans smiled. 'I haven't had a chance to compliment you on your work. It is excellent. Superb, in fact.'

The old aristocrat thawed a little at that, and smiled in a deprecatory way.

Evans went on with his explanation. 'M. Paty de Pussy furnished the forged Old Masters, for a consideration which I fear was not adequate, in view of the final prices. These were delivered by Gring to one of a number of dealers or galleries, among them being our late lamented friends, Abel Heiss and Dodo Lourde.

'I'll not bore you with needless details,' Evans said. 'At the time this case began, there was to be a wholesale disposal of false El Grecos. Stables had run up the listed prices to a total of three million dollars, and had offered a candlelight Greco apiece to six different museums, widely separately geographically but all more or less under his thumb. At the most inopportune moment for the conspirators, who on this side of the water were to use the proceeds of the sale for a purchase of arms and ammunition, Mr Weiss appeared in Paris, innocently enough. His presence was fatal to the scheme if he got a look at the paintings or even heard about them, since an unscrupulous dealer had tried to sell a Greco by Paty de Pussy to Weiss some years before. I was, in fact, the one to detect the fraud.'

He turned to Paty de Pussy, who was bristling again.

'Very careless with that crimson, you were,' Evans said, chidingly. 'Not up to your usual standard. Greco, as you know by this time, did not use cochineal until just before his death.'

'To continue,' said Homer, 'Haute Costa de Bellevieu was faced with a desperate situation. He made a deal with a band of professional kidnappers of whom we have six members with us, one of them, Eloi le Mec, being dead, the others, at least for the time being, alive.

'The hour of kidnapping was fixed with reference to the

banquet of the *Société des Artistes Français*, and it was purely by chance that Mr Weiss chose to visit Mr Jansen's studio just previously. The investigating authorities, naturally, were misled into believing that Jansen and his friends, including me, were responsible, particularly as Jansen had cashed two cheques under circumstances that looked suspicious.

'Gring had been ordered to find out, if possible, whether Mr Weiss was intending to visit picture galleries and whether he knew about the shower of Grecos by which Mr Stables was to refresh the American world of art. Gring failed to make a satisfactory report, and was intimidated by Heiss and Lourde into disclosing the identity of Paty de Pussy.

'Mr Weiss was kidnapped, as you all know. He and Colonel Kvek were both drugged by means of a hypodermic, and were loaded, taxi and all, on the waiting barge which is so nobly bearing us home to triumph and to victory. For a time the police and the authorities generally were completely up in the air. None of the suspects had the remotest connexion with the case except Gring, and he had not known about the kidnapping. At that point I took a hand in the case because it seemed my obvious duty. I convinced Sergeant Frémont, here, to leave me at large and he had the good sense to do so and to render me every possible service. The credit should go to him.

'Now how did Gring die, and why, and at whose hand?'

The prefect hung his head in utter despair. 'I didn't ...' he began.

'Don't be unduly disturbed,' Evans said, kindly. 'I know the exact extent of your guilt and of your innocence. The demise took place because of a series of coincidences that nearly baffled me, in fact, that had me gasping for air and praying for light during a considerable period of time. My barber, one Henri Duplessis, is an amorous chap with a taste for expatriate American girls. He is tender-hearted. In order not to cause his wife unnecessary worry Henri was wont, when a-wooing, to leave his spouse in a drugged and peaceful state, and for this purpose he used an old Inca remedy known in the States as a Mickey Finn.'

242

'Ah,' the sergeant sighed, and barely restrained himself from a gambol or two on the deck.

'On the day of Gring's death, Henri entered the Dingo to obtain from the bartender a Mickey Finn and was observed in the act of pocketing the phial by a member of the prefect's drug squad. The barber was nabbed and grilled, and in order to escape a serious charge was obliged to tell the prefect about the Mickey Finn and its uses and qualities. The prefect took the phial away and placed it in the third drawer, right, of his desk. Later he filled it with typewriter oil.'

The prefect, paler and more agonized, tried to rise.

'Patience,' said Evans. 'Meanwhile, de Bellevieu, who seemed to know everything, found out that Gring had been talking too much and decided to do away with him.

'Now I must explain to those of you who don't know it that our prefect is an ardent royalist, and has worked for the restoration of the Bourbons many years. He was pledged to carry out the orders of his chief, Haute Costa de Bellevieu, but had never been ordered to commit murder before. He knew that if he rebelled, the matter might come to public attention, the coveted arms would never be obtained, disaster would follow. When Henri the barber turned in the Mickey Finn, the prefect thought he saw a way out. He decided to administer the knock-out drops and later have Gring shanghaied to some distant port, so badly frightened that he would never return. Haute Costa de Bellevieu would not know Gring was alive. With this in mind, the prefect went to Montparnasse, found Gring at his accustomed table, slipped the Mickey Finn into the *crème de cacao* and hurried back to the prefecture. There he found an order from the minister of justice to rearrest Gring at once. Unfortunately, Gring was dead.

'No other case of death from a Mickey Finn has ever been reported in the course of history, but Gring's condition at the time he drank the Mickey verged on collapse. He was wild with anxiety about a girl and some oil fields, had had no proper sleep for days. The Mickey Finn, which (and the doctor will bear me out), would not kill a ladybug or a white-footed mouse, extinguished Ambrose. Dr Hyacinthe Toudoux acquitted himself with glory in the autopsy. He analysed correctly the oil of the prairie rattler and another ingredient, which in fairness to the bartending profession I must not disclose.

'Let us now review the search for Hugo Weiss.'

'Not too much at once, boy,' the ambassador said. 'Let's snatch a quick drink.'

'Da, da,' roared Colonel Kvek, and the prisoners croaked their approval. Everyone had a drink except Sergeant Frémont, who passed the recess cutting capers in the bow.

When all were in their seats again, Evans glanced from one to the other and resumed his explanation. 'In order to get Mr Weiss out of the way, de Bellevieu got in touch with a notorious gang known as the St Julien rollers, whose specialty had been jewel robberies. This gang was one of the few in Paris which used the river as a means of escape and the transportation of stolen diamonds toward Antwerp. The leader is one Barnabé Vieuxchamp, the third from the left among the prisoners, and a distant relative, I believe, of the illustrious Barney Oldfield, the American speed king. Am I right, Monsieur Vieuxchamp?'

'I'm not saying a word,' the head gangster said.

'Of course, Weiss was shadowed. A car blocked the passage of the Colonel's taxi on the Pont Royal, it was easy to jab the victims with a hypodermic, take possession of the taxi, drive it on the quay and load it with its unconscious driver and passenger. I was able, quite early in the game, with the help of Miss Leonard, to eliminate all other avenues of egress from the city excepting the Seine. At that time I didn't know which gang was involved, so I couldn't say for sure whether they had gone up river or down toward Havre. Colonel Kvek's ingenuity, in sending me the message, saved the day.'

'It was nothing,' the colonel said. 'I punched a hole in the forehead with a small stick I found in the hay and tossed it overboard on the chance that someone would find it and recognize the subject. I had only faint hopes that it would come into your hands but anything was worth trying.'

'Once I had fixed the town of Frontville as the hiding place, the rest was simple, although mishaps occurred,' Evans said. 'Hjalmar knew about the island and that it had been an ammu-

244

nition dump during the war. The obsolete type of hand grenade thrown at us in the Rendez-vous des Imprévoyants led me to fear that explosives had been left in the dugouts and were at the gang's disposal. That being the case, I surmised correctly that the dugouts would be mined and wired for destruction if danger threatened. Had not the horse of Miss Leonard, our trigger-woman, tripped over a brier there would have been no explosion at all, but in that instance our luck, which had been running well, deserted us.

'It was not at first the intention of Haute Costa de Bellevieu to murder Mr Weiss or later to kidnap and try to do away with Miss Leonard, the prefect, and M. de Pussy. He had to act hastily, and once the kidnapping was done he soon saw that the jig was up if Weiss should return. These undesirable citizens of the St Julien mob did not agree to kill Mr Weiss and were double-crossed by de Bellevieu and threatened with denunciation and arrest on other charges if they would not put Weiss to death.'

Homer turned to the sergeant. 'I hope, Sergeant, you will have the prosecution take that factor into account. If our fellow voyagers are guillotined they will never see Devil's Island. That would be a pity.'

'Ah, boa constrictors, tarantulas, Corsicans with whips, stale bread . . .' the sergeant intoned.

'Don't rub it in,' said Vieuxchamp, defiantly. 'And let me tell you wise guys something. If Devil's Island's tough, we'll make it tougher.' And he spat within an inch of the prefect's toe.

'Ho, ho,' chuckled the ambassador, nudging the minister of justice in the ribs.

'We now come to Monsieur Paty de Pussy,' Evans said, smiling at the furious old aristocrat.

'Swords, pistols. What you like. In the Bois, early morning,' the old man muttered. Evans smiled.

'I was led to the studio of Paty de Pussy by a series of coincidences, although I should have found it sooner or later. You see, when Messrs Heiss and Lourde, now deceased, were released from the *préfecture*, marked for death, they left behind

245

six false Grecos which had been intended for immediate shipment. I interviewed Dinde, got a look at the books, and for
reasons of my own which Mr Weiss will understand, retrieved
the false Grecos from the prefect and shipped them to their
several destinations. In doing so, I was surprised to learn that
identical shipments had just been sent to the six museums in
question. I found the expressman who had carted them, got the
address of the house where he had picked them up and was
astonished to find they had come from the studio of Paty de
Pussy and that Abel and Dodo were hiding there.'

'They forced their way in,' said Paty de Pussy. 'Served them
right to be hanged. Don't know who did it, but I approve.'

'Rather drastic punishment for small-time peccadillos,'
Evans said. 'I believe, with the Mikado, that the punishment
should fit the crime.'

'You're an interloper and a busybody,' Paty de Pussy said.

Evans flushed. 'I'm afraid that is true,' he said. 'I assure you
that I shall never try sleuthing again. But to resume. What puzzled and excited me most was the speed with which de Pussy
turned out Old Masters.'

At this, Hugo Weiss was all attention. 'How, my boy ? Tell
us how ?'

'Monsieur Paty de Pussy had had long practice with Greco's
palette. For him to match colours was easy, and he has remarkable talent for imitating the Master's brush strokes. It seems
that Abel Heiss and Dodo Lourde had got track of a process by
which canvas may be sensitized to receive a photographic impression.'

'I'll be damned,' Weiss said. 'Not even a straightforward
copy.'

Paty de Pussy could contain himself no longer.

'That shameful expedient was forced on me by those ruffians.
I had never stooped to such a trick before. Indeed, my
draughtmanship has passed for Rembrandt's, Titian's, a score
of masters, and hangs on many museum walls,' he said.

'That's interesting,' Evans said. 'You were aware, then, that
the copies were to be used for illegitimate purposes ?'

The old man spluttered. 'If I'd known the prices that scoun-
246

drel, Haute Costa de Bellevieu, received, I would have called him out. I got five hundred francs a metre, not a cent more. I never knew what de Bellevieu was up to until he had me tied up by his lackeys.'

'I understand that,' Evans said. 'You were approached by Gring with orders for copies. He delivered them and brought you your inadequate pay. Up to the evening of their death, you had never seen Heiss and Lourde? Am I right?'

'That is correct,' admitted Paty de Pussy.

'It may make you feel better to know that the late Haute Costa de Bellevieu sealed his doom when he telephoned you, preparatory to having you mishandled and trussed up,' Evans said. 'The man had been fiendishly clever in covering his tracks. Not even M. Crayon de Crayon was aware of the machinations of his leader, nor the miraculous sources from which dollars poured into the coffers of the royalist cause.'

The prefect groaned.

'M. le Prefect is next in order,' Evans said. 'I am not a moralist but an observer of human antics. M. Crayon de Crayon will pardon me if I remark at the outset that he is a psychological curiosity. He has sown no wild oats in his youth, formed no pernicious habits, has been in minor matters punctiliously honest. Yet he could serve one government in a responsible post, while planning and working for its overthrow.'

Crayon de Crayon made a gesture as if to interrupt.

'I know what you are about to say,' Evans continued. 'You believe in the divine right of kings, that a monarchy would improve the lot of the people of France. That is your conviction. Whether a man as ignorant of history and economy as you are has a right to form opinions or convictions is a moot point. We cannot discuss it here. The problem with which we have to deal centres around the death of Ambrose Gring. Gring died from a mild soporific administered by the prefect of police. M. Crayon de Crayon, however, in slipping the Mickey Finn into Gring's glass thought he was doing the chap a favour, in fact the prefect intended to save the life he unwittingly destroyed. In the case of Heiss and Lourde, the prefect got them out of custody as quickly as he could, fearing any moment that he would be ordered to execute them. Later, they were hanged by de Bellevieu, whose false phone call had trapped de Pussy.

'That the prefect is implicated in the attempt to smuggle arms into France and to start a bloody revolution is unquestionable. That he will resign before leaving this barge is also unquestionable. He is dangerous because of arrested development and perverse education. Who can say what punishment is just and reasonable for having been born among has-beens and having absorbed their ideas ?'

The ambassador, who had been increasingly moved to pity by the prefect's discomfiture, said: 'Not too brutal, my boy. None of us are any too bright, you know. Make a frightful hash of everything.'

'Da, da. Another drink. I've just remembered it's my name day. Everyone must drink. I insist on it. We are all unfortunates and sinners. Brandy ! Whisky ! Applejack ! On my saint's day no one must be sad,' bellowed Colonel Kvek.

'I shall be prime minister,' the minister of justice said, shaking Evans by the hand. 'Sergeant, I'll see that you are named prefect.'

Sergeant Frémont's honest face showed real dismay.

'I implore you, not prefect. Only chief of detectives. That is a non-political job I can handle. I know my limitations. As prefect I should rapidly go mad.'

'I forbid any man to go mad on my name day,' said the colonel, tickling Mme Sosthène playfully with his gold-headed cane. They were passing the fragrant Halles aux Vins behind which could be heard the roaring of lions, jackals, hyenas, tigers, and the cries of exotic birds. The lusty timbre of the colonel's voice set off the elephants and all the wild boars to add to the din. Along the quays, the *Presque Sans Souci* was greeted by admiring throngs waving handkerchiefs, parasols and the like and shouting, 'Vive Frémont ! Death to traitors ! Long live the American and his millions.' For the news of Frémont's triumph in the matter of the murder, the kidnapping, the arms plot and the Old Master racket had travelled from Charenton faster than the huge grey barge.

'I'm ready for questions while there's yet time,' Evans said.

CHAPTER 31

In Which Many Hearts Are Gladdened

'FIRST,' said the ambassador, 'will you tell us why the devil you sent two sets of false Grecos to those six museums ? One would have been enough. Everything in moderation. . . .'

'That was to aid Mr Weiss and Mr Jackson. When Mr Weiss leaves these shores bound for the U.S.A. he will have complete proofs and documentation with which to confront his old enemy, Mr T. Prosper Stables. What he does with them is his own affair, but I hope he will not let that arch-hypocrite off too lightly.'

'Never fear,' said Weiss, accepting a bottle from Kvek. 'I'll make him pray and sweat as he never has before. I'll even make him pay his back taxes, which will leave him practically penniless, less than fifty million dollars if I figure it right.'

'Don't make us weep,' said Barnabé.

Evans smiled and continued: 'Mr Jackson, if I mistake me not, will, upon landing, hasten to tip off all the American editors and news services to be on hand when the shipments of fake Grecos pour in. They'll make Stables' life a hell with questions. In that way, our friend Oklahoma Tom will make himself solid with everyone who matters in the newspaper game.'

'What a story !' Jackson said.

'No one must work or worry on my name day,' shouted Kvek. He had just been informed by Weiss that a good executive job was open for him in the States if he wanted it, and the ambassador had assured him that the visa would be fixed up in a jiffy. There were men who had less cause for rejoicing.

Hjalmar at the wheel suddenly began to wave his arms and shout. 'Where are my 250,000 francs, by God. I'll get 'em or the prefect goes overboard.'

The prefect indicated an inside pocket he himself could not reach, tied up as he was, and Hjalmar turned over the wheel to

Jacques Goujon, vaulted tables and chairs, and nearly tore the prefect's coat inside out. Sheaves of bank notes were scattered all over the deck but Hjalmar's companions retrieved them gaily. He counted them, and the total was correct within a few thousand. From that time until they docked, he outdid even Lvov Kvek among the brandy bottles.

'Don't forget my portrait. Next trip I'll sit for it,' said Hugo Weiss.

'By the way,' asked Evans, 'did you get a written statement from me ?'

The ambassador grinned a little shamefacedly.

'Forgive me, boy. What with one thing and another, business, pleasure, and all that, the thing slipped my mind. My secretary does most of my reading, you know. Anything in it I ought to know ?'

Homer turned to the minister of justice. 'Did you receive your copy ?'

The minister was apologetic, too. 'Must have got mixed up with some other papers. Sorry. I'll try to find it, but nobody ever finds anything in my office. Sometimes it's just as well.'

'Exactly,' chimed in the ambassador. 'Nothing like papers for getting a man into trouble.'

The sergeant was hopping and skipping around the bow, humming snatches of song from the Blackbirds' Revue. When he caught sight of Melchisedek he called to him and appointed him chauffeur to the chief of detectives, at which the ex-serviceman began to dance the Black Bottom. Kvek, not to be outdone on his name day, performed a rollicking Kazotzky with butcher knives from the galley in his mouth, behind his ears, and in both hands.

Would it be too depressing to leave the scene of festivity aboard the *Presque Sans Souci* to spend a moment with one member of the cast who was consumed with grief and sadness – none other than Gwendolyn Poularde ? She was seated on the cot in her shabby garret, weeping softly and wringing her shapely hands. Her life's work, the hours of toil and privation she had suffered in order to learn to paint, had gone for nothing. No one in the Louvre would even listen to her plead-

250

ings any longer, and in fact, the attendants had threatened her with arrest if she entered the museum again. Rosa Stier, Simon, Sturlusson, all her friends in Montparnasse had tried to cheer her in vain. Gwendolyn was sunk.

At perhaps the lowest moment of her suffering and agony, a rap sounded on the door.

'Who is it ?' she asked.

'Telegram,' a voice replied.

Listlessly she dragged herself to the door and took the message. No use opening it, she thought. It must be from Chicago. The Arson Galleries inquiring about her show. However, she tore open the telegram and sank to the cot, almost fainting, not with despair but joy.

CANVASSES SUPERB TEN GARAGES SOLD BE-
FORE OPENING SEND EVERYTHING YOU PAINT
IN FUTURE THANKS FOR SHIPPING AIR MAIL
GLAD TO FOOT BILL

ARSON

Weeping and laughing hysterically, she hurried to the *terrasse* of the Café du Dôme.

'Of course,' said Rosa Stier, reaching for her twelfth Pernod. 'You didn't think Homer Evans would let you down.'

By the time the *Presque Sans Souci* was made fast to the stanchions at the Pont Royal, such a throng had gathered that double police cordons had to be drawn around the area. Hugo Weiss, when he walked the plank to the quay, was given such a hearty ovation as only Parisian crowds can give. The cheering was spontaneous and in every way sympathetic, which so warmed the heart of the genial multi-millionaire that he decided to demand, as a part of his pound of flesh from T. Prosper Stables, the real No. 1 candlelight Greco for the Louvre.

As the prefect, handcuffed inconspicuously, was about to be helped into the wagon, Hjalmar thought of his friends in Montparnasse and particularly of Messrs Chalgrin and Delbos. Well he might, for M. Chalgrin, at his cashbox in the Dôme, was declaiming with feeling Harpagon's immortal soliloquy from 'L'Avare,' Act IV, Scene VII.

CHALGRIN, *crying from the cashbox:*

'Alas, my poor money, my poor 125,000 francs. My dear friend. I have been deprived of you; and since you were taken from me, I have lost my support, my consolation, my joy; all is over for me, and I have nothing left to do in the world. Without you, it is impossible for me to live. It's done, and I no longer exist; I die, I am dead, I am buried. Is there no one who will bring me back to life, by giving me back my money . . .'

In the Coupole, a similar heart-rending scene was taking place, but since M. Delbos had not taste for the classics he was cursing Hjalmar and his own proper folly in modern style, with a somewhat staccato rhythm beautified, however, by a generous sprinkling of the names of the Saints.

On the quay, Hjalmar yelled, 'Hey, you, wait a minute,' to the prefect, rushed to the back door of the wagon and nearly tore the prefect's pants off retrieving the two cheques. He and Lvov lifted off the taxi, amid the plaudits of the crowd, and the convivial Russian vowed he would take one last ride at the wheel of his old machine before turning it in to the company. With Hjalmar in the rear seat, he set out for the corner of the boulevards Raspail and Montparnasse. With a roar the Norwegian embraced M. Chalgrin and handed him the rumpled cheque.

'It's O.K.,' he said. 'Hugo Weiss is back in town.'

And he rushed to the Coupole to gladden the heart of M. Delbos, who, quite unjustly, was in the act of wishing on Hjalmar an assortment of social diseases.

The two proprietors held their cheques to the light and gurgled like babies staring at a photographer's canary bird. They began to turn them, veer them, frisk them, jumble and shuffle them, all the while murmuring and chuckling with joy. They huddled them, rustled them, inverted and subverted them, tapped them, twisted them upside down, topsy-turvy, arsiversy. Finally, they raced for the bank across from the Dôme to cash them, and since Hugo Weiss was so well known and the news of his safe return had spread to all branches of the Crédit Lyonnais, the bank clerks and officials outdid themselves and it only took Messrs Chalgrin and Delbos the remainder of that happy day to get the money in their hands.

When the ambassador's turn came to walk the plank, Homer Evans felt called upon to go with him and steady him a bit, and the cheer that greeted the ambassador's difficult feat of balancing attested the appreciation of the crowd.

Sergeant Frémont got the biggest hand, when he descended from the barge with Miriam on his arm. Once the ambassador was safely away, Evans approached the sergeant and spirited him to the rue Delambre where an introduction to Joe ensured him a perpetual supply of Fine Michel or Mickey Finns.

'You're sure . . . er . . . there'll be no other accident?' the sergeant asked, hesitantly, his mind for an instant on the late Ambrose Gring.

'Positive, old man,' said Evans, and the sergeant set off happily for Le Havre where, when the *Ile de France* reached the breakwater, he could easily distinguish his darling Hydrangea in the midst of the passengers grouped at the rail. The idyll that followed and the success of the new chief inspector in suppressing crime is too blissful to relate.

Agents Bonnet and Schlumberger were promoted at once and given a roving commission which took them into all the rural museums in France. Whenever they found a canvas signed H. Jansen, they returned it to its proper author, and the fame of the fifty stray paintings grew to such an extent that art dealers bid high to possess one. Of course, the breakage of glass in the Dôme and the Coupole rose correspondingly.

Imagine Hjalmar's relief when he found waiting for him, in his accumulated mail, two letters: one the announcement of Maggie's engagement to a swain, the other from the British embassy enjoining him against following the girl to England.

It was a jolly sight, indeed, to see Melchisedek Knockwoode strutting up and down the main boulevards, the cynosure of all feminine eyes from the large and expensive cafés. His new British officer's uniform fitted him like a glove and he quickly acquired skill with the swagger stick.

Dinde, at Evans' suggestion, took possession of the Heiss

253

and Lourde galleries and their contents, and no one seemed to know the difference. Adolphe, rescued from the Goldfish Bowl, became Weiss's valet.

The good doctor, Hyacinthe Toudoux, won more fame and considerable fortune with his masterpiece *Observations divers sur quelques ivrognes d'Amérique du Nord* with case histories of the hangovers of the Montparnasse group which had been under his care in the prefecture. Also, he fought and won a duel in the Bois de Boulogne against a jealous rival physician who accused him of having thrown an important fencing match in 1910.

CHAPTER 32

The Boyish Silhouette Gives Way to the Curved Outline

THE last brief and final chapter is in the nature of a postlude. Sufficient time for rest and refreshment having elapsed since the adventures just related, Miriam Leonard was standing by an open window, looking at the stars and caressing gently with her fingertips the folds of a small American flag attached to the casement of a certain high window.

She had been wearing a costume which had gracefully expressed the return of the curved outline, without resort to corselette, wrap-around, combinaire, or any of the other strange and complicated inner garments so much in demand that summer. Tea-rose scanties of a light and supple silk jersey had been hidden by her chic frock. They had been, strictly speaking, only necessary to Miriam as a means of attaching her beige silk stockings which had matched her suède gloves with scrupulous perfection.

Her jumper frock, which lay limply across the back of a chair, was of pale sorrel *crapella frisca* and had a box-pleated skirt and a fitted blouse with long full sleeves falling in soft folds above tight cuffs. From the neat hip-level pocket, embellished with a Czerny motif embroidered in chestnut roan stitching, her automatic had fallen into one of Evans' shoes.

Beneath the broad bed in which Homer at last was sleeping with unusual soundness, were a pair of slippers of Java lizard with Louis XV heels. Her narrow-brimmed high-crowned hat of rengale straw was set off by a scarf of grosgrain ribbon in four shades of horse colours as it snuggled jauntily on the hook beside a certain panama.

A light night breeze cooled her strong young limbs and she threw back her head happily to gaze at the Milky Way.

'Now I know,' she murmured, 'exactly why I came to Paris.'

THE END
*of everything
except Problem 'C'.*